BRIDES OF ARKANSAS

THREE-IN-ONE COLLECTION

JANET LEE BARTON

BARBOUR
PUBLISHING

A Love for Keeps © 2009 by Janet Lee Barton
A Love All Her Own © 2009 by Janet Lee Barton
A Love to Cherish © 2009 by Janet Lee Barton

ISBN 978-1-60260-638-8

Scripture quotations are taken from the King James Version of the Bible.

This book is a work of fiction. Names, characters, places, and incidents are either products of the author's imagination or used fictitiously. Any similarity to actual people, organizations, and/or events is purely coincidental.

Cover Design: Kirk DouPonce, DogEared Design

Published by Barbour Publishing, Inc., P.O. Box 719, Uhrichsville, Ohio 44683, www.barbourbooks.com

Our mission is to publish and distribute inspirational products offering exceptional value and biblical encouragement to the masses.

ecpa Member of the
Evangelical Christian
Publishers Association

Printed in the United States of America.

Dear Readers,

Thank you so much for choosing to read *Brides of Arkansas*. This collection is one of my favorites. While I was born and raised in New Mexico, we lived for several of my childhood years in Arkansas when my dad wanted to try his hand at farming. I loved it there. But the farming didn't work out and we returned to New Mexico when I was in second grade. Still, I have so many warm childhood memories from our time in Northeastern Arkansas where some of my family still reside. I love the state!

Then, after I married my husband, we moved to North Little Rock for a while. That is when we visited Hot Springs for the first time. But It wasn't until we moved to Oklahoma—the first time—that we visited Eureka Springs. I loved both places. It was like taking a step back in time to visit each place and I loved the differences between the two towns. I remember taking notes on our visits for research for future stories.

I hope you enjoy *Brides of Arkansas*. It is a collection of closely linked novels revolving around two families who have experienced loss and heartache. *A Love For Keeps* takes place in 1886 Eureka Springs. The story is about Meagan who struggles to keep from falling in love with the widowed banker who loans her the money to start a business to help her struggling family. *A Love All Her Own* takes place in that same year, when Abigail runs away to Hot Springs and comes to terms with her past, but has a tough time forgiving herself and a harder time believing the man she loves could care about her—once he finds out about her past. The series continues into 1902 with *A Love To Cherish*, about Meagan's little sister Becca, now all grown up, who's moved from Eureka Springs to Hot Springs after a devastating loss—only to find herself falling in love against her firm resolve not to. It is only with the Lord's help that each one can find their own true love.

What a blessing to know that the Lord always has a plan—even if it is as simple as starting a series about a family and two towns in Arkansas, only to find that the real stories in the series is about learning to lean on the Lord when you don't know what to do, accepting the Lord's forgiveness and learning to forgive oneself, and learning to trust the Lord's plan for your life. What a joy and a blessing to be able to write for Him.

I hope you enjoy reading these stories as much as I enjoyed writing them.

Janet Lee Barton

A LOVE FOR KEEPS

Dedication

To my Lord and Savior, for showing me the way. To Dan, who has encouraged me from the beginning; Nicole, who reads even when she doesn't always feel like it; and Mariah and Paige, who give me a wealth of ideas.
I love you all—with all my heart.

Chapter 1

Eureka Springs, Arkansas
February 1886

Meagan Snow walked out of the bank, trying not to let her mother know how discouraged she felt. All she had to do was look at the older woman to see she felt the very same way, if not more so.

"Meagan, I don't know why I let you talk me into doing this," Elsie Snow said as they walked down Main Street to the third bank they would try that morning. "We've already been turned down by two different banks. We should probably just go on home."

"Mama, I am not giving up until we have no choice." She couldn't. It had been one thing for her mother to take in wash to help ends meet since Papa died. Meagan and her sisters, Becca and Sarah, could help her with that. However, the fact that Mama felt she had to take a part-time job helping to get the newly built Crescent Hotel ready to open was more than Meagan could take. It was time, as the oldest daughter, to help more than she had been. The mending she took in wasn't enough. God had blessed her with a talent, and she intended to put it to use to help provide for her family. She could do no less. If they were successful in getting a loan, her mother would be able to quit the hotel position before long.

They entered the Connors Bank and walked up to the receptionist. "Good morning. I'm Meagan Snow and this is my mother, Elsie. We'd like to see a loan officer, if possible," she said.

The receptionist gave Meagan and then her mother an appraising look before answering, "I'll see if Mr. Brooks has time to see you. Please take a seat right over there." She pointed to several settees in what Meagan assumed was a waiting area.

"Thank you," Meagan's mother said. One settee had a cuspidor sitting to the side of it. Meagan and her mother chose the other one. The way Mama twisted her lace-trimmed hankie between her fingers told Meagan how nervous she was.

Meagan covered those fingers with her hand and squeezed. "It's going to be all right, Mama. This bank is much bigger than the others are. It surely has more money to loan." She tried to sound positive, but the truth was she didn't know what they were going to do if they couldn't get a loan from this bank.

"I don't think it's that the other bankers didn't have the money, dear. I'm sure they think we are a bad risk. Moreover, I'm afraid this one isn't likely to be any different. The look on the impertinent young woman's face tells me that."

"Yes, I know. However, we know that we are not bad risks! And I will do my best to convince the bank manager of just that."

It seemed they waited for a long time, but it was really only a few minutes. A nice-looking man followed the receptionist out of a nearby office, and as she pointed in their direction, he nodded and headed their way. He didn't seem at all like the other two men they'd met with that day. Those men had been much older and. . .*stuffy* was the word that came to mind. The younger man who was striding over to them was of medium height, broad shouldered, and had deep brown hair. When he reached them, Meagan observed that his brown eyes had flecks of gold in them, and he was quite handsome when he smiled and held out his hand to her mother.

"Good morning, ladies. Mrs. Snow, Miss Snow, I'm Nate Brooks. What can I do for you today?"

"We need to apply for a business loan," Meagan stated, bringing his attention to her.

"I see." He paused and looked from Meagan to her mother and back again. "And what kind of loan are you looking to procure?"

"My daughter is a wonderful seamstress. She would like to start a dressmaking business in our home."

"Oh, I see." He nodded and motioned for them to follow him. "Please, come into my office and we'll see what we can do."

Meagan was afraid to get her hopes up, but this was the first time they had been invited inside an office and the first time anyone had seemed willing to listen to them. She prayed silently. *Dear Lord, please let this man see that we can make this business work. Please let him sense that we honor our word and will pay back every penny we borrow. Please let him lend us what we need, Father.*

Her opinion of the banker raised another notch when he held out a chair for her mother. She started to pull out her own chair, but his hand brushed hers as he did it for her. Meagan wasn't prepared for the way her pulse began to race at the slight touch. She took the seat and tried to compose herself. This was a business meeting, after all.

❧

Nate had held his office door open for the women, and once they were inside, he pulled out chairs, first for Mrs. Snow and then for her daughter, who'd started to pull out her own. He wasn't sure if he could help them at all, but he hadn't been able to turn them away. The expression on the older woman's face was one of gracious resignation, and his heart had gone out to her. The daughter had more of a look of determination, and he was curious to hear what she had to say. She was lovely with black hair worn up in the style of the day. He wasn't sure what they called it, but nearly every young woman he knew wore theirs dressed similarly. The style was very flattering to Miss Meagan Snow. She was quite striking with her big blue eyes and long dark lashes, and she'd smelled good when he pulled out the chair for her. . .of lavender water or some such thing. Nate brought his thoughts up short. He needed to keep his mind on business. "Please, tell me a little about yourself," he said to the older woman.

"Well, I am a widow. My husband passed away a couple of years ago. He worked for the railroad. Then he came down with rheumatism, and for a while, it looked as if he was going to get better. But even the springs couldn't help him. He came down with the influenza and never recovered."

"I'm so sorry." That explained why these two women needed a source of income.

"Thank you. He did provide a house for us, free and clear, but we need income and we're willing to put our home up as collateral."

He glanced at the younger woman and saw that she was watching her mother closely. It was obvious that she felt protective of her. He focused his gaze on Mrs. Snow, also. "You say you want to start a dressmaking business in your home?"

"Yes, we do. Well, it will be my daughter's business. She's the dressmaker. And a better one I've never seen. She's even designed a few of her own."

"Is that right, Miss Snow?"

"Yes. My mother has taken a *temporary* position at the Crescent. But I feel it is my duty, as the oldest child, to help bring in an income, and I believe I can make this work." Her blue gaze met his from across the desk. "I don't want Mama working outside the home any longer than necessary, and I'd never agree to us putting our home up to secure the loan if I didn't believe I could make the shop a success."

"Have you had any formal training?"

"No, Mr. Brooks, I have not. But I learned the basics from my mother—"

"She's gone well past the basics," Meagan's mother interrupted. "She's being much too modest. She's expanded her knowledge well past mine by keeping up with the styles and making clothes for the whole family—I have two other daughters. And she's even been paid to make frocks for some of our neighbors and friends."

"I see." He looked at Miss Snow. "So this will be your business?"

"Yes, sir. It will be."

"And what is it you need to set this dressmaking shop up?"

"Well, we would need to turn one of our parlors into the actual shop or add on to our home." Miss Snow took a folded sheet of paper out of her reticule and handed it to him as she continued, "I'd need a new sewing machine and enough fabrics and trims to be able to offer my clients good choices."

He glanced at the paper. That she'd looked into what it would take to open her own shop was very apparent as he asked more questions.

"What kind of frocks do you specialize in?"

"I can make anything from everyday frocks to ball gowns."

She seemed quite confident of her capabilities, and Nate wanted to give them a chance. "I think that your idea may be a good one. Still, before I could commit to lending you the money you need, I would want to visit your home and see what would be involved in turning part of it into a shop. And"—he looked at Miss Snow—"I'd need to see some samples of your work."

He wasn't sure if she would raise any objections but didn't see how she could.

"That would be fine," she said. "When would you like to come to our home?"

He looked at his schedule. "Would tomorrow at three o'clock be all right?"

"Will that be all right with you, Mama?" the daughter asked.

"I'll be home from the Crescent by then. Three will be just fine," the mother replied.

"Good." Nate stood, signaling the end of the meeting. The two ladies did the same. "I'll see you tomorrow at three, then."

He showed them out of the office, and as they thanked him and walked away, they looked so very happy that he hoped he didn't have to disappoint them.

❧

Meagan felt almost giddy when they walked out of the bank and started for home. "Oh, Mama, I think he's going to loan us the money!"

Her mother's smile told her she was every bit as hopeful as Meagan was. "I hope so, dear. He has kind eyes, and he certainly listened to us. He could have told us no today, so he must seriously be contemplating making us a loan."

"I'm sure he is." Meagan silently prayed that Nate Brooks was as good a man as he appeared to be and that he would approve the loan. Otherwise, she wasn't sure what they were going to do. But she knew that God would provide a way for them to get by. He always had.

It was amazing how much brighter the mid-February day seemed as they branched off Main at Spring, continuing past some of the homes that were built on the rocks above. Most of the houses had wide porches overlooking the road below. Meagan loved the way Eureka Springs was built on winding roads up and down the mountainsides. They continued on Spring, up the hill to Mountain, and then to the corner of Mountain and Montgomery, where they lived. The air seemed a touch warmer and the sky bluer than when they'd first started out. The pine trees even seemed greener. It wouldn't be long until winter gave way to spring, and Meagan could feel the change beginning. She'd been so concerned with the business of the day and worries about her family that she hadn't taken time to enjoy the beautiful day.

Her sisters must have been watching for them because as soon as Meagan and her mother rounded the corner, the girls ran out of the house to meet them.

"Well," ten-year-old Becca said, "did you get a loan?"

"And is Mama going to get to quit working so hard?" fifteen-year-old Sarah asked.

"We're hoping so," Meagan said. "Mr. Brooks will be coming tomorrow to look at the house and see how we mean to turn part of it into a shop. And he wants to see samples of my work."

"And then we'll get the loan?" Sarah asked.

Mama put an arm around her as they walked up the steps to the front porch and inside the house. "We hope so. But we want to make sure the house is as clean as it can be and that there aren't any stains on the dresses Meagan has made us."

"Mama, our home is always clean," Sarah said.

"I know. But we want it spotless for tomorrow." Of one accord, they headed to the kitchen, where they always discussed important things.

"We'll help, Mama," Becca said.

"I know you will, dear," their mother said, putting on the teakettle. "Let's have a bite to eat, and then we will get busy."

"What are we going to do if he says no?" Becca asked. "Before long, I'll be able to work at the Crescent, too."

"Maybe I can help clean Mrs. Elliot's house," Sarah added. "She's gettin' old and—"

"Girls, you aren't going to have to go to work. If Mr. Brooks says no, I'll keep working at the Crescent Hotel. It's not bad, really."

"And I can still sew for people. I just won't be able to charge as much."

"Everything is going to be all right, girls. I'm sure Mr. Brooks is going to loan us some money. We just have to make the best impression we can." Mama let out a big sigh and smiled. "But let us pray about it." She bowed her head, and her daughters did the same. "Dear Father, You know what we want and need. You've given Meagan a wonderful talent, and she wishes to use it to help this family. We pray that, if it's in Your will, we will get the loan we need to get Meagan started in her dressmaking business. But we only want it if it be Your will. It is in Jesus' name we pray. Amen."

"Amen," Meagan and her sisters said in unison.

"It's time to get to it," Mama said. "I'm so thankful I don't have to go into work today. We have much to do."

Meagan put on an apron and began cutting thick slices of bread to go with the soup her mother had put on before they left the house that morning. They enjoyed their meal but didn't dawdle over it. They had a lot to get done in a short amount of time.

Sarah was right. Their home was always clean. Still, so much counted on Nate Brooks's impression of it and them, that they did a thorough cleaning much like what they'd done just a few weeks ago. The good thing was that they *had* cleaned so well then. While Meagan took the rugs outside and beat them until there was no dust left to fly, Mama went over to Mrs. Morrison's to ask if Meagan might be able to borrow the dresses she'd made her so that she could show them to Mr. Brooks the next day. Becca mopped floors, while Sarah dusted every inch of the house.

By the time their mother returned from Mrs. Morrison's, they were ready for a break. Meagan brewed a pot of tea while her mother told her about the visit. "Nelda said she would run the dresses over in the morning. She wants to make sure they are pressed. She is so excited for you, dear."

"Mama, we don't even know if we'll get the loan. It's a little premature for her to be excited."

"She's sure we will get the loan and even offered to come tell Mr. Brooks how much she loves your creations, if we need her to."

"That's very sweet of her. I hope he'll be able to tell the quality of my work by looking at it himself. But it's nice to know that Mrs. Morrison will give me a good recommendation, if we need it." Meagan smiled and took a sip of tea.

"If we had more time, we could go all over town collecting what you'd made. You'd have more frocks to show him."

"It will be fine, Mama. We have a lot to show him. And I have some of my designs I can bring out, too."

"He's going to love them all," Sarah assured her. "Why, we look as good as anyone else at school or at church."

"Thank you, Sarah." Meagan gave her younger sister a hug. "I'm very hopeful all will go well."

They finished their tea and then pitched in to shine the windows. By early evening, they were all ready to stop for the day as they heated up the soup left over from their noon meal.

"The house fairly shines, it's so clean," Becca said.

"Yes, it does. Mr. Brooks will find no dust in this house tomorrow," Meagan said. "Now all that is left to do is to look over the clothing and make sure it looks fresh and clean. I'll do any mending needed tonight before I go to bed."

"I don't think there will be much mending—you always keep up with that so well," Mama stated. "But we'll check, just to make sure, and I'll brush whatever needs only that. Tomorrow we can take turns pressing."

"Thank you, Mama." Meagan sent up a silent prayer. *Dear Father, thank You for Mama. Please help us to get this loan so that she doesn't have to work so hard. You know what we need, Lord. I trust that You will provide.*

Meagan sighed as she headed upstairs to see what needed mending. So much depended on the outcome of Mr. Brooks's visit. It had been so hard to lose Papa. And then to see her mother so willingly give up the household help they'd had ever since Meagan could remember. . .well, that was hard to watch. Meagan didn't mind helping her mother at all. What she did hate was the way some of her mother's friends had just quit calling on her or had stopped sending her invitations. To make things worse, her mother felt it necessary to get a job at the hotel.

Meagan had been trying to help, taking in mending for neighbors and sewing for them. But she didn't charge much because she felt they were doing her a favor by hiring her. She could make more money for the family, but she would have to go into business to do so. Their future hinged on tomorrow's meeting.

Chapter 2

Nate wouldn't have gone to Abigail's that evening except that she made it so very hard for him to say no. She was his late wife's sister and the aunt of his six-year-old daughter. They were family, and she never failed to remind him of it. Not to mention that she was the daughter of the owner of the bank Nate managed. Mr. Connors had made no secret that his daughter knew many rich people who were always in need of a banker. To Jacob Connors's way of thinking, Nate needed to mingle and make friends of them all.

Abigail always wanted Nate there for a number of reasons. For one thing, she needed his support at these social functions, and his presence was a way to help the bank's business, too. After all, she invited people who were Nate's clients—or certainly should be. Of course, she was a banker's daughter and thought along the same lines as her father—or so she said.

Nate sighed as he raised the knocker on her front door. Abigail had moved into her own home several years before when she'd inherited it from her grandmother. It wasn't a large home, but it was very nice and in one of the well-to-do neighborhoods in Eureka Springs.

Normally, she hired a butler for her parties, but tonight she opened the door herself and greeted him with a kiss on the cheek, as she always did. It never failed to make him uncomfortable. He had a feeling that she would like him to make it a real kiss, but she was Rose's sister and he just couldn't do that. He had no doubts that if he asked Abigail to marry him, she'd have them walking down the aisle in a matter of weeks. He wasn't ready for that step.

"I'm so glad you came, Nate. Thank you for arriving early."

"You say that every time, Abigail."

"I mean it every time." She smiled and batted her eyelashes at him as she took hold of his arm and led him into her large parlor. "How is my Natalie tonight?"

"She wanted to come, too. I told her it was one of your stuffy adult parties and she wouldn't enjoy herself."

"Nate!"

"Well, she wouldn't. And she agreed. I promised her I wouldn't be late."

"You always manage to leave early, Nate."

"I have a daughter to take care of, Abigail."

"I know that. You could have brought her over and put her to bed here."

"We've been over that before, Abigail." Occasionally, he had let Natalie stay overnight with her aunt Abigail, but that was only when he felt Abigail could give her the attention she needed.

"I know. I'll have just the two of you over for dinner later in the week."

"I'll tell her."

Nate was relieved when a knock at the door announced her other guests were beginning to arrive. He became weary of one-on-one conversation with Abigail after a few minutes. He greeted the others and mingled as much as he could before they were called to dinner. Two of her best friends, Jillian Burton and Rebecca Dobson, had come with their current suitors. Nate knew them through banking, too. Jillian's beau was Reginald Fitzgerald, who ran his family's jewelry store. Rebecca's current beau was Edward Mitchell, who'd just opened a new furniture store in town.

Several other couples whom he'd only met a time or two showed up, but he was certain that if they were anyone he needed to know better, Abigail would see that he did. For now, he just wanted to eat and get home to his daughter. Abigail employed a housekeeper and hired an extra cook for her parties. When the housekeeper let Abigail know that dinner was ready to be served, Nate was glad. He would get home that much sooner.

The help served several courses that included roast duck and creamed potatoes with tiny English peas and crusty rolls. The food was wonderful, and Nate was able to enjoy it as he only needed to give half an ear to Abigail and her friends discussing the upcoming spring social season in Eureka Springs. The ladies' talk about ball gowns and dressmakers, however, caught his attention and held it.

"I don't know what we are going to do with Miss Elliot marrying and moving away at the end of the year," Jillian said.

"We must get orders in quickly if we are to have the newest styles for this season," Rebecca added.

"This town could use several more dressmakers. I don't want to have to start going away to get my frocks," Abigail said, "but I don't know that we'll have much choice if we keep losing seamstresses."

Nate didn't say anything, but if Miss Meagan Snow was as good a dressmaker as her mother claimed, setting them up in business might prove to be a good risk—a very good one, indeed.

∽

Meagan woke on Tuesday, feeling both excited and apprehensive. She and her mother had worked into the night, too wound up to sleep, but they had only a few frocks to press. They felt confident that Mr. Brooks would appreciate their efforts.

As she pulled on a wrapper and hurried downstairs to finish the pressing before getting dressed, Meagan took a deep breath and tried to appear calm. She didn't want her mother or the girls to see how nervous she was. That would only make them apprehensive. Besides, she'd prayed and put it all in the Lord's hands, and He would take care of it. They'd cleaned the house until it sparkled, and she was making certain that she would be showing Mr. Brooks her best work. There wasn't anything else she could do except wait on his decision.

"Good morning, dear. Mrs. Morrison brought over the morning dress and the dinner dress you made her. She made sure they were clean and pressed. She said if we need her to come meet Mr. Brooks to let her know. She'll be glad to."

"That's very nice of her." Meagan looked over the two dresses: the dinner dress, a crimson-and-cream-striped sateen; and the morning dress, a blue-and-green-checked gingham. "She has taken very good care of them. They look like they did the day I finished them."

She carefully laid them in her room until time to bring them out to show Mr. Brooks. While her mother made breakfast for the younger girls, she finished the pressing. Then her mother went to work, the girls went to school, and Meagan spent the rest of the morning laying out everything she planned to show Mr. Brooks. She loved the last housedress she'd made for Becca. It was of patterned blue and white batiste with three rows of pleated ruffles at the hem, the neckline, and wrists, and a skirt that draped gracefully in the back. Meagan was happy with the way her mother's new brown brocade visiting dress had turned out, too, with its side drape, trimmed in gold. She looked lovely in it.

After making sure everything looked as good as it could, Meagan put on her favorite afternoon dress. It was brown, cream, and blue plaid gingham, with a front drape. She went down to the kitchen to heat up her curling irons and put her hair up, curling a few tendrils around her face. Finally, there was nothing more to do but wait until Mr. Brooks arrived. . .except to pray that he would decide to approve their loan.

❧

Mr. Brooks arrived promptly at three o'clock. When Meagan opened the door to him, she found him looking around the partial wraparound porch. She wasn't worried. The cottage was in good shape, and the neighborhood always well kept. He'd find nothing to be critical about there.

"Good afternoon, Mr. Brooks." She hoped she didn't sound too nervous.

He turned back to the front door with a smile. "Good afternoon, Miss Snow. How are you this beautiful spring day?"

Meagan had barely noticed how sunny and warm the day had become. She'd been too busy getting ready for his visit. But she didn't want to appear too apprehensive. "I'm quite well, thank you. Please, come in."

"Welcome to our home, Mr. Brooks," her mother said from behind her. "Meagan has much to show you."

"Thank you, Mrs. Snow. I'm anxious to see Miss Snow's work." He handed his calling card to her and then turned to Meagan. "Did you, perhaps, fashion the frock you are wearing?"

"Yes, I did." Meagan turned slowly, her arms outstretched so that he could see how the skirt was draped.

He nodded. "It's a lovely dress."

"We're both wearing afternoon dresses that she designed herself," Elsie said, turning gracefully so that Mr. Brooks could see how the skirt of her dress draped across the front and tied on the left side.

"These are both quite nice. What else can you show me?"

Meagan led him into the parlor where they'd laid out the rest of her work. She motioned for him to move around the room. "I've made more, but they were for other people and I didn't have time to ask if we could borrow them."

"No need. I wasn't expecting to see this much." He walked over to the frocks she'd made for Becca. "You make children's clothing, too?"

"Of course," Meagan said.

"I have a six-year-old, and she's been growing quite fast. I'm going to have to replenish her wardrobe soon. These look every bit as nice as anything we've had made for her. Since my wife passed away, her family has been helping me choose her clothing."

Meagan wasn't sure what to say—or even how she felt about the fact that he wasn't married. While she felt badly for him and his child, she couldn't deny that knowing he was a widower made it easier to accept the fact that she found him quite attractive.

He smiled. "My Natalie is very vocal about what she likes to wear. I'm sure that together, she and I could manage her wardrobe."

"I'm sure you could, too."

Mr. Brooks looked everything over carefully and listened as Meagan pointed out a certain style or a special drape or ruffle on each outfit she showed him, from school dresses to walking dresses, to Sunday dresses she'd made for her sisters.

"While Meagan is showing you around, I'm going to put on a pot of water to heat. I hope you'll join us for afternoon tea after you are through here, Mr. Brooks."

"I'd love to, Mrs. Snow." He smiled at her mother and then turned to

Meagan. "Let's see the rest."

It was hard to tell what he was thinking, but that he could tell the quality of the fabrics and trim she'd used and commented on the quality of her work gave her hope.

Meagan had just finished showing Mr. Brooks the rest of her work when the front door flew open and Becca and Sarah burst in from school. They stopped short when they saw the banker in the parlor.

"Oh!" Becca said.

"It is all right, Becca. Girls, this is Mr. Brooks. He's the banker who came to see my work.

"Mr. Brooks, these are my sisters. Sarah is the older one, and Becca the younger."

Both sisters gave a quick curtsy, making Meagan smile with pride at their good manners. "How do you do, Mr. Brooks?" Sarah said.

He smiled and bowed from the waist. "Sarah and Becca, is it?"

Becca giggled and bobbed her head.

"It is nice to meet you both. Your sister is a very talented dressmaker and she's made you some lovely things."

"Oh, we know," Sarah said. "She's a wonderful seamstress."

Sarah could be quite outspoken at times, and Meagan was afraid she'd ask outright if he was going to loan them money. "Mama is in the kitchen, making tea for us. Would you girls go let her know that we are ready?"

They hesitated only a moment, just long enough for Meagan to incline her head in the direction of the kitchen. "Please?"

It was obvious that Sarah wanted to stay, but she sighed and nodded her head, pulling Becca, who was no more anxious to leave the room than she was, with her.

"I'm sorry. They are—"

"They want to know my decision almost as much as you and your mother, I'm sure. That is quite natural. They live here, too, and all of this affects them as well. Why don't we go have that tea and talk about it?"

"Yes, of course," Meagan said. "Please follow me."

"Do you have any sketches of your designs that I could look at?"

"I do. I meant to give my sketch pad to you. I'll get it while Mama pours your tea."

She led him down the hall to the back parlor. It was cozy and bright, and her mother was sitting in her chair, the tea tray in front of her.

"Mr. Brooks, I'm so glad you could join us; please take a seat anywhere you'd like," Mama said. She poured him a cup of tea. "Would you like cream and sugar?"

He sat down in the chair on the other side of her. "Yes, please." He took the proffered cup and took a sip.

"Mama, I forgot my drawings; I'll be right back," Meagan said. By the time she returned, Mr. Brooks seemed right at home. Becca was serving him a tea cake, and he was smiling.

Meagan took the cup of tea her mother had prepared for her and handed the banker her designs.

"Thank you, Miss Snow." He plopped the rest of the tea cake in his mouth and opened her sketchbook. He turned the pages slowly and looked over each design carefully. "This is the frock you have on, isn't it?"

"Yes, it is." He had a good eye for fashion, but he still hadn't given any indication as to what he was going to do.

He closed the sketch pad, handed it to Meagan, and smiled. "Relax, ladies. I'm very impressed with Miss Snow's designs and the quality of her work. Your front parlor is amply big enough to turn into a shop. I'm going to give you the loan."

For the first time that day, Meagan felt her smile was genuine. "Oh, thank you, Mr. Brooks. You won't be sorry!"

Her mother was up out of her chair, pumping the banker's hand up and down. "Thank you, thank you. Have no worries. We will pay back every penny."

Sarah was barely able to contain her excitement, and Becca was clapping and jumping up and down with excitement.

Mr. Brooks chuckled. "I am not worried. With the support system you have here, I have no doubt that you will make your business a success."

Meagan looked at her mother and sisters. She had a feeling they all helped him make his decision. She nodded. "I'm blessed, that's for certain."

"Come into the bank tomorrow morning, and we'll get your signature." He pulled out a piece of paper and handed it to Meagan. "This is a list of building contractors I think you can trust to do the work you need. I'll need to approve the plans you come up with, of course, but you can rest easy tonight. You have the loan."

Meagan took the paper from him, and as her fingers brushed his, she was taken aback by the electrical jolt that shot up her arm. Her gaze met his and she wondered if he'd felt the same thing.

Chapter 3

The next day, the receptionist jumped to her feet as soon as Meagan and her mother approached her desk. "Mrs. Snow, Miss Snow, Mr. Brooks has been expecting you. Please, come right this way." The woman smiled and led them to his office.

He seated them once again and put Meagan and her mother both at ease with his smile. Meagan didn't like the way her heartbeat sped up at that smile, though. He was such a nice man and—

"It's not often I feel as good about loaning money out as I do today," Nate Brooks said as he took his seat behind his desk. He handed Meagan a card. "Be sure to have some business cards made up and leave them wherever you go. This company is known to do beautiful cards at a reasonable price."

"Thank you," Meagan said, taking the small card from him. "I'll go see them this week."

"Well, ladies, let's get started. The sooner we get this paperwork done, the sooner you'll be able to start your business."

For the next half hour, papers passed back and forth as signatures were put to them. Meagan had a moment's misgiving when her mother handed over the deed to their home. If only they'd been able to secure a loan without putting up their home as collateral. It was all very sobering. Her family's future was at stake. If she failed in this endeavor, they could lose their home.

Mr. Brooks seemed to sense her mood. "I believe you are going to build a thriving business, Miss Snow. Otherwise, I wouldn't be lending you the money. I don't do business like that. Try to think of it as placing your deed in my hands for safekeeping."

"I'll try," Meagan said. She wanted to believe him, but she sent up a silent prayer to the One who knew for sure what kind of man Mr. Brooks was. *Lord, please let him be telling the truth. . .that he believes in us and that our deed is in a safe place. I pray that I can make this business successful so that my family won't have to worry about the future, so that Mama can quit working at the Crescent very soon, and so that we can pay back this debt and get our deed back. Please help me, Father.*

When they had signed the last paper and seen for themselves the amount of money that had been put in their account, Meagan and her mother breathed a sigh of relief. It was going to be all right. The Lord would see them through.

Mr. Brooks stood up. "When do you think you'll be contacting the contractor? Did you decide who you might use?"

"I thought I'd go see Mr. Adams. One of our neighbors gave him a very good recommendation, just as you did."

"He is a good man. If he has time, you won't be disappointed in his work."

"We'll go see him first, then."

Mr. Brooks saw them out of his office. "I'll be checking in from time to time to see if you need anything, if it is all right with you."

"Of course." How could she tell him no? His bank had just loaned them a substantial amount of money. She expected him to take an interest in the business.

"I'll be seeing you, then. Good day, ladies."

"Good day, Mr. Brooks. Thank you for your help."

He bowed slightly. "It's been my pleasure."

Meagan and her mother left the bank and lost no time in going to Mr. Adams's business to ask him about turning their parlor into a dressmaking shop. His place wasn't all that far from where they lived, just over Owen Street near the Josephine Hotel, so he agreed to come out the next morning to look around and discuss the needed changes to their home. They bade him goodbye, and Meagan's mother went on to work at the Crescent.

Meagan stopped at home to put a roast in the oven for a celebration supper, and then she hurried back downtown to do some shopping. First, she ordered a new Singer sewing machine and a large folding screen to put in one corner of the room, so that her clients would be able to change for their fittings.

Next, she went to her favorite dry goods store to order yard goods she wanted to have on hand. She also ordered fabric samples in case what she had in the shop or could find in town didn't suit a client. She bought spools of thread, buttons, trims, and everything else she could think of that she might need. Her fabrics would take several weeks to come in, but she arranged for the other things to be delivered to the house. She couldn't remember when she'd ever had more fun shopping in her life.

❧

"How do I look, Papa?" Natalie Brooks asked Nate. He watched her twirl around and give a cute curtsy. Thankful that he had a housekeeper to help him—he'd never be able to put Natalie's hair up in those curls—he took his daughter's hand in his and bowed to her.

"You look lovely this morning, my dear."

"And you look quite handsome, Papa."

"Thank you. I believe it is time to go to church." Nate helped his daughter with her light cloak, and they headed outside. He assisted her into the runabout and took his own seat. It was a beautiful day. Some of the oaks were beginning to leaf out, and the sky was a clear, cloudless blue. He looked down at his daughter and smiled. "This is the day which the Lord hath made; we will rejoice and be glad in it!"

"Yes, let's, Papa!"

"Are you ready?" Nate asked.

Natalie nodded and grinned. "I am."

"So am I!"

With a flick of Nate's wrist, they were on their way to church. He knew many people in Eureka Springs, either from doing business with them or through his late wife's family. Natalie waved right along with him each time they were greeted by the passengers of a passing buggy.

They were among the last to arrive at church, and Nate and Natalie hurried down the aisle to sit with the Connors family.

"Good morning, Nate," Abigail said with a smile.

"Good morning. We are running a little late this morning."

"No matter," Georgette Connors said, motioning for Natalie to come sit by her. The Connors family gathered his daughter into their circle immediately.

Georgette Connors hugged her close. "You look lovely today, dear. We're having your favorite Sunday dinner."

Natalie looked at her and asked, "We're having roast chicken and apple pie?"

Her grandfather, Jacob Connors, nodded and chuckled. "Well, I like the chicken, but the pie is my favorite."

"It is my favorite, too, Grandfather. But we can't have it until last."

"I know." Jacob shook his head.

Nate sometimes wished that he didn't feel he had to sit with the Connors family, but they were the only relatives Natalie had besides him. His parents had passed away before she was born, and she adored her grandparents and her aunt Abigail. That they loved her could never be in doubt. And Nate wanted them in her life; he just didn't always want them in his. But he didn't know how to separate his life from theirs—wasn't even sure it was possible. Still, they were family, and he enjoyed their affection and care, too. He supposed he should be counting his blessings instead of wishing for more. He wasn't sure what had him so unsettled lately—

"Mama, there seems to be a crowd today," a familiar voice said from behind him. "I hope we don't take someone else's seat."

"Well, if we do, they are later than we are. Besides, we don't pay for them, Meagan. God just wants us here. He doesn't care where we sit."

Nate chuckled silently. Mrs. Snow was a very practical woman. As the family slipped into the row behind him, he could see from the corner of his eye that it was indeed the Snow family.

The service began, and Nate tried to concentrate on it. The singing lifted him up as always and the prayers touched his soul. The sermon about reaching out to others and helping them spoke to his heart. He couldn't help but think of the Snow women sitting behind him, and he prayed that their endeavor would be a success, not because they owed the bank money but because they seemed to be a lovely family without a man to lead them, and his heart went out to them.

As soon as the service was over, Nate stood and turned to the women behind him. "Good day, Mrs. Snow, Miss Snow. How nice to have you visit with us today."

"Why, Mr. Brooks. I thought that was you," Mrs. Snow said. "Thank you for the welcome, but we aren't visitors. We've been coming here ever since we moved to Eureka Springs."

"Oh, my. I am sorry." Nate felt awful. How had he not noticed that they attended the same church?

"Don't worry about it. We usually sit toward the back," Meagan Snow said. She looked exceptionally lovely in one of the frocks she'd shown him this past week.

"Papa, who are these ladies you are talking to?" Natalie asked, tugging at his sleeve.

"These are nice ladies I met through the bank, Natalie. They are going to be starting a new dressmaking shop. Mrs. Snow, Miss Snow, this is my daughter, Natalie."

"Why, hello, Natalie, how nice to meet you."

"I'm pleased to meet you, ma'am," Natalie said, looking curiously at the family.

As his in-laws turned from talking to the people in the pew in front of them, Nate made the introductions all around, from Mrs. Snow and her daughters to the Connorses and back again. Jacob and Georgette were gracious, but Nate wasn't pleased when Abigail practically brushed the introductions aside by only saying, "Pleased, I am sure."

She nudged him to move out of the row and said in a loud whisper, "We need to hurry, Nate, dear. You know how Mama gets upset if we dawdle. She likes us to be on time for Sunday dinner."

Nate didn't know what she was talking about. Georgette had never acted upset about how long they stayed after church. She usually did her own socializing before they left. As the rest of the Connorses followed Abigail out into the aisle, he wasn't sure what to say. "Natalie and I will be along shortly."

Abigail sighed. "Very well. Try to hurry, though."

Nate was at a loss as to what to say to the Snow family. "I. . .ah. . ."

"Oh, we quite understand, Mr. Brooks," Meagan said, and he had a feeling she was trying to ease his discomfort at his sister-in-law's rudeness. "We have a Sunday dinner to take out of the oven, too."

Nate and Natalie walked down the aisle with the Snow ladies. He could see that Abigail looked a bit put out as she left with her parents, but he wasn't inclined to hurry on her account. He wasn't inclined to hurry at all.

∾

Abigail fairly fumed on the way out of church. Who were those women Nate was being so friendly to? Oh, he'd said that they were going to open a dress-making shop, but how exactly did he know them? The way they looked at him, you'd think they were old friends. The oldest daughter—what was her name? All she could remember was their last name was Snow. Most likely, Nate was still talking to them. That thought didn't sit well with her. She knew nearly everyone Nate socialized with, and she'd never seen these women. She didn't like the way Nate had looked at the oldest daughter, either. She didn't like it at all.

Abigail wasn't the least bit happy that Nate hesitated when she suggested that they leave. He always left with them—usually she rode back to her parents' home with him, and Natalie rode with her parents. But not today. He didn't suggest it, and she wasn't going to wait on him.

Her mother looked at her closely as they rode home in their buggy but didn't say anything until they were home and in her kitchen. "Abigail, dear, what is wrong? You seem quite out of sorts. And what was all of that about my being upset if Nate isn't on time. I'm not like that, and you well know it!"

"I'm sorry, Mother. I just know how much you put into preparing Sunday dinner before you go to church. It isn't right for you to have to keep it warm."

"Dear, it is no problem to keep dinner warm. The chicken will be fine until Nate and Natalie get here, and I still need to cream the potatoes and warm the bread."

"I don't know why you let your help have Sunday off when you always have company over, Mama."

"I don't need Laura on Sundays, Abigail. I think she should be able to go to church with her family the same as I do. Besides, I didn't always have help, and I don't want to forget completely how to cook. And you let your house-keeper off."

"Well, yes, most times I do. But I'm here most of the day or out with friends." Abigail did count herself very lucky. She'd received a substantial inheritance from her paternal grandparents and the house from her mother's mother. With that, and the fact that her papa had invested wisely, she was independently wealthy in her own right, even without what she would inherit from her parents one day. She'd been used to wealth all of her life, unlike her mother, who married into it. Abigail sighed. She really had no choice but to offer to lend a hand. "Well, what can I do to help? It appears Nate is going to keep us waiting all afternoon."

"Dear, he'll be along any minute. He really hasn't kept us waiting."

Abigail sighed. *Oh, yes, Mama, he has. He's kept me waiting for a very long time. I've been patient way too long. It is time to find a way to persuade him to marry me . . .and not just for Natalie's sake, but for my own. If I wait too much longer, it might be too late. I must find a way.*

⤲

Nate wasn't sure what kind of welcome he was going to get when they arrived at the Connorses' home, but he really wasn't that much later than usual. He lifted Natalie up so that she could use the knocker and let her grandparents know that they had arrived.

"We're here!" Natalie said as her grandfather let them in.

"That you are. Are you hungry?" her grandfather asked.

"I am!" She sniffed. "It smells really good in here!"

"It does, doesn't it?" Jacob said. "I'm a bit on the hungry side, too."

Georgette and Abigail came in from the dining room. "Well, it's about time!" Abigail said. Nate knew she wasn't upset with Natalie, but he didn't like that she'd managed to take the smile off his daughter's face.

"It's not Natalie's fault, Abigail."

"Oh, I know that." She gave him a look that told him she was not pleased with him at all. He just wasn't sure why. They really weren't that late.

"We hurried, Aunt Abby. Honest we did."

"There just was a clog-up getting out of the building." Nate turned to his hostess. "I'm sorry if we've held things up, Mother Connors. Is there anything I can do?"

"It isn't a problem, Nate dear. Really. Abigail is just having a bad day. We rarely get things on the table until one o'clock, and it's not even that now. Natalie, would you like to come help finish up?"

"Oh, yes!" Natalie said, following her grandmother to the kitchen.

"Nate, come tell me about your week while our women get dinner on the table," Jacob called.

Nate looked from Abigail to her papa, shrugged, and followed Jacob to the drawing room. Some days there was no pleasing Abigail, and he'd learned not to worry overly much about it. He certainly wasn't going to start now.

Chapter 4

Nate was glad for Monday to arrive. Abigail had been decidedly cool all through Sunday dinner, and he didn't enjoy being around her at all when she was in that kind of mood. The Connors parents had talked him into letting Natalie stay the afternoon with the promise to bring her home after supper, and Nate had been glad to take off. He'd tried to relax and read his Bible for a while when he got home, but he kept thinking about Meagan Snow and her family. He still couldn't quite understand how they'd been attending the same church all this time without him knowing it. Yet he supposed there really was no reason he would have known them had he not begun doing business with them.

As he headed to work on Monday morning, Nate reflected that, most Sundays, he spoke to the people who sat around them and then hurried off to the Connors home for Sunday dinner. He couldn't remember when he'd done things any differently until yesterday. That was probably why Abigail was upset with him. With reason, he supposed, as she most often rode with him after church. She could have done so yesterday, too. He'd been polite to people doing business with her father's bank. It was what he was supposed to be doing.

Later that Monday, he told himself it was what he should do when he went to check on how things were going at the Snow home. Meagan had told him that Mr. Adams was going to start on the renovations today, and he wanted to see firsthand how it was going. Mr. Adams's work wagon was outside, and Nate was sure he was still hard at work.

"Mr. Brooks, please come in," Meagan said as she opened the door. "Mr. Adams has been working all day!" Her eyes sparkled with excitement as she led him into the parlor. The older man stopped working and came to shake his hand.

"Miss Snow said you'd recommended me, and I thank you for it, Mr. Brooks."

"You're welcome. It looks like you are making good headway." Nate entered the parlor to see that the carpenter was building shelves all along one wall, where Miss Snow could store her sewing supplies.

They'd also decided to turn one of the side windows into an entry door, and Mr. Adams would be installing that by the end of the week. "I should have everything Miss Snow asked for finished by the middle of March," the man said.

Nate nodded. He knew Adams would keep his word; that was the main reason he'd recommended him.

"It is looking great, isn't it, Mr. Brooks?" Meagan asked.

"It is. I think you are going to have a lovely shop here, Miss Snow." She was the one who was lovely. Her hair was upswept, and the afternoon dress she wore was one of the ones he'd admired the day he'd inspected her work. It was made of a blue and cream stripe that brought out the color of her eyes. Her cheeks were flushed pink, and he was sure it was from the excitement of seeing her plans come to life.

"Thank you. I already have a few orders even before the shop opens. Of course, they are from friends and neighbors. But they wanted to be the first to be able to say they bought from our shop. I'll be getting clothing labels to put inside all my work soon, and these dresses will be the first to have them."

"But the shop isn't quite ready."

"No. But I have my old sewing machine set up in the dining room. I don't want to lose any time. And these ladies will be wonderful to spread word about the shop opening."

"Sometimes that's the best kind of advertising."

"That's what I thought. I've had flyers and business cards made up to leave with some of the dry goods stores for people who ask about seamstresses, and I've paid for some newspaper advertising to come out the day the shop opens."

"It seems you've thought things through. I'm sure you will build up your clientele in no time." As he spoke, Nate reminded himself to urge Abigail and her friends to give Miss Snow some business. They spent untold money on their wardrobes. Surely, they'd be glad to know there was a new dressmaker in town. As far as that went, his daughter needed new clothes, too. Even though Abigail and her mother had seen to having Natalie's clothes made, he was her father, after all. "I'd like to bring my daughter around to see you. She's growing so fast these days, and I'm sure you could help us choose some styles and fabrics that she would love."

"I would be honored to make something for your little girl, Mr. Brooks."

"When would be a good time for you to see us?"

"Whenever it is convenient for you," Meagan said.

"I'll wait until the shop is open and bring her in then."

"Wonderful! She can be one of my first clients. I'll pull out some of my most recent ladies' magazines and patterns and designs, and we'll see what she might like."

"She'll love that," Nate said.

"Why, Mr. Brooks. How nice to see you," Mrs. Snow said on entering the house. He supposed she was coming in from work. She peeked inside the parlor to see the work that had been completed. "Isn't it all so exciting?"

"It is that. I wanted to see what Mr. Adams had done and was talking to Miss Snow about bringing my daughter in to see her. She is in need of some new things, and I am sure your daughter can please her."

"Oh, I'm sure she will. Meagan will listen carefully to what your little girl likes and will come up with some beautiful ideas."

"I'm certain of it." Nate pulled his watch out of his pocket. "I'd better be leaving now. I'll be back to see how things are going, and if you need anything, please don't hesitate to get in touch with me."

"Oh, we won't," Meagan assured him. "You've helped us so much, aside from approving our loan. With Papa gone, it gives us peace of mind to know that we can come to you for advice."

Nate felt a swell of pride at her words. It felt very good to feel needed. "I'm more than pleased to help. And Miss Snow?"

"Yes?"

"Your papa would have been very proud of you and your mother's decisions, I am sure."

Meagan ducked her head, but not before he saw a tear spring to her eyes. "Thank you."

"I've been trying to tell her how proud her papa would be, Mr. Brooks. Thank you for your kind words."

"You're very welcome."

❧

Over the next few weeks, Meagan began to look forward to Nate's visits. Just when he'd become Nate to her, she couldn't say, but somewhere along the way, they'd begun to call each other by their first names. As she began to stock the shelves that Mr. Adams had just finished that morning, she found herself humming and wondering if Nate would be by that afternoon.

He'd been visiting often to check on the work being done, and while Meagan couldn't wait to open her shop, she was afraid she wouldn't be seeing much of Nate once she did. Her humming stopped, and then she remembered that he was bringing in his daughter, Natalie, once the shop opened. She would be seeing him at least some after the opening. That was set for the very next Monday, March 22. She shivered with excitement as she put a bolt of copper silk atop a bolt of nutmeg brown brocade. She stepped back and looked at the bolts of fabric she'd arranged by color. They were the latest colors and fabrics, and they'd just come in on the train the day before. More and more, her family parlor was taking on the look of a real dressmaker's shop.

Not only had Mr. Adams made shelves to hold her fabrics, he'd also made drawers for all her notions and trims. He'd put the most beautiful glass-windowed door in the place where a full-length window had been. The man was a wonderful craftsman, and he took into account all of her suggestions and ideas. But he'd be through here before long. He'd be moving his work outside tomorrow, as they'd decided to have him paint the porch railing to freshen it up.

Meagan's new sewing machine had come in, too, and it was set up in front of the south-facing bay window where she'd have good light all day and could see anyone coming up to the shop. It was so easy to use, she'd almost finished the frocks that had been ordered before Mr. Adams had begun transforming their parlor.

She loved her shop. It was coming together even better than she'd imagined. Their own settee and two chairs with round tables sat in the front of the shop where her clients could look at the ladies' magazines and fashion plates and the sketches of her own designs. The settee had been recovered in a rose damask and looked lovely. She and her mother decided that she needed two screens in case she was taking measurements of a customer and another came in at the same time for a fitting. Meagan could only hope she'd become that busy. But just in case, and so they'd both be alike, she'd ordered another screen. It had come in today, and Mr. Adams had put both screens up in opposite corners. She only had to organize and put up her trims and notions to have everything in place.

Mr. Adams had hung a bell above the shop door to alert Meagan to arriving customers, and she turned in surprise now as it rang. Nate Brooks entered with a smile on his face, and Meagan's heart felt all fluttery as it always did when she first saw him. She'd been trying to tell herself to quit being so silly, but she really had no control over the way her heart beat faster in his presence.

"Good afternoon, Meagan. Mr. Adams said he thought you were in the shop."

She loved the way he said her name. "Good afternoon, Nate. I've lost track of time today, but look how much I accomplished!" She swept her arm around the room. "Isn't it looking wonderful?"

His deep laugh had her heart doing a little flip. "It is. Mr. Adams says he's nearly through here, and I can see that he is. It looks as if you are ready to open today."

"Oh, I still have some things to be delivered from the dry goods store, and Mr. Adams has the railings to finish up. I actually could open now, but we want to make sure everything is as clean as it can be. We'll have it completely ready on Monday. I'll use the extra time this week to finish up the frocks I've been working on."

"I'm sure your open house will be very successful. I'm handing out the cards you gave me. Perhaps I should wait until the next day to bring Natalie. Although, she is so excited I hate to disappoint her."

"Why don't you bring her tomorrow and then again on Monday for the open house, so that she can enjoy that? If you bring her in early, I'll be able to give her my undivided attention. And she can be the first real customer to come to the shop."

"Oh, she would love that! Thank you for suggesting it, Meagan. Will this time tomorrow be all right?"

"Of course it will be. Or you could bring her a little later—whatever works with your schedule."

"How about around four thirty, is that too late?"

"That would be fine."

"Wonderful. I'll have the housekeeper bring Natalie to the bank, and we'll come over from there. I'm not going to tell her until tomorrow, though. It will be a great surprise for her."

"I look forward to it," Meagan said.

Nate nodded. "Yes, well, everything seems to be going according to plan. I'm very happy for you. And I hope that your mother will be able to quit her position at the Crescent before too long, as I know that is your wish."

"I pray that she will be able to," Meagan said as she saw him out. "And thank you for your consideration of her."

"You're welcome. I'll see you tomorrow."

Meagan watched him leave and was glad she hadn't gone back inside when he turned and gave her a wave from the street. She'd come to like Nate Brooks quite a bit in the last few weeks.

❧

The next afternoon, Meagan watched from the window and saw Nate with his daughter as they came up the walk. They went around to the shop door and used the knocker instead of just entering.

"Good day." Meagan opened the door for them.

"Natalie, do you remember Miss Snow from church?"

"Yes, Papa, I do. She's pretty."

Meagan could feel the color flood her face.

"Yes, she is," Nate said.

"Why, thank you." She was glad Natalie was there so that she didn't have to look at Nate. "You are very pretty yourself."

Natalie giggled. "Thank you. Papa says you make beautiful clothing and that you are going to make something for me."

"I am, if you think you might like some of my ideas."

"Oh, I'm sure that I will," the little girl said.

"Well, let's go sit down, and I'll show you some of the new styles and find out what you like and don't like."

The child followed her and took a seat on the settee, where her father joined her. Meagan had only seen Natalie briefly that day in church. Since then, she and her family had sat in the back where they usually did. And normally, they left right after church, before Nate and his daughter came up the aisle. Natalie looked a lot like her father with her dark hair and brown eyes, and she seemed very sweet.

Meagan pulled out several ladies' magazines. She looked at Natalie and asked, "What is it you need right now?"

"I would like a new walking dress, and I heard Aunt Abby tell Grandmother just the other day that I could use a new Sunday dress."

Meagan looked at Nate for guidance.

"I think she could use more than that, but it will be a start."

"That is where we will begin, then," Meagan said. Turning to a page, she showed them some of the newest styles for young girls. One was a walking dress made of a dark blue cashmere and had a finely pleated vest, with three wide rows of pleats at the hem. White lace trimmed the pleated collar and the cuffs.

"Oh, how pretty. Could it be in another color?"

"Of course. We can make it any color you like," Meagan assured her as she turned to another page and showed her a dress of cream foulard with a heavy green band at the hem.

"I like that, too, Miss Snow! I even like the colors," Natalie said.

"I do, too. Let us see what else we can find that you like."

With Nate looking on, Meagan showed his daughter more styles and brought out the newest dresses she'd made for her sisters. By the time they were through, they'd decided on a walking dress and a dress to wear to church. She took Natalie's measurements and gave her some swatches of the fabric in the colors she liked to take home with her. She would let Meagan know which ones she wanted when they came to the grand opening.

When it was time to leave, Nate turned to Meagan. "Natalie quite enjoyed herself today—and I enjoyed watching the two of you decide on the items to add to her wardrobe. If that is the way you are going to treat all of your customers, I have no doubt that you are going to do quite well. No doubt at all."

Chapter 5

By the end of the next week, Nate could no longer deny that he was very attracted to Meagan Snow. His daughter had taken to her immediately, and he understood why. Meagan was a warm and lovely woman, who treated Natalie as if she was just as special as the wealthiest client she might have. He also liked her family almost as much as he liked her.

He'd waited late in the day of her open house to take Natalie in, not wanting to detract from what Meagan needed to do in trying to obtain clients. Quite a few women were still there. While he hadn't felt out of place in the shop when he'd taken his daughter to meet Meagan, today he did. Meagan greeted them, but with so many women to serve, it was impossible for Natalie to receive the same kind of attention she'd had the first time he brought her in.

Mrs. Snow was helping her daughter, and she must have sensed Nate's discomfort. She came over and offered her hand. "Good afternoon, Mr. Brooks, how nice to see you and your daughter again."

"Thank you, Mrs. Snow." He looked around the room and lowered his voice. "It appears that the open house is a success. I think I should bring Natalie in another day to discuss her fabric choices."

"Oh no, Meagan would feel terrible if you do that. She doesn't want to disappoint Natalie. The shop is due to close shortly. Why don't you and your daughter come out to the kitchen with me? I just took some cookies out of the oven, but it is so close to closing I don't believe we are going to need them."

"Oh, please, Papa," Natalie said with the look that rarely failed to get a yes out of him. "I want to show Miss Snow the colors I decided on."

Nate nodded, and before long, he and Natalie were sitting at the kitchen table, eating warm cookies and watching Mrs. Snow start dinner. She reminded him of his mother. Becca and Sarah took Natalie under their wing, and Nate listened to them talk about school and church and any number of other things until Meagan rushed into the kitchen.

"I am so sorry, Natalie. I wasn't expecting so many people."

"It appeared to be a great success." Nate smiled at Meagan. Her face was flushed, and she was smiling. One only had to look at her to realize that it had been a very good day for her and that she was very happy.

She nodded. "I have appointments set up for the rest of the week with ladies who want to order some of their spring wardrobe from me! But I would love to see what fabrics you've chosen for your dresses, Natalie."

"Why don't you and Natalie go do that now? Supper will be ready in about a half hour, and Mr. Brooks and Natalie can join us."

"Oh, we can't intrude like that, Mrs. Snow," Nate said, although the smell of the stew she was stirring had his mouth watering.

"You won't be intruding. We would like your company. Unless you are due to be somewhere else?"

Nate shook his head. "No, we aren't." He'd told his housekeeper not to worry about dinner, that he would take Natalie to her favorite restaurant for dinner. Sharing a meal with the Snow women seemed a much better choice.

"Please, Papa," Natalie said. Apparently his daughter agreed with him.

"Thank you, Mrs. Snow. We gladly accept your invitation."

He couldn't remember the last time he had such an enjoyable evening. He watched as Meagan and Natalie discussed the colors and styles. By the time they'd settled on everything, Mrs. Snow was calling them to supper in the dining room. The table had been set with china and lit with both candles and gaslight. The atmosphere was warm and inviting.

Once seated, Mrs. Snow asked Nate to say the prayer.

He gladly obliged. "Dear Father, we thank You for this day and for the many blessings You've bestowed upon us. We thank You for the food we are about to eat. Most of all we thank You for Your Son and our Savior. In His name we pray. Amen."

He totally enjoyed the informality of the simple meal. The beef stew was well seasoned and served with a fresh salad. For dessert, they were treated to bread pudding. Nate was amazed that Mrs. Snow, even with the help of her daughters, could prepare such a meal and set so nice a table without the aid of hired help. Perhaps he'd been around the Connors family too long.

～

During the rest of March, Nate and Natalie visited Meagan's shop often, usually on a Saturday, but sometimes during the week. They had the first fitting of the first dress, then more fittings. By the time they arrived at the shop, Mrs. Snow, whom he'd found didn't work on the weekends, was usually taking a pan of cookies, a cake, or a pie out of the oven. She never failed to ask them if they wanted some of whatever she'd baked.

On the weekday fittings, they almost always were asked to stay for dinner, and Nate thought he would have agreed to stay even if it wasn't for his daughter's pleading expression. He enjoyed being there as much as Natalie did. It was more than a little refreshing to see how the Snow family had coped with the loss of a husband, father, and breadwinner. They might have had household staff at some point, judging from the home and the furnishings. They talked about Mr. Snow often, and Nate could tell they loved him and missed him greatly, but they honored his memory by getting on with their lives the best they could. He never heard them complain. Maybe he related so well to them because they'd suffered a loss just as he did when he lost his wife, Rose, in the fire.

Whatever the reason, he liked being around the Snow family. He didn't feel that he had to be constantly on guard as he did most times with Rose's family. He supposed that was because he'd always felt guilty that he hadn't been able to save her. By the time he'd reached their home, it was engulfed in flames, and Abigail was outside holding Natalie. He'd tried to go in, but some of his neighbors had stopped him. In shock, all he could do was join Abigail, taking his daughter in his arms as they watched the flames.

Something died in him that day, but he'd struggled through, questioning God, reading and praying—and doing his best to raise the daughter he adored. He knew now that the Lord had never left his side, and while he still wondered why his Rose had to die, he knew she was in a better place. He strived to raise Natalie the way he thought Rose would want him to. . .trusting in the Lord to help him.

Since he'd met Meagan Snow and her family, he'd felt more alive than he had since the day of the fire. And it felt really good to be looking forward rather than backward.

"Papa, do you like the Snow family as much as I do?" Natalie asked when they were on their way to the shop for a fitting of her new Sunday dress.

He looked down and smiled at his daughter. She was always in a good mood when they were on their way to the Snows' home. "Well, I'm not sure how much that is, but I do like them very much."

"They are so nice, and they like to talk to me, and I like talking to them. I just enjoy being there. It's very. . .homey, isn't it?"

That is it, exactly, Nate thought. "Yes, it is."

"I like being there almost as much as at home. . .and much better than any other place."

As she skipped and chattered alongside him, Nate realized that Natalie was always very happy and talkative when they left the Snow home, but she didn't have much to say when she left her aunt Abigail's. He began to wonder why that was. Natalie had always been close to Abigail, but not quite as open or happy around her aunt as she was around Meagan. Maybe it was a difference in personalities. Or perhaps it could be the different way each woman treated her. Abigail sometimes treated Natalie as if she were younger than she really was, and Meagan treated her. . .like a person in her own right. Nate shook his head.

Mulling it over wasn't telling him anything. Perhaps his daughter just liked Meagan better than she did Abigail. *That* he could certainly understand.

❧

Meagan began looking forward to Natalie's fittings more each time she came in. Her heart went out to the child and her papa. It had been so hard for Meagan's family when her own father had passed away, but how very hard it must be for Nate to raise a child on his own, or for Natalie to barely remember her mother. Yet Natalie was a delightful child and a joy to have around.

Nate, however, made her pulse race and her heart beat faster these days. Something about the man's slow smile never failed to make her smile back—and her heart seemed to do little flip-flops at the sight of him. He was such a gentleman, and he treated her mother and sisters with a gentle grace that touched her heart. He was extra nice to her mother, and that meant so much to Meagan. More than likely, his own loss made him relate to them and be so considerate. Whatever it was, she found her respect growing for him each day—as well as her attraction to him. She tried not to show how she felt and lived in fear that she wouldn't be able to hide those feelings much longer.

At this fitting, she concentrated on Natalie and how well the new suit dress fit. It was in the child's favorite colors, blue with green trim. Its bodice was fitted, and the skirt was tucked in the front and pulled to the rear to form a modified bustle, nothing the size of what women were wearing these days, but enough of one to make Natalie feel she was wearing the latest style. The collar and cuffs on the dress matched the green inserts of the jacket. To Meagan, Natalie looked adorable.

Apparently, Nate thought so, too.

"You do wonderful work, Meagan. Nothing we've had made for Natalie in the last few years can compare to the quality of your work."

"Thank you. I love doing this. I am so happy you made it possible. I talked Mama into giving her notice at the Crescent. Today is her last day."

"Oh, I'm happy to hear that news!"

"Somehow, I thought you might be."

Nate nodded. "Your mother reminds me of my own at times. I'm glad she will be able to stay at home again."

"I convinced her that I'd be needing her help here. I do think the business will grow enough that I will need some extra hands. I hope so, anyway."

"Once word gets out from the ladies you are sewing for now, you'll need her."

Natalie had been turning this way and that in front of the mirror. "I love this dress, Miss Meagan! I can't wait to wear it. When do you think it will be ready?"

"You may take it home with you."

Natalie clapped. "I can wear it on Sunday. Oh, I can hardly wait!"

"I look forward to seeing you in it," Meagan said.

"I can't wait to see what Grandmother and Aunt Abby say! I haven't told them about it because I wanted it to be a surprise."

Nate chuckled. "They certainly will be surprised, mostly because you and I did this without their help."

He sounded proud that he'd been the one to help his daughter, but Meagan wondered if his in-laws would feel the same way. She'd watched them in church more than she should have, she supposed. It was obvious that Nate's sister-in-law wanted everyone to think she had some kind of claim on him. Perhaps she did. If so, Meagan needed to quit weaving daydreams about the man. Perhaps she needed to assume that he was taken, for even if he wasn't, she'd be silly to think that a man like him would be interested in her.

Chapter 6

When he and Natalie went to dinner at Abigail's the first Saturday evening in April, Nate was still wondering about Natalie's differing moods when with Abigail or the Snows. It wasn't that Natalie didn't want to be with her aunt—she was excited to be spending the night there.

Abigail had also invited her parents, which was a big change from her usual dinner parties, so the evening was more enjoyable than usual for Nate. . .until his parents-in-law went home and Natalie went up to get ready for bed. Then he was left alone with Abigail.

"That was a wonderful meal, Abigail. And it was nice that it was just family tonight."

"I thought so, too," she said, leading him into the front parlor. She took a seat in the ladies' chair flanking the fireplace, and Nate sat down in the gentleman's seat across from her. It was a nice room, elegantly furnished, but he'd never really felt comfortable in it. Now he knew why. It didn't have that homey feel that the Snows' home had. Maybe it was because Abigail lived by herself or because she was too concerned about nothing getting messed.

"Nate, dear," Abigail began, "don't you think it's time you thought of marrying again?"

It had been a while since she'd brought up the subject, but he'd been expecting it for some time. He answered the way he always did. "No. Natalie and I are getting along quite well. I have a wonderful housekeeper who takes good care of us."

"But don't you get lonesome?"

He had been lonesome for a long time, but only for Rose. Now he realized that thoughts of her had somehow been replaced by Meagan Snow, and he wasn't quite sure how he felt about that.

"Don't you?" Abigail prodded.

"Everyone gets lonesome from time to time, Abigail. Of course I do. That certainly isn't a reason to get married, though. There needs to be more—"

"What about for Natalie's sake? She needs a woman's influence in her life."

Nate chuckled. "She has that. She has you and your mother, and even my housekeeper, who is wonderful with her." She also had the Snow women, but

Nate felt it best not to mention them.

"Nate." Abigail had that exasperated tone in her voice. He seemed to bring it out in her. "You know that Rose would have wanted you to remarry, and you know that I love Natalie as my own. I care for you—"

"Abigail, we have this discussion on a regular basis, and I haven't changed my mind. I—"

"Papa, I'm ready for bed," Natalie interrupted, and Nate had never been happier to have a conversation cut short. "Are you going to hear my prayers?"

"I certainly am," Nate said, getting up to follow her upstairs.

Abigail did love Natalie, there was no denying that and never had been. She'd furnished a room specifically for her niece and had chosen everything with the little girl in mind. Nate did appreciate her love for his daughter. But that was all.

Natalie knelt beside the bed as she always did, and Nate knelt next to her as she prayed.

"Dear God, thank You for Papa and for Grandmother and Grandfather and for Aunt Abby. And thank You for all the Snow ladies, especially Miss Meg. Please watch over them all and keep them safe. Please forgive me for my sins and help me to do Your will. And please let Papa get home safely. Thank You for everything, dear God. In Jesus' name. Amen."

"Amen." Nate echoed. He realized that Natalie must like Meagan a great deal when she called her Miss Meg. She always shortened the first names of the people she cared a lot about.

Natalie jumped into bed, and he helped her pull the quilt up to her neck. He bent down and kissed her brow. "Good night, Natalie."

"Good night, Papa. I'll see you at church tomorrow."

He nodded. "Yes, you will. Sleep tight, and sweet dreams."

"Thank you." Natalie yawned.

Nate met Abigail in the hall. "I'll go in and tell her good night and be right back. Would you like a cup of chocolate before you go?"

Nate didn't want to continue the conversation they'd begun earlier. He shook his head. "No, thank you. I'm quite full from that excellent dinner you served. Thank you again, Abigail. There's no need to see me to the door; I can let myself out."

"Yes, well, all right," Abigail said a bit coolly.

He knew she was unhappy with him, but if he stayed and continued the conversation, her mood would only get worse. "I'll see you and Natalie at church tomorrow." Nate didn't wait for an answer. He hurried down the stairs, gathered his overcoat, and took his leave, shutting the door behind him.

As soon as he arrived at church the next morning, Nate could tell Abigail still wasn't happy. The tightness around her lips had proven over time to be a signal that she was in a bad mood. He decided to ignore her moodiness and hoped she would get over it.

"Good morning!" he said to no one in particular, but with a smile and a wink for his daughter.

"Good morning, Papa," Natalie said, scooting over on the pew to make room for him. "Aunt Abby and Grandmother and Grandfather think my new outfit is beautiful!"

He was almost certain he heard a *huff* coming from Abigail as he replied to his daughter, "You do look quite lovely this morning."

"Thank you. I feel pretty in the dress Miss Meg made me!"

Georgette Connors leaned forward, looking past her daughter and granddaughter to address Nate. "I want to know where to find this new dressmaker you've found. The quality of her work is superb!"

"Her name is Meagan Snow, but you've already met her, Georgette," Nate said. "She and her family attend church here. I introduced you to them."

Georgette look confused and cocked her head to the side. Nate could tell she was trying to remember.

"They sat behind us over a month ago. The bank is financing her new business endeavor."

"Oh, yes. I remember now. Well, I'll talk to you about it later."

Nate nodded. Thankfully, he was on the outside of the row by his daughter and not beside Abigail. She'd barely acknowledged his greeting, and she looked stiff as a board. He had a feeling it was all this talk about Natalie's new dress. She was probably angry that he hadn't consulted her about the addition to his daughter's wardrobe. Well, she would have to get over it.

When the service was over, Nate looked around for the Snow women so that he could point them out to Georgette again, but they were out the door before he could get her attention.

Natalie rode with her grandparents back to their house, and Nate offered Abigail a ride, as she and Natalie had been picked up by her parents that morning.

"Yes, thank you," she accepted a bit coolly.

Nate sighed inwardly. Sometimes he wished they didn't have a standing date to eat with his in-laws every Sunday. He helped Abigail into his surrey and wondered if she was going to tell him why she was angry. He took the reins in hand and flicked his wrist. Once they were moving, Abigail lost no time in letting him know what her problem was.

"Who is this Meg that I've been hearing about from Natalie?"

"Why, she's the dressmaker who made her new dress," Nate answered.

"I know that, Nate. But where did she come from, and how do you know about her?"

Nate tried to tamp down his growing irritation that neither Abigail nor her mother remembered meeting the Snows. "You've met her at church, Abigail. I introduced you all back in February."

Her brow furrowed, trying to remember.

Nate sighed. "They were sitting in the pew behind us."

"Oh, yes. Now I remember. But I don't recall you saying she was a seamstress."

"Well, I did. She is a talented dressmaker who's opened her own shop. The bank loaned her the money to get it started—"

"Oh, I see." Abigail sounded a little less cool. "So you are just helping her get started and making sure that our bank gets a return on the investment."

Maybe that's how it had started out, but Nate knew that wasn't the reason he was taking Natalie to Meagan's shop now. There was much more to it, but it wasn't something Abigail would want to hear, and it wasn't anything Nate wanted to tell her. . .not yet, anyway. "I'd appreciate it if you would spread the word about the shop and the quality of Miss Snow's work. A word from you would help a lot."

"I suppose I could do that," Abigail said. But she didn't sound too happy about it.

Nate decided it was time to change the subject. "I received my invitation to the grand opening gala at the Crescent on May 20th."

"Oh, good. I received mine, too. Everyone is talking about how it's going to be the event of the season!"

Nate was sure it would be. He wanted to bring up Meagan and her shop again and how he was sure there would be women wanting new ball gowns. But Abigail's mood had lifted with talk of the Crescent, and for everyone's sake at dinner, he felt it best not to change subjects. Somehow, he managed to keep up with the conversation while his thoughts were on Meagan.

Abigail's assumption that he was taking Natalie to Meagan's shop to insure the success of her business had him facing the truth. He'd come to care for the Snow family, and he wanted the business to be a success for their sake. Yet that wasn't the reason he kept ordering items for his daughter's wardrobe. He was beginning to care for Meagan more each time he was around her. That was why he would keep taking Natalie to Meagan for all of her wardrobe needs. It was that simple.

Chapter 7

The next week, Meagan and her mother went to order more fabric and trims. Several of the ladies who'd come in the day she'd opened had ordered afternoon dresses, and one had ordered a dinner gown. Nate had also decided to order several more items for Natalie. Meagan was thrilled, and it did look as if her mother had quit working at the Crescent just in time. There was no doubt she was needed.

Celebrating this change, Meagan and her mother decided to have lunch at the Southern Hotel. Many of the hotels were located near the springs so that their guests wouldn't have to go far to take advantage of what many thought to be healing waters. Being located adjacent to the Basin Spring, the Southern was no exception.

As they entered the hotel, Meagan felt wonderful to be able to treat her mother to a luxury they hadn't been able to afford since Papa's death. The girls were in school, but hopefully, she'd be able to treat them one day soon, too.

After the two ladies were shown to a table in the elegant dining room, a waiter handed them each a menu. Meagan looked it over and ordered a cup of bouillon, an egg sandwich, and tea.

"I'll have the same, please," her mother requested. When the waiter left, she chuckled. "We could just as well have had this meal at home."

"I know, Mama. But we still have more shopping to do, and you deserve a treat."

"Thank you, dear. You've been working so hard so that I could quit working at the Crescent; I think it is you who deserves a treat."

"I know there is nothing wrong with you working outside the home. The Crescent Hotel is beautiful, and I'm sure it is a nice place to work. But Becca is still young, and, well, we all just want you at home," Meagan said. "The house doesn't feel the same if you aren't there."

Her mother reached over and patted her hand. "You are a wonderful daughter, Meagan. I am proud of all my girls, and your papa would be so proud of all of you, too."

"Thank you. We've been very blessed to have parents such as you and Papa. I hope that he would approve of what we—"

"Why, good day, ladies," a voice from over Meagan's shoulder interrupted.

Her mother smiled in recognition, but Meagan knew who it was even before she turned around to see. She'd know that voice anywhere—even if her pounding heart hadn't recognized it. She smiled and said, "Good day, Mr. Brooks."

"We're treating ourselves to celebrate that I can stay at home and help my Meagan," her mother added. "Thank you for making that possible, Mr. Brooks. Would you like to join us?"

Thank you, Mama. Meagan held her breath, waiting for his answer.

"Actually, I would like that, if you are sure?"

"Please do," Meagan's mother said. "We would like the company."

He looked at Meagan for confirmation.

"Please do." She sounded a little breathless to her own ears.

Nate smiled and took a seat. The waiter seemed to come out of nowhere with a menu. Nate brushed it away with a smile and said, "I'll have the gentleman's plate, please. And please add the ladies' ticket to mine."

"Oh, no!" Meagan said. "We can't let you do that."

"After the wonderful meals I've enjoyed at your home? I can't join you if you won't let me pay for your lunch." He half stood before Meagan's mother shook her head and chuckled.

"Please sit, Mr. Brooks. We'll be honored to have lunch with you."

"Good." He sat back down and grinned at Meagan. "It's not often I have the opportunity to have lunch with such lovely ladies."

His glance captured Meagan's, and she could feel the warm rush of color steal up her cheeks. The man had a way of making the blood race through her veins.

He smiled and took a sip from his water glass. "What brought you out and about besides your celebration?"

"We ordered some fabric, and we're going to buy some trim and notions this afternoon. I need trim for the coat you've ordered for Natalie."

"Natalie's grandmother loved the new Sunday dress. I gave her your name and the address of your shop. I'm hoping she and Natalie's aunt Abigail will spread the word about the shop. The women in their circle seem to have a new outfit every time I see them. I've also heard that one of the dressmakers in town is getting married, and everyone is worried that there just aren't enough seamstresses in town. I'm getting word out as fast as I can."

"Oh, thank you for telling me. I'll give your friends a discount if they come in."

Nate shook his head. "There is no need to do that."

"But—"

"Most of these women can well afford your prices. Don't worry about that."

"All right, I'll charge them what I charge you."

Nate raised an eyebrow and grinned at her. "No. I have a feeling you are giving me a very good discount. You charge them the going rate."

Meagan sighed. She did give him a discount from what she normally charged. How could she not? He was the reason she'd been able to start her shop in the first place. "All right, I will."

"Good."

The waiter brought their meals out and served them. Once he was gone, Nate asked, "May I ask a blessing?"

"Of course you may," Meagan's mother said, and they bowed their heads while he did.

Meagan couldn't remember when she'd had a better time. Nate was attentive to her and her mother, and the conversation flowed smoothly. Of course, she gave the credit for that to her mother. They talked about the Crescent Hotel, which looked down over the town, and about what a beautiful addition it was to the landscape.

"It really is quite lovely on the inside. And the management is very dedicated to seeing that the guests are treated like royalty," Meagan's mother said.

"The opening gala is coming up soon. I'm sure it will be very lavish," Nate said.

"Oh, it will be. They were planning it before I left."

Meagan could only imagine what a gala at the hotel would be like. She'd heard it was by invitation only and was sure that only the richest and most influential people in town were invited—which certainly didn't include her.

That Nate knew many people in town became obvious as they enjoyed their meal, because several diners came up to their table and spoke to him. He was diligent in introducing them—never failing to mention her dressmaking shop.

A nice-looking couple stopped at the table, and Nate introduced them as Mr. and Mrs. Richardson.

"I've heard wonderful things about the quality of your work," Mrs. Richardson said. "I do need a few things for this spring and summer. Would it be possible for me to make an appointment to see you later today?"

"Of course. I should be back at the shop by three o'clock," Meagan said. "Could you come then?"

"I will be there. It was very nice to meet you and your mother," Mrs. Richardson said. "I'll call on you this afternoon, then."

The couple took their leave, and Meagan smiled at Nate. "Thank you. Again."

"You are very welcome. She's a very nice woman, and I'm sure she will be very pleased with the work you do for her. She'll also help spread the word."

Meagan hated to see the meal end. It was the first time she'd spent any time in Nate's company outside of the shop, besides at his bank and that one day at church. But that couldn't even be counted because he'd only been introducing them. This was different somehow.

They said their farewells outside the hotel, and Meagan spent the rest of the afternoon thinking about Nate and what a very nice man he was.

Over the first couple of weeks in April, Meagan ran into Nate at several other places, and she liked him more each time. First, they saw each other at the post office, where they spoke for several minutes. He asked about her mother and sisters and told her how much Natalie was looking forward to her next fitting. The next time she ran into him was at Martin's Dry Goods where she was picking up some thread and buttons and he was trying to select a doll for Natalie's birthday.

"Is her birthday coming up soon?" Meagan asked.

"It is two weeks from this Saturday. She is so excited. I hope she likes this doll. Do you think she will?" He held it up for her inspection. The lovely doll had hair the color of Natalie's and eyes the same shade as hers, too. She was dressed in the little girl's favorite color and the latest style.

"Oh, I think she will love it. It is beautiful."

"Good." He smiled and nodded. "I trust your judgment. I'll have it wrapped and sent to the house. My housekeeper, Mrs. Baker, will put it in my study."

He was through with his transaction before she was, but he waited for her to finish and walked out of the store with her. "Would you have time for a soda? There is a soda shop just across the street by the Perry House Hotel."

Meagan hesitated for only a moment. Her mother would be the first to encourage her to go. "I–I'd like that."

He put a hand on her elbow while they crossed the street and went into the shop. It was fairly quiet this time of day, and most of the seats at the counter were free, as were the small round tables. Nate led her to one of those and pulled out a chair for her. She'd been in the shop several times, but it had been a while, and she'd never been in there with a gentleman.

That's exactly what Nate Brooks was—a very nice, gentle man. Yes, he was a banker, and she would always be thankful for all the ways he'd helped her and her family. But lately, she was seeing him as more than just a businessman. He was a wonderful father to Natalie, and he was easy to be around. *Much too easy to be around,* Meagan thought as he ordered their sodas and began telling her a funny story about Natalie. She was laughing when their sodas were brought to the table.

Meagan felt more at ease around Nate each time she saw him, but this was the first time she'd actually had any real time with him alone. Conversation flowed easily between them until a clock in the shop chimed the hour.

Meagan realized they'd been there for over an hour. "Oh, I must be getting home. Mama will be getting worried about me."

Nate stood and pulled out her chair immediately. "I'll accompany you home and explain."

"Oh, no, that's not necessary. She will understand. But I'm sure she's beginning to wonder what has kept me so long."

"Well, I'd better let you go, then. Thank you for joining me this afternoon. I quite enjoyed it."

"You are welcome—so did I. Enjoy it, I mean. Thank you for treating me. Sodas are one of my very favorite things."

"I'll have to take you to the Crescent one of these days. I've been told that they have a wonderful soda shop there."

Meagan's heart felt all fluttery at the thought of him actually taking her to the Crescent. As they left the shop and she started home, however, she told herself it was time to quit daydreaming. Nate Brooks was a wonderful man, but they weren't in the same social circles, and nice as he was to her, it didn't mean that he was interested in her in any way other than seeing that her business was a success. *I need to remember that. Just because I find myself dreaming about him day and night doesn't mean he's dreaming about me. . . .*

❧

Nate went back to the bank for an hour before going home. He'd enjoyed the afternoon even more than the lunch he'd had with Meagan and her mother. He wished that Meagan had let him see her home. He hadn't wanted the afternoon to end. It was always that way when he was with her.

From his observations, most of the women in his social circle visited with each other, entertained each other, and gossiped about each other. At times, he just wanted to leave the room. . .and often did. Meagan was so very different from them. It was refreshing just to be near her.

She was working to help her family, to keep her mother from working outside the home, and to give them all a future. He ventured to guess that none of the women he knew would handle the death of a parent and all the changes Meagan's family had gone through since then with such grace. He admired her greatly, and he hoped that by seeing him outside of the bank or her shop, she would get to know him better.

He thought back over the afternoon as he had his runabout brought around and headed home. He really cared about Meagan Snow. She was the first woman since his Rose that had touched his heart. He hoped she might begin to feel the same way about him.

He traveled up Spring Street to his home and prayed as the sun set behind the hill. *Thank You, Lord, for allowing me to run into Meagan the way I have been lately. I pray that if it be Your will, she will see me as a man who would like to court her. And I pray that You help me find a way to ask her if she will allow me to. In Jesus' name I pray. Amen.*

Chapter 8

"Aunt Abby and Grandmother, when are you going to visit Miss Meg's shop and have her make something for you?" Natalie asked at Sunday dinner the next week. "She makes such lovely things, and she showed me a ball gown she's making for someone. It is so beautiful."

"I am beginning to hear very good things about her," Abigail's mother said, ladling gravy over the potatoes on the plate she was serving to Nate. "I'm thinking of asking her to make me a new summer walking dress."

Inside, Abigail fumed, but she tried not to show it. As if she didn't hear enough about Meagan Snow from Natalie, now she was beginning to hear it from some of her friends *and* her mother. By all accounts the woman was a very good dressmaker—obviously word was getting around if her mother was thinking of doing business with her—but Abigail was sick of hearing her name.

"You should, Grandmother. She is making me one."

It seemed that Natalie was a one-woman advertising agency for that Snow woman's shop. *One would think she was being paid*, Abigail thought.

"I ran into Meagan and her mother having lunch the other day, and the Richardsons were there, too. Myla made an appointment to go see her." Nate's comment added to her irritation.

"Yes. Myla is having Miss Snow make her a new tea gown and a walking dress."

Abigail didn't much care—she just didn't like Natalie talking about her all the time, and she especially didn't like the fact that her niece saw so much of the woman. Suddenly, Abigail realized that if Natalie was going for fittings, unless the housekeeper was taking her, Nate was seeing an awful lot of Miss Snow, too.

"Does Mrs. Baker take Natalie to be fitted?"

"No." Natalie answered the question that had been directed to Nate. "Papa takes me."

"Oh, well, I know how busy you are, Nate. I'll be glad to take Natalie in for her fittings."

"Thank you, Abigail, but that won't be necessary. Miss Snow is very good about scheduling the fittings for when it is convenient for me."

"I see." And she didn't like what she was thinking. Not one bit.

"That's very nice of her," Abigail's mother said, handing Abigail her plate. "I've heard she is just a lovely woman."

Abigail made up her mind right then and there that it was time for her to get to know Miss Snow. And she would start tomorrow.

❧

Meagan couldn't be much happier with the way her business was growing. Mrs. Richardson had ordered several things from her, and through her word of mouth, two of her friends had come in and ordered new afternoon dresses. Occasionally, someone would see the sign outside and come in.

She was just finishing up the trim on a dinner dress she'd made for Mrs. Sinclair, one of the ladies who had come in the day of her opening, when she looked out the window and saw a woman approaching the shop. She came up the steps and around to the door. Meagan had a sinking feeling as she got up to greet her.

Abigail Connors swept into the shop as if she'd been coming for years. Meagan would know her anywhere. She saw her each Sunday, sitting on the same pew that Nate and Natalie used. . .often next to Nate. That she had a proprietary air toward Nate and Natalie was a big understatement. Now, here she was, in the one place Meagan had begun to weave dreams about herself and Nate.

Meagan forced a smile to her lips and held out her hand. "Good afternoon, Miss Connors. How nice to see you. How may I help you?"

"Thank you." The expression on the woman's face didn't match the tone of her voice at all. "How do you know who I am?"

"I've seen you at church with Mr. Brooks and Natalie. I've been doing some sewing for her."

"Ah, yes. I know," she said in a dismissive tone. "I've been hearing about your work. I'd like to see some samples of it if you have any to show me. I might decide to place an order with you if I like what I see."

Meagan could feel her face turn hot with indignation. How dare the woman take that tone with her? For a moment, Meagan thought she'd actually spoken aloud, and oh, how she wanted to. Instead, she silently prayed, asking for help not to lose her temper. This woman was Natalie's aunt and the daughter of the man who owned the bank that gave her the money to start this business. She could not afford to make her angry.

"I'd be glad to show you some of my work." She opened the wardrobe she and her mother had decided to put in the shop for just that reason. They used it to store some of the things Meagan had made for herself and other family members, rotating them with other outfits.

"Are you interested in anything in particular? An afternoon dress? Dinner dress?"

"Just show me what you have," Abigail said, pulling off the gloves that matched her afternoon dress of blue taffeta trimmed in gold. Meagan knew it was of the very latest style and fabric.

Thankful that she could show Abigail several things that were of just as good quality as what she was wearing and in the latest styles, as well, she pulled out an afternoon dress to show her. It was made of red-and-white-striped serge with matching red trim at the neck and wrists. A solid red over-skirt gathered up and draped to the side.

Abigail turned it this way and that, looking closely at the stitching. "This is very nice," she said. "What else do you have?"

Meagan showed one of her morning dresses and a walking dress that belonged to her mother. She also pulled out a dinner dress and a Sunday dress. Abigail went over each one as if she were buying them for herself or perhaps, given the way she was inspecting each one, the queen of England! Meagan had never had her work scrutinized quite so thoroughly.

When she'd hung them all back, she turned to Abigail. "I hope you are satisfied that I do my best on each outfit I make, Miss Connors?"

Abigail rewarded her with a very slight nod. If Meagan had blinked, she would have missed it.

"You do fine work, Miss Snow. I can see why I've been hearing good reports about your skill as a dressmaker and why Nate keeps telling me to let all of my friends know about the shop."

Meagan's heart warmed at the thought that Nate was trying to send more business to her.

"I would like to have a new dinner dress. Do you have some fashion plates available for me to look at?"

"Certainly." She motioned to the settee in front of the fireplace. "Please, make yourself comfortable. I just received the latest *Harpers Bazaar* and there are some lovely plates in it."

She handed the magazine to Abigail and then reached for another. "And here is the latest *Godey's* that I have. I'm sure we can find something in these."

As it was teatime and her mother always insisted that she stop working and take a brief break in the afternoon, Meagan wasn't surprised to see her enter the shop with a loaded tea tray. She'd taken to bringing in extra, just in case Meagan was with a customer, and she had never been so glad to see her mother as now.

"Mama, thank you. I didn't realize it was teatime already. Miss Connors, would you like a cup of tea and a tea cake?"

Abigail looked up from the magazine. "I—yes, I suppose I would."

"You do remember my mother from church, don't you?"

"No, I'm afraid I don't," Abigail said quite bluntly.

"There's no reason you should, Miss Connors," Meagan's mother said. "We only met that one time."

Meagan wanted to shout that there was every reason to remember her sweet mother, but she kept to the manners she'd been raised with and said nothing. Nevertheless, she certainly wasn't going to let her mother serve the woman.

"How would you like your tea? With cream and sugar?"

Abigail had gone back to perusing the magazine and didn't look up. "Yes, that will be fine."

"Would you like a tea cake?" Meagan asked. She could feel her eyebrow rise.

"No. Just tea."

Meagan looked at her mother and found her with a smile on her face and a twinkle in her eye as she fixed the cup of tea. Meagan sighed inwardly and smiled back as she took the cup of tea and set it down beside Abigail. "There you are."

The woman looked up from the magazine once more. "Yes, well, thank you."

"You are welcome. Have you seen anything you like?" Meagan took a sip of her own tea.

"Yes, in fact, I have." Abigail showed Meagan a fashion plate picturing a beautiful dinner dress in peacock blue satin trimmed in black Chantilly lace.

"That is lovely."

"Can you make something like that for me?"

"Of course. Would you want it in the same fabric? Or if not, I have several samples of other colors and different fabrics you may choose from."

"Let me look at those."

Never had Meagan dealt with a ruder woman. She wanted nothing more than to tell her so, but she couldn't. Instead, she sighed as she went to get her samples. Her mother just shook her head and left the room.

By the time Abigail left, Meagan had shown her every bolt and sample of fabric in the shop. After much deliberation, she finally decided that the design of the fashion plate would look better on her if it was made of a red-striped silk and black lace. Although Meagan thought it might be a little daring, she wasn't about to argue with the woman's choice.

"When can you start on it?" Abigail asked.

"I'll have to order the fabric and trim, but it shouldn't take more than a couple of weeks to come in. I can start on it then. I will need to take your measurements, though."

"Oh, yes. Can you do that now?"

"Certainly."

"It won't take long, will it? I'm having dinner with Nate and Natalie, and I don't want to be late."

Meagan's heart gave a sudden little twist. She didn't much like the idea of Nate having dinner with this woman—even if they were related by marriage. "It won't take long at all. You may use the screen behind you to remove your dress. Just let me know when you are ready."

When Abigail called, Meagan made quick work of getting her measurements. She wrote them down carefully in the notebook she kept for such purposes. "That will do it. I'll make note of these with your order. I'd like to make a muslin pattern and fit it to you. Can you come for a fitting a week from now?"

"I should be able to," Abigail said from behind the screen. "If not, I'll let you know."

"I'll give you an appointment card with the time before you leave."

She couldn't leave too soon for Meagan. When Abigail dressed and was ready to go, she took the card from Meagan and walked out the door without a word. Meagan released a huge sigh of relief. The very last thing she wanted was to sew for that woman, but there was absolutely no way to get out of it.

She locked the shop door and pulled down the shade that said Closed on the other side before gathering the teacups and tray and heading to the kitchen to see her mother. She set the tray down and dropped into a chair at the table.

Her mother turned from shaping the bread she was making for supper. "Her majesty has taken her leave, has she?"

"Finally. Oh, Mama! I do dread having to try to please her. I've a feeling there will be no way I can do it."

"Just do the best you can, dear. It's all you can do."

"But what if she hates my work for her and spreads a bad word about me?"

"Her papa owns the bank that gave us the loan. She's not going to risk causing him to lose money by hurting your business, dear," her mother assured her.

"Surely she wouldn't." Meagan got up to heat water for a cup of fresh tea.

"You needn't worry anyway, dear. You are an excellent seamstress. She won't find anything to complain about."

"Oh, I hope you are right, Mama. She is one of the rudest women I've ever dealt with! I'm sure she was taught better."

"I certainly hope so." Her mother chuckled and shook her head. "Evidently she didn't learn it very well."

Meagan's sisters burst in from school just then, and the talk turned to their day. It seemed there was a new boy at school, and Becca kept teasing Sarah about him. From the color flooding her sister's cheeks, Meagan had a feeling that she might have taken a liking to him. She visited with the girls for a while and then went to finish trimming the dinner dress she'd been working on when Abigail came in. Her thoughts wandered as she hand stitched the trim around the bodice. Could it be possible that Nate had sent Abigail to check on her? No! He came in with Natalie often enough to know how her business was going. Besides, he wouldn't do that. Perhaps it was just because she wanted to find out herself how Meagan did business. Or perhaps it was because she wanted to make it very clear to Meagan that she had claim to Natalie and Nate. . . .

Chapter 9

It seemed to Nate that he only saw Meagan when he took Natalie in for a fitting or briefly at church—although he never had a chance to speak to her there. Abigail saw to that. She seemed to be at his shoulder, slipping her hand through his arm as soon as the service was over. She always had something "important" to tell him or someone to introduce him to. By the time he got free, Meagan and her family had already left.

He was beginning to feel frustrated with the whole situation. He hadn't run into Meagan since the day he treated her to a soda, and just seeing her in the shop wasn't enough for him. She seemed to be in his thoughts often during the day, and he'd even begun to dream about her. He wanted to spend more time with her, but he wasn't sure how she might feel about that.

When Nate took Natalie in for a fitting of her new spring jacket the day before her birthday, Meagan seemed glad to see them. Her mother had made a special supper for Natalie, including her favorite cake. She would have a family celebration the next day, but Nate had a feeling that this was the one Natalie would enjoy most.

Before her mother served the cake, Meagan presented Natalie with a new reticule to match the jacket she'd just finished. Her mother and sisters had small gifts for her, too. Nate had never seen his daughter so happy and excited.

"Oh, thank you so much!" Natalie said. "I love it all. I'm having a party at my aunt Abby's tomorrow evening, but I know it's not going to be as nice as this."

"Oh, I'm sure it will be," Meagan assured her. "We just didn't want your birthday to come without giving you a little celebration."

"Thank you," Natalie said again. "I can't wait to show Grandmother and Aunt Abby my gifts!"

Nate heard Meagan's quick intake of breath, as if she were about to say something, but when he looked at her, she just gave a little shake of her head and began to hand out the cake.

Something about her seemed different though, and he wasn't sure what it was. When he and Natalie got ready to leave, it was even more apparent that something was different. While her attitude toward his daughter was still

53

warm, he sensed a certain coolness toward him. Nate wanted to ask if something was wrong, but with his daughter and Meagan's family right there, he didn't feel it was the right time.

"Thank you all for helping to make Natalie's birthday so special."

"Yes, thank you!" Natalie said. "It was ever so much fun! And I love my gifts. Thank you so very much!"

"We were happy to be able to celebrate with you," Mrs. Snow said.

"And I love my new coat, Miss Meg. It is just like I pictured it, only better. And thank you again for my reticule!"

Meagan's smile for his daughter was completely genuine, of that Nate had no doubt.

"I'm glad you are happy with it. It was a joy to make it for you." She bent down and gave Natalie a hug. "I hope you have a happy day tomorrow."

As Nate watched the expression on his daughter's face when she hugged Meagan back, he knew he wasn't the only one who cared for Meagan Snow.

❧

Meagan blew the hair off her forehead as soon as the door closed on Nate and Natalie.

"Come have a cup of tea, dear," her mother said. "I can tell you are upset."

Meagan let out a ragged sigh and followed her mother to the kitchen where Becca and Sarah were cleaning up. She didn't know who she was trying to convince when she said, "I have no right to be upset, Mama."

"That may be so, but you are. What is wrong?"

"It was the mention of Abigail Connors," Meagan said, dropping into a chair at the table. "I do not see how she could be related in any way to Natalie. That child is so sweet and her aunt is. . .a. . .a viper!"

"Now, Meagan, dear, that's a bit strong, don't you think?" Her mother made a cup of tea and handed it to Meagan, then poured herself one and joined her at the table.

"I suppose it might be. But she is just so condescending and rude. And she acts as if she owns Natalie and Mr. Brooks. She never fails to point out how often she spends time with them and all they do together, or how she's always been there for the two of them ever since her sister died in the fire." Meagan sighed and began to rub her temple. "When Natalie tells Abigail about her party here and what we gave her. . .well, I don't think she's going to be happy. She isn't going to like the fact that we celebrated Natalie's birthday here at all."

"Ahh, I believe I'm beginning to see."

Meagan shook her head. "No, Mama. I know my place. Mr. Brooks will not be courting me—I don't belong in his social circle. Abigail Connors has a way of making me realize that. Besides, I—"

"Meagan Snow, I'll not have you talking like that. You are just as good as that Connors woman and anyone in her circle. When he worked for the railroad, your papa was just as well thought of as Mr. Connors is. Don't you ever think you have to belong in a certain circle before you are good enough for anyone. The only circle you need worry about is the one that God is at the center of."

"I know, Mama. I'm sorry. I didn't mean to upset you."

"Just don't talk like that again. Nate Brooks would be a very lucky man indeed if you cared for him."

Meagan took a sip of her tea, afraid that if she looked her mother in the eye, she'd be able to see that Meagan already did care for Nate—much too much for her own good.

❧

Meagan couldn't deny that she'd been cool toward Nate after Natalie's birthday celebration. She didn't mean to be. She felt badly about it, yet events of the weekend had her feeling even more upset.

On Sunday, Nate had somehow managed to get out of his pew and head back toward her and her family before Abigail could grab him. She was, however, right behind him.

Meagan's first instinct was to flee, but her mother put a constraining hand on her shoulder, and she realized she couldn't be that rude.

"Good morning, Mrs. Snow, Meagan, Becca, and Sarah," Nate said with a smile.

Her family greeted him the same way they always did.

His eyes were on her, however, and as Abigail was sidling up to him, all Meagan could muster was a weak smile and a quiet, "Good morning."

"I just wanted to thank you again—"

"Oh, dear Meagan," Abigail interrupted Nate, "the jacket you made our Natalie is just beautiful. I can't wait to have the first fitting of the dress you are making me!"

"Thank you," was all Meagan managed to say.

Nate looked irritated as he continued, "I was thanking you for helping to make Natalie's birthday even more special than usual."

The subject of the conversation came running up the aisle. "Miss Meg, everyone loves my jacket! I've been telling everyone who asks that it was you who made it!"

Meagan couldn't help but smile at the child's sweetness. "Why, thank you, Natalie. That is very nice of you."

"Well, yes, it was, dear," Abigail said, pulling Natalie close to her side. "We're getting out the word as fast as we can. But now we must leave. Mama and Papa will be wondering what is keeping us today."

Nate let out an audible sigh but nodded. "I suppose we should be going. I hope you have a very nice day, ladies."

"Thank you," Meagan's mother said. "You have a wonderful one, too."

Abigail put her hand on Nate's arm and turned to Meagan. "Good-bye. I'll be in for my fitting this week."

All Meagan could do was nod at the woman and try to smile.

It certainly wasn't a great afternoon for her. She was out of sorts the rest of the day and even into the next. With Abigail and some of her friends as her clients now, Meagan was reminded almost daily that Nate's social life wasn't the kind she led. Her life was filled with family, work, and church. And while she wished she were going to the Crescent's Grand Opening Gala, it wasn't the kind of thing she would want to do often. Yet from what she heard from Abigail and some of her friends, their lives seemed filled with parties and elegant dinners and—

She had to chuckle. It was all those things that would keep her in business. She was fortunate to be able to sew for the ladies who attended all of those social gatherings. They were the ones who paid more for their outfits and would get her business on sound financial footing. One day, she'd be able to pay off the bank loan. Then, perhaps she could ask Miss Abigail Connors to find someone else to sew for her.

Meagan sighed and shook her head. No. Not even then. She still couldn't risk making Abigail angry. The woman would waste no time trying to get her friends and acquaintances to go elsewhere, too. Meagan was just going to have to put up with Abigail and be thankful for the business she might help bring in. Most importantly, she needed to pray for the Lord to give her patience and a proper attitude toward Abigail.

She was also bothered by how she had been treating Nate recently. It wasn't his fault she didn't like his sister-in-law, and she shouldn't be letting those feelings have anything to do with how she treated Nate. He probably thought she was awful. Perhaps he even regretted giving her the loan—

The bell over the shop door rang, and Meagan looked up to see the man in her thoughts come inside. "Nate. . .is something wrong? I don't think Natalie is due for a fitting."

But Natalie wasn't with him, and she felt silly for mentioning it.

He smiled. "Everything is fine. . .at least with me. I was wondering the same about you. You've seemed a little. . .as if something is bothering you the last few times I've seen you, and I wanted to make sure that I haven't offended you in some way."

She jumped up from her sewing machine and assured him, "Oh, no, Nate. You haven't offended me at all."

"I'm glad. I've wanted to ask you something for several weeks now."

"Oh? What is it?" Her heartbeat sped up.

"Well, you know the Grand Opening Gala at the Crescent is being held next month?"

"Yes, I know." She held her breath, waiting to hear what he was going to say next.

"I was wondering. . .would you accompany me to it?"

For a moment, Meagan couldn't breathe. He was asking her to the biggest event so far in the season. "I—I—"

"I know it is late notice, with it being only three weeks away, and I apologize for that. If you already have an escort, I understand. But if not, I would be honored if you would be my guest."

Meagan felt as if her heart were going to pound right out of her chest. She had assumed he'd be taking Abigail and had never thought that he might ask her. . .although she couldn't deny that she'd dreamed about it several times. And much as she wanted to go, she felt she should say no—

"I would really like you to go with me, Meagan. I never feel quite comfortable at these things, yet I'm expected to go to them. I think it would be so much easier if you were there with me."

"Oh, I. . ." That he felt uncomfortable at something like that touched her. "But I can't dance. I don't know how."

"It doesn't matter. We don't have to dance." He tilted his head and grinned at her. "Please?"

Her heart turned to mush. There was just no way she could bring herself to say no. "I would love to go with you, Nate."

Chapter 10

Dinner was almost over before Abigail remembered to ask what time Nate would be picking her up for the gala the next week.

"I'm not escorting you, Abigail," Nate said.

"You aren't escorting me? Why, you always. . ." What was he thinking?

"No, Abigail, I don't," Nate said. "We are usually at the same gatherings, but I rarely escort you to them."

"Well, I assumed you would be taking me to this. It's the biggest event of the year! Why aren't you going?"

"I am going. I'm sorry, Abigail, but I've already invited someone else."

"Who?" She could feel a severe headache coming on. This couldn't be happening. How was she going to find an escort at this late date? It was only a week until the gala.

"I invited Miss Snow to accompany me."

"Meagan Snow? The *seamstress*?"

"She is the owner of a dressmaking shop. . .not just a seamstress, Abigail."

Abigail could feel the color rushing to her face. "Well, whatever she is—"

"Abigail, dear," her mother interrupted, nodding her head in Natalie's direction. "Now is not the time to discuss this."

Natalie's eyes were big and round, and she looked as if she were about to cry. Abigail took a deep breath and tried to tamp down her temper as she knew her parents expected. She sighed and nodded. "Very well."

If it hadn't been for her parents stepping in, total silence would have reigned at the table. Abigail didn't know what the conversation was about, and she let it flow around her. All she could think of was that Nate had chosen Meagan Snow over her.

The more she thought about it, the angrier she became. How dare Nate not take her? What was he thinking? He should have known she expected him to accompany her. This was the biggest event in Eureka Springs this season, and Nate was aware that she wasn't being courted by anyone. Of course, it wasn't for lack of trying on several of her men friends' parts—particularly Robert Ackerman. He'd made no secret that he was very interested in her. The only man she'd ever been interested in, however, was Nate. Now, instead of taking her to the gala, he was taking a mere seamstress. Why? Perhaps it was to help her business by introducing her to the wealthy women in town. But that was already happening. No. Much as she hated the very thought, Abigail was afraid it was simply because he cared about Meagan Snow and wanted her to go with him. That was not going to do. It just wasn't going to do at all.

❧

Nate knew he would remember the Crescent opening for the rest of his life. Meagan was more than lovely in her porcelain blue silk ball gown. Her hair was dressed in a more elaborate style than usual, and her eyes were bright and shining. He was sure it was just in excitement about the gala, and not necessarily because she was going with him, but he was glad he was taking her.

He'd rented a carriage to take them in style, and it wasn't dark yet when they started up the hill to Prospect Avenue where the Crescent, built out of limestone, appeared to be almost castlelike, looking down over its village below. When the driver stopped at the entrance to the Crescent, attendants helped Meagan out of the carriage before Nate had a chance to.

He pulled her hand through his arm, however, and led her up entrance steps into the huge foyer where people were arriving and meeting up with others they knew. He began to introduce her to his friends and some of the bank's customers but was pleased that she recognized other people whom she felt comfortable around, too.

Her neighbors Mr. and Mrs. Morrison were attending. Mrs. Morrison was wearing the ball gown that Meagan had made for her, and she looked lovely. "I've had so many compliments on my gown, and I'm taking the opportunity to tell everyone who asks about your shop, dear. Now that I know you are here, I can send them your way," Mrs. Morrison said.

"Oh, thank you!"

They made their way to the Grand Ballroom. Tables had been set up around the huge room, and they found one that had an opening for Nate and Meagan and the Morrisons. Nate knew several others at the table and made introductions.

It was very relaxing to be at a different table than the one Abigail and her friends were at. He'd spotted her across the room, and if her expression was anything to go by—and it usually was—she still wasn't happy with him. He didn't want to upset her, but she'd become much too possessive of him, and it was time she realized he wasn't her property. He turned his attention to Meagan and the people at his table.

Mr. Powell Clayton, the president of the railway and one of the town's outstanding citizens with the Eureka Springs Improvement Company and various other endeavors, stopped by the table with his wife. Nate was somewhat surprised when Mr. Clayton began talking to Meagan about her father.

"He was a good railroad man, your papa," Mr. Clayton said. "We've missed him greatly. I was honored to have known him."

Nate saw tears well up in Meagan's eyes, but she got them under control and smiled. "Thank you. That means so much to me."

"I've heard that you have gone into business for yourself?"

"Yes, sir, I am a seamstress and—"

"She is not just a seamstress," Mrs. Morrison said. "She also designs some of her creations. She is a dressmaker whose name will always mean quality workmanship and exquisite design."

Nate smiled and added his opinion, even though it wasn't needed. "Miss Snow has quite a talent. I don't think there is anything she can't make. And whether her own design or from a fashion plate, the end result is always better than expected."

"I take it you made the gown you have on?" Mrs. Clayton asked.

"She made mine, also. It is one of her original designs," Mrs. Morrison said before Meagan could answer.

"You made both of them?"

"Yes, ma'am, I did," Meagan answered modestly.

"I'll be in to see you next week."

"I'd love that. The dress you have on is very lovely."

"Yes, well, it's seen its best day. I think it is time I have a new ball gown, don't you, Powell, dear?"

"Anything you want to have Miss Snow make for you is fine with me, dear."

One of the other men at the table laughed. "Spoken like a smart husband."

"I take it I'll get the same answer if I order something from Miss Snow?" his wife asked.

"Of course you will," he answered.

More laughter followed the Claytons as they rushed to their table for the first course of oysters in half shells, which was just arriving. Nate could see that Meagan was having a good time, and he let himself relax and enjoy the evening, too.

Mock turtle soup arrived next, followed by lobster farci and then fillet of beef with mushroom sauce. Nate lost count of the side dishes but enjoyed the lemon pie.

Once they finished the meal, Reverend McElwee gave the invocation and then Mr. Clayton took to the podium to introduce the guest of honor, the Honorable James G. Blaine, the Republican presidential nominee of 1884. After he spoke, there would be a brief break while the tables were cleared, and then the popular Harry Barton and his orchestra would begin the night's entertainment.

A LOVE FOR KEEPS

Nate took that opportunity to take Meagan around and introduce her to some of the people he knew. First, they went to a table across the room, and he introduced her to Mr. and Mrs. Connors. They were very gracious to her.

"I've been hearing good things about the dress shop you've opened, Miss Snow. Connors Bank is glad to have had the chance to be a part of it."

"Thank you, sir. I can't thank you enough for giving me the opportunity to go into business."

"The credit isn't mine. Nate saw the possibilities. He's also a great asset to Connors Bank. I wish you much success."

"Thank you," Meagan said once more before Nate led her away.

"I have to do this or I'll not have any friends left," he said as he led her over to the table where Abigail and his friends sat. As he introduced Meagan, he realized that most of the people he socialized with were Abigail's friends. . . and he wasn't all that fond of most of them.

But they were all very nice to Meagan, and for that he was grateful. He would have hated for them to snub her or treat her with disdain because of Abigail's attitude.

Abigail spoke but was very cool. Meagan didn't seem to let it bother her. She was polite to her and the others, and when several of the women asked about her shop, he knew that fashion had triumphed over loyalty to Abigail.

As they were on their way back to their table, Meagan excused herself to go to the ladies' room.

It was then that Abigail cornered him.

"Why didn't you sit at our table tonight, Nate? Were you embarrassed by your companion?"

"Not at all! I thought she might be more comfortable with people she knew. If I were embarrassed, I wouldn't have introduced her to everyone. They seem to like her."

"Yes, well I'm sure she'll fit right in," Abigail said a bit sarcastically. "I still can't understand why you brought her."

"You don't have to, Abigail."

"Well! You don't have to be rude!"

Nate sighed. "Abigail, I'm sorry you are upset with me. I'm not trying to be rude. But who I choose to bring is really none of your business."

"I'm family, Nate."

"That doesn't mean you have to approve of whom I choose to keep company with."

Saying nothing, Abigail swept her skirts around and flounced off in a huff in the direction of the ladies' room. Nate had a feeling she wanted to stomp her feet. He could only hope that Meagan wasn't still there.

Lately Abigail had an edge to her that he didn't like. He wasn't sure she was a good influence on his daughter, either. Abigail had become quite snobbish through the years. Or had she always been that way? Perhaps he should think about limiting the time Natalie spent with her aunt.

✑

Meagan had never had an evening such as this one. She felt like a princess. She'd met many of Eureka Springs's most prominent citizens and was especially impressed with Mr. and Mrs. Connors and the Claytons. She'd been stopped on the way to the ladies' room by first one lady and then another to ask if she was the one who made Mrs. Morrison's gown.

By the time she got to the ladies' room and to the mirror, she found there was no need to pinch her cheeks to put a little color to them. Her face was flushed with the sheer excitement of the evening. She'd had two women ask if they could come in on Monday, and another asked the same for Tuesday.

She was just turning to leave when Abigail Connors entered the room. Meagan's heart seemed to stop beating at the look in the woman's eyes. She nodded and tried to smile, but Miss Connors was not smiling. She barely nodded as she swept past Meagan. That she was angry was obvious, and Meagan was sure the fact that she'd come with Nate was the reason. She was thankful other women were milling around—she felt that might be the only reason Abigail hadn't told her just what she thought of her being here with Nate.

Meagan rushed back to her table as fast as possible. She wanted to get as far away from Abigail Connors as she could.

Nate looked at her closely when she got back to their table, but she smiled and took her seat without mentioning Abigail. She hoped that she hadn't made life harder for Nate by coming with him. Even if he never asked her anywhere else, she would be thankful to him for this evening.

The orchestra added to the enchantment of the evening, and Meagan began to tap her foot in time to the music.

"Would you like to learn to dance?" Nate leaned near and asked. "I could teach you a few steps."

At the very thought of being held in Nate's arms, Meagan's heart began to beat so fast it was hard to speak. All she could manage was, "You could?"

"Certainly. I would love to teach you."

"I would love to learn," Meagan admitted. She looked around the room at the couples who seemed to be floating across the floor. "But not here in front of everyone." She shook her head. "Maybe another time?"

Nate scooted back his chair and stood. "Perhaps we can get some air, then." He pulled out her chair. "Come with me."

Meagan felt his hand at her elbow as he steered her toward one of the double doors leading out of the ballroom. Then he led her down the stairs to an outside terrace where several other couples had decided to get some fresh air, too. They could still hear the orchestra in the quiet of the evening.

"Oh, it's lovely here," Meagan said. The fragrance of blooming flowers lent sweetness to the night air, and the lights from residences up and down the hillside made her realize just how far up they were.

"It is, isn't it? Not near as lovely as you, though," Nate said.

Meagan caught her breath at his words. She wasn't sure what to say, except, "Thank you."

Following a lull in the music, the orchestra began to play again, and Nate turned to her. "A waltz. Perfect. Won't you let me show you some steps now?"

"I—yes, please," Meagan said. How thoughtful of him to get her away from any chance of ridicule for her clumsiness.

He bowed and slipped his right arm around her waist, holding out his left hand for hers. Meagan slipped her hand into his, and he drew her nearer. "One, two, three," Nate began to count as he showed her the steps. "One, two, three." The pressure from his hand told her when to turn. "One, two, three. You're getting it. One, two, three."

Meagan found it quite easy to follow his lead, the slight pressure on her back telling her when and in what direction he wanted her to turn. She lost track of time and was quite disappointed when the music ended. Nate sighed and kept his arm around her for a moment before letting her go. "You are an excellent student. Would you like to go in and dance around the ballroom floor now?"

"Oh. . .I'm not sure I'm ready for that—to dance in front of everyone. But thank you for the lesson. I enjoyed—"

"Another waltz," Nate interrupted as the music began again. "Let me have one more dance out here, then." He looked down into her eyes and smiled. Reaching out and tucking an errant curl behind her ear, he whispered, "Please."

He was asking her to do the very thing she wanted—to step into his arms again. "All right."

Nate's arm encircled her once more and pulled her close. Meagan's heart began to pound in time to the music as they floated around the limestone terrace. She wished the evening would never come to an end.

Chapter 11

Nate hated to see the evening end—he hated to part company with Meagan. Even Abigail's bad mood hadn't put a damper on his evening. All he need do was look at Meagan, and all thoughts of Abigail's anger disappeared.

"Oh, what a lovely evening," Meagan said as he helped her into the carriage.

It was beautiful. The moon was huge, and the stars bright and numerous. The air was balmy and fragrant.

"It is, isn't it?" Nate took his place beside her and motioned for the driver to take off. "Lovely as it is, though, the night sky really doesn't compare to how you look tonight, Meagan," he complimented her once more.

"Oh, why. . .thank you, Nate."

The way she ducked her head, he had a feeling she was blushing as she often did when he paid her a compliment. If so, he wished he could see the captivating color flood her cheeks. "You're welcome. I thank you for accompanying me this evening, Meagan. And thank you for letting me teach you to dance the waltz. I can't remember when I've had a better time."

"It was a wonderful evening. I've never been anywhere as nice as the Crescent before. Obviously, I'd never danced before tonight. Thank you for teaching me and for asking me to accompany you, Nate."

"Please—quit thanking me. I was honored to be your escort." *More than honored.* He was also proud just to be seen with her. More than one man had come up to him and asked who she was while she was in the ladies' room. The whole evening had been one to remember, but the highlight for him was waltzing with Meagan on the terrace. No. He would never forget this night.

"Everyone looked so elegant, and oh, the food was so delicious."

Nate chuckled. "It was very good. They hired an excellent chef." He loved Meagan's fresh perspective on the evening. When the carriage stopped at her house, Nate helped her down and asked the driver to wait for him. He walked her to the door and admitted, "I hate to see the evening end."

"Mama and the girls will be up, wanting a full account of the opening. Would you like to come in and have some lemonade? I'm sure Mama has some made."

"I would love some if you are sure your mother won't mind."

"She'll be happy to see you."

Meagan opened the door, and her mother must have been listening for the sound, because she came out of the kitchen, followed by Sarah and Becca.

"Mama, I asked Nate in for lemonade or something cool to drink, but he wants to make sure it's all right with you."

"Of course it is." Mrs. Snow smiled. "You are always welcome in this home, Nate. We've all been waiting to hear about the evening. Please, come on back to the kitchen."

Nate was beginning to feel at home in this kitchen. He loved it there. It was warm and welcoming, even when nothing was on the stove or in the oven.

Meagan looked beautiful as he held out a chair for her. She didn't look out of place at all sitting at their kitchen table in all her finery. Her sisters helped her mother, and soon he had a glass of lemonade sitting before him.

"Thank you," Nate said and took his first sip. "The last time I sat in a kitchen and drank lemonade, I was about Sarah's age. This takes me back to my mother's kitchen, Mrs. Snow. It's a good memory. Thank you."

"You're welcome, Nate."

As they all sat around the table, he and Meagan filled the others in on the Crescent gala. He mostly listened unless Meagan asked for his input.

She described the inside of the Crescent in detail, although her mother knew what it looked like from working there. But it hadn't been quite as dressed up then, she said. Meagan went on to describe the gowns some of the women had been wearing and how they'd sat at the same table as their neighbors, and she told them about meeting the Claytons.

It was while Meagan described the women and how lovely they all looked that Nate realized how very different she was from Abigail. Abigail would have been critical of each and every woman there and what she had on. It was what she and her friends always did, and then when one of them left the table or room, the others talked about that one. He often wondered how they could not recognize that they were all talking about each other.

Even if Meagan and her family didn't like someone, he didn't think they would talk about them that way. He'd never heard any of that when he was around them. Sitting in this kitchen with this family made him aware of the fact that he really hadn't been true to himself or his upbringing in the last few years.

When the clock struck the hour, he knew it was time to leave. He certainly didn't want to wear out his welcome. As Meagan and her family saw him to the door, Nate realized he had a lot to think about. Perhaps it was time he made some changes. He left the house that had become some kind of haven for him and headed home.

He was falling in love with Meagan Snow, but he wasn't sure she was even aware of how much he cared for her. Part of him was afraid to let her know, and the other couldn't wait to tell her how he felt. He wasn't sure the time was right. He prayed for the Lord to help him sort it all out and to be able to find a way to convince Meagan that he truly cared for her.

Once Nate and that Snow woman left the gala, Abigail was no longer interested in staying. She insisted her escort take her home, although he wasn't happy about it. She didn't much care. All she wanted to do was get home. She wasn't in the mood to make small talk when all she could think of was Nate and the fact that he appeared to be very interested in Meagan Snow. That just wasn't going to do at all.

Millie helped her out of her gown and brought a pot of tea to her room as Abigail always expected. "Here you go, Miss Abigail. How was the gala? You looked so beautiful tonight—I'm sure it was an evening you'll never forget."

"No. I never will, Millie." Abigail couldn't hold her anger in any longer. "Actually, it was one of the worst nights of my life!"

"Oh, I'm so sorry. What happened?"

"Nate and that—"Abigail caught herself before she confided in her hired help. "I don't want to talk about it."

Millie nodded and poured a cup of tea for her. "I understand. Would you like anything else, ma'am?"

"No. You may retire for the night."

"Thank you, Miss Abigail. Good night."

Abigail sighed as her housekeeper left the room. She did like tea; it usually settled her nerves. Not tonight. She sipped from her cup as she looked out the window into the night.

She was too keyed up to stay still, and she felt like a caged tiger as she paced her room. *There must be something I can do to nip this little romance in the bud.* She couldn't just let Meagan Snow win Nate's heart!

Abigail had been biding her time ever since her sister, Rose, had died, hoping that one day Nate would realize how much she loved him. She'd resented Rose since the day Nate began to court her and even more once they'd had a child. Nevertheless, she loved her niece. That day of the fire was one she rarely let herself think about, but now she couldn't keep the memories back.

She'd stopped by to bring a present to three-year-old Natalie. When the fire broke out, there was confusion. She and Rose ran from one window to the next, trying to see where it was. When they found that the flames were jumping from one building to the other up the hillside, they knew they didn't have much time to salvage anything.

"Abigail, the fire will be here any moment. We must get Natalie to safety!" Rose handed the child to her. "I have to get the picture albums. I'll hurry!"

Rose started up the staircase. Hugging the child close, Abigail followed. "No, Rose. There isn't time! We need to go now."

"It won't take a minute. I must get the mementos that mean so much to us. Take Natalie to safety. I'll be right behind you."

"No, Rose, you must come now! The fire is almost here!" Abigail grabbed Rose's arm, but her sister pulled away, losing her balance. Abigail screamed as she watched her sister tumble from the landing to the bottom of the staircase. She rushed to help her, but Rose was badly hurt. By then the flames had reached the house.

"Get. . .Natalie to. . .safety," Rose whispered before she passed out. Abigail grabbed the child and ran, intending to come back to help Rose, but when she turned back, the house was engulfed in flames. Nate showed up and rushed past her, trying to save his wife. But flames surged out of the house, and it was too late.

As she and Nate tried to comfort each other in those moments, hugging Natalie close, Abigail hated herself for the errant thought that came to mind. *Finally, Rose is out of the way.* Maybe now, Nate would make her his wife.

Abigail shook her head, trying to push away the guilt she'd felt that day. She had loved Nate long before he married her sister. And ever since Rose's death, Abigail had hoped that one day Nate would look at her and realize he loved her, too. Yet it had been four years since her sister died—four years of waiting and hoping.

It hadn't been terribly hard. Nate wasn't interested in anyone else. His life revolved around Natalie, and that was all right with Abigail. She loved her niece as if she were her own. Life hadn't been bad. She spent a great deal of it with Nate and Natalie, and she had been hopeful that he would finally see it was in Natalie's best interest for them to marry. Now time seemed to be running out, and she must do something. She hadn't waited all these years to let some new woman come in and take away the only man she'd ever loved. It just wasn't going to happen.

✎

After Nate left, the girls went upstairs to get ready for bed, and Meagan helped her mother clean up the kitchen. It was then that she told her about running into Abigail.

"She's not happy with me at all, Mama. I probably shouldn't have accepted Nate's invitation." She put up the last cup and leaned against the doorframe.

"She's not married to him, Meagan. He was free to ask anyone he wanted to accompany him to the gala. It was you he wanted to go with."

"I know. But she is one of my customers now—not to mention that her father owns the bank that gave us the loan."

"I doubt her father does business according to his daughter's moods, dear. Besides, Nate runs that bank. I don't think that Mr. Connors is that involved in the day-to-day managing of it anymore."

"But he—"

"Meagan, I'm sure he has Nate's welfare to consider also. After all, he's the father of Mr. Connors's granddaughter. He has her welfare to take into consideration, too."

"That's true. I just hope tonight doesn't cause problems for Nate. Will you help me out of this gown, Mama?"

"Of course I will. I'm ready to go up, too."

Meagan didn't bring up the subject of Nate again while her mother helped her out of the gown. She hung it in the wardrobe while Meagan changed into her gown and wrapper. "You looked lovely tonight, my Meagan. I'm sure there wasn't a woman there who looked any prettier than you did. I'm so glad you got to go."

"Thank you, Mama. Many women there looked more elegant than I did, but I had such a wonderful time. It's a night I'll never forget."

"I'm glad. Good night, dear."

"Good night, Mama."

After her mother left, Meagan read her Bible and said her prayers, but she still had a hard time getting to sleep. She was much too excited to settle down. She went downstairs and made herself a cup of tea, then took it back to her room and sat down in the chair beside her bed. It had been a night to remember. Nate had treated her as if she were the most special woman in the world, and for a while, she had felt as if she were. . .particularly when he'd held her in his arms and danced with her.

Then she remembered running into Abigail. Meagan took a sip of tea. She wasn't sure how to act when the woman came into the shop this next week for a fitting, but she couldn't worry about it now. What she must do was realize that she could never fit into Nate's social group. She had enjoyed the evening and knew it was a night she would never forget. But she was beginning to care too much for Nate Brooks, and there was no future in that. Oh, how he made her stomach flutter when she was around him.

Meagan sighed and took another sip of tea. Although she was glad she'd accepted his invitation, part of her wished she hadn't gone with him this evening. It was only going to make it harder to accept the fact that there was no future in giving her heart to him. There would only be heartache ahead.

Abigail Connors had not liked it at all that Nate was with Meagan tonight. And even if he wasn't interested in Abigail, she was part of his daughter's family and could make life miserable for him.

No. For everyone's sake, she had to stop dreaming about a future with Nate. It was going to lead nowhere. She took one more sip of tea and then got on her knees.

"Dear Lord, You've been with me through all the heartaches in my life, and I know You will help me now. I'm afraid I'm falling in love with Nate Brooks, but I would never fit into his social circle. . .nor would I really want to. We live in two different worlds, and I don't see how they can ever merge. Please help me to accept that and quit thinking of him night and day. In Jesus' name, I pray. Amen."

Chapter 12

Knowing that she needed to put Nate out of her mind and quit dreaming about him was one thing, but during the next few days, Meagan found doing it was quite another. She saw him and Natalie at church, but Abigail had a grip on his arm as soon as the service was over, and they were out the door before Meagan had a chance to even wave. Natalie wasn't coming in for a fitting until later in the week.

Abigail, however, would be in for a fitting on Wednesday afternoon. She brought her mother with her, and Meagan found that Mrs. Connors was nothing like her daughter. She was gracious and kind and had only good words to say.

"I've been meaning to come in and see about having you make me a few things. After I saw samples of your work at the gala, I didn't want to delay any longer, so I insisted Abigail bring me with her today."

"Thank you, Mrs. Connors. I have several magazines with the newest fashion plates. Would you like to look at them?"

"I'm not sure we have the time, Mother," Abigail said.

"Of course we do, dear. I can look at them while you are changing and having your fitting. If I need to make an appointment to come in by myself, I'll do that. But yes, Miss Snow, I would love to look at your magazines." She settled herself in the settee and took the magazines from Meagan.

"My mother will be in shortly with tea, Mrs. Connors. She always brings some in this time of day."

"That will be lovely, dear," the older woman said. "I'd enjoy a cup of tea."

"Very well, Mother." Abigail sighed in resignation as she went behind the screen to change into the dress Meagan was making for her.

While Meagan could tell Abigail wasn't very happy, she was quite relieved that Abigail's mother was with her. Meagan had been dreading this fitting ever since the evening of the gala. From Abigail's attitude, Meagan was fairly certain that if it hadn't been for Mrs. Connors's insistence, Abigail would have come by herself—probably to warn her away from Nate.

When her mother brought in the tea tray, Meagan introduced the two women and was very pleased that they seemed to like each other. She left her mother to serve tea to Mrs. Connors while she went to help Abigail with the hooks on her dress.

But even with both of their mothers in the room, Abigail managed to get in her barbs.

"How did you enjoy the gala?" Abigail asked.

"I enjoyed it very much."

"I thought it was very nice of Nate to introduce you to so many people. Of course, that's Nate. He's always looking after the bank's interests."

Meagan took a sharp intake of breath at Abigail's words. Was that why Nate had asked her to accompany him? It easily could have been. Her heart twisted at the very thought.

She didn't know what to say, so she said nothing. Still, Abigail didn't let up. For the rest of the time she was there, Abigail managed to let Meagan know that she had a prior claim to her brother-in-law. As she swept around the screen to show her mother the dinner gown Meagan had made her, she turned this way and that. "I think this will work for the dinner I'm hosting for Nate's birthday, don't you, Mother?"

She stood on the small platform Meagan had asked Mr. Adams to build for her to make it easier to pin hems. Abigail turned when Meagan asked her to, while she pinned the hem of the garment.

"It's beautiful, dear. It would work for any dinner you might host," her mother replied, watching her daughter turn slowly as Meagan pinned.

Once she was finished, Abigail slowly turned again, looking in the mirrors Meagan had set up in the shop. The red-on-red-striped silk did look wonderful on her, bringing out the blue in her eyes and her blond hair.

"I think I'll have you make me a new gown to wear to the opera, too, Miss Snow," Abigail said. "When Nate took me, although he told me I looked lovely in my blue silk, I realized I needed something new to add to my wardrobe for the upcoming season."

Meagan felt another twinge at the mention of Nate taking Abigail to the opera. Obviously, the woman was trying to let Meagan know that just because he'd taken her to the gala didn't mean that he was going to be escorting her anywhere else. Abigail was getting her message across quite well.

Making the woman another gown was the last thing Meagan wanted to do. She had been hoping that Abigail would satisfy whatever curiosity it was that brought her into the shop and have her make just this one dress and then leave Meagan alone. But it seemed she wasn't going to do that. And as she was the daughter of the man who owned the bank and her mother was sitting in the very same room, Meagan couldn't very well say no. "You are welcome to look over the new plates. I'm sure we can find something to please you."

"I've found a few I like already. I'll look them over again when I come for my next fitting."

"Well, I've already found a few things I love," Mrs. Connors said. "But I know my daughter is in a hurry, so I'll come back in to see you next week if you have a time available for me."

Meagan checked the appointment book she'd just begun to need. "Monday at two will work for me, if that is convenient for you."

"That will be fine."

"Miss Snow!" Abigail called from behind the screen. "Are you going to help me get out of this gown?"

"Of course," Meagan said, hurrying to do just that. Abigail Connors couldn't leave fast enough to please her.

"Abigail! Miss Snow was taking care of me."

"I'm sorry, Mother. But we do have to change before we meet Papa for dinner at the Crescent," Abigail said from behind the screen.

Meagan helped her out of the dress. "I should have this ready for you by Saturday. Would you like me to have it sent to your home, or do you want to pick it up and look over the plates again then?"

"You may have it sent to my home. Since I won't need to come in for another fitting now, I will find the plate I like and pick out the fabric before Mother and I leave. I want to look my best this season." She turned and looked Meagan in the eye and lowered her voice. "I plan on being Mrs. Nate Brooks by this time next year."

Meagan held up the dress Abigail had worn into the shop, thankful for the yards of material that kept Abigail from seeing the tears that had quickly formed at her words. She blinked quickly and turned to hang up the garment she was making for the woman. *Please, Lord, help me to hide how this woman's words have hurt. Please help me deal with all of this later.*

After Abigail's hatefulness to her, the fact that she didn't want to give her mother time to decide anything but was willing to stay a little longer for her own interests didn't surprise Meagan one bit. Nor did it seem to surprise her mother, for she said nothing as Abigail picked up *Godey's* magazine and flipped the pages.

"Here," she said, finding the fashion plate she liked. "I like this one."

It was a beautiful gown of gold and white brocade. "That will look lovely on you," Meagan said. "I believe I have fabric similar if not exactly like this."

She led the way to her stock of fabric on the shelves and pulled out several bolts. "Will this work for you?"

"Yes, I believe so. It looks like the fabric in the picture."

"I think it will work up beautifully."

"Very well, then. You have my measurements. When do you want me to come for the first fitting?"

Meagan looked at her appointment schedule once more. "I should be ready for your first fitting by next Friday afternoon about three."

Abigail nodded and pulled on her gloves. "Are you ready, Mother?"

"No, dear. If you can place an order with Miss Snow, I can, too. Sit down and have a cup of that delicious tea Mrs. Snow prepared. I have found a few gowns I want to talk to Miss Snow about."

Abigail shrugged and took a seat and the cup of tea Meagan's mother brought to her. She seemed quite content to be late, now that she'd said what she wanted to say. One glance at her told Meagan that she was feeling quite smug about the dart she'd shot into Meagan's heart.

Meagan was determined not to let her know how direct a hit she'd made. She managed to avoid looking at her, giving all of her attention to Mrs. Connors, instead. She couldn't help but wonder how Abigail had turned out the way she was when her mother was so gracious and kind.

The fashion plates Mrs. Connors chose were lovely, the afternoon dress in a brown print crepe and the dinner dress in a blue silk. It didn't take long for the woman to choose fabrics similar to the ones used in the pictures, and since she'd made an appointment for the next week, they decided she could come in for measurements then.

Meagan had never been so glad to pull down her Closed sign. She turned to her mother. "That is it for today. Abigail can ruin a day faster than anyone I know."

"I can understand that. Abigail Connors certainly is an unpleasant young woman," her mother said while gathering up the teacups. "I don't understand it at all. Her mother is very nice."

"She is. I think she was a bit. . ."

"Put out with her daughter. If Abigail had been younger, I think she'd have received a nice spanking. She could use one now, as far as I'm concerned. Your papa would never have let you girls talk to me the way she did her mama. Wonder what kind of man her father is?"

"He seemed very nice when I met him at the gala." Meagan shrugged. "Maybe her upbringing doesn't have anything to do with it. She just isn't a very pleasant person."

"Maybe there's a reason for it."

"I'm sure there is, Mama. There must be. Still, I wish I didn't have to have any dealings with her. Apparently, that isn't going to be the case."

That wasn't what was really bothering her, though. It was trying to come to grips with the fact that Abigail Connors was determined to marry Nate and had done all in her power to let Meagan know it.

Once a month or so, Nate had Natalie's grandparents and Abigail over for dinner. Rose had asked them over at least once a month for dinner when she was alive, and Nate had kept the practice up for Natalie's sake. He wished he could stop it—or at least stop asking Abigail—but he hadn't found a way to do it. He always hoped she'd have another engagement, but she never did.

When Abigail arrived early, informing him that her parents were under the weather and wouldn't be able to come, he felt a little put out that no one had notified him before now. He would have canceled until they felt better. He tried not to show his irritation that he evidently was going to have to spend the evening with Abigail. "I hope they are better soon. If I'd known, we could have put this off until next week."

"Oh, don't worry about it, Nate. I'm sure they will feel better very soon. They hated for Natalie to be disappointed, so I told them I would come."

Nate inhaled deeply, telling himself that he'd have to suffer through the evening on his own. He wasn't comfortable around Abigail when her family or friends weren't around. He had no doubt that she still wasn't happy with him for taking Meagan to the gala instead of her, yet she'd been overly sweet to him lately, and he was not sure what was going on with her.

Tonight she seemed her usual self during dinner, talking about the upcoming parties her friends had invited them to and a surprise birthday party she and her mother were planning for her father.

Natalie loved hearing all about the parties and Abigail's social life, listening intently to every word her aunt said. Nate had come to the conclusion that he'd rather Natalie *not* take after her aunt Abigail in that regard, however.

"Are you going to the party Jillian is hosting, Nate? If so, will you accompany me?" Abigail asked.

He shook his head. "I'm not planning on going to that, Abigail. I'm about partied out." And he had no desire at all to take her.

"But, Nate, you have to keep up with what is going on in town for the sake of the bank. Please reconsider," she implored him.

She'd used that reasoning on him too many times, and he was getting quite tired of it. "I do what I need to do for the sake of the bank, Abigail. I always have. I don't believe, however, that I have to attend every social event that comes along. I have a daughter to raise and—"

"Yes, and I'd like to talk to you about that," Abigail said, a slight smile on her lips.

Nate groaned to himself. He'd just given her an opening to talk about her favorite subject. . .and the one he most disliked. Well, he wasn't going to have that conversation in front of his daughter.

"Not right now, Abigail," he said as Mrs. Baker came in and served a dessert.

"I understand. We'll talk later."

Nate had no doubt that they would. He'd given her the opening, and she wouldn't leave until she had her say. He might as well prepare himself for it.

They took turns playing checkers with Natalie after dinner, but finally, Nate could put it off no longer. "It's time to get ready for bed, Natalie, dear. I'll be up soon to hear your prayers."

"May I stay up a little longer, Papa? I'm having so much fun!"

If he hadn't wanted to get the inevitable conversation with Abigail over with, he might have let her talk him into staying up later.

"Not tonight, dear," Abigail said before he had a chance to answer his daughter. "Your papa and I need to have a talk."

It was on the tip of his tongue to say that talk could wait a little longer and that Natalie could stay up, but he wanted the talk over with as much as Abigail wanted to start it. Probably even more so.

"Aunt Abigail is right, sweetie. You go on, and I'll be up soon."

"All right, Papa. Good night, Aunt Abby." She gave her aunt a hug.

"Good night, dear. Sweet dreams."

Nate watched his daughter scamper up the stairs before turning back to Abigail. She looked like a cat who'd swallowed a canary, thinking she was getting her way.

She sat down to pour the coffee his housekeeper had brought into the room and handed him a cup, as if she were the lady of the manor. She'd made him well aware that was what she wanted. But it was her dream—not his.

He sat down on a chair across from her. "What is it you wanted to talk about, Abigail?"

"Well, you brought it up, Nate, dear. You do have a child to raise, and you need help doing it. Natalie needs a mother."

He couldn't deny that—but he had someone he could see in that position, and it wasn't his sister-in-law. "Abigail, we've had this conversation many times."

"Yes, I know. Still, you don't seem to understand how badly a girl needs a mother. Nate, dear, just because you've taken over her wardrobe doesn't mean she doesn't need a mother. There are things you just aren't prepared to teach her and—" Abigail pulled a hankie from her sleeve and dabbed at her eyes. "Ever since the day Rose put Natalie in my arms and asked me to take care of her, I've felt as if she were mine."

The guilt and sorrow Nate felt that he hadn't been there to save his wife washed over him in waves, as it never failed to do when Abigail brought up that day. And when she did, he always felt even worse because his father-in-law thought he'd gone in and tried to save Rose, instead of just not being there in time. Abigail had let him think that, and when Nate wanted to tell him the truth, she'd talked him out of it, telling him that her father had gone through enough heartache in losing Rose, and they couldn't give him more.

"I think it's time we told your father the truth about the day Rose died. I was too late. I just didn't get there in time, and the house was in flames when I arrived. I don't know why you ever let him think I did. And I certainly don't know why I didn't correct it immediately! We need to tell him, Abigail."

"Nate, we can't do that! It would break his heart all over again. And what if he got so mad that he hadn't been told the truth that he fired you?"

"I'd be free from the guilt of not telling him the truth."

Abigail jumped to her feet and began to pace in front of his fireplace. "Well, we can't tell him now. Think of how it would hurt the family relationship! Besides, it would hurt my own relationship with him, Nate! I was only trying to protect you, to keep Father from blaming you for not being there—you know how hard he can be."

Actually, Jacob Connors had never shown that side to Nate, but Abigail seemed so distraught, Nate agreed not to tell her father the truth of that day . . .at least not yet.

"How did we get on this subject anyway?" Abigail asked. "We were discussing Natalie's need for a mother. How did we get to this?"

Nate sighed and shook his head. She'd brought up that day his life had changed forever. "Well, we aren't discussing it anymore," Nate said firmly.

"Nate. She needs a mother. She needs someone who is with her and will listen to her and give her advice and love her."

"Natalie has you and your mother, Abigail. It's not as if she has no women in her life. And that is the end of the discussion as far as I am concerned." He didn't mention that the Snow women had been a very good influence on his daughter, too. He had a feeling Abigail wouldn't take very well to that information just now. "I need to go up and hear Natalie's prayers. I'll see you home as soon as I do."

"No, Papa told the driver to come back for me at ten. It's nearly that now."

"That was thoughtful of Jacob. If I'm not down before the driver gets here, please tell your parents I hope they recover quickly."

"Yes. I will," she replied, her tone cool.

Nate knew she was angry with him again. She didn't even want to come up and kiss Natalie good night. Well, there was nothing to do about it except wait out her bad mood. She'd get past it eventually, and they'd have the same conversation again. That is the way it always was with Abigail.

Chapter 13

A few days later when Nate took Natalie for a fitting, she mentioned that her aunt Abigail had been grouchy lately. Nate hoped the woman hadn't taken her aggravation with him out on his daughter. "What has she seemed upset about?"

Natalie twisted her hands together and looked up at him. "She's sharp with me sometimes, and she doesn't want me to talk about Miss Meg anymore. She says that's all I talk about." Natalie did a good imitation of her aunt as she continued, "She said all she hears is 'Miss Meg this and Miss Meg that.' She said no one is that nice. But Papa, Miss Meg *is* that nice."

"Yes, she is. Your aunt Abigail just doesn't know her as well as we do, dear. Don't worry so about it."

"But Papa, I really like Miss Meg, and it's hard for me not to mention her name." Her eyes were big, brown, and sad.

"I'll talk to your aunt Abigail, Natalie. And I'm your papa. You can talk about Miss Meg all you want, anytime you want. I'll see that your aunt Abigail understands that." He flicked the reins to his horses and they took off in a brisk trot.

Natalie rewarded him with a huge smile. "Thank you, Papa!"

How dare Abigail tell Natalie that she didn't want her talking about Meagan! If Natalie had been misbehaving, that Abigail would admonish her would be one thing, but just because she was in a bad mood or didn't want to hear what the child had to say, why that was something entirely different!

By the time they arrived at Meagan's shop, Nate was very angry, but he tried not to let it show as she opened the door of the shop to them. "Good afternoon! I saw you coming around the porch."

She smiled at Natalie and at him, but her smile didn't seem as large or bright for him. Maybe it was just his imagination, or maybe his anger at Abigail was coloring his mood. He decided not to carry it into her shop. "Natalie has been looking forward to her fitting for days."

He didn't add that he had been looking forward to it, too. He just was not seeing enough of Meagan. He wanted to court her very much—but he was getting mixed messages from her and didn't know how to broach the subject. Still, he enjoyed watching her with his daughter.

He could hear giggling from behind the screen as Meagan helped her out of her day dress and into the new walking dress she was making for her. "Oh, it's beautiful, Miss Meg! I can't wait to wear it!"

"It is going to look lovely on you, Natalie."

"May I show Papa? I know the sleeves aren't in yet, but I'd like him to see it."

He heard Meagan chuckle at her enthusiasm. "Of course you may."

Natalie ran out from behind the screen and twirled in front of him. "Do you like it, Papa?"

It was a very pretty dress, and she looked adorable in it. He couldn't remember what kind of fabric Meagan had said it was, but it was of a red-and-white-striped material that reminded him of a candy cane. "I do like it, Natalie! It looks wonderful on you."

"Thank you, kind sir." She giggled and curtsied, causing both him and Meagan to chuckle.

"Why, Natalie, dear, how nice that dress looks on you." Mrs. Snow entered the room with a smile. "Are you going to stay for dinner with us tonight?"

Natalie swung around to him. "Papa?"

Nate hesitated in answering, knowing his daughter wanted to stay, but waiting for Meagan to add her voice to the invitation as she normally did. Only she didn't, and the silence felt uncomfortable. "I think not tonight. But thank you for your invitation. Perhaps next time?"

"Of course. You and Natalie are always welcome at our table, Nate."

Nate waited a moment to see if Meagan would add anything to that. When she didn't, he simply said, "Thank you, Mrs. Snow. That means a lot to both Natalie and me."

"You are quite welcome. It's the least we can do after all you've done for us. Besides, we enjoy your company."

Somehow, Nate didn't think Meagan quite agreed with her mother, and he began to wonder if she'd gone to the gala with him because he gave them the loan. He sincerely hoped not.

❧

Frustrated that he didn't know how to approach Meagan and still upset at Abigail for telling Natalie not to talk about her, Nate went to see Abigail after work the next day.

Her housekeeper showed him into her parlor, and Abigail glided over to greet him. "Why, Nate, what a nice surprise. . .unless—is something wrong?"

Nate wondered if she could tell how upset he was by his expression. "There is something I would like to talk to you about."

"Oh?" She motioned to the settee. "Please, take a seat and tell me what is on your mind."

Her voice sounded hopeful, and he hated to ruin her pleasant mood. He really did appreciate Abigail. She'd been there to help him with Natalie through her own grief. But she wanted him to feel something he didn't feel for her, and he wished she would just accept it. It would make being part of the same family so much easier. But as he knew all too well, life wasn't always easy, and it was for his daughter's sake he was here today. He might as well get straight to it. He took the chair beside the settee and waited for Abigail to sit down before he said anything.

"Natalie says you don't want her talking about Miss Snow anymore."

"What?" Her right eyebrow went up as it always did when she felt defensive.

"Did you not tell her that you didn't want her talking about Miss Snow?" He knew that Natalie didn't lie. He waited for Abigail's answer, well aware that he couldn't rule out that she would.

"Perhaps she misunderstood me, Nate. I did tell her that Miss Meg seemed to be all she wanted to talk about anymore."

"She likes Miss Snow and considers her a friend. It's no different than you talking about your friends all the time."

"It is different, Nate."

"How so?" Let her explain further if she would.

"It just is. She seems quite taken with the woman, Nate. I don't want her to get hurt. You might want to guard against Natalie becoming too attached to her—she's a mere seamstress!"

If he only knew how Meagan felt about him, Nate would gladly tell Abigail that if he had his way, Natalie would be seeing much more of the *seamstress*. But something in his sister-in-law's demeanor kept him from doing so. He did make one thing clear. "I don't want you ever to tell Natalie that she can't talk about someone she cares about. If she can't feel free to talk to you, then how can you possibly think you are—"

"Oh, Nate dear," Abigail interrupted him, her tone suddenly sweet as honey. "This has just been a misunderstanding on Natalie's part. I will tell her I never meant to upset her and assure her that she can always talk to me about anything."

Nate stood. He felt he'd accomplished the main thing he came here for. He was pretty certain that Abigail wouldn't be telling Natalie that she couldn't talk about Meagan or anyone else she might wish to talk about again.

❧

If Meagan's mother had wondered why she hadn't insisted that Nate and Natalie stay for supper, she hadn't said anything, and for that Meagan was very grateful. She didn't know why she hadn't tried to get them to stay. . . . Well, maybe she did. She just wasn't sure how Nate felt about her. There was a time when she'd thought he might care about her as much as she did him, but Abigail's insinuations had her doubting his motivation in asking her to the gala. Had it only been to help her business out that he'd asked her to accompany him?

Meagan hoped not. She prayed not. But there was no denying that it well could have been for that reason. He hadn't asked her to accompany him anywhere else, so how could she be sure? And if he was not interested in her in the way she was him, it was better for her to steel her heart against the love she could no longer deny she felt for him.

Meagan kept telling herself that as she cut out the muslin pattern for Abigail's new gown. Oh, how she wished she could tell the woman to take her business elsewhere. But for the sake of her business and her family's future, she could not. It was time to face reality and quit dreaming.

She was face-to-face with reality when Abigail came in for her fitting that very afternoon. She'd brought a friend with her, Miss Rebecca Dobson.

"Oh, what a nice little shop you have here," Miss Dobson said. "I've been hearing all kinds of good things about your work. I'm still using Mrs. Sparrow for now, but Abigail insisted I come with her and keep her company."

Meagan was immensely relieved that the woman had a dressmaker of her own. She liked Mrs. Connors a lot, but her daughter was another matter entirely, and Meagan wasn't interested in acquiring any of Abigail's friends as customers.

"Please, make yourself comfortable, then. There are some of the latest fashion magazines to look at, or if you and Miss Connors prefer to talk, she'll be able to hear you through the screen."

Evidently, that is what they did prefer because she'd barely started pinning the muslin on Abigail before she began to talk about Nate.

"Nate came by to see me yesterday afternoon, right out of the blue, Rebecca," Abigail said.

"Oh? What did he want?"

"He is concerned about Natalie. He wants her to be able to come to both of us with anything. He said he wants her to be able to talk about the things that mean a lot to her."

"Hmm. That sounds as if he's. . .thinking about the future, doesn't it?" Miss Dobson asked.

"I certainly hope so!" Abigail giggled, and Meagan had to struggle to keep from purposely sticking her with the pin she was holding.

"I've been telling him how much Natalie needs a mother. Perhaps he's finally taking me seriously," Abigail continued.

Her friend laughed. "And I know just who you have in mind."

"Well, who better to raise Natalie than the sister of her mother?"

"You have a point. Besides, Natalie has always been close to you, and you've loved Nate for a very long time."

Meagan took the pins out of her mouth and swallowed hard. She was glad she was behind Abigail so that the woman couldn't see the tears that formed. Abigail was trying to get a message across to her; there was no doubt about it. Well, it appeared she did have a prior claim to Nate, and no amount of wishing or dreaming was going to change that. It was time Meagan accepted the fact that she would never have a future with Nate Brooks. She blinked back the tears, stuck the pins back in her mouth, and finished pinning the pattern on Abigail. By the time she was done, Meagan had her tears under control and was resolved to get through the afternoon. Knowing she wouldn't be able to do it on her own, she prayed silently for help to do just that.

"I think that's it. The gown is going to fit you nicely, Miss Connors. Now all I have to do is mark the pins and take them out. You can come back for a fitting a week from today, if that is convenient for you."

"That will be fine," Abigail said. "I think Nate will really like it."

The woman loved to shoot darts, and her aim was perfect, Meagan thought. Oh, how she wished she never had to pin another thing on her! But she couldn't get out of it. There was still the loan to pay off and the fact that Abigail could cause problems with that loan—not to mention her customers. Over half of them were Nate and Abigail's friends or business acquaintances. No. Much as she would like to tell the woman to find someone else to sew for her, she just couldn't do it. All she could do was pray for the strength to keep her thoughts to herself. . .and to put Nate Brooks out of her mind.

Chapter 14

Nate was on the way to Meagan's shop with Natalie for a fitting when he realized that he wasn't going to have an excuse to go to her shop much longer. At least, not nearly as often. There wasn't much more he could have Meagan make Natalie. She had nearly a whole new wardrobe.

He'd hoped it would become obvious to Meagan that part of the reason he'd ordered so much from her was so that he could see her on a semiregular basis. . .especially after he'd taken her to the Crescent. He thought she would be aware that he wanted to court her. If she'd come to that conclusion, she certainly showed no sign of it. Feeling that his time was running out, he was determined to find a way to tell her how he felt and that he wanted to see more of her.

He hoped to have that chance today. His daughter had come to feel so comfortable and welcome at Meagan's shop and home that she ran ahead of him and burst into the shop. He could hear their conversation as he approached the door.

"Good afternoon, Miss Meg! I'm here for my fitting!" he heard Natalie say.

He heard Meagan chuckle. "So you are," she said. "Good afternoon to you! I have everything ready, so come on and we'll get started."

Nate entered the shop just as they disappeared behind the changing screen. He took his normal seat in one of the chairs and waited for Natalie to come around the screen and twirl in front of him. When she did, it was worth the wait. She looked adorable in the silk dress she could wear for dinner or to church. Meagan only needed to put the hem in and finish the matching jacket.

Natalie twirled this way and that in front of the mirror, admiring herself.

"I think she likes it," Meagan said.

He chuckled. "Now whatever gave you that idea? She looks adorable, Meagan. And she loves everything you've made her."

"Thank you. She's a pleasure to sew for."

Mrs. Snow entered the room just then. "Oh, Natalie dear, I knew that would look lovely on you, and it does!"

Natalie curtsied prettily. "Thank you, Mrs. Snow. I feel like a princess in everything Miss Meg makes for me."

"And you look like one," Nate added.

"Nate, it's good to see you. Are you able to stay for supper with us?"

"Oh, Papa, can we? Please?"

His daughter's eyes implored him to say yes, but he wasn't sure what to do—

"Please do join us," Meagan said, looking at Natalie.

Nate wondered why she didn't look at him and had a feeling she'd added her invitation to her mother's just for Natalie's sake, but he wasn't going to turn it down. Hopefully it would give him the opportunity to be able to talk to her later. "Thank you, then. We'd be honored to join you."

❧

As she and her sisters helped get the meal of roast pork, mashed potatoes, and green beans on the table, Meagan wondered why she hadn't told her mother earlier in the day not to ask Nate and Natalie to stay for supper. Once the invitation was issued, however, she couldn't bear disappointing Natalie again. She kept telling herself that it was the child she was concerned with, yet if she were being honest with herself, she had to admit that she truly wanted them to stay—in spite of the fact that Abigail was making her life miserable each and every time she came into the shop.

Meagan had come to the realization that Nate hadn't meant to hurt her. It wasn't his fault that she'd begun to care for him so much. She shouldn't have read so much into the outing for a soda or the invitation to the Crescent gala . . .or the dance lessons in the moonlight. She told herself that the first had just been out of politeness and the second had most likely been to help her business out. The third, well, he hadn't given her any real encouragement that he cared about her the way she did him. Not really. She'd just hoped.

And now, looking at Nate from across her dining room table as they all enjoyed the apple pie her mother had made earlier in the day, she told herself to let go of the hope. Much as she cared for Nate and his daughter, his sister-in-law was part of their family and there was really no way to compete with Abigail Connors. She was a determined woman, and she wanted Nate. Of that there was no doubt. She'd come out and told Meagan that she planned to be married to him. How much plainer could it be? If Abigail was that certain, she must know how Nate felt about her.

Yet the way Nate looked at Meagan, off and on throughout the meal, continued to make her pulse race and turn her heart to mush. When he asked if he could have a minute with her after supper, while Sarah, Becca, and Natalie were helping to clear the table, she wasn't sure what to think. All a tremble on the inside, she led him to the family parlor where they'd had tea the day he'd decided to give them the loan.

She motioned for him to take a seat in the same chair he'd sat in the first time he'd come to this room, and she seated herself on the settee. "What is it you want to talk to me about, Nate?"

"It's of a personal nature, Meagan."

"Oh?" Her heart seemed to stop the slow somersault it had begun, and she held her breath, waiting for his reply.

"For some time now, I've wanted to ask you to have dinner with me. There is a new restaurant in town that I've wanted to try, and I'd very much like to take you with me if you would like to go. I was wondering if you would be free to accompany me tomorrow evening."

Oh how she wanted to go! With every fiber of her being, she wanted to accept his invitation. But from all of Abigail's accounts, they were practically engaged. If so, he certainly shouldn't be asking her to go to dinner with him. Who did he think he was? He might be the banker who loaned her money to start her business, but he was also the man who'd stolen her heart when he was almost engaged to another. Nate had no business playing with her feelings.

She might be risking her business, but she couldn't risk more heartache. Disappointment in him pierced her heart as she jumped up from the settee and answered, "I'm sorry, but I won't be able to accompany you, Nate." Meagan was well aware that she sounded angry, but she couldn't help it. She was.

Nate stood also, looking a bit surprised and. . .there was something else in his eyes as he looked at her. "I'm sorry. I—"

The girls entered just then, and Meagan didn't know who was the more relieved at the interruption—she or Nate.

"Papa, may I play one game of checkers with Becca? I'm getting much better at it, and I know it is from playing with her," Natalie said.

Nate glanced at Meagan and then back to his daughter. He shook his head. "Not tonight, dear. We need to be getting home."

Meagan's heart twisted in her chest. She didn't want things to end like this between her and Nate. She didn't want them to go. But they weren't hers to keep, and it was becoming more painful by the day to want something so badly and know that she couldn't have it. A life with Nate and Natalie wasn't going to happen for her, and she had to accept that fact. Abigail had a stronger claim, and there was nothing Meagan could do about it except perhaps to lower her standards—and that was something she had no intention of doing.

❧

Nate listened to Natalie's prayers, trying to hide his heartache at Meagan's refusal to have dinner with him. But his daughter was quite intuitive and put her small hands on each side of his face as he kissed her good night. "Papa, are you all right? You seem sad tonight."

He was sad. But he didn't want his daughter taking on his mood and becoming dispirited herself. "I'm fine, dear. Just a little tired, I suppose."

Nate told himself that it wasn't really a lie. He was tired of being lonely and tired of not knowing what direction the Lord wanted him to go in. He'd thought it was to pursue Meagan Snow, but after tonight, he thought that perhaps he'd been wrong.

"Well, you'd better turn in yourself and get a good night's rest," Natalie advised with a giggle.

"I might just do that, sweetheart. You sleep tight and have sweet dreams."

"You, too, Papa," Natalie said as he turned down the gaslight and left her door ajar so he could hear if she called out in the night.

He went back downstairs and entered his study to find that his housekeeper had left him a pot of hot cocoa. Mrs. Baker knew he liked the beverage any time of year and especially before bed. Perhaps it would help him sleep, but he doubted he'd have sweet dreams tonight. It appeared that he'd been living on dreams ever since he met Meagan Snow. At first, she'd reminded him of his Rose, and then as he'd come to know her, she'd become a gracious, beautiful woman in her own right—at least in his thoughts and dreams. But when she'd turned down his invitation to dinner, he'd come to the realization that perhaps she wasn't interested in him as a man, but only as the one who had approved her bank loan.

No, he told himself. That was being unfair to her. She'd never acted as if she was only kind to him because he was a banker. He knew she cared about Natalie, and he'd come to think she might care about him. But perhaps that was only wishful thinking on his part. Perhaps she simply was not impressed with the man he was.

She was used to being around real people instead of the kind he'd introduced her to at the gala. Most of them were superficial, going about their days with only one thing in mind: to be entertained, to have a good time. Why, most of the people he'd associated with since Rose's death had too much time on their hands, and they didn't use it for much good.

He wanted something different for himself and his daughter. Perhaps he'd read too much into Meagan's refusal tonight. The girls had interrupted them before he could find out why she was turning him down. Meagan had looked weary. Maybe that was all it was. She worked very hard, and if the conversation at the supper table had been any indication, her business was growing. Perhaps she was just tired and had a lot of work to do.

Nate leaned back in his office chair and took a sip of cocoa. It was still very warm and comforting. He took another sip and began to feel better. He wasn't going to give up on Meagan—not now—and not until he had no other choice.

Chapter 15

Meagan barely managed to make small talk with her mother and sisters after Nate and Natalie left. She didn't want them to see how upset she was. She flipped through one of her newest magazines while she kept them company in the parlor. That way she didn't have to look up every time they asked her a question and she answered or made a comment.

"Mr. Brooks seemed in a hurry to leave tonight, didn't he, Meagan?" Becca looked up while she and Sarah played a game of checkers in the family parlor. "Natalie asked if we could play a game of checkers, but he barely let her finish her cookie before they took off."

"Maybe he had work to do at home, dear," her mother answered.

"He didn't look too happy about leaving," Sarah said. "Did you make him angry, Meagan?"

Her sister's question took her by surprise, and Meagan inhaled sharply. *Did I? Well, if so, it was no more so than he'd made me.* The more Meagan thought about their conversation the more upset she became, and she was glad her mother spoke, saving her from having to answer her sister.

"Meagan make Mr. Brooks angry?" Their mother chuckled. "Now, Sarah, you know better. Your sister goes out of her way not to anger anyone."

"I know. But he looked. . ." She shrugged. "I don't know. He just didn't look as happy when he left as when he came in for supper."

"Hmm," Mama said. "I'm sure he's fine, dear. He probably just wanted to get Natalie home and ready for bed. And that's just what you girls need to be doing now. Don't you have some studying to do?"

"I do have a test at the end of the week," Sarah admitted.

"Well, go on, then. I'll be up to say good night soon."

Meagan was relieved the conversation about Nate had ended. Just hearing his name made her want to cry. She released a sigh and turned to leave the parlor. "I think I'll go straighten up the shop, Mama."

"Have a cup of tea with me first, dear," her mother said. "You haven't had much time to relax lately."

"That sounds good." Meagan followed her mother into the kitchen.

Once they sat down at the table with their tea, her mother said, "Tell me what's bothering you, dear. You've looked so sad this evening."

"Oh, Mama." Meagan sighed and shook her head. "It will do no good to discuss it."

"It's as I suspect, then. It's matters of the heart you are dealing with."

She should have known she couldn't keep anything from her mother. At her gentle words, Meagan began to talk about it all. "Nate asked me to go to dinner with him tomorrow evening, and I turned him down."

"But why, dear? I know you care for the man."

"And so does Abigail Connors. She is determined to have him, Mama. And from what she tells me, she's practically engaged to him. She's let me know in no uncertain terms that she plans to marry the man."

"But that could just be her dream, dear."

"Mama, she sees him all the time. If she didn't believe it, then why would she say it?"

"Perhaps she said it to keep you from accepting a dinner invitation from him?"

Oh, how badly Meagan wanted to grasp at the hope her mother was handing her. But she was too afraid to. Yet there was a flicker. . . . "Mama, do you think that could be true?"

"I think it could be, yes. But I could be wrong. You are right to protect your heart, dear. But while doing that, you need to realize that not all things are as they seem."

"I've been hoping that she was just trying to upset me. But Mama, she is his sister-in-law and Natalie's aunt. She will always be part of his family, a tie that I do not have."

"I understand that. Still, true love is very strong. I do not get the impression that Mr. Brooks is smitten with Abigail Connors. And I can't think that he would ask you to dinner if that were so. But I don't have all the answers except the most important one."

"What is that, Mama?"

"You know yourself what it is, my Meggie. Take it all to the Lord, and trust in Him to work it out."

Meagan nodded. "I will, Mama. I'm going to straighten up the shop and then turn in. Thank you for listening to me."

"I'm always here for you, dear."

Meagan kissed the top of her mother's head. "I know you are. And I don't know what any of us would do without you."

She started to rinse her cup and saucer, but her mother shooed her out of the kitchen. "I'll do this. You go take care of the shop, and spend a little time with the Lord."

Meagan did just that, praying as she worked. She didn't know what the Lord's plan for her and Nate was. Hearing Abigail go on about her and Nate and the places they'd gone and the future she hoped for—it was hard not to believe her. Yet. . .there was a look in Nate's eyes tonight that had made Meagan want to cry. He seemed disappointed that she refused his invitation. Perhaps he was. But even if he was, that didn't mean he wasn't planning a future with Abigail. Meagan simply did not know what was going on, and she prayed that the Lord would help her through the pain if there was no future for them.

❧

Nate and Natalie had supper at the Connorses' home several nights later, and to his happy surprise, Abigail wasn't there. It was a rare event when she wasn't at her parents' house when Nate and Natalie came for dinner.

"Where is Aunt Abby tonight, Grandmother?" Natalie asked when they entered the dining room.

"A friend of hers is having a dinner just for the women they socialize with. Caroline Atwell has become engaged to be married, and it's a celebration of sorts," Georgette informed her once they were at the dinner table.

"I'm sure they'll have a delightful time," Nate said. He had noticed that the women Abigail was with most of the time just loved to talk about weddings.

"I'm sure Aunt Abby will enjoy helping to plan the wedding," Natalie said.

Nate was sure of it, too. The only thing she'd like better would be to be planning her own wedding to him. The cook served them Natalie's favorite meal of chicken and dumplings, with peas and baby onions on the side. Fluffy rolls completed the course.

As the meal progressed, Nate began to relax and enjoy himself. He could only wish Abigail had more outings with her friends on the nights that he and Natalie were invited to her parents' home for dinner. Then he felt bad at that thought. Abigail had been a great blessing to him right after Rose passed away. It was only in the last few years that he'd realized she wanted to replace her sister in his affections. That was something he was finding very hard to think about at all. Especially as he'd already put Meagan Snow in that position. . .even if she didn't return his feelings.

Natalie's laugh brought him out of his depressing thoughts. She did enjoy being around her grandparents.

"Oh, Grandpa, that was funny," Natalie said. "Will you play checkers with me after dinner? I'm getting much better at them."

"Of course I will. Soon we'll have to teach you to play chess," Jacob said.

"I'd love to learn chess!" Natalie said. "But I want to beat you and Papa at checkers before I do."

The cook came in to clear the table and serve bread pudding and coffee.

"Oh, thank you," Natalie said as her dessert was placed in front of her. "Everything has been delicious! Thank you for making my favorites!"

"You're welcome," the Connorses' cook said. "Your grandmother asked me to make them especially for you, Miss Natalie."

"Thank you, Grandmother. It's probably a good thing Aunt Abby wasn't here tonight. You know how she feels about dumplings!"

"You are welcome, dear. And yes, I do know how your aunt Abigail feels about them. She doesn't like them very much, does she?"

Natalie giggled. "No, she sure doesn't."

"But you know what?"

Natalie shook her head. "What, Grandmother?"

"She would have had to fill up on peas and onions, because I was going to serve it anyway. The best thing about her being otherwise engaged this evening is that we haven't had to hear her complain about the meal."

Everyone got a chuckle out of that, even the cook who was placing Nate's dessert in front of him. Georgette was exactly right. Abigail would have complained all evening. That his in-laws loved Natalie very much was always apparent, and tonight was no exception.

"You may call it a night, Mrs. Jackson. Natalie will help with the cleanup."

"Thank you, ma'am. Everything is washed and put up except what's on the table."

"Thank you." Georgette smiled at the woman. "Have a nice evening."

"I will. Good night."

Nate and Jacob retired to the study while Natalie and her grandmother cleared the table after dessert. "It's always a pleasure to have you and Natalie over, Nate. It brings a little life into this house."

"It's been a most enjoyable evening, Jacob. Natalie loves coming over." He did, too, most of the time. It was only Abigail's company that put him on edge at times. But he was thankful for Jacob and Georgette. "I'm blessed that you and Georgette have always been so kind to me and welcomed me as much as you do Natalie."

"Nate, you are like a son to us. You are the father of our only granddaughter. You'll always be part of this family. But you need a life outside of us, too. You need to remarry, son. You need to for your sake *and* Natalie's."

He could honestly answer Jacob. "I've been thinking about it." The only problem was, Nate couldn't help but feel that Jacob was hinting for him to marry Abigail. He couldn't blame the man. He wanted his daughter to be happy, too. And he wanted to keep his granddaughter close to the family. Nate understood all of that. He just wasn't sure he could give Jacob and

Abigail what they wanted. He wasn't sure at all. The only woman he wanted as a wife was Meagan Snow, and if he couldn't get her to go to dinner with him, he didn't know how it was going to be possible to ask her to become his wife. He could think about getting married all he wanted, but at the moment, it didn't look like marriage would ever be to the woman he'd come to love.

❧

Later, after they'd returned home and Natalie was ready for bed, Nate went up to tuck her in. They both knelt beside her bed as she said her prayers.

"Dear Father, thank You for this day and for everyone I love. Especially Papa. Thank You for my grandparents and for Aunt Abby, too. Please forgive me for the things I did wrong today and help me to do better tomorrow. Thank You for everything—especially for Jesus. Amen."

Nate was always touched by her simple prayers, and he had a feeling that the Lord was, too. Natalie scrambled up into her bed and pulled the covers up around her neck.

"Did you have a good time at your grandparents' tonight?" Nate asked as he brushed his lips across her brow.

"I did. I love playing checkers with Grandfather. I'm glad he doesn't let me win. I want to beat him fair and square one day!"

"I'm sure you will. You are getting better all the time." Nate sat down on the side of the bed and thought a minute before he spoke. "Natalie, dear, would you like for me to marry again one of these days?"

She sat straight up in bed and clapped her hands. "Oh, Papa, yes I would! I would love to have a mama like all of my friends! It would be so nice!"

"Do you think so?"

"Oh, yes! And you wouldn't be so lonesome when I grow up or when I'm not here."

Now how did she know I get lonesome? Nate wondered. "Well, I'll tell you what. I will do some thinking about it, all right?"

"Oh, yes, Papa. Please do think about it!"

She settled back down on her pillow, and Nate kissed her once more before turning down the light and going back down to his study.

He had been thinking about marriage a lot lately. Abigail had been bringing up the subject more often over the last few months, but it was Meagan he envisioned as his bride. But if Meagan didn't care about him the same way, what was he to do?

Abigail had been right about Natalie. She did need and want a mother. Yet the only woman he wanted to fill that position seemed cool and distant to him. Until the other day, he truly thought Meagan was beginning to care about him, too. Now he wasn't so sure.

He didn't want to give up on Meagan yet. Maybe she was just having a bad day when he asked her to dinner. That might be all it was. Natalie had her last fitting set for the next day. Perhaps he would be able to ask Meagan out again. If she turned him down this time, well then, he'd just have to accept that he'd been mistaken about how she might feel toward him and get over her.

But he wasn't ready to give up tonight. He bowed his head and asked for guidance. "Dear Lord, I'm in a quandary here. I have no idea if Meagan cares for me as I do her, but I need to find out. My daughter wants a mother, and I need a wife. I want it to be Meagan. But if that is not Your will, please help me to accept what is and go on. In Jesus' precious name, I pray. Amen."

Chapter 16

Meagan greeted Natalie and Nate when they came in the shop on Saturday morning, feeling both sad and relieved that this was Natalie's last fitting for a while. Much as she loved this child—and her papa—it had become painful to see them both when she knew they would never be hers.

"Good afternoon, Natalie. Are you ready to try on your new dress?"

"Oh, yes, I am!" Natalie hurried behind the changing screen. "I can't wait to wear it to church."

Meagan's mother came in with a pot of coffee and tray of cookies just then. She'd known the Brookses were coming, and Meagan had asked her to bring in some cookies for the child.

"Good morning, Nate. Would you like some coffee while Natalie is trying on her outfit?"

"Good morning, Mrs. Snow. I'd love a cup. It is such a beautiful spring day out. I think I'll take Natalie over to Basin Park after lunch. They sprayed the streets this morning to keep down the dust, so even if a breeze comes up, it should be pleasant out. A concert band is performing today, and I've heard they are very good."

"It's been a while since I've gone over there, but it is a nice day for it. I'm sure Natalie will enjoy it."

While her mother was entertaining Nate, Meagan helped Natalie change out of her walking dress and into her new lightweight wool church dress. Before she sent the child out to show her papa, Natalie motioned for her to bend down.

"Guess what, Miss Meg?" she whispered in her ear.

"I don't know. What is it?" Meagan whispered back.

Natalie cupped both hands around her mouth as she got close to Meagan's ear. "My papa is thinking about getting married again!"

Trying to hide the pain that splintered her chest at the child's excited whisper, Meagan asked, "Are you happy about that?"

Natalie smiled and nodded. "I'll have a mommy like all of my friends. And Papa won't be so sad all the time."

If Nate was thinking of remarrying, Meagan was certain it was to Abigail.

After all, that was all she'd been hearing from the woman for weeks now. She didn't quite know for whom her heart was breaking—herself or Natalie. The child did need a mother, and it was obvious that she wanted one badly. But even if Meagan hadn't wanted Nate for herself, she'd be disappointed in his choice of a wife and mother. Abigail was not the woman Meagan could imagine Nate with, and she certainly couldn't picture the woman being the kind of mother Natalie needed.

But the decision wasn't hers to make, and it appeared that Nate had already made it. She prayed for the Lord to help her accept that her dreams weren't going to come true and to not let Nate see how brokenhearted she was.

She gave the child a hug and sent her out to show her finished dress to her papa.

"Natalie, you look too grown-up," Nate said. "I can see that I'm going to have to watch you closely around all those suitors who'll be coming to our door a few years down the road."

"Oh, Papa," Natalie said with a laugh. "You are silly. I don't like any old boys, and they don't like me. They are too busy catching frogs to notice what I'm wearing!"

Nate laughed. "Well, that's quite a relief. They'll be noticing much sooner than I'll be ready for them to."

"Oh, Papa!" Natalie giggled again. "Are Becca and Sarah here? May I go show them my new dress?"

"I believe they are upstairs, but you may go, if it is all right with your papa," Mrs. Snow said. "Be sure to get a cookie before you leave."

"I will. Thank you!" Natalie said as she ran into the foyer and up the stairs, calling, "Becca! Sarah!"

Meagan was thankful that her mother remained in the room, but her relief was short lived as the knocker on the front door sounded. Her mother went to answer the door, leaving Meagan and Nate together.

"I—I'm not sure Natalie and I are going to know what to do, now that her wardrobe is filled for this season. She's growing much too fast to have you make anything for fall."

Relieved that the conversation centered on Natalie, Meagan felt herself relax a bit. "Yes, she certainly is. I did put deep hems in everything I've made her so that it won't be a problem should they need to be let down."

"Thank you. I do appreciate that." Nate's glance caught hers. "Meagan, you'd mentioned once that you liked to close the shop early on Saturdays, if possible. Do you think—would you be able to go to lunch with Natalie and me and then to Basin Park to hear the concert today?"

For a moment, Meagan's heart sang with joy at his invitation—then it plummeted. How dare he ask her to spend the day with him and Natalie when he was practically betrothed to another woman? She steeled her heart for what she had to do, no matter how badly it pounded for her to accept his invitation.

"No, thank you." She knew her voice sounded very cool. The look of disappointment in his eyes was almost her undoing, but she had to remain strong if she was to avoid even more heartache. "I'll not be able to do that."

Nate's heart felt as if a vise were squeezing it. It appeared that Meagan had no interest in going out with him. . .yet she looked so sad. He had to ask. "Meagan, have I done anything to offend you? If so, please tell me and please forgive me."

"I. . .you. . ." Meagan shook her head as Natalie rushed back into the room in her new dress with Becca following close behind. She gave her attention to the girls, and Nate tried to do the same. It appeared he wasn't going to get any answers—at least not today.

"Becca wants a dress like this one, Miss Meg," Natalie said as she went behind the screen.

"Oh does she now?" Meagan asked. "I'll see what I can do, Becca. Think about what color you would want."

Nate didn't hear the rest of the conversation as Natalie went behind the screen to change and Meagan went to help.

"Good day, Mr. Brooks," Becca said. "Natalie said you are going to Basin Park today. She's very excited about it."

"Yes, we are going after lunch. It's quite nice out even for early June, so we're going to take advantage of the sunny skies and balmy day."

"Papa?" Natalie said from behind the screen.

"Yes, dear?"

"Could Becca come with us?"

Why not? Nate thought. Her sister certainly didn't want to. He looked at Becca and could tell that she really wanted to go. "We'd love to have you come with us and share lunch with us. Sarah is welcome to come, too, if she'd like. Run and ask your mother—or better yet, let's both go ask your mother if you can accompany us."

"Oh, thank you, Mr. Brooks. I've done my chores this morning, so perhaps she'll say yes!"

Nate heard Natalie from behind the screen. "Do you think you could come too, Miss Meg? It's going to be such fun!"

He held his breath, waiting to see what Meagan said. "I'm afraid not, Natalie. But it was nice of you to ask Becca. I know she will enjoy it."

He followed Becca out of the room. There was no need to hear any more. The disappointment Nate felt dug deep into his heart. For whatever reason, Meagan wanted nothing to do with him socially. He was going to have to accept it and get on with his life.

❧

Meagan didn't know how she managed to refuse Natalie's invitation. She *wanted* to spend the afternoon with Natalie and her father. *Wanted* to go to lunch with them and then over to Basin Park to hear the concert. Yet it would only mean more heartache for her.

She helped Natalie change back into the dress she'd worn to the shop and then carefully folded the outfit she'd made her and wrapped it in tissue and placed it in a bag. "I hope you'll enjoy your new dress as much as I enjoyed making it for you. If the hem needs to be taken down, I'll be glad to do that for you."

"I'll wear it to church tomorrow!" Natalie promised.

Meagan was relieved that her mother came back into the shop with Nate, Becca, and Sarah. That way she wouldn't have to speak to him alone. She had no idea what to say to him anymore.

"I have some shopping to do this afternoon," her mother said. "I can meet you at the park and bring the girls home. That way you won't have to go out of your way to bring them back."

Thank you, Mama. Meagan wasn't sure she could face seeing Nate again that day. It hurt too much to see the look in his eyes.

"I don't mind bringing them home, Mrs. Snow."

"I know you don't, and I appreciate your willingness to get them back, but I'll meet you there about two, if that is all right."

"That will be fine. The concert should be about over by that time."

"I'll see you then. Thank you again for asking them. They don't get many outings like this."

"Natalie is thrilled to have some company other than her boring papa, I believe," he said. He stood a moment as if he didn't quite know what else to say.

Meagan's mother rounded up the girls and led them outside. *Dear Mama, she is trying to make this all easier on me.* Yet Meagan knew that nothing was going to help her heart stop aching—at least not yet, and probably not for months to come.

Meagan handed Nate the bag with Natalie's dress in it. "If the hem needs to be taken down, I'll be glad to do that for this or any of her other frocks."

"Thank you. I'll remember," Nate said, taking the bag from her.

Their fingers brushed, and the electric shock that flowed from the tips of her fingers straight to her heart astounded Meagan. She couldn't help but wonder if Nate had felt it, too. If so, he didn't mention it as he followed her mother and the excited girls out the door. But he turned back with a look in his eyes that almost had her changing her mind and saying she'd go with them. It was only with the Lord's help that she bit her tongue.

He did look disappointed—just like she felt. Only she was disappointed in him. That he could be involved with someone else and pursuing her at the same time. . .well, she just couldn't understand it. She'd thought he was much more honorable than that. Still, he looked so sad.

Could she be wrong about it all? With Abigail talking about how much time she spent with Nate and Natalie and that she expected to be married to him by next year. . .why would she be telling Meagan and anyone else within hearing distance about it if it weren't true? Could she just have wanted Meagan to think that so that she wouldn't accept Nate's invitations?

Surely not. No. That is just wishful thinking on my part, Meagan told herself. Yet. . .should she have done what she truly wanted to do and gone to lunch with him and Natalie? She stood at the side of the window and watched as Nate helped all of the girls into his buggy, her mother looking on.

No. She did what she had to do for her own sake, but her heart broke as she watched him drive away.

Chapter 17

During the next couple of weeks, Nate thought about the last few months repeatedly. He didn't see how he could have offended Meagan. He'd only wanted to see more of her. He hadn't treated her or her family badly. He liked them much too much to do so. The only thing he could come up with that made any sense at all to him was that Meagan Snow just was not interested in him the way he was in her. Yet when she'd refused his invitation to lunch that day, she'd looked. . .almost as sad as he felt. *Sad.* How could that be, and why?

All Nate really knew was that his dreams of a life with Meagan weren't coming true, and he had to get on with life. It didn't help him at all that Natalie kept asking when they were going to visit the Snows. He had no reason to take her now that Meagan had finished her wardrobe for the spring and well into the summer. He could only hope that Natalie grew enough to need the hems in her dresses let down an inch or so.

Life seemed to have reverted back to where it was before he'd met Meagan and her family, only Nate felt his loneliness as he'd never felt it before. He was even thankful for the invitation to Abigail's for dinner that evening.

One thing he'd found out about himself was that he didn't want to be alone for the rest of his life. He was extremely grateful that he had Natalie, but she would grow up, get married, and start a family of her own one day. Then he would be all by himself except for when invited to dinner or when they came to visit him.

Nate shook his head to rid himself of his maudlin thoughts. Natalie was still a little girl, and it would be a long time before all of that happened. But even now, he longed for someone to share his life with, and he knew Natalie wanted a mother. He'd loved Rose with all his heart, and then Meagan had come along. That he was in love with her there was no doubt. But she obviously didn't return those feelings. . .and he didn't think the love he'd felt for Rose and then for Meagan would come more than twice in a lifetime. Was it possible that he could learn to care about someone enough to share his life with her? Natalie did need a mother.

He sighed as he stopped his rig outside Abigail's and hitched his horse to the post. He helped Natalie down and watched as she ran to her aunt's door.

He was a bit surprised when Abigail opened the door herself. She enveloped Natalie in a hug and then smiled up at him.

"I'm so glad you could come. I haven't seen you in several days."

Her words seemed balm to his battered ego. At least Abigail was glad to see him. Normally he wouldn't have been thrilled that it was just the three of them for dinner, but tonight he was relieved that he didn't have to put up with her friends.

It was a surprisingly relaxed atmosphere. Instead of eating in the dining room, Abigail had set a smaller table in her parlor for just the three of them, and there was much more of a family feel to the evening than her elaborate parties. The first course was mulligatawny soup, followed by veal cutlets with brown sauce, rice, potatoes, and string beans.

"This is very good, Aunt Abby," Natalie said.

"Thank you, dear. Of course, when Millie knew you were coming, she took extra care. She wondered if you would like to help her make some cookies after supper."

"May I? Papa loves gingersnaps. Could we make those?"

"Of course you may. And you can take some home with you, too."

"Thank you, Aunt Abby!"

Any hopes Nate had of leaving early disappeared, but Natalie was happy and excited, and he supposed there were worse things than spending an evening in Abigail's company. Being alone and spending too much time thinking of Meagan, for instance. Perhaps it was time he thanked the Lord for the blessings he had instead of longing for something that could never be his.

The meal was quite pleasant, and once they'd finished, Natalie ran off to help Millie in the kitchen while he and Abigail went into the parlor.

Abigail breathed a sigh of relief. The family supper she'd planned had worked out well, and Nate seemed quite relaxed and at ease tonight. With Natalie in the kitchen with Millie, she might not have a better chance to broach the subject dearest to her heart.

She sat down on the settee and poured coffee from the pot her housekeeper had set on the table beside her. She put just a dollop of cream and two teaspoons of sugar in the cup, just as she knew Nate liked his after-dinner coffee, and handed it to him.

"Thank you, Abigail. Supper was delicious. And it was nice and peaceful."

"Did you have a bad day today, Nate? You seemed a bit dispirited when you arrived."

"It has been a busy week. Perhaps I'm just tired. I do appreciate that you weren't throwing a dinner party tonight. I enjoyed the quiet evening."

Maybe she'd been going about things all wrong, Abigail thought. It had never occurred to her that he would enjoy a quiet, family-type meal more than one in the company of others. Maybe he was just now beginning to appreciate that kind of thing. Whatever it was, he seemed quite at ease with her, and she was going to take advantage of his mood.

"You know, Nate, I think you are just lonely. I think you miss being married. You need a wife as much as Natalie needs a mother."

For once, Nate didn't argue with her. "I've been thinking about that."

Abigail caught her breath. For a moment she was afraid she'd heard wrong and was afraid to speak. "That's good. That you've been giving it some thought."

He nodded and took a sip from his cup.

The thought that he might have someone—that Snow woman—in mind had her asking point-blank, "And is there someone you—"

"No." It came out rough and firm and told her more than she wanted to know.

He was hurting. Something had happened, but she wasn't going to ask about it. Instead, she was going to fight for what she wanted. She rose from the settee and went to sit on the footstool at Nate's feet. She looked him in the eyes and spoke from her heart. "You know, Nate, you will never find anyone who cares about you and Natalie the way I do. I've loved you both for a very long time."

"Abigail—"

"Please hear me out, Nate. Think about Rose. Can you think of anyone she would rather you marry than someone who loves you and Natalie as much as she did?" She didn't wait for his answer but continued, afraid he'd stop her at any moment. "It's what she would want, Nate. I know that you don't love me the way I love you. . .but I will try to make you happy."

There. She'd done it. She'd laid her heart at his feet.

Nate stood and pulled her to her feet. "You deserve more—"

"No." She shook her head. She had no time to lose. "Nate, think of Mama and Papa. They were devastated when Rose died. If you were to marry someone outside the family, they might lose some of the closeness they have with Natalie and you. And. . .well, married to me, you would never have to worry about your position at the bank. Think about it, Nate, dear. The best thing you could do for all of us is to marry me."

She held her breath, waiting to hear what he had to say, but Natalie burst into the room just then. "Papa, Aunt Abby! The cookies are nearly done. I can't wait to taste them!"

Abigail had never been more relieved in her life. At least she'd been saved from an outright refusal. "I can't wait, either, Natalie, dear."

"Neither can I. Should we go to the kitchen and grab one hot out of the oven?"

"Oh, let's!" Natalie said.

Abigail laid a hand on Nate's arm as they headed out of the room. "Just think about it, please."

Her heart leaped with joy as he nodded his head. He'd listened without getting angry and without telling her no. She could only hope that her plan to come between him and Miss Snow had worked. Now, maybe, just maybe, he'd come to his senses and see that he needed to keep his love and his daughter in his wife's family.

❧

For the next few days, Nate mulled over all Abigail had said. He'd been surprised when she dropped the conversation once Natalie came to get them. It was as if she'd made her best case for marriage, and she was going to let him think about it.

Now as he left the bank and started walking home—it was too nice a day not to—he thought about it all over again. He'd been thinking about the past and the fire and how guilty he had felt that he hadn't been there when the fire reached his home, that he hadn't been able to save his wife. If only he'd gotten word about the fire earlier! But all the *if onlys* in the world could not change the events of that day, and he had accepted that long ago.

Still, he'd always wished for a different outcome. There was no way to get around the fact that, without Abigail, most likely Natalie would have died in the fire that day, too. A shiver went down his spine at the very thought. He would be forever grateful that Abigail had gotten his daughter to safety. He thought back over the last few years, back to the first few weeks when he'd been numb with pain. The whole family had been, but somehow they'd all managed to give Natalie the love and attention she needed, and no one gave her more attention than Abigail. There was also the fact that her father still thought Nate had gotten there in time to save Rose. Nate was sick of the guilt he felt that he couldn't save Jacob's youngest daughter. All Abigail had talked about had been true.

Normally, he would have brushed the conversation of the other night off and put it out of his mind until she brought it up again. But she'd been so right in many areas. Her parents would love nothing more than for Natalie to stay close, and the best way for that to happen would be if he and Abigail got married. This was also the first time she'd mentioned his needs, that he was lonely and needed a wife as much as Natalie needed a mother. The fact that the only woman he'd ever come to love besides Rose didn't seem to want to have anything to do with him. . .well, that most likely did play a part in his thinking these days, too.

If he thought for one moment that he had a chance with Meagan Snow, he would not even be giving the conversation with Abigail a second thought. But much to his disappointment, Meagan had made it quite clear that she wasn't interested in his courting her at all.

Natalie needed a mother, and he needed a wife. Abigail was quite right about all of that. She was also right about the fact that he didn't love her. . .not like she loved him. He wasn't sure he ever could. She seemed to understand that and still wanted them to marry. Could she be happy in a marriage to him under those circumstances? There was only one way to find out. She was having a dinner party the next night. He'd be the last one to leave for a change, and he would ask her.

❧

Once Nate told Abigail that he wanted to talk to her after everyone left, he began to have second thoughts. She had a look of expectancy about her, and he wasn't sure he was doing the right thing. But it was too late to change his mind now.

Abigail obviously wanted to know what he had to say, because she made sure no one lingered very long after dinner. As soon as the last couple took their leave, she led Nate into her parlor where she'd instructed her housekeeper to bring in coffee and the tea cakes she knew he was fond of.

"What is it you want to talk to me about, Nate?" She fixed his coffee for him and handed it to him along with one of the small cakes.

"I suppose it is about our conversation the other night."

Her cup rattled in its saucer before she steadied it. "Oh?"

"Yes. I've been giving everything you said some thought. I would like to remarry one day. It would be good to have someone to talk over the day with, to come home to at night."

Abigail kept silent, which surprised him. She nodded and took a sip of her coffee.

"And you are right about Natalie. She does want a mother. She would like me to marry again."

"I thought she would," Abigail said. She set her coffee down and clasped her hands together in her lap. "What else have you decided?"

Nate took a deep breath. "It will require both of us to make this decision."

She sat up straighter, and he knew he had her complete attention. "And what is that?"

"First—you said you know that I don't lo—"

"Love me like I love you?"

"Yes."

"I do know that."

"And you are willing to marry me anyway?"

Abigail joined him on the settee and took his hands in hers. "I am. Nate, I believe you will learn to love me."

At that moment, Nate truly hoped he could as he looked into her eyes. "In that case, then, will you marry me?"

Abigail leaned her head to one side and looked at him. Then her lips turned up in a smile. "Yes, Nate, I will marry you."

Chapter 18

Meagan's heart continued to break a little more each day after she turned down Nate's invitation to lunch. At church, she couldn't help but notice that Nate had stopped looking in her direction since she'd turned him down twice. She told herself it was best that way, but her heart told her differently.

While Nate wasn't looking for her, Abigail seemed intent on catching her eye and then pulling Nate a little closer as she placed a possessive hand through the crook of his arm. Her look seemed to say, *I told you so*.

Natalie always waved, but she didn't look as happy as she had just a few weeks ago, and Meagan's heart went out to her.

It came as no surprise when Abigail came into the shop the next day to pick up the last outfit Meagan had made for her to find that Nate was indeed getting married to her. "I want you to make my wedding dress, Miss Snow." She seemed to stress the *Miss* while she continued, "What plates do you have that I can choose from? But then, I've heard you are quite the designer. Do you think you could come up with a design for me?"

For a moment, Meagan was speechless. *Make this woman's wedding gown for her marriage to Nate?* If a knife had pierced her heart and been given a twist, she did not think it could give her any more pain than she felt at that moment. "I don't think I'm the one to make your wedding gown, Miss Connors. That is something I've never made before and—"

"Oh, nonsense! You do work comparable to some of my friends' gowns from Paris. There is no reason for you not to make my wedding gown unless. . ."

She paused, and Meagan held her breath. This woman was being much too nice.

"Unless you are hoping that Nate will change his mind and marry *you* instead of me?" Abigail continued.

She got right to the point, and she was exactly right. Meagan had wanted the first wedding gown she made to be her own. She'd been dreaming of walking down the aisle toward Nate for months. . .even after she knew it was hopeless.

"Miss Snow? Is that your problem? I do hope not. I want you to make this gown. And I'm sure my papa would not be pleased if you turn me down."

Turning her down was the very thing Meagan wanted to do. She'd never wanted to tell anyone to get out of her shop and never come back as badly as she did right at this moment. Abigail, however, was right. Her papa wouldn't be happy, and since Meagan still owed the bank on her loan, she couldn't risk making him angry. She'd already lost any chance for a life with Nate. She couldn't risk losing her family's livelihood.

"All right, Miss Connors. I'll make your gown."

"Good. That is what I was hoping to hear. I've set a wedding date for the seventeenth of July."

"That's very soon." It was June now, but Meagan told herself the sooner Nate was married, the sooner she could put him out of her mind. And the sooner she could finish Abigail's dress, the better. Perhaps once the woman had what she wanted, she would find another dressmaker to suit her needs. "But I will not design it. I won't have time. You'll have to choose from the plates I have."

Abigail made an irritated sound but didn't argue. "Very well, let's look at what you have."

Meagan pulled out several magazines for her to look at. After poring over the different plates for the better part of the afternoon, Abigail finally decided on a lovely gown made of ivory satin draped with Brussels lace. Meagan was thankful that it wasn't anything like the gown she had pictured as her own. Abigail's choice was intricate, but Meagan had no doubt that she could make it.

Since she had no other appointments that day, they took careful measurements and found that there would need to be no changes from the last dress. That would make Meagan's job much easier, and for that she was extremely thankful.

By the time Abigail left the shop, Meagan was totally worn down. She was fully aware that the only way she'd been able to manage to act as if she wasn't heartbroken that Nate was marrying that woman was with the Lord's help. She prayed He'd be with her during the next month, giving her the strength she needed just to get through each day as she worked on the bridal gown for Abigail.

❧

Even though Meagan prayed each night for strength to get through this trying time, it was all she could do to get through each day. Word of the upcoming marriage between Nate and Abigail had spread all over town.

She was worried about Natalie. At one time, the little girl had seemed so excited that her papa might marry again, but Meagan's mother told her she'd run into Natalie and her grandmother in town and asked if she was excited about all the wedding preparations and she had just shrugged. "She didn't look very happy to me," Meagan's mother had said.

And she didn't. At church, she looked sad, Nate looked resigned, and Meagan wasn't sure that even Abigail looked all that happy. Yet she had what she'd evidently always wanted. Hard as it was, Meagan began praying that Nate and Natalie would be happy, although she couldn't bring herself to add Abigail to that prayer, not yet—and she wasn't sure she'd ever be able to.

When Abigail and her mother brought Natalie in to ask if Meagan would make her dress, also, there was no way Meagan could turn them down. It was wonderful to see Natalie again, and she seemed happy to see Meagan. Still, there was a sadness in her eyes that Meagan didn't like. She wished she could ask Natalie what was wrong, but with Abigail and her mother within hearing distance, there was no way to do it. All she really could do was pray that the little girl would be happy with the new developments in her life. The one bright light in all of it seemed to be that she got to see Natalie again.

With all the heartache involved in making clothes for the wedding of the man she loved, taking care to make Abigail's dress come up to the high standards she'd set for herself when she went into business was one of the hardest things Meagan had ever done. But her reputation and her family's livelihood depended on her. She didn't for one moment think that Nate would let the bank foreclose on her, but Abigail could make sure no one would want to come to her shop if she wasn't satisfied with her dress.

So Meagan stayed up late, working to make sure that the trim was just so, that the lace draped perfectly on the mannequin she'd padded out to match Abigail's measurements. She did take part of Independence Day off to watch the parade and have a picnic at Basin Park with her family; then it was back to work as soon as they got back home. Sarah had shown a great interest in learning to sew and helping Meagan in the shop, and Meagan was grateful. She could use all the help she could get.

When Abigail insisted that Meagan come to Nate's house for her and Natalie's last fittings a week before the wedding, she agreed only because Nate would be at work. Abigail seemed intent on rubbing salt into the wounds she'd already inflicted. But the thought of being alone with Abigail at Nate's home was just too intimidating, so Meagan took Sarah along for support.

Nate's housekeeper, Mrs. Baker, showed Meagan and Sarah up the stairs and to Natalie's room. Nate's home was beautiful, and Meagan wondered if Abigail would move in after their wedding or if Nate and Natalie would live in her home. Somehow, she couldn't think that Abigail's home would be as warm and inviting as Nate's. His housekeeper had a knack for making it feel homey, and then there was the fact that Natalie lived there.

"Miss Meg, I've been waiting for you to get here," Natalie said when Meagan entered the child's room. "I wanted to run down and greet you, but Aunt Abby said no." The look the little girl gave her aunt spoke volumes to Meagan. Natalie was not happy with her aunt at all.

"She's here now, Natalie. I told you to quit whining, and she'd be here soon."

Tears welled in Natalie's eyes, but she answered Meagan's smile with one of her own.

"Sarah, would you please help Miss Connors try on her dress while I get Natalie's on her?"

"Natalie can wait—"

"There's no need for that. I brought my sister to help me out today."

"Very well." Abigail's tone was unusually sweet. "She can help Natalie while you help me."

Meagan nodded at her sister. There was no point in irritating Abigail more than she already seemed to be.

Meagan would have preferred to be helping Natalie. But as they were all in the same room, there was no way to have a private conversation with her and ask how she was doing. She could only hope the little girl knew how much she cared that she was upset.

Abigail stood in front of the corner mirror while Meagan helped her off with her wrapper and on with the bustle she'd need for the wedding dress. Then she stood on a stool to raise the dress over Abigail's head and down over her corset, chemise, petticoats, and bustle. It was going to look wonderful on her. Meagan could tell as she buttoned the tiny buttons up the back and settled the skirts around her. It fit her to perfection, and hard as it was to say, she told the truth. "It looks beautiful on you, Miss Connors."

Abigail turned this way and that in front of the mirror. The train was just the right length, and the veil framed her face perfectly. "I do look wonderful, don't I, Natalie, dear?"

Natalie ran over to her aunt. "It's very pretty, Aunt Abby. May I see how my dress looks?"

"In a moment, Natalie." Abigail twisted and turned once more before moving out of the way.

"I'll help you out of the dress, Miss Connors," Sarah said. "My sister needs to check the hem on Natalie's dress."

"Why it looks perfectly straight to me," Abigail said, but she let Sarah help her out of the dress while Natalie preened in front of the mirror.

"Oh, it's beautiful, Miss Meg! I love it," the young girl said. The dress was of satin and lace but was a soft buttery yellow, fitting for a young girl.

"Thank you, Natalie. I'm glad you like it. It fits you perfectly, and you look beautiful in it. I just need to make sure the hem is right." Meagan had her make slow turns until she was certain the hem was level. "It is just right."

"You need to take if off if Miss Snow is through inspecting it. You don't want to get it dirty, Natalie."

"I won't get it dirty, Aunt Abby."

"Natalie, take it off, now."

Meagan wasn't sure who she was trying to impress by her tone, but it certainly wasn't her. She didn't like the way Abigail was speaking to her niece.

"Do I have to?"

"Natalie! I can't believe your impertinence! Now go change!"

Meagan held her breath and glanced at her sister. How dare the woman speak to Natalie like that? She was just a child excited about a new dress.

Natalie turned to do as she was told, but then she began to cry. "I wish my daddy never said he would marry you, Aunt Abby! I wanted him to marry Miss Meg—not you!"

Abigail grabbed her arm. "I'll not have that attitude, either. You—"

Natalie pulled her arm away and ran for the bedroom door. She ran out of the room, yelling, "I don't want you to be my mama!"

Meagan followed her first instinct to run after the little girl, but she wasn't fast enough. A scream she knew she would never forget sent chills down her spine as she reached the landing. At the bottom of the stairs lay Natalie.

Chapter 19

Meagan went into action as soon as she reached the bottom of the stairs. Natalie was breathing, but she wasn't responding. Her arm seemed bent at an odd angle, and Meagan was afraid to move her. As Abigail seemed incapable of helping her, Meagan hurriedly sent her sister for Nate and asked the housekeeper to get the doctor.

Abigail began sobbing and couldn't seem to stop. It seemed forever before Nate burst through the door. He arrived out of breath and with fear in his eyes. Bending over his daughter, he took one look at Abigail and then looked to Meagan to tell them what happened.

"It was an accident. She got upset and ran out of the room, and then we heard a yell and. . ." Meagan prayed for the Lord to keep her tears at bay. She had a feeling Nate couldn't take that right now. "When I got to the landing, she was at the bottom of the stairs." Her heart twisted just seeing the pain in Nate's eyes.

The doctor arrived and quickly checked for broken bones. He tried to rouse Natalie once more to no avail. Afraid to jostle her into a carriage or wagon for the trip to the doctor's home, he had the child transferred to her bedroom. Abigail managed to go up to turn down the bed, but Meagan thought she was suffering from shock.

Meagan knew she would never forget the look on Nate's face when he gently picked up his limp daughter and carried her upstairs. It was only then, as she stayed behind for a few minutes to pray, that she let the tears flow.

She sent Sarah to tell Abigail's parents and their mother. "Let Mama know I might be here awhile. I think Abigail is in shock and I. . .I just can't leave right now."

Sarah gave her a hug. "I will. We'll be back to check on you all."

Meagan nodded and hugged her back. Then she gave her a little push. She rushed up the stairs. This wasn't her family and maybe it wasn't her place to stay, but she had to find out how Natalie was and see if Nate or Abigail needed anything.

When Meagan stopped just inside the bedroom door, she saw the doctor bent over Natalie. Nate and Abigail stood at the foot of the bed. Meagan waited to hear what the doctor had to say.

He turned to Nate. "Her left arm is broken, and I'll need to set it. But I'm more concerned that she's not responsive. Most likely, she is suffering from a concussion. We'll have to watch her closely. I'd prefer to have her in my office, but I don't want to move her right now." He looked at Abigail and then over at Meagan. "Would you get Nate's housekeeper? I'm going to need her help setting the bone."

Meagan nodded and turned to find the housekeeper right behind her. "The doctor needs your help."

Mrs. Baker nodded and hurried to the doctor's side. "What do you need me to do?"

"Get some water for the plaster and help me set her arm. Do you think you can do that?"

"Of course. I'll be right back with the water." She took one look at Natalie, shook her head, and hurried out of the room.

Meagan was right behind her. "Can I help?"

Nate's housekeeper was on her way to gather a pail of warm water from the stove's reservoir, along with several rags. She shook her head. "Just pray. Poor baby. I just hope she won't be feeling the pain of having that arm set."

A shiver shot right through Meagan at the very thought that Natalie was suffering, and she sent up a silent prayer that the child would be all right.

Meagan followed the housekeeper out of the kitchen, and when the door knocker sounded, Mrs. Baker turned to her. "I'm sure that's Mr. and Mrs. Connors. Will you show them upstairs?"

"Of course I will." Meagan hurried to answer the door, and it was Mr. and Mrs. Connors. Sarah had filled them in on the accident, and Meagan led them up even though they knew the way. They looked so worried, she didn't want to send them up by themselves. She could see that Nate was standing at the end of his daughter's bed and Abigail was just staring into space when her parents arrived. Meagan's heart went out to her. She knew it had been an accident, but she had a feeling Abigail would be blaming herself.

The housekeeper was bustling around getting things ready for the doctor when he turned and said, "All right, everyone. It's time to leave the room until we get this arm set. Then you can come back in."

"Doc, I don't want to leave. I can help."

"I know you don't want to leave, Nate. But it would be hard on you to stay, and it will make my job quicker and much easier if you go. I'll let you back in as soon as I'm done."

Abigail's mother took her arm and led her into the hallway. Her father put a hand to Nate's shoulder. Nate simply nodded and turned to leave the room. Meagan stood slightly away from them all but couldn't bring herself to go downstairs.

Nate moved to the staircase and looked down. What must be going through his mind? Meagan couldn't keep herself from going to him. "You know that we're all praying she comes through this."

He looked down at her. "I know you are. I. . .thank you for being here and for sending for me."

"You are welcome. I—" Meagan broke off, unable to continue. Just the look in Nate's eyes had tears welling in hers. *He's lost a wife, dear Lord. Please don't let him lose his daughter, too.* She didn't know what else to say or do.

"Is there any tea made, do you know?" Mrs. Connors asked.

Relieved to have something to do, Meagan said, "I'll go make some tea and bring it up, if that is all right?"

Nate didn't seem to hear her, and Abigail only stared at her. Mrs. Connors nodded and said, "That would be very helpful. Thank you, Miss Snow."

Meagan hurried back to the kitchen and put water on for the tea. While it was heating, she readied a tea tray with cream and sugar, cups, and saucers. She prayed while the tea was steeping. "Dear Lord, please let Natalie be all right. I don't know what it would do to this family if they lost her. And I—my whole family has come to love her, too, Lord. And You know how I feel about Nate. Please keep him from any more heartache. Please let Natalie heal and come back to us. In Jesus' name I pray. Amen."

She turned and gave a start to see Nate standing there looking at her.

"Meagan. . .I. . .thank you for that prayer. I—" He stopped and sighed. "I couldn't stand there just waiting for Doc to let me back in. Let me carry the tray up for you."

"All right." She handed it to him. She didn't know whether to go or stay until he looked back.

"You're coming, too, aren't you?"

"Of course." There was no way she could let this family go through this alone. She followed Nate up the staircase.

❧

The doctor was just coming out of the room when Nate and Meagan got to the landing. Nate quickly set the tray on a table outside Natalie's door. "How is she?"

"She's still unconscious. But her arm is set, and she's breathing normally. I believe she will come out of this, Nate. I've seen cases similar to this too many times not to believe she'll be all right. I'll check in later."

Nate knew there was no guarantee, but suddenly he felt hope. "Thank you. I pray you are right. I'll see you out."

"No. I can see myself out. You stay with your daughter."

For the first time since Nate got there, Abigail spoke. "Miss Snow can go with you. She's not needed anymore."

"Abigail!" Mrs. Connors protested. "Miss Snow's presence has been comforting. And she's made some tea which will taste mighty good to me right now." She turned and looked at Meagan. "I'm sorry about my daughter's rudeness. She's just upset about Natalie."

"That's understandable," Meagan said. "I can go home. My mother and I will check and see if you all need anything a little later."

"No." Nate put out a hand to stop her. He wanted her here beside him. . . just in case. "I don't want you to go. Natalie will want to see you when she wakes up."

Abigail shrugged before following him back into the room. Nate pulled a chair close to Natalie's bed and took hold of her hand. She looked so small and defenseless lying there. He heard Meagan say, "I'll get Mrs. Connors some tea. Would you like a cup, Miss Connors?"

Abigail was silent.

"Nate?"

"Not just yet, thank you." It gave him comfort to hear her voice in the room.

"I'll take a cup," Abigail's father said.

Nate glanced over at his in-laws and could see the pain in their eyes. They'd lost their youngest daughter and now there was the possibility—no! He couldn't think that way, wouldn't think that way.

His glance slid to Abigail. She was just staring into space. She seemed near collapse. Anyone could look at her and see that.

Meagan took the tea to Mr. and Mrs. Connors, and Nate heard them whisper their thanks. The wait was grueling. Nate bowed his head and whispered, "Dear Lord, please be with my Natalie. I can't lose her, Lord. Please heal her and bring her back to me. You said You won't give us more than we can handle, and Lord, I don't think I could stand it if—please, Lord, I beg You to let my baby be all right."

Suddenly he heard the crash of a teacup, and then Georgette exclaimed, "Nate! Natalie's eyes are blinking!"

His head came up, and he looked closely at his daughter. Everyone else in the room gathered around the bed, looking at Natalie. . .even Meagan. There was a flutter, and then another. The little girl's eyes slowly opened and then shut. Opened and shut again. . .and then opened. "Papa?"

"I'm—" Nate's voice broke. "I'm here, my precious girl."

"My arm hurts, Papa."

"I know. You fell—"

"Down the stairs. I was running away from Aunt Abby and I fell. . .

just like Mama did."

Nate caught his breath. This was the first time Natalie had ever mentioned her mother or the fall. "But you are going to be all right, Natalie, dear. You have a broken arm, and once it heals, you'll be fine."

Natalie didn't seem to hear him. Instead, she was looking at Abigail. "I fell, Aunt Abby. Just like Mama did. And it was all your fault!"

"No!" Abigail screamed. "It was *not* my fault. I was trying to keep Rose from going back upstairs for her precious mementos!" She began to cry deep, wrenching sobs. "I was trying to get us all out of there. But. . .but. . ." She sobbed again. "When I grabbed her, she tried to pull away from me and lost her balance. Then she. . .I. . ." Her voice trickled away.

"Abigail, dear, we know you didn't mean to. . . " Her mother put an arm around her, but Abigail pulled away.

"I don't want you to marry Aunt Abigail, Papa!" Natalie was crying now. "I want you to marry Miss Meg!"

"Oh, Natalie. I'm so sorry. I'm an awful person. I've made Nate feel guilty for not being there to save her. All the time I resented that he loved Rose and not me! And then. . .I made Miss Snow think that he was. . .in love with me so that she wouldn't give him the time of day—so that he would finally realize it was me he needed to marry. But he loves her! I'm sorry. I'm so sorry!" She yanked the engagement ring Nate had given her off her finger and forced it into his hand, tears flowing down her face. Then she turned and ran out of the room.

Holding the ring he'd given Abigail, Nate felt an overwhelming sense of relief that she'd broken the engagement, but he was speechless as he watched her run out of the room. He knew that Abigail could be manipulative, but to go to such lengths to get her way? And to purposefully add to the guilt he'd felt that he couldn't save Rose? It was hard to take it all in. But what pained him most was that she'd set out to ruin his relationship with Meagan so that he would ask her to marry him. Anger deep and hot rose up, and all he could do was look at Meagan. The color was high on her cheeks, and she looked as shocked as he felt.

"Abigail!" Mrs. Connors looked totally taken aback at her daughter's words. She didn't seem to know what to do.

"I'll go after her. She's in no shape to be by herself," Jacob Connors said. He crossed the room to kiss Natalie. "I love you, and I'll be back in a little while, all right?"

Natalie nodded. "Yes, Grandfather."

Georgette hurried over to the bed and gave her granddaughter a kiss on the cheek. "Natalie, dear, God has answered our prayers that you will be all right. We love you so very much. And your aunt Abigail loves you with all her heart." Georgette wiped the tears streaming from her eyes. "She never meant to harm anyone. I—Nate, I must go with Jacob and Abigail. We need to get her home. She's not—"

He nodded. Abigail was in no condition to be alone, but he wasn't the one who could help her. He needed to stay with his daughter and Meagan. "She needs you. Go to her. Natalie knows you'll be back soon."

It was quiet in the room once the Connors family left. Nate wasn't sure what to say, and Meagan didn't seem to know what to do as she stood beside Natalie's bed, wiping tears from her own eyes. But when she finally looked at him, Nate began to hope.

Chapter 20

Meagan's heart was thumping so hard she could barely breathe, seeing the look in Nate's eyes. He approached her slowly, his lips turning up in a slight smile. She couldn't take her gaze from his.

"Was Abigail right? Did she make you think I was in love with her?"

Meagan bit her bottom lip and nodded but couldn't find her voice.

"It all makes sense now. You must have thought me quite the cad when I kept asking you to have dinner and then lunch with me." He lifted her face to his. "I'm sorry. I certainly helped her cause when I asked her to marry me, didn't I?"

"I didn't know what to think. I. . .didn't think you were the kind of person who would act that way, yet everything Abigail was saying to me when she came into the shop told me something completely different from what I thought was happening between us."

Nate shook his head and looked deep into her eyes. "I can see how you would be confused and not want to have anything to do with me. But when you kept refusing to see me, I thought you didn't care."

"Oh, Nate." Meagan shook her head. "I'm sorry, I—"

"It isn't your fault, Meagan. But I knew I would never find anyone like you again. And if you didn't want me, as I thought, well, I hoped I could one day come to love Abigail. Natalie needs a mother, and. . .I thought I was doing the right thing. I didn't treat her right, either. I was just so. . .heartbroken. I had no hope that you would ever return my feelings, and—"

"Oh, Nate, I don't know what to say. I did—I do care about you very much. I just didn't know what to think, and then once you were engaged, there was nothing more to do."

Nate bent his head and whispered in her ear, "You are the woman I want to marry. I love you, Meagan Snow. I've loved you for quite a while now, and I wish I'd told you long ago. I love you with all my heart. Do you think you can give me another chance to win yours?"

Meagan pulled back just enough to look him in the eye. "My heart is already yours. You won it a long time ago. I love you, too, Nate."

His lips claimed hers softly at first until Meagan returned the pressure, and then he deepened the kiss. Meagan's eyes filled with tears. Nate loved her. Not

Abigail—but her. Her world righted itself for the first time in weeks.

She broke the kiss and looked into Nate's eyes. She could see the joy she felt reflected in his eyes.

"Will you marry me, Meagan? Will you take my heart as your own and be my wife and Natalie's mother?"

"I love you, Nate. I will be honored to become your wife and the mother of your daughter, whom I love, also."

His lips found hers once more in a kiss meant to assure her of just how much he loved her. Time forgotten, they were broken apart by the child they both loved yelling, "Yippee! We're going to marry Miss Meg!"

Nate chuckled and looked a little embarrassed. Apparently Meagan wasn't the only one who'd forgotten that Natalie was in the same room and overheard everything they said.

When they hurried over to Natalie and included her in a hug, Meagan was more than a little aware that if Natalie hadn't taken that fall, she and Nate might never have known how the other felt. She thanked the Lord once again that Natalie was going to be all right. How doubly blessed they were this evening.

❧

The doctor arrived at the same time Meagan's mother and sisters did. They were all in the room while the doctor looked into Natalie's eyes and checked her cast before pronouncing her on the mend. He recommended a light supper if she was hungry but told Nate not to worry if her appetite wasn't up to par. He gave her some medicine that would ease her pain and help her sleep during the night, should she need it.

"It does my heart good to see you awake, child," he said to Natalie. "You look quite chipper for someone who broke an arm and had a concussion to go along with it."

Natalie's smile was huge when she nodded. "I'm very happy!"

"I'm sure you are no happier than your papa and these good folk here with him."

"Can I tell them, Papa?" Natalie giggled excitedly.

Nate grinned and pulled Meagan into the crook of his arm. "Go right ahead."

Meagan's mother and sisters looked at her curiously. She just smiled back.

"Tell us what, Natalie, dear?" Mrs. Snow asked.

"Papa and Miss Meg are going to get married! She's going to be my new mama! And I will be part of your family!"

"You are? How wonderful for us!" Meagan's mother seemed truly confused when she looked at Natalie. "But what? How?"

"It all happened 'cause of my fall," Natalie said. "Aunt Abby gave Papa his ring back, and then after she left, Papa and Miss Meg said they love each other, and I saw them kissing!"

Meagan couldn't contain her joy any longer. "Nate asked me to marry him, Mama. And I told him yes."

"Oh, my dears. That is wonderful news. But what about—"

"We'll tell you later," Meagan said.

Her mother nodded, and Meagan knew she understood that there was quite a bit left unsaid.

"My, we do have much to celebrate!"

It was a while later before Meagan and Nate could discuss wedding plans. By the time her family had left, with Nate promising to bring her home once Natalie was asleep and his housekeeper could watch her, Meagan had begun to believe it was all true and not part of her dreams.

After a light supper, Meagan had helped Natalie get ready for bed, and the child was so sweet even with her pain, that she knew Natalie truly loved her. It felt very natural to kiss the child good night and wait for Nate to do the same. They didn't go far in case she called out. Instead of going downstairs, they took a seat on a settee in the wide hallway. There was so much to talk about as she told him how Abigail had gone about convincing her that Nate and she were going to be married.

"I can't help but feel sorry for her," Meagan said.

"I know. I never realized how guilty she felt about Rose's death. I was too busy blaming myself for not getting there in time, I suppose. I should never have asked her to marry me when I didn't love her like I do you."

"You need to talk to her, Nate. She's devastated that Natalie is upset with her. I saw her face when Natalie told her she wanted you to marry me."

Nate rubbed a hand over his face and shook his head. "I still can't believe this day. I was so afraid I was going to lose my daughter and to end it with her all right and knowing I have you. . .I have so much to thank the Lord for!" He bent his head and captured her lips with his own.

Meagan wondered if there would ever be a sweeter kiss between them. But when he raised his head for only a second and then kissed her again, she knew there could be.

"When are you going to become my wife? I don't want to wait long. I don't want to take a chance on anything going wrong again."

She kissed his cheek. "Nothing is going to go wrong—not now. We'll get married as soon as I can get my wedding gown made and you can talk to Abigail and let her know that she will always be part of Natalie's life. I would never want Rose's family to think that they couldn't come around or be as much a part of her life as they always have been. Please, Nate, let them know."

Nate cupped his hand around her chin and looked down at her. If she'd ever doubted his love for her, she no longer did. It was shining from his eyes.

"I'll let them know," he promised. . .just before he kissed her, telling her in his own way just how very much he loved her.

❧

Nate didn't see Abigail or her parents for the next several days, but Jacob and Georgette came to see Natalie often, bringing her a toy or some other treat. He'd talked to them briefly, but he didn't feel any animosity from them about the broken engagement to Abigail. Georgette stayed most of the day while Nate was at work, but she usually left just before he got home, and he hadn't been able to really talk to them about their daughter. Abigail hadn't come to see Natalie at all. Natalie didn't seem too concerned about it. Nate tried to tell her that her aunt Abigail loved her, but Natalie didn't want to talk about it just yet.

By the end of the week, Nate was determined to keep his promise to Meagan. He left work on Friday and went to Abigail's home. She did need reassurance that Natalie still loved her, and he'd promised to let her know that she would be a part of Natalie's life always. But Abigail wasn't at her home, or at least that's what her housekeeper told him. Nate sought her out at her parents' home. He was shown into the study where Mr. Connors seemed to be waiting for him.

"Good evening, Nate. Please, take a seat. I suppose you've come to talk about my daughter."

"I've come to see her, sir."

"She's had a hard time. I had no idea she blamed herself for so much." Jacob sighed deeply.

Nate nodded. "I. . .know. Neither did I. I want to assure her that Natalie will come around. I know she didn't mean to make Rose fall down the stairs that day. And I should have told you earlier that as much as I wanted to save Rose, I didn't get there in time. The house was engulfed in flames when I got there."

"I know that, son."

"You do?"

"I know most people in this town, Nate. They tell me things. But I also know how much you loved Rose. I know you would have gone in there and dragged her out if there were any way you could have."

Nate blinked against the tears that threatened. "I would have."

Jacob nodded. "Abigail isn't the woman for you. I know it, and you know it. You never had to marry her to stay part of this family, Nate."

"Thank you, sir. I am sorry I hurt Abigail. I prayed that I was doing the right thing when I asked her to marry me. What I should have done was pray for the Lord to guide me in doing the right thing. I didn't wait on Him. It would have been easier on Abigail if I'd done that."

"One day, she'll get what she needs. A love all her own—not one that loved her sister first or who is in love with someone else, but one who loves her."

"I'll pray she does. I would like to apologize to her. Do you think she'll talk to me?"

"Not now, Nate. She doesn't want to talk to anyone—not even her friends."

Nate sighed, whether from frustration or relief he didn't know, but at least he could tell Meagan that he had tried. "I understand. I—"

"I'll tell her you came by, Nate. She'll be all right. We're going to see to it that she is."

Nate couldn't help but wonder whom Jacob was trying to convince. . .Nate or himself.

"I like Miss Snow." Jacob changed the subject, taking Nate by surprise. "Natalie told us about you asking her to marry you. We'll be invited to the wedding?"

"Oh yes, you will. Meagan wanted me to assure Abigail, and you and Georgette, that she wants you all to be as much a part of Natalie's life as you always have been. She knows how deeply you love Natalie."

"That does my heart good to hear, Nate. Let her know she'll be part of ours, too. I think Rose would have liked her."

Nate left the Connors' home feeling blessed, indeed. Blessed that Natalie was all right, blessed that Jacob and Georgette would continue to be part of his life, and blessed to be in love with a woman who wanted it no other way.

Epilogue

September 3, 1886

Meagan's wedding day dawned bright and sunny. She'd finished her dress only two days before, but it was just as she'd imagined it. She'd made it as different from Abigail's as she possibly could. It was of white satin and lace, but it was much simpler than Abigail's, and she loved it.

Now as she waited to walk down the aisle toward her husband-to-be, Meagan felt completely blessed. Nate was the most wonderful man in the world. When she'd expressed a worry about her mother and sisters, he'd taken her in his arms.

"Meagan, my love, don't you know that I would never let them suffer because of our marriage? My home is large enough for you all. However, what I thought I might do is pay off your loan and give the title to your home back to your mother free and clear. She and the girls could continue to live in the home they love if that is what they wish."

"But I don't want her to have to work—I mean I love the shop and. . .I don't—"

"Meagan. Your mother will never have to work outside the home again. And you have a talent. If you want to continue with the business you've worked so hard to get started, that is fine with me. I would hope that you wouldn't feel you must work night and day, though. I'd like to spend time with you. Perhaps you could continue to teach Sarah to sew, if she's interested, and she could help out. Then she would have a career until she finds some nice young man whom we approve of."

He did care about her family, and he'd been thinking about their future just as she had. Having answered all her worries, Meagan had reached up and pulled his dear face down to hers so that she could look him in the eye. "You are the dearest man in the world. Oh! How I love you."

Nate had taken advantage of their close proximity and claimed her lips in a kiss that more than convinced her he felt the same toward her. She had no complaints at all.

Now, as the wedding march began, she slowly followed Natalie down the aisle to Nate, who was standing at the front of the church. Her eyes on him, she barely noticed who was there to witness the happiest day of her life. She did see her family on one side of the aisle and Mr. and Mrs. Conners on the other side. She felt additionally blessed to see Rose's parents there to witness their vows. Those were the only people she was concerned with today—their loved ones witnessing her and Nate's vow to love and honor each other for the rest of their lives.

As the minister pronounced them man and wife, Meagan raised her face to Nate.

"I love you, my wife," he whispered just before his lips met hers. Meagan thanked the Lord above for all of her blessings and most especially that He had given her a love for keeps.

A LOVE ALL
HER OWN

Dedication

To my Lord and Savior for showing me the way
and to my family for their love and support always.

Chapter 1

Abigail Connors sniffed and threw off her covers. She was through with this crying. It wasn't going to change a thing. She'd done enough of that over the past week and a half—ever since her world had collapsed around her. Much as she wanted to pretend it was all a nightmare, there was no denying it. She'd lost the man she'd loved for years and the love of the niece she adored—all in one afternoon. And she had no one to blame but herself.

Fresh tears threatened, even when she thought she couldn't possibly have any left, but she swiped at her eyes and held her weeping at bay. It wasn't going to do her any good, and she couldn't stay in bed forever. As it was, enough talk about her was probably circulating around town, now that her wedding had been called off. She pulled on her wrapper and yanked the cord to summon her parents' housekeeper.

In minutes, Laura appeared. "Miss Abigail, I'm so glad to see you up and about! Would you like some breakfast?" It was obvious that the woman had been worried about her. During those first few days when Abigail couldn't have cared less if she ever ate again, everyone in the house had practically begged her to eat. Laura had prepared all her favorites to no avail. But the woman looked so hopeful this morning that Abigail couldn't disappoint her.

"Perhaps after I've had a bath, Laura. Please prepare that for me now, and then you can make me some tea and toast."

The housekeeper set about doing as asked at once. By the time Abigail was finished bathing and was trying to decide what she needed to do next, Laura arrived with a tray laden with tea, toast, and an egg cooked just the way Abigail liked it. For the first time in days, Abigail felt hungry. "Thank you, Laura. I think I'll be going home today, so if you would just see that my things get home, I would appreciate it."

Laura didn't say anything, but Abigail had a feeling the housekeeper didn't approve and would go running to her mother with the news. Nevertheless, it was time. She had to make plans. She could not stay in Eureka Springs and watch Nate Brooks start a new life with Meagan Snow. She couldn't stay and see the disgust in her niece Natalie's eyes when the little girl looked at her. Nor could she stay and be laughed at behind her back. She could not, would not do it. Going anywhere would be better.

Abigail ate her breakfast and was on her second cup of tea when her mother's light knock sounded on the door. "Come in, Mama."

"Abigail, dear, what's this Laura tells me about you going home?" her mother asked, gracefully sweeping into the room. She looked lovely as always, dressed in a green-and-white-striped morning dress, with not a hair out of place. "I'm not sure you are ready to—"

"It's time, Mama. I can't stay with you and Papa forever, and I can't stay in Eureka Springs, either. Not with the. . ." She couldn't finish the sentence. She didn't even want to think about Nate's upcoming marriage to Meagan Snow.

"But dear, you don't want to make a hasty decision. Give yourself time—"

"Mama, please. I just can't stay here. Don't you see?" Her parents had been so very kind and patient with her the last few days, even after she'd admitted what an awful person she was. They had assured her of their love and insisted she stay with them until she felt she could cope with her heartache, but she knew she'd disappointed them. Abigail felt she had to get away, but she wasn't quite sure where to go. "Mama, I must get out of Eureka Springs."

"Why don't you get dressed and then come down to your papa's study? We can talk to him about it. He'll know what to do."

"Mama, he's not going to want me going anywhere. I—"

"Abigail, dear, your father and I have your best interests at heart. You know that. We will hear you out, and then together, we'll all decide what is best."

Abigail sighed. There was no way around it. She was going to have to discuss this with her father. She needed a plan, and she needed it quickly.

❧

Abigail dressed in a pale blue morning dress, and Laura dressed her hair for her, arranging it on top of her head as was in fashion. Before leaving the room, Abigail pinched her cheeks to give them a little color, knowing her papa would try to find a reason to keep her under his care a little longer. Taking a deep breath, she opened the bedroom door and went down to his study.

Her father was sitting at his desk, writing, while her mother was looking out the front window, a cup of tea in her hand. "I just don't know, Jacob," her mother said but cut her sentence off when she noticed Abigail enter the room.

"Don't know what, Mama?" Abigail mustered a smile. "What to do with me?"

Her father rewarded her with a chuckle. "That would probably sum it up nicely, dear. You have presented us a challenge from time to time."

Abigail went over and kissed the top of her father's head. "Yes, I know. Mama has been telling you that I think it's time to leave, hasn't she?"

"She has. I don't think it is a good idea."

"Somehow that doesn't surprise me, Papa. But I must find a way to. . .get on with my life." Abigail heard the wobble in her voice and hoped her parents didn't notice it.

Her mother poured a cup of tea and handed it to her. "Here dear. We'll figure out something."

"Thank you, Mama." Abigail took a sip and continued. "I'd like to get away for a while."

"Away? You aren't just talking about going back to your house, are you?"

"No, Papa. I—I want to get out of Eureka Springs for a while." *Maybe for the rest of my life,* Abigail thought. But she didn't voice the wish.

"Georgette dear, I'd like a cup of that tea, please." Abigail's father waited until he'd taken a sip from the cup her mother handed him. "Where are you thinking you'd like to go?"

She took a deep breath. "Europe."

Her father almost choked on the warm liquid he'd swallowed. "Europe!" He stood up and began to pace the room. "Abigail, Europe is much too far away. What if something happened and you needed us?"

"Papa, I'm sure I'd be all right." But the thought did give her pause. Much as she thought of herself as independent, Abigail had never really been away from home without her parents.

He shook his head. "No. I don't think that's a good idea at all. Please dear, just give things time."

"Oh Papa, I don't think I can stand staying in the same town where everyone knows me—and knows that my engagement has been broken *and* that Nate will be marrying Meagan Snow very soon. Everyone I know will be laughing and talking behind my back." Abigail could feel the tears and knew she couldn't hold them at bay much longer. "I can't stay knowing that my Natalie doesn't want anything to do with me—" Her voice broke on a sob. "I just can't do that. I need a change. I have to get away, Papa. I just have to."

Jacob Connors gathered her in his arms and rocked her back and forth. "Oh, my Abby. Just let me think on it a little while. I believe I can come up with something closer than half a continent and an ocean away. Don't go home just yet. Have dinner with us, and I'll try to have an answer for you by then."

Abigail sighed in relief. Her father was going to help her. She was going to be able to get away from all the hurt and humiliation. "Thank you, Papa," she whispered.

⌘

Marcus Wellington stopped by Western Union as he did first thing every morning, noon, and afternoon. In his business, he was liable to get several telegrams a day. The telegrapher handed him two new ones.

"This one from Mr. Connors in Eureka Springs just came in a few minutes ago, Marcus," Harold Dillard said.

"Thank you, Harold." Marcus took the telegrams and moved over to the end of the counter to read them. He tore into Mr. Connors's first. He hadn't heard from the man in several months, but whatever he needed, Marcus would get to first. He read:

> *Marcus, need your help. Daughter is coming to Hot Springs soon. Need you to have protection for her. Can you take care of it for me?*

Marcus waited until the customer Harold was helping left. "I need to reply to this one right away, Harold."

The clerk gave him a pad and pencil, and Marcus wrote: *Jacob. Will be glad to. Let me know the details. Marcus.* He handed it to Harold. "This needs to go out right away."

"I can do that, Marcus." Harold read it over and began transmitting.

"I'll wait a few minutes—just to make sure he's not on the other end waiting for my reply—to send another," Marcus said, walking over to look out the window. He couldn't help but wonder why Jacob's daughter would be coming to Hot Springs by herself, but it didn't matter. The man had asked him a favor, and there was no way he'd turn him down. If it hadn't been for Jacob Connors, the Wellington Agency wouldn't exist. Marcus had just about exhausted his resources two years ago when he'd finally approached his father's good friend and banker, Jacob Connors. He wasn't sure if that was the only reason the man had lent him the money to start his detective/protective agency, but they both had reason to be glad he did. Many people had thought that his business would fail within a month or two, but they'd been wrong. The Wellington Agency would never compete with the Pinkerton Agency, and that was fine with Marcus. He had no desire to be that big. Still, his business was doing so well he was making plans to open offices all across the state, and he owed it all to Jacob Connors.

The telegraph machine started working, alerting Marcus that a message was coming in. Harold was writing out the code. "You were right. He must have been waiting for you." Harold handed Marcus the paper:

Thank you. Will be sending details in the next day or so.

Marcus sent a reply saying, *Message received. Will be looking for next one.* There was nothing else to do until he knew when Jacob's daughter would be arriving. He'd check his schedule and think about whom he could trust to watch over Miss Connors. He folded the message and headed for the door. "See you later, Harold."

❧

When Abigail joined her parents for dinner, she couldn't tell if her father had come up with a plan or not, but she knew he would let her know in his own way and his own time. She just hoped it would be before she lost what appetite she had for the meal she knew Laura had prepared with her tastes in mind. It was the first time since she'd been staying with her parents that she had joined them for dinner, and the housekeeper had made her favorites, from baked ham to scalloped potatoes and rolls.

Her father seated her mother and took his place at the head of the table. Then he looked at Abigail. "I think I have a plan. But let's ask a blessing for our food first, and then I'll tell you all about it."

Abigail bowed her head while her father gave the blessing.

"Dear Lord, we thank You for this day. We thank You that our Abby is joining us for dinner tonight. Father, we ask that the plans we draw up for her are in Your will. And we ask You to bless this food we are about to eat. In Jesus' name. Amen."

As her mother began to dish up the meal, her father laid out the plan he'd come up with.

"For some time now, I've been thinking about investing in a bathhouse in Hot Springs. I believe the town could support another one, but I want it to be very nice."

"But Jacob, what does that have to do with Abigail?" his wife asked, handing him his plate.

"Well, I don't know who I'd trust more to investigate the bathhouses already in business than my daughter. Abigail wants to get away. I don't think it really matters where, does it, daughter?"

Abigail shrugged. "Not particularly. I've heard that Hot Springs is a very nice place to visit. I'm not sure it's far enough away, though. Some of my friends are the ones who told me about it."

"Dear, I know you wish to get away." Her mother handed Abigail a filled plate. "But I would rest so much better if I knew you were in the state. I would worry so if you were to travel abroad."

"Well, I suppose I could check out the bathhouses for Papa. If I hate it there, I'm sure I can go somewhere else."

"I think you'll like it fine," her father said. "There is even more to do there than in Eureka Springs. And we have friends who you could go to if you needed anything. Your mother and I have known the Wellingtons for a long time. They will show you around and help you get acquainted quickly."

Abigail wanted to protest, but deep down, she had to admit that she'd feel more comfortable if she knew some people in the area whom she could turn to if needed. It appeared that her parents understood her need to get out of town. That alone had her appetite coming back, and Abigail found she was actually very hungry.

"That will be nice. The Wellingtons. I'll look for them," Abigail said before taking a bite of ham.

"You won't have to. Their son will be meeting your train," her father said. "He owns the Wellington Agency. It's a detective/protective agency, and I've asked him to watch over you while you are there."

Abigail almost choked on the ham she'd just swallowed. "Papa, I don't need someone to watch every move I make!"

"Abigail, dear. You are my daughter, and you stand to have a sizable inheritance one day. I don't want anything happening to you," her father said quietly.

"But—"

"Abigail, Marcus Wellington is going to make sure you are safe. That is all. More than likely, you won't even know who it is he has watching you at any given time. His agency is growing and getting good reports from all over the country. Your mother and I know his family, and I know him to be an honorable man."

"But, Papa—"

"Abigail. It really isn't going to matter whether you are here in the States or in Europe. Be assured I will hire someone to watch over you no matter where you go. And you are going to have someone to turn to if you need them—whether you like it or not."

Chapter 2

The trip by train to Hot Springs was long, but Abigail was so relieved to get out of Eureka Springs she hardly noticed. It had taken longer than she expected—or wanted—to pack and close her home for an extended stay away, but finally she had left on the evening train on Thursday, August 5. From Eureka Springs, she'd gone through Fayetteville and on to Fort Smith. Arriving there late that night, she switched from the Frisco line to the Iron Mountain line, where her father had booked a sleeping berth for her. She'd thought she wouldn't be able to sleep, but the rocking motion of the train lulled her into a deep slumber so that she woke refreshed and excited to finish the last leg of the trip. After freshening up and eating breakfast at Malvern, she switched trains for the last time and watched the scenery pass by, glad that she would be at Hot Springs that afternoon.

Abigail had been very busy ever since she agreed to go to Hot Springs instead of Europe. The relief she felt that she wouldn't have to stay in Eureka Springs and be humiliated further by the gossip and speculation as to why Nate was going to marry Meagan Snow instead of her was huge. It energized her enough to decide what to take with her and arrange to have her home closed until she returned—if she ever did. At the moment, she couldn't imagine wanting to go back to Eureka Springs, but she wasn't about to voice that opinion to her parents.

As the train neared Hot Springs, Abigail looked out the window and could see the edge of the Ouachita Mountains getting closer. She wondered if Hot Springs was going to be that much different from her hometown and then decided that it didn't matter. What did was that she didn't know anyone here. There would be no one to know her background or to gossip about her.

She could feel both the excitement and apprehension of being on her own in a strange place begin to mount as the train slowed down and entered Hot Springs. The city seemed to be situated in a narrow valley between mountains, with pines scaling one mountainside while hickory, oaks, and other hardwoods covered the opposite mountainside. She caught glimpses of pink and purple flowers here and there. As the train eased to a stop and blew its whistle at the train depot, Abigail stood and shook out her skirts. She was glad she'd chosen a frock of brown and beige foulard. It didn't show the dust and ash from train travel quite as badly as other colors.

Her papa had told her that there would be someone to meet her at the train depot, and as she gathered her parasol and reticule and made her way to the exit, she hoped he was right. Suddenly, the fact that she was alone in a strange place weighed down on her, and she realized that she wasn't quite as brave and independent as she wanted everyone to think. She stepped off the train and looked around, only she wasn't sure whom she was looking for or what he might look like.

$\backsim$

Over the last two weeks, Marcus had received a detailed letter and several telegrams from Jacob Connors. He'd found out that Miss Connors had been planning on getting married recently but that the marriage had been called off and she wanted to get away. She'd be checking out some business dealings for her father while she was there. The man didn't expect her to be watched around the clock—he just wanted her safe. Although Jacob didn't give Marcus any more information than that, they'd kept the telegraph lines busy while they came up with an elaborate plan to make sure Abigail Connors got to Hot Springs safely—and hopefully without her suspecting anything, at least while she was traveling. Jacob had told Marcus that Abigail knew someone from the Wellington Agency would be watching over her—whether she liked it or not—once she got to Hot Springs, but she wasn't to know that she'd be watched all the way to Hot Springs.

From what Jacob had told him, Marcus had a feeling Miss Connors was quite independent and, if he wasn't mistaken, quite a bit spoiled. Still, she was Jacob's daughter, and he was going to do all he could to keep her safe and out of trouble during her stay in Hot Springs.

With most of his agents on assignment or on much-needed leave, Marcus had assigned Luke Monroe, a young man whom he'd been able to clear of a crime he didn't commit but had served time in prison for, to see that Miss Connors reached Hot Springs safely.

At twenty, Luke had no living relatives and no place to call home. Marcus had found he just couldn't let the young man fend for himself. Although his name had been cleared, Luke would have a hard time finding a job, and Marcus had wanted to help.

When he'd asked Luke if he wanted to join the Wellington Agency and learn the business from desk clerk up, Luke hadn't hesitated a moment. "Oh, yes, sir! I'd love to help somebody one day the way you helped me," he'd said.

That was all it took. Marcus owned the building that housed his office and his own apartment, and he happened to have a vacancy *and* a need for a building manager. He offered the apartment as part of Luke's pay, along with a salary. In the meantime, he'd train the young man to be a good agent.

When he offered Luke the position, he'd thought he'd seen the sheen of tears in the young man's eyes. "Sir," Luke had said, "I'll never make you sorry for helping me. I promise you. I want to be one of the best agents you have, and I'll work hard to become just that."

"I can't ask for more than that, Luke. You can move in the apartment to-day—it's furnished. And you can start work tomorrow."

That had been six months ago, and although this was Luke's first real assignment, Marcus didn't have one doubt that Luke would do all he could to do the job right, to see that Abigail Connors got on the right trains and that she was not bothered by anyone on her way, all without her knowing she was being watched.

Marcus had sent Luke to Eureka Springs two days before Abigail was to leave. Jacob had met him, and they'd arranged for him to be at the train station when Jacob and his wife took Abigail to catch her train so that he would know exactly who it was he'd been hired to keep safe.

Afterward, Jacob had sent Marcus a telegram letting him know that Abigail and the agent were on their way. All Marcus had to do was meet her train when it came in that afternoon.

Normally, Luke did a lot of the mail and telegram sorting from the desk across the room. Then he'd give it to Marcus in order of importance. Marcus had gotten used to the young man sharing the office with him but knew that since he'd put him in the field, the young man would be wanting another outside assignment soon. Marcus read the other telegrams he'd received that morning and decided what needed to be answered right away, keeping an eye on the clock so that he wouldn't be late to meet the train. When his telephone rang one quick and two sharp rings, he jumped and hurried over to the wall where it was installed. He still wasn't used to the modern convenience, but his parents had convinced him that if he was planning to expand his business, he really should have one put in at his office. It stood silent most of the time, and when it did ring, most times it was his mother—making sure it worked.

Marcus wasn't the least bit surprised to hear her voice on the line now. "Marcus dear, what time is it that Jacob and Georgette's daughter arrives today?"

"She's coming in on the afternoon train, Mother."

"Are you sure you don't want to bring her by this afternoon, dear?"

"Jacob said she would most likely be tired from travel and that she would probably want to get settled into the hotel."

"I do wish he'd just have sent her here. We have plenty of room and—"

"Maybe you can convince her to stay with you and Papa once she gets to know you, Mother."

"Perhaps. When your father telegraphed Jacob, though, it sounded as if he thought she'd want to stay in the hotel. But we'll see what we can do to change her mind."

Marcus smiled, knowing that his mother would do just that. "I'm sure you will, Mother. I'll bring her by tomorrow as planned, all right?"

"That will be fine, son. I have a nice dinner planned. Will you be over for dinner tonight?"

"Not this evening, Mother, but thank you. I need to make sure the arrangements I've made for Miss Connors will work out."

"All right then, son. I'll see you tomorrow. I am so glad you had a telephone put in."

Marcus couldn't contain his chuckle. "Yes, I know. I am, too, Mother." He replaced the receiver and looked at the clock. He'd finish the schedules he made each week for his agents and then head down to the depot. He was anxious to meet Abigail Connors and try to figure out what he'd be requiring the agents he assigned to her to do. He prayed that she wouldn't be too much of a handful, but in reading between the lines of Jacob's correspondence, Marcus had a feeling she would be.

✒

Abigail stood at the bottom of the steps for only a minute or two before a man whose size alone was slightly intimidating approached her. He was broad shouldered and dressed impeccably. . .and he towered over her. He took his hat off and addressed her.

"Miss Connors? Abigail Connors?" He looked down at her with a smile that brought out a dimple in his cheek and made her catch her breath.

He must be the man her father had arranged to meet her, Abigail thought. She found herself looking into the bluest eyes she'd ever seen, and they seemed to be looking right into her soul. "Yes, I'm Abigail Connors."

"I'm Marcus Wellington of Wellington Agency. Your father—"

"Yes, I'm aware that my father hired you to watch over me. I tried to tell him that your services weren't needed, but he insisted."

"He just wants to make sure you are safe while you are here."

"Yes, well, I'm sure I will be."

Marcus chuckled. "I know you will be as long as I'm responsible for seeing that you are."

How dare he laugh at her! "You are quite confident of yourself, aren't you, Mr. Wellington?"

He irritated her even further by grinning at her. A dimple appeared near his mouth. But his tone was serious when he answered, "My business depends on me being able to do what I say I will, Miss Connors. And I've promised your father that you will be safe while under my agency's watchfulness. Now, let's get your bags, and I'll see you to your hotel."

It appeared Mr. Wellington was as bossy as he was confident. There was no point, however, in arguing with the man. Her father had hired his agency, and she really couldn't do anything about that. Besides, he was the son of good friends of her parents, and she'd given her parents enough to go through lately. She would put up with him if she had to, but she didn't like his cockiness one bit—even if he did try to cover it with the most beautiful smile she'd ever seen.

Marcus led her into the train depot, where they waited for her baggage to be unloaded from the train. Once it was brought over and he saw the trunk and bags she said were hers, Marcus arranged for the luggage to be sent over to the Arlington Hotel, where she would be staying. Then he hired a hackney to take them to the hotel. That he knew how to take charge couldn't be disputed—he seemed to command respect without demanding it.

He helped her into the cab and then took a seat beside her. "I do hope you enjoy your visit to our city, Miss Connors. Your father said you would be taking care of some business for him while you are here."

Dear Papa. "Yes. He's thinking of investing in a bathhouse venture and wants me to look into the ones here in Hot Springs."

"The hotel where you are staying is on what we call Bathhouse Row. You'll see that there are a few new bathhouses under construction. You do have them in Eureka Springs, don't you?"

"Just a few, although our hotels are built near the springs for the guests' convenience." Abigail glanced about as they rode through downtown and noticed that Hot Springs seemed to be way ahead of her hometown in some ways. The boardwalks that were only talked about in Eureka Springs were a reality here and were uniformly wide. Her mother would love them. She'd be sure and write her parents about it. Perhaps they could nudge the city leaders to move a little faster.

Mr. Wellington pointed to the buildings they were passing by. "Here are the bathhouses. There is the Palace Bathhouse, and the one right next to it is the Independent. Then there is the Hale Bathhouse and the Big Iron."

As he pointed them all out, Abigail was impressed with how nice they looked standing in a row with magnolia trees lining the street that ran in front of them. The huge white blossoms of the magnolias smelled wonderful. Pine trees grew up the mountain behind them, yet on the mountain behind the buildings across the street, there seemed to be mostly oak and hickory trees, leafy and green. It really was a beautiful setting, and Abigail looked forward to visiting each bathhouse to see what it offered.

"Here we are," Mr. Wellington said as the hackney pulled up in front of a very nice hotel. "I think you'll enjoy your stay at the Arlington. It's one of the nicest in town. The Hays will be even nicer once they get through remodeling, but it isn't due to open until next year. For now, you are staying at one of the best hotels in town."

He paid the driver and helped her down from the cab. Abigail didn't offer to reimburse him—she supposed it would be included in what her father paid the man. He did see her into the hotel, and she was impressed by the lovely interior. The desk clerk was very nice when she registered, and a bellboy came immediately to show her to her room.

"Her bags will be sent over from the train depot. Please see that she gets them as soon as they arrive," Marcus said to the man at the desk.

"Certainly, Mr. Wellington."

Marcus Wellington followed her and the bellboy up the stairs to the second-floor rooms she'd been given. When she looked at him questioningly, he bent and whispered in her ear, "I make it a practice to check out the rooms of my clients to make sure there are no surprises."

"What do you mean?"

"Just to make sure your windows lock, the door locks properly, that kind of thing."

"Oh, all right. Thank you."

The bellboy stopped outside a door just two away from the main staircase, and Mr. Wellington waited until the boy unlocked and opened it for Abigail. They entered a small sitting room with a bedroom off to the side. While the bellboy was explaining where everything was, Marcus made sure the locks on the windows were secure. He took the key from the young man and made sure that the door did lock, and then he handed it to Abigail.

The bellboy left, promising to bring up Abigail's bags when they arrived, and Marcus stood just outside the door. "Is there anything I can get you, Miss Connors? Would you like company for dinner?"

"No, thank you. I'll eat here at the hotel and have an early evening. I'm rather tired from the travel."

"I've promised your father and my parents that I will bring you over tomorrow to meet them."

Abigail had also promised her father that she would meet the Wellingtons and check in with them from time to time, so she agreed. "What time will be best for your mother?"

"She thought you might take tea with them in the afternoon, if that appeals to you."

"Yes, that will be nice. What time?"

"I'll pick you up about three o'clock, if that is acceptable."

"That will be fine."

Marcus turned just in time to see the bellboy and another young man bringing up a trunk. "Is that for Miss Connors?"

"Yes, sir. There are several more pieces, too."

Marcus waited until the trunk and two more bags had been delivered to Abigail's room. She had to admit she was glad he was there. She wasn't used to strange men handling her things. She tipped the young men when the last bag was set down. "Thank you. Will you please ask the desk clerk to send someone up to help me unpack?"

"I'll be glad to. Thank you, ma'am," the first young man answered. They both smiled as they turned to go back downstairs.

"Everything is here?" Marcus asked her.

"Yes, I believe so. I'll let you know if I find anything missing."

He nodded. "Good. I'll see you tomorrow then. And Miss Connors. . ."

"Yes?"

"Be assured that you'll be safe here." He tipped his hat and turned to leave.

Abigail still wasn't sure how she felt about all her comings and goings being watched, but her father had insisted. "Thank you. I'm sure my father will be pleased."

"Have a good evening." Mr. Wellington tipped his hat to her and turned to go back downstairs.

Abigail closed her door and locked it. Then she crossed over to the windows that looked down on the street below. She wondered what was taking so long, but she watched until Mr. Wellington finally came out of the hotel. He was with several other men, and Abigail wondered if they would be some of the men he assigned to her. When he got to the street, he looked up toward her window, and Abigail quickly moved behind the drapes so that he wouldn't know she saw him. He pulled out his pocket watch and looked at it then turned. He did not use one of the hackneys lined up outside, taking off on foot, instead. He crossed the street and headed back in the direction of the train depot. She wondered where his offices were. And she couldn't help but wonder who he'd have watching over her. What surprised her most, however, was that although she didn't like his cockiness one bit, she couldn't deny that it made her feel better knowing he was in charge of making sure she was safe.

❧

Almost as soon as he'd met Miss Connors, Marcus had decided to make some changes in the assignments he'd given his men. Once downstairs in the lobby, he met with the agents he'd assigned to watch over Abigail Connors during her stay. His free agents had been there, reading papers when he brought her in so they could see what she looked like.

Now he handed out assignments on what days and times they'd be responsible for watching her—with one change. "Benson, I'm going to take over the responsibility of escorting her wherever she needs to go, and it has nothing to do with your capabilities. I have a feeling Miss Connors could be slightly demanding, and since she is the daughter of the man who helped me get this business started, I feel I'm the one who should deal with all that. I'll have you assigned to watch her while she's here during the day. Nelson, you have evening duty for this week. You can leave at midnight. Morgan, you're in charge of days this weekend. Ross, you'll take the evenings. If anything changes or I think we need to make adjustments, I'll let you know. I'd like a report on my desk from you all an hour after your shift is finished." They each nodded their agreement, and then, Marcus and all but Benson headed outside.

He stopped outside and looked up to the window of Abigail Connors's room. Marcus had had many a client stay in the same hotel and knew right where to look. He and his men were all going in different directions, and Marcus's long strides took him straight to the telegraph office, where he sent a telegram to Jacob Connors to let him know his daughter had arrived in Hot Springs and settled in her hotel safely. All this would be much easier if there were long-distance lines between the two cities—but Eureka Springs didn't even have phone service yet.

After meeting Abigail Connors in person, Marcus could certainly see why Jacob wanted someone to watch over her. On first meeting, she seemed quite confident and independent, but looking into her eyes, Marcus could see a sadness and vulnerability that told him there was much more to her than first appeared. He fought the urge to go back and check on her; she would be safe with Benson. Instead, he went back to his office and looked over the telegrams he'd just picked up. Evidently, Luke was back in town because the agent reports had been sorted and put on his desk. Marcus looked them over and studied his scheduling for the rest of the week. Abigail Connors wasn't the only client he was responsible for, and he needed to check in with other agents before he could call it a night.

Through it all, in the back of his mind, he kept thinking about the beautiful woman in his care, and he couldn't help but wonder just who broke the engagement and why.

Chapter 3

Abigail wasn't quite sure what to do with herself once Marcus Wellington left. She liked the rooms she'd been given. The small sitting room had a settee in front of a fireplace and a writing desk by the window. A nice round table sat in the center of the room, with two chairs on either side of it, where she supposed she could have breakfast if she didn't want to go to the dining room downstairs. The room was beautifully decorated in different shades of blues and greens and felt soothing to her.

Abigail went into the bedroom to find the same colors on the drapes at the windows and on the bed. It was a very nice room. She spotted her trunk and bags at the end of the bed and quickly realized that the desk clerk had not sent anyone up to help her yet. She found the electric bell that she'd been told rang through to the office about the time a knock sounded on the sitting room door.

It was the maid come to help her. The young woman smiled. "Good evening, ma'am. I've been sent to help you get settled in."

"Good. I'd just rung the bell to remind the clerk." Before Abigail could let her in and shut the door, the bellboy who'd brought her things was there. "You rang, ma'am?"

"I did. I suppose I should have waited five minutes longer. I don't need anything now, thank you."

"All right. Just ring again if you do decide you need anything."

"Thank you, I will." Abigail noticed that his parting smile seemed to be centered on the young maid waiting for Abigail's directions. She waved to the bellboy and turned to the maid. "Will you be on duty tomorrow?"

The young woman bobbed her head. "Yes, ma'am, I will."

"I'd like you to arrange for my frocks to be pressed, then."

"Yes, ma'am. I'll do that first thing tomorrow morning."

She opened the trunk first as it held all of her frocks, and she would need one to change into when she went to dinner. Even though the maid was helpful, Abigail wondered why she hadn't brought her housekeeper. Abigail wasn't used to doing things like this herself. Well, she wasn't exactly doing it by herself, but neither was she used to doing things like this at all.

But she had assured her parents that she was self-sufficient, and she was determined to be just that—no matter how inconvenient it was. They thought she couldn't look after herself as it was; otherwise, they wouldn't have hired Marcus Wellington's agency to keep an eye on her.

She shook out one of her favorite walking dresses and handed it to the maid to hang in the wardrobe. Then she brought out a dinner dress for the girl to hang beside it. It took over an hour just to get her trunk unpacked, and her stomach was beginning to rumble. "Thank you, Miss—what is your name?"

"My name is Bea, ma'am. It's short for Beatrice. Fielding is my last name."

"Well, Bea, my name is Abigail Connors. Do you work every day?"

The young maid shook her head. "No, ma'am. I've just been hired to fill in when the other maids are off work."

"What kind of work have you done?"

"I was personal maid for Mrs. Rothschild until she passed away a few weeks back. I took care of her clothing and helped her with her hair. . .and was there when she needed me."

"Hmm," Abigail said. "When you have free time, perhaps I'll be able to use you to help me from time to time with my hair, to keep my frocks pressed, and to run errands. Would you be interested in doing that?"

"Oh yes, ma'am! I'd love to help you when I can."

"I'll need to check your references."

"Yes, ma'am. I understand. I can give you a list. Would you want it now, or is tomorrow soon enough?"

"Tomorrow will be fine."

"Thank you, ma'am."

"You are welcome." Abigail looked around at her baggage. The trunk was empty, and she thought she could manage her bags. "I'll finish this up myself. Just stop by tomorrow to see about getting the most wrinkled frocks pressed for me and to give me your references."

"I will. Have a good evening, Miss Connors."

"Thank you. You have a nice one, too."

After the maid left, Abigail checked her hair and pinched her cheeks. She was starving and didn't have the energy to change for just an hour. Normally, she never would have thought of having dinner in the same dress she'd been traveling in, but the freedom of not knowing anyone in town was very liberating. Tired as she was, all Abigail wanted to do was have a good supper and come back to her room.

She headed down to the dining room, and once there, she was shown to a table in an alcove and seated facing out into the room. She was quite pleased. It was out of the way enough that she wouldn't feel out of place eating alone, yet she could see other diners plainly so that she didn't feel quite so alone.

The waiter handed her a menu, and she was impressed with the selection the hotel offered.

She chose the veal cutlets with brown sauce and riced potatoes. For dessert, she chose lemon pie. As she waited for her meal, she took in the luxurious decor and was quite happy with her selection of hotels. She didn't think any of the others in town could be any nicer.

From the soft murmur of voices and the gentle clink of silverware, the hotel's clientele seemed quite sophisticated and genteel. Abigail was not made to feel uncomfortable at all for being by herself, and for that, she was quite thankful. She did see a man across the way keep looking at her, but she had a feeling he was the agent hired to watch over her. She had the impression from meeting Marcus Wellington that he didn't do anything by half measure, and she was certain that he would have her watched no matter where she went outside her room. She was a little surprised by the comfort that thought gave her.

Abigail actually enjoyed her dinner. The meal was delicious and the service outstanding. Best of all, she was able to watch the other diners without worrying that they might be discussing her broken engagement. If they were discussing her at all, they might be wondering who she was, but as she was at a hotel and the other guests weren't from Hot Springs, they probably weren't thinking of her at all. There was something very freeing about that thought.

That the wealthy frequented Hot Springs was evident in the way the guests were dressed, and Abigail would be certain to dress in a like manner while she was at the hotel. But as no one knew her, she wasn't going to worry about wearing her traveling clothes this evening. Instead, she just let herself enjoy the meal and the comings and goings of the other guests.

❧

Marcus had supper at one of the restaurants down the street from the Arlington Hotel. He hadn't been able to get Abigail Connors off his mind all evening, and it bothered him a great deal that he was still thinking about her. At first, he told himself it was because she was a new client and he just wanted to make sure everything went well—as he would any other client.

But from the moment he'd first seen Abigail, he knew she would be no ordinary client. Maybe it was because she was Jacob's daughter, or maybe it was because she was alone here in Hot Springs and he felt even more responsibility for her. He didn't know. All he was certain of was that he'd been thinking of her ever since he left the hotel. In the back of his mind were all the questions he'd like answered. He wanted to know why her wedding had been called off and why she was traveling alone. Why did she feel the need to leave Eureka Springs? And why was he so interested in her?

Marcus chided himself. Probably his investigative personality had his mind working overtime—that was all. But when he left the restaurant in time to meet his agents as they switched shifts at eight o'clock, he had a feeling it was more than that.

Benson was in the lobby, waiting for Nelson, when Marcus arrived. He put down the paper he was reading when Marcus took a seat beside him. "How's it going?"

"It's been quiet. Miss Connors came down for dinner and just went back up about ten minutes ago."

"Hmm. I would have thought she might eat in her room tonight."

"No, sir. She came down and had a leisurely meal. She seemed interested in watching the people around her and appeared quite at ease at a table by herself."

Perhaps she was more confident and independent than her father thought she was. "Well, I'm glad she had a good evening and is safe and sound back in her room," Marcus said. "I'm not sure everything will be quite so calm in the days to come."

"Most likely not," Benson said. "In this line of work, it usually isn't." Nelson arrived just then, and Benson filled him in on the calm night.

"I could use some quiet time after the last client I was assigned to," Nelson said as he settled into the chair Benson had just vacated. It had the best view of the stairs and the front desk.

They all laughed. Nelson's last client had been a wealthy woman with three spoiled children. As it turned out, her husband had apparently hired the Wellington Agency to watch his children while his wife went to the bathhouses for relaxation. Marcus assured both men, "Don't worry. I've got that name on my never-again list."

"Good thing, 'cause I'd have to decline the opportunity to do it again," Nelson said.

"Can't say I'd blame you," Marcus said as he and Benson turned to leave. "Have a good night."

He and Benson parted ways just outside the hotel, and Marcus found himself looking up at Miss Connors's hotel window. He wondered what she thought of Hot Springs and what kind of mood she'd be in the next day. He couldn't deny that he was looking forward to finding out.

❧

By the time Abigail got back to her room, she was ready for a good night's rest. She climbed into bed and pulled up her covers, but it didn't take long before Abigail realized that she wasn't going to drift off into a peaceful sleep as she'd hoped. In the dark of the night and alone in a strange place, she began to think about home and all she had lost in the last few weeks.

Abigail fought the sudden urge to cry, but the hot tears won and cascaded down her cheeks. Brushing them away with the back of her hand, Abigail turned over and crunched her pillow, but she couldn't turn off her thoughts. The past was over with, and she needed to get on with her future. She wasn't sure she could.

For so long, she'd felt guilty about her sister's death. . .and now she knew her niece blamed her for it as well. . .even though it hadn't been her fault. She truly had been trying to save Rose when she'd followed her up the stairs and grabbed her arm and tried to get her to come with her the day of the fire. When Rose pulled away, she lost her balance and fell down the stairs. It hadn't been Abigail's fault, yet she knew she would always feel she could have, should have done something else—only she didn't know what.

Rose had been determined to save her keepsakes, telling Abigail that she'd be right back. But even had Abigail left her alone and let her go, she wouldn't have gotten out in time. The result would have been the same, and Abigail still would have blamed herself. If there was anything she should feel guilty about that day, it was that she'd envied her sister and wanted the life she had, but she had never *ever* wished her gone. And she had truly tried to convince Rose to get out in time.

Deep down, Abigail knew all that, but she would never forget seeing her sister fall down the stairs, rushing to help, only to find that Rose was badly hurt. All she could do when Rose told her to get Natalie to safety was just that—and hope she'd have time to come back and get her sister out. But that wasn't to be. By the time she'd turned around, the house was in flames. Abigail shuddered, remembering that sight in vivid detail. She would never forget that day. What really broke her heart was that now her niece remembered that day, too, and she wasn't likely to forget it. And in Natalie's mind, Abigail was to blame.

Abigail wished she could change the past, but there was no way that could be done. And she had no one but herself to blame for the heartache. There was no keeping the tears back, and she began to sob for the past, for the present, and for the future she'd wished for but lost.

❧

Abigail didn't wake until midmorning, but she was relieved to have the night over with. Even after her tears had subsided, she'd tossed and turned. Now she washed her face and could only hope that some of the puffiness around her eyes would go down before she met the Wellingtons.

She was pleased when Bea kept her word and came to take her dresses to be pressed. Bea handed her the list of references and told her that she'd try to come back that afternoon to help with her hair. As it was past midmorning but she was still not very hungry, Abigail sent a lunch order of tea and the soup of the day down to the kitchen with Bea, to be sent up at noon.

Abigail finished unpacking the bags she'd been too exhausted to deal with the night before, quite pleased that she managed to do it all herself. The thought that she really was quite spoiled came to mind, but she didn't let it stay there long. She didn't much like the picture it gave of herself.

After she'd freshened up, she was pleased that her lunch arrived right on time, and she thought about the day ahead as she ate her split pea soup and enjoyed her pot of tea. She was looking forward to meeting the Wellingtons. She'd realized just how alone she was during her long night, and she would be glad to have someone to call on if needed. At least they were old friends of her parents, and she hoped that would make it easier to get to know them.

Bea brought her gowns up just after one o'clock and was able to stay and help with preparations for attending the Wellingtons' tea. She brushed Abigail's hair to a bright shine and then pulled it up, twisted and turned it, and pinned it on top of her head. Bea explained each step so that Abigail could attempt to do it herself if Bea wasn't available. The maid pulled a few curls out around Abigail's face, and Abigail was very pleased with the results.

"Thank you, Bea. I'll try to do it myself tomorrow morning for church."

"I'm sure you'll be able to. Just brush, pull up, and twist."

"I think that sounds easier than it is, but I'll try." After all, she was going to be here awhile. She wasn't going to have someone at her disposal all the time. She thought of hiring a personal maid—after all, many people traveled with their personal staff. Somehow that only reinforced the fact that she *was* very spoiled, and for some reason, she didn't want the Wellingtons to see her that way.

Bea helped her into a visiting dress, a pale blue crepe de chine draped to the side and trimmed with gold embroidery. By the time Bea left, Abigail thought she looked as nice as she could.

Marcus Wellington arrived promptly at three, and when Abigail opened the door to him, she was a little surprised at how nervous she was.

"Good afternoon, Miss Connors. It is a lovely day out. Are you ready to go?"

"It is, Mr. Wellington. And I am ready and looking forward to meeting your parents." She gathered her parasol, reticule, and key. After locking the door, she dropped it in her small bag and took the arm Marcus held out to her as they went downstairs to the lobby.

He led her out to a surrey with a fringed canopy top, helped her in, and then rounded the vehicle to take his own seat. With a flick of his wrist, they were off, down Central Avenue back toward the train depot. Abigail quite enjoyed the ride while Marcus pointed out several businesses to her. A general store owned by a Mr. E. Burgauer was said to have a varied stock, and according to Marcus, the William J. Little Grocery at the junction of Central and Reserve was one of the largest in the city.

He also pointed out the post office and Cooper and Johnston's Stationery and Bookstore. A photographer and a large jewelry store occupied the same block. And they passed several banks, too. There was so much to look at—and Abigail was seeing just part of the town. She looked forward to learning her way around.

Marcus turned off Central Avenue and made several more turns before he stopped the surrey at a large home on a quiet street. He tied the reins to the hitching post at the street and helped her down. Before they got halfway to the house, the door was thrown open and a woman who reminded Abigail of her own mother stepped out onto the wide porch. "Marcus, dear, don't dawdle. Bring Miss Connors inside—I've been waiting all day to meet her."

When Abigail stepped up onto the porch, Mrs. Wellington gave her a quick hug. "I am so glad to finally meet you, dear. You look just like your mother at your age! Isn't she lovely, Marcus?"

Chapter 4

Abigail held her breath, waiting for Marcus Wellington's answer to his mother's question.

"Yes, Mother, she is very lovely. And she's been looking forward to meeting you and Father, too, so let's get her inside out of the heat."

Abigail felt the color rise up her neck and onto her cheeks. She wondered if Marcus was just being polite or if he was being sincere. She had a feeling he was uncomfortable in having to answer his mother's question. But Mrs. Wellington paid no attention and pulled Abigail inside the large foyer.

"Your father is in his study; would you go get him, Marcus? We'll be waiting in the parlor," Mrs. Wellington said. She led Abigail over to the right and into a parlor that made her feel right at home. It was so much like her parents' parlor that her mother could have decorated it. Obviously, the two women had similar tastes.

"Please, dear, take a seat anywhere," Mrs. Wellington said, sitting on the burgundy-colored settee. A tea tray laden with all kinds of sandwiches and sweet treats rested on the round table in front of her. "I'll pour tea as soon as Marcus and his father join us. I can't tell you how pleased I am that you are here. I'm hoping that your parents will pay us a visit soon. Although we keep letters going back and forth, it's been much too long since we've seen them in person."

Marcus and his father entered the room, and Abigail could see that Marcus looked very much like Mr. Wellington. They both had that engaging dimple when they smiled.

"Well now, how pretty you are," the older Mr. Wellington said as he came over and took Abigail's hand in his. "You do look like your mother. We are so glad you are here in Hot Springs and we have this chance to meet you. You were only a child the last time we saw you."

Abigail couldn't remember actually meeting them, so she must have been young.

"I'm very pleased to meet you all, too, Mr. Wellington. My parents think of you as among their closest and dearest friends."

Mrs. Wellington poured their tea, and Marcus handed round a tray with delicate sandwiches and little iced tea cakes. The afternoon passed pleasantly with the Wellingtons telling her stories about her parents when they were all younger. When it was time to leave, Abigail hated to depart. The evening loomed long and lonely to her.

"We'd love to have you join us for church tomorrow and for dinner here afterward, if you would be so inclined," Mrs. Wellington invited.

Abigail didn't hesitate to accept. "I would love to. Thank you for the invitation!"

"Wonderful! Marcus will pick you up in the morning, then, won't you, dear?"

"I'll be happy to," Marcus answered.

For a moment, Abigail's heart skipped a beat. Then she remembered that he was actually working for her father and escorting her would be part of his job. Still, she managed a smile. "I'll be ready. Thank you again for the invitation, Mrs. Wellington."

"You are quite welcome, dear. We are looking forward to introducing you to our church family and others in town. We really are quite excited about having you here."

The older Wellingtons followed them out onto the porch, and Abigail waved to them as she left. She dreaded the long evening awaiting her back at the hotel after Marcus dropped her off.

Once they were on their way, Abigail turned to Marcus and said, "Your parents are wonderful, Mr. Wellington. They made me feel very welcome. Thank you for taking me."

"They felt the same about you. I could tell," Marcus replied. And his parents did. It was obvious that they liked Abigail Connors from the first. Perhaps it was because she was their good friends' daughter, but he had a feeling his parents would have taken to Abigail even if she weren't. "Thank you for going to see them."

"I'm glad I did—and that I get to see them again. Are you sure you don't mind picking me up and taking me to church—"

"Of course not. I'll be happy to. I'd be—"

"Oh yes," Abigail interrupted. "I'd almost forgotten you are being paid—"

"Miss Connors, I'd be happy to take you to church even if your father hadn't hired my agency to protect you while you are here." Marcus had a feeling that he knew what she was thinking and wanted to assure her. "I will be more than glad to take you to church and back to my parents' home for Sunday dinner."

She was silent for a moment, and then she said, "Thank you. I will be ready."

"Good." Marcus hoped that she'd seen she was more than just a client to him. "Since there is that family connection, do you think we might be able to call each other by our first names?" He grinned at her, hoping for a smile.

"I suppose we could. It would certainly be easier if we are to see much of each other while I am here."

"Oh, we're going to see each other, Abigail—aside from the fact that my firm is in charge of protecting you, you are also a friend of the family."

"Then we can go by first names. Marcus it will be."

He liked the way she said his name.

"Well then, Abigail, would you care to have dinner at your hotel with me tonight?"

"Marcus, you don't have to watch me every waking hour."

"I know that. The invitation wasn't part of the job. We both have to eat, and I often eat at the Arlington. The food is excellent." They arrived at the hotel just then, and the topic was dropped for the time being. Marcus, however, had every intention of getting back to it.

He helped Abigail down from the buggy and walked her inside the hotel. But before he saw her to her room, he took hold of her arm and steered her toward Morgan, who'd come into the hotel just ahead of them. Marcus had let him know earlier that he could take a few hours off. Now he was sitting in a chair that had a good view of the staircase, reading—or pretending to read—a paper.

"Morgan, I thought Miss Connors should meet the men I have assigned to her. Miss Connors, this is Alan Morgan. He is on day duty this weekend."

"How do you do, Miss Connors? Be assured that if you need anything, I'll be right here."

"Thank you, Mr. Morgan. I'm glad to know who you are and that I can call on you if needed."

"Anytime, ma'am." The agent bowed at the waist.

"Your relief will be here shortly, Morgan, and I'll be talking to you later."

"Yes, sir," Morgan said. He went back to his paper as Marcus led Abigail away.

He accompanied her up to her room and took the key from her. After unlocking the door and giving a look inside, he handed the key back to her. "You know, you never answered me. Will you have supper with me? We both have to eat, and while those little sandwiches my mother served are delicious, they didn't do much to fill me up." He looked down at her with a grin.

"I'd like to change first. Can you wait for me to do that?"

She looked up into his eyes, and Marcus felt something he'd never experienced before. He wasn't even sure what it was. He only knew he badly wanted her to say yes, and he'd wait for however long it took.

"I can. Will an hour be enough time?" He'd wait longer if needed.

"Yes, I can be ready by then."

"I'll be back up to get you"—Marcus looked at his watch—"at seven o'clock."

"I'll be ready."

He nodded and turned to leave, grinning as he did so. He didn't have much time either, if he was going to change and get back by seven.

❧

Abigail was extremely proud that she'd managed to get ready with five minutes to spare before Marcus would be knocking on her door. Thanks to Bea's help earlier that day, her hair still looked quite nice. And due to Bea, all of her frocks were pressed and ready to choose from, so it made an easy time of it for Abigail. Thankfully, she didn't have to change undergarments, and she chose a dress of peach satin with a brown overskirt that draped to the back. She'd just finished putting on her jewelry when Marcus arrived.

From the look in his eyes, she felt she looked quite presentable.

"You look lovely." He smiled into her eyes. "And I am starving. Are you ready?"

"Yes, I am. And I'm a little hungry, too."

"I told you those little sandwiches don't fill one up. Let's go." He took the key from her and locked the door behind them before handing it back to her. She took the arm he offered, and they descended the stairs and walked to the dining room.

Abigail had thought she'd been treated well the night before, but evidently coming in with a gentleman did gain one a higher level of service. Or perhaps it was because of the man she was with. Marcus seemed to garner respect wherever he went. She'd noticed it from the train depot to the hotel clerk and bellboys, and now—here at the restaurant. They were seated at a table in front of the windows, where Abigail could be seen as well as see most of the other diners in the room. She took the seat the waiter held out for her and glanced around. Satisfied that she was dressed in a similar style to the other women in the room, she felt herself relax, only briefly letting herself wonder why it mattered more tonight than it had the night before.

They looked over the menus the waiter had left. "I had the veal last night, and it was delicious, but I'd like to try something different tonight."

"I can recommend the filet of beef with scalloped potatoes and brown sauce," Marcus said. "It is one of my favorite dishes."

Abigail scanned the menu before nodding her head. "I'll try that, then. Do you really eat here often?"

"I do—several times a week, in fact. It's near my apartment and office."

"You don't eat at your parents'?" Abigail was curious about this man who'd been hired to protect her.

"Of course I do. But many times I am working late or in a hurry, and it's easier to eat out."

The waiter came back to the table, and while Marcus gave him their order, she was able to look at Marcus without his knowing. He looked quite handsome in his black wool suit and crisp white shirt. She could feel the color creep up her face when he looked back to see her watching him, and she quickly turned her head and looked out the window while he finished their order.

She liked Hot Springs at night. The streetlights made it easy to see who was out and about, and she felt almost as safe as when she was at home in Eureka Springs. But was that because of the lighting outside or the man across from her? She knew. Much as she didn't want to admit it—and sometimes resented it—part of her was glad that Marcus Wellington was in charge of her safety.

"What time do you want to start checking out the bathhouses on Monday?" Marcus asked once the waiter left the table.

"I thought around ten in the morning." Abigail had slept in that day, but normally, even if she was up late the night before, she was a fairly early riser. And even if she weren't, she wouldn't want Marcus Wellington to think she was lazy. After all, she'd promised her father that she would check into things for him, and he would want to think she was acting in a professional way.

"That should be a good time. If not, I'm sure you can set up appointments with the managers for another time."

"That is true. It isn't as if I have to do it all in one day." After all, she had no intention of going back home anytime soon.

Their first course of cream of asparagus soup arrived, and while they ate, Marcus pointed out several people he knew. Actually, it was more than several; it seemed he knew most of the people in the dining room. She supposed it was no different than when she was out in Eureka Springs. She'd been born and raised there, and while she knew many people, she couldn't recall ever being treated with such open respect and friendliness as she'd seen Marcus treated with. It wasn't a thought she wanted to explore—not at the moment anyway—and she was relieved when the waiter brought the next course and broke into her thoughts.

The filet of beef was the most tender she'd ever eaten, and she was glad Marcus had suggested it. "This is wonderful. I can see why it is one of your favorites."

"I'm glad you like it. Thank you for agreeing to have dinner with me. It's nice to have company."

Abigail had a feeling he could have company any time he wanted, but she didn't say so. "You are welcome. I don't really like eating alone, either." *Now why did I say that?* Marcus didn't need to know that.

"I'm sure you don't have to do it often. And once you meet people here, you won't need to anymore. I'm sure you'll have invitations from many people and keep me quite busy."

"What do you mean?"

"I will be the one accompanying you most of where you go while you are here."

"I'm sure you have more important things to do. I assumed you'd assign one of your agents to watch me."

"I thought about it, but I've decided to do that myself. You are the daughter of the man who helped me start my business. My father makes a good living, but I didn't want to take money that he might need in his own business. Your father loaned me money when no one else would. . .not to mention that he is an old family friend. And I'm sure that by the time you leave Hot Springs, you will be considered a family friend in your own right."

While Abigail hoped he was right—she really liked his parents and could see why her parents regarded them so highly—she reminded herself that in escorting her around town, Marcus would only be doing the job her father was paying him to do. That thought dampened her mood somewhat, and she was glad that their dessert of orange and cream coconut cake was served so that she didn't have to talk—but she found she'd lost her appetite. She mostly pushed the cake around on her plate until she looked up to find Marcus watching her.

"Are you all right? This cake is delicious, and you've barely touched it."

He really had the most brilliantly blue eyes Abigail had ever seen, and looking into them did funny things to her heart. "I guess I'm still a little tired from the travel and all."

"That is understandable. Would you like some coffee or tea before we leave?"

"No, thank you. I've asked for tea to be brought to my room each night before bedtime. It helps me sleep better." At least it usually did. Abigail hoped it would settle her down tonight and make her sleepy. She didn't want another night like the last one.

Marcus motioned the waiter over and paid for their meal.

"You don't have to pay for mine. They can put it on my hotel bill."

Marcus shook his head as the waiter left the table. "No. I asked you to have dinner with me." He got up and pulled out her chair.

As Marcus guided her through the dining room, they were stopped several times by diners who knew him, and he made sure to introduce her to the people at each table. By the time they left the dining room, she knew she'd never remember all their names; Marcus knew them all, and she'd just have to count on him to remind her.

He walked her to her room and, after taking her key, unlocked the door. "Wait here." He entered, and Abigail assumed he was checking the room to make sure no one was there. When he came out, he handed the key back to her. "Everything is fine. I hope you sleep well."

She took the key and was surprised when an electric spark shot up her arm at the brief touch of his fingertips against hers. "I—thank you for dinner. It was delicious."

"You are welcome. Thank you for putting up with my company." He grinned at her, and that dimple at the corner of his mouth seemed to deepen as he looked down at her.

She couldn't help but smile back. "It was nice to have company. What time should I be ready in the morning?"

"I'll be here to pick you up at nine o'clock."

"I'll be ready." *I did it today; surely I can do it tomorrow.*

Marcus gave a little salute and turned to leave. "It looks as if your pot of tea is arriving."

Sure enough, a bellboy was bringing her tea tray. Marcus waited until he set it down on the table in Abigail's sitting room and left. Then he turned to Abigail again. "You sleep well. I'll see you in the morning."

She nodded and stepped inside the room. "I'll see you then."

"Lock the door. I won't leave until you do."

"All right." Abigail stepped inside and shut the door. Then she turned the key in the lock and wondered if he was waiting to hear the click it made.

"Good girl. Good night, Abigail."

"Good night, Marcus."

It was only when she crossed the room and took out her earrings while looking in the mirror that she realized she was smiling. She moved to the side of the window and pulled the drapes aside just a bit to look down at the street, wondering if Marcus was still in the hotel talking to the agent who was in the lobby that night or if he'd already left.

She watched for a moment longer until a man who looked to be about Marcus's size walked out. From the gaslight below, she was pretty sure it was he, and when he turned and looked up, her heart did a flip. Was he looking up at her room? She quickly dropped the drape and moved away from the window. Even though she didn't think he could see her looking out, she wanted to be sure.

She poured her tea and sipped, thinking back over the evening. If she had to be protected, she supposed it could be worse. Marcus was actually very easy to be around—not to mention how entertaining it was to watch for that dimple. *All in all, maybe it won't be so bad having someone to watch over me.* Especially since Marcus had decided he would be the one to escort her around town.

❧

Marcus walked outside the hotel and didn't try to stop himself from looking up at the windows of Abigail's room. Watching over her was his job, after all. The light still glowed, and he imagined her sipping her tea. Was she thinking back over the evening?

He hoped she enjoyed herself as much as he did. It had been a treat to have such a lovely woman sitting across from him for dinner. Most of the time, he ate alone, and he'd found Abigail to be quite captivating as a dinner companion.

She seemed to want to come across as tough and independent, but he had a feeling she was anything but. Something in the expression in her eyes made him want to know more about her—something that reached out to him in a way he'd never experienced before.

He felt protective of her, and this feeling had absolutely nothing to do with the fact that her father had hired him to do just that. He wanted to know what it was that made her look so vulnerable and why her wedding had been called off. Perhaps it was time to find out more than what Jacob had told him. Marcus felt an urgent need to know all he could about Abigail Connors because she was quickly becoming more than just a client to him.

He headed home, determined to find out all he could about her and looking more than a little forward to the next day. While he walked, he prayed that the Lord would help Abigail with whatever it was that made her look so sad when she thought no one was watching her.

Chapter 5

Abigail was proud of herself the next morning. She managed to put her hair up the way Bea had explained to her, and she was dressed in her favorite Sunday dress when Marcus picked her up for the ride to church.

His parents were waiting for them, and while Mr. Wellington greeted her by clasping her hand in his, Mrs. Wellington gave her a hug as soon as Abigail turned to her. Then she took over from Marcus and led her into the church. From the moment Abigail entered the church, she felt at home.

Mrs. Wellington introduced her as they made their way to a pew near the front of the building. Over and over again, Mrs. Wellington said, "Please meet Abigail Connors, the daughter of dear friends of ours in Eureka Springs." She'd give the parishioners' names, too, and Abigail could only hope she would remember some of them. As she took her seat beside Mrs. Wellington, she realized that she hadn't been to church since she'd broken her engagement to Nate. She couldn't face having to explain everything to the people she'd gone to church with all her life.

Now she wondered why. Had she been afraid that they'd be talking about her behind their hymnals? Or that they might be thinking that the broken engagement was what she deserved? She'd known those people all her life, yet. . .had she really? As the service got underway with prayer and singing, Abigail realized that through the years she'd gone to church more because it was expected of her than because she wanted to be there. . .needed to be there. *Oh, dear Lord, please forgive me. Please help me to become the child You want me to be, and please forgive me for putting everything else in front of You.*

Abigail blinked back tears and hoped that no one noticed. She'd been so concerned with herself she couldn't even remember the last time she'd prayed. Nor could she really recall listening to a sermon all the way through. But today was different, and she found herself holding on to every word the minister was saying about forgiveness of others and oneself. She was beginning to realize that she had much to ask forgiveness for.

She was still thinking about the sermon when the service ended and she and Marcus followed his parents back to their home. Mrs. Wellington's dining table was set with fine china and crystal—for twelve. Before Abigail had a chance to become nervous, several of the people she had been introduced to earlier arrived, and she strived to remember their names. The minister and his wife arrived last, and everyone seemed to want to talk to Abigail.

"We are so glad to meet you, Miss Connors," a man she'd been introduced to earlier said. "I've heard wonderful things about your family. How long are you planning on staying in Hot Springs?"

"I'm not certain. I'm looking into some things for my father." Abigail spoke the truth. She was going to do as requested, and she had no idea when she was going home. No time soon—that was for sure.

"Would you happen to know the Joneses? They are dear friends of ours and moved to Eureka Springs a couple of years ago."

"No, I don't believe I've met them. It's possible my parents would know them, though." Abigail felt faint for a moment. If they knew people in Eureka Springs, it was possible they'd heard about her wedding being called off and had heard any number of things about her.

"We'd love to have you to dinner one evening soon," his wife said.

Her tone was very nice and friendly, and Abigail tried to put her fears to the back of her mind. "Why, thank you." At least it would get her out, and she supposed she should get to know some of the people in town. It might be that she would be staying for quite some time. Abigail just wished she could remember their names. "That would be lovely."

"I'll send you an invitation this next week, then."

"I look forward to it." She was going to have to ask Marcus who the couple was, because hard as she tried, she couldn't recall their names.

But she did remember the next person who came up to her and asked if she'd be free for lunch during the next week. Abigail had been introduced to the young woman and her husband before church—and recalled that her name was Sally Andrews.

"I'm certain I will be available," Abigail said. Sally appeared to be about her age, and she was quite nice. "I'd love to have lunch."

"How about Tuesday? I could meet you at your hotel, and we could have lunch there."

"That should work fine." They set a time, and Abigail found herself looking forward to getting to know Sally better. She didn't really miss her friends in Eureka Springs as much as she thought she might. And that, too, was strange to her for she saw some of them almost every day.

Mrs. Wellington called everyone to the table, and Abigail wasn't disappointed to find herself sitting next to Marcus. He'd almost disappeared into the background while others had come up to speak to her. Now he leaned near and whispered, "How are you doing?"

"I'm fine. I just wish I could remember that couple right across from us."

"They are the Bransons: Peter and Emily." His voice was low and for her ears only.

"Oh, thank you. They want me to come to dinner soon."

"You'll enjoy yourself. They are very nice people."

As the meal progressed, they all seemed to go out of their way to make Abigail feel welcome in their town. The minister and his wife were very nice, also.

"We're very glad you joined us today. It's sometimes hard to go to church when you are away from home."

Abigail didn't want to admit that there'd been times at home when it had been hard for her to go. "Your church has a very good feeling to it. Everyone was very friendly and welcoming."

"We hope you'll join us again."

"I'm planning on it."

The afternoon passed quickly. After dinner, they played a game of croquet in the big, shady backyard, and Abigail enjoyed herself immensely. After everyone else had left, the Wellingtons insisted that she stay for a light supper, and by the time Marcus took her back to the hotel that evening, she didn't feel quite so alone in a new town.

He walked her to her room and, after checking inside, joined her just outside the door once more. "What time do you want me to pick you up tomorrow? Didn't we decide on around ten?"

His smile showed his dimple, and as Abigail looked into those blue eyes, her heart fluttered against her ribs. "Yes, we did. I'll be ready."

"Good."

"I'm sure you've had second thoughts about telling my father you'd be responsible for me. Between doing what you've been hired to do and doing what your family expects you to do, you certainly have your work cut out for you."

He leaned against the door frame and looked into her eyes. "Yes, ma'am, I believe I do."

The look in his eyes kept her from taking offense.

He shoved himself away from the door frame and gave her a push. "Lock up. Sleep well, and I'll see you in the morning."

"See you then," Abigail breathed as she backed into her room. She shut the door and turned the key.

"Good night," Marcus said from the other side.

She could hear him walk away as she whispered, "Good night."

❧

Marcus walked out of the hotel after he'd had a word with Morgan and Ross, who were changing shifts. Abigail didn't know just how true her words were. He certainly did have his work cut out for him...and the biggest part of it was making sure he didn't begin to care too much for his client.

He'd watched her this afternoon at his parents'. She wasn't nearly as confident as she would like everyone to think she was. And she seemed a little ...apprehensive, especially when the Bransons had first gone up to talk to her. She'd turned quite pale for a moment. He wondered why. There was so much he didn't know about Abigail Connors, and the more he was around her, the more he wanted to know about her. He'd put a man on it first thing tomorrow.

Marcus glanced up at her window and fought the urge to wait until her lights went out before heading for home. He had an agent there in case she needed anything, and he'd see her the next day. He chuckled and shook his head. Abigail Connors was taking up entirely too many of his thoughts.

❧

Abigail was glad to see Bea early the next morning. She'd washed her hair and needed the maid's help in making herself presentable. Bea also gathered the gowns that needed to be pressed and the other garments that needed to be washed and took them down to the hotel laundry for Abigail.

"Thank you, Bea," Abigail said as the young woman put her hair up for her.

"You are welcome, Miss Connors. I'm glad to do it. I talked to the manager, and he said that if you need me to help you on my days off, I could. So just let me know what you might want me to do for you and what time you need me. One of the regulars who'd taken a month's leave is back, and I'll only be working on Tuesdays and Thursdays now."

"Oh, well that will work out wonderfully for me. What are you being paid for your day here?"

Bea told her, and Abigail nodded. "I'll pay you that for each day you come to help me out. I'd like you on Saturday mornings and the weekday mornings that you aren't working. If I need you to help me get ready for a special evening function, do you think you could do that?"

"Of course! I'd be happy to." Bea's smile was wide.

"Good. I've been able to make myself presentable, but I have to admit that I've missed my housekeeper. She always helped me get ready to go out. I'm hoping to learn more from you so that I can manage on my own better."

"I'll be glad to help," Bea said. "It's really not that hard. You'll do fine."

Her sweetness touched Abigail. It was nice to hear encouraging words, even if they were from someone she barely knew—and a maid at that. Not normally one to exchange small talk with servants, Abigail surprised herself by confiding in the young woman, "Thank you, Bea. I hope so. But I'm afraid I've been quite spoiled."

By the time Marcus came to pick her up to visit the bathhouses, Abigail felt she looked very nice. She'd chosen a blue and brown plaid walking dress, accessorized with a blue hat and parasol. Bea had arranged little curls to peek out from under the hat on Abigail's forehead, and she felt quite stylish when Marcus arrived.

He looked quite nice and professional in his suit and bowler. Seeing that dimple flash as he smiled gave her that fluttery feeling again, and she wasn't sure she welcomed it. She wasn't even sure what it meant as she'd never experienced it before.

"You look very nice this morning," he said as they went downstairs. "Have you decided which bathhouse you want to visit first?"

She shook her head. "I thought maybe we'd just start out from here and visit the closest one first."

"That sounds good to me. It's a lovely day out. Would you like to walk?"

They stepped outside. Noting the blue, cloudless sky, Abigail nodded. "Yes, let's. It will be easier than getting in and out of a buggy, anyway."

Marcus chuckled. "That's what I thought. Besides, this way you can see more of the city up close."

Abigail did feel a little nervous as she and Marcus set out for the first bathhouse. This was the first time her father had ever sent her to look into any kind of business venture for him, and she wanted to make him proud. "What is the difference between the springs at home and the ones here in Hot Springs?" she asked as Marcus took her arm and steered her out onto the walk.

"They are totally different. The springs here are hot." He grinned down at her. "Hence the name of the town. The springs in Eureka Springs are not hot. They are known for what many believe to be their mineral healing properties. Our springs start out at around 143 degrees and have to be cooled before they can be used in the bathhouses. Many people who have suffered from ailments have found that the hot waters have helped them. Others come because they think the hot baths are good for them and that they make them feel better."

They arrived at the Big Iron Bathhouse first, and after introducing herself to the receptionist, Abigail asked if she could make an appointment.

"For a bath? My dear, look around you. We have several people waiting now. No, we cannot accommodate you now."

"No, I don't want a bath. I'd like to make an appointment to tour the facility."

"You mean you don't want a bath? You just want to look around?"

"That's right." Abigail didn't feel she needed to explain any more than that.

"Well, I'm not sure. You'd have to talk to the manager about that."

"That's what I'm wanting to do. Is he in?"

"No. He won't be back until this afternoon."

Abigail didn't want to lose her temper with Marcus standing right beside her. "All right. May I make an appointment for tomorrow?"

The receptionist looked at her book. "He can probably see you this time tomorrow."

"That will be fine. Please put me down for that." She handed her a business card her father had made for her, calling her a representative of the Connors Bank of Eureka Springs. "Please tell him I am representing my father's bank."

The receptionist's tone quickly changed. "I'll be glad to, Miss Connors. We'll see you tomorrow."

The lobby had been somewhat dim, and Abigail opened her parasol against the brightness of the light outside.

"You handled that very well."

"Thank you. She wasn't very helpful, was she?"

Marcus chuckled. "Not until she found out your father is a banker." He shook his head. "It always bothers me when people are treated differently depending on their circumstances or how they look. I guess that is why I think so much of your father. When I went in, he didn't know that I was the grown son of his good friends. I didn't want that to be a factor in whether or not he gave me a loan."

"He is a very special man." It suddenly struck Abigail that the deferential treatment she'd always received had been more because of her father and his position in town rather than anything she'd ever done. She wondered why she'd never really thought about it before. Deep down she knew the truth, but had she thought it was her right to be treated so well just because her father was so well thought of—or because of how wealthy he was? If so, how impertinent of her.

They were at the next bathhouse before she had time to reflect further, and Abigail was relieved. She didn't much like the turn her thoughts had taken. The Old Hale Bathhouse was nicer than its name implied, probably because it had been renovated.

"There are regulations and inspections on a regular basis. If the government decides improvements need to be made, they are made. Otherwise, their licenses can be taken away," Marcus explained.

The manager was available, and he showed her what he could while they waited for one of the rooms and a tub to be cleaned so that she could see that. "When bathers come in, their valuables are given to us, and we put them in our safe," the manager explained. "Then they are provided with fresh sheets and towels. The towels are to dry off with after the bath, and the sheets are to wrap in for the rubdown. The bathers provide their own mitts and bathrobes. An attendant oversees the bath. The tubs are scrubbed clean after every bath, and the rooms cleaned and readied for the next bather."

"And how long does the bathing take?" Abigail asked.

"Around twenty minutes, a little more or less, depending on the bather."

They toured the facility and then saw the room that had just been cleaned. The marble room had a stall.

"The stall is at about 150 degrees, and the baths are at 98 degrees," the manager explained. "Obviously, going from one to the other creates a kind of shock to the body, but it is what invigorates our clients—once they've perspired out the impurities, relaxed in the bath, and been rubbed down by our attendants."

By the time they arrived back at the front desk, they'd seen several people emerge from their rooms, some looking invigorated and others quite drained.

"I assure you that those who look a bit the worse for it will be feeling totally different after a rest."

Abigail certainly hoped so. She might be looking into this business venture for her father, but after this morning, she had no intention of trying it out for herself. She thanked the manager for his time, and she and Marcus walked out into the bright sunshine.

"Do you want to go to the next bathhouse, or would you like to take time for lunch?" Marcus asked. "There is a restaurant down the street a little ways that I think you'd enjoy."

"Yes, I think I'd like that. Thank you. I feel a little drained myself."

"It's because of the heat and the humidity inside the bathhouses. There's no way to get around that."

"I suppose not, with the water so hot. I don't think I realized just how. . . muggy it would feel inside one of those rooms."

Marcus led her farther down the street to a small restaurant, and Abigail breathed a sigh of relief that it felt cool inside. After looking over the menu, she chose a French salad, a cup of bouillon, and tea.

After the waiter left, Marcus turned to her. "We have several more bathhouses. Do you want to continue to visit them today?"

"Maybe one more, if we can see the manager. The rest can wait until tomorrow or the next day. I'm sure you have other things to do."

Marcus looked at her and shook his head. "Whatever else I might need to do can be worked around you."

"But—"

"Abigail, are you trying to get rid of me?"

His dimple flashed, and her heartbeat sped up. "No, of course not. Besides, I know that if I should go anywhere without your knowledge, one of your agents will be right behind me."

"I'm glad you realize that. It will make me worry a little less when I'm not there."

"Then I take it that I *can* leave the hotel should I need to do some shopping?"

"Of course you can. I don't want you to feel as if you are a prisoner, and I'm certain that's the last thing your father intended when he asked me to make sure you are safe while you are here."

"Good." Abigail found herself smiling at him. "I'm glad you realize that."

Marcus threw back his head and laughed. "I think we are beginning to understand each other. I will be accompanying you to any events you may want to attend, though. Parties, the opera—that kind of thing. We need to be clear on that."

Somehow the idea of him escorting her only gave her a warm feeling and a sense of safety. "We're clear. I suppose you need to know that I've hired one of the part-time maids to work for me on her off days. And should I go out to the post office or shopping, she will most likely accompany me."

"I'd like to have her credentials checked out."

"All right. I'll get them to you. She seems very nice and has been quite helpful to me. I'm sure she will check out just fine."

"In the business I'm in, I've found you can never be too sure. I hope she does check out."

Abigail did, too. While she didn't want to go home, she was used to a life filled with friends and family. To her surprise, she even missed her housekeeper. Abigail had confided in her from time to time, and although she never really asked for her opinion, still she was someone to talk to. Now, Abigail found that she did miss all that. She liked Bea and was looking forward to having someone to talk to when she wasn't with Marcus or his family.

And she was relieved that she would be able to come and go from the hotel for more than one reason. She didn't want to count on Marcus for everything. She'd looked forward to seeing him much too much today, and she didn't welcome that feeling. . .not at all.

Chapter 6

A bigail gave Bea's references to Marcus when he came to pick her up the next day to visit several other bathhouses on her list.

He handed the papers to the agent. . .she believed his name was Nelson. She'd been introduced to him the day before, but because Marcus had someone at the hotel nearly twenty-four hours a day, she was still a bit confused on who was who.

Bea had helped her get ready for the day, and Abigail felt confident that she looked her best. She found that because she was doing business for her father, she wanted to look professional, not just for her sake, but for his as well.

"You are awfully quiet this morning. Are you all right?" Marcus asked as they started down the street.

"I'm fine, thank you. I forgot to tell you that I'm meeting Sally Andrews at the hotel for lunch at noon. She'd asked me about it at your parents', and I had a note reminding me of it first thing this morning."

"I'll be sure to have you back in plenty of time. We can visit one or two bathhouses this morning and another this afternoon or tomorrow. But before I forget, my mother wondered if you'd have dinner with us on Saturday evening."

Abigail had been wondering when she would see Mr. and Mrs. Wellington again and was quite happy to receive the invitation. "I'd love to."

"Good. I'll let her know." He gripped her elbow as he accompanied her inside the Big Iron Bathhouse. After a quick tour of its facilities, they agreed they had time to visit the Independent Bathhouse. Marcus led Abigail up to the reception desk.

"Good morning, can we see the manager, please?" Marcus asked.

"I'll see if I can find him. Please have a seat." It was apparent that the young woman was attracted to Marcus by the smile on her face. She appeared to be about Abigail's age. When she got up to go find the manager, Abigail could see that she was a bit taller. She had dark hair and brown eyes and was quite pretty. Abigail couldn't help but wonder if the young woman and Marcus knew each other—and then she wondered if he was courting anyone.

Knowing it really wasn't any of her business and trying to ignore a little niggle of jealousy at the thought that he might, Abigail turned and looked around the foyer. "This is nice. All the bathhouses seem to be a bit different inside, but I suppose it is that and the way each are managed that draw in different people."

"That is true. The city also has a free bathhouse for those who can't afford to come to the nicer ones."

"Oh? I didn't know that."

"With Hot Springs being inside the National Reservation, and even though it has its own city government, the federal government oversees the springs and anything to do with them."

"I see. Papa will have to take that under consideration, too."

"Yes, he will. I can set up an appointment with the park superintendent, if you'd like. He can tell you all you'll need to know."

"I might need to do that. I'll let you know." Hard as she tried, Abigail couldn't keep the coolness out of her tone, and she wasn't sure why it was there.

When Marcus raised an eyebrow and looked at her questioningly, she realized he'd heard it, too.

She quickly added, "I need to check with Papa, first. Then if he thinks I need to meet with the superintendent, I'll ask you to make an appointment."

"Good enough," was all Marcus said.

The receptionist returned, and Abigail caught the smile that passed between her and Marcus. She didn't like it, and more. . .she didn't like that she didn't like it. What was wrong with her? This man had been hired by her father to make sure she was safe. He was the son of dear friends of her parents. That was all. She and Marcus had no relationship, and she wasn't looking for one. Not after loving someone for as long as she'd loved Nate and then to have it all for naught. No. She didn't need to think along those lines.

The receptionist turned to her. "Mr. Martin asked if you could come back a little later. He's showing a prospective client around."

"That's all right." Abigail wasn't sure she wanted to come back. At least not soon. And possibly not with Marcus. "I'll check back or make an appointment for another time."

"We can make an appointment now, if you'd like. That would probably be best," the young woman said.

She was being nice, and Abigail didn't want to appear rude—especially not in front of Marcus. "Can we make it for around three today?"

The receptionist consulted her appointment book and nodded. "Yes, he is free at that time."

"We'll be back then," Marcus said, taking Abigail's arm. "Thank you."

"You're welcome." The receptionist's smile seemed meant only for Marcus.

Deep down, Abigail couldn't blame her. He was a very nice-looking man.

Once they were outside, Marcus turned to Abigail and asked, "Do you want to try the Palace?"

"Why don't we just make an appointment there for this afternoon or later this week? I think my chances of getting a good tour will be better if we set up a time instead of hoping for the manager to be free. Then we can head on back to the hotel. It will almost be time for lunch by then."

"I think that might be for the best, too." He led her to the next few bath-houses where they set up appointments for the next several days. Then they started back to the hotel. "I'll pick you up this afternoon around a quarter of three and tomorrow around ten again, if that is all right with you?"

"That will be fine. Oh, and thank your mother for the invitation on Saturday. I'm looking forward to seeing your parents again."

"You'd be welcome to call on them anytime, you know."

She did know. She'd felt it that first day when she'd met them. "I do. I just wouldn't want to interrupt their daily schedule."

"You needn't worry about that. If Mother were going out for the day, you'd be welcome to accompany her anywhere. You'll see as you get to know her."

His words made Abigail feel better. She had begun to feel a little awkward after seeing Marcus and the receptionist's reaction to him. After all, this was *his* town and a lot of these people were *his* friends. She was the stranger in town, and at the moment, she felt a little lonely.

It was nearing noon when they got back to the hotel and parted ways. She barely had time to freshen up before meeting Sally in the lobby. The other woman looked fresh as a daisy in a yellow and white dress, with a sheer over-skirt in yellow draped to the side. Once they were seated at a table in front of one of the windows overlooking the street, Sally smiled at her. "I am so glad you were able to meet me for lunch. How are you liking Hot Springs?"

"Thank you for inviting me," Abigail said. "I like your town a lot—although all I've mostly seen are the bathhouses I'm checking out for my father. I'd like to see some of the shops, but I'll get to them."

"I'd love to go shopping with you anytime. I can show you where I like to shop."

"Wonderful! I'd love to do that."

"I also wanted to invite you to a dinner I'm giving a week from Friday evening, if you are free. You may bring an escort, of course."

"Why, thank you. I'd like that. Perhaps Mr. Wellington will come with me." Abigail didn't really want to get into the fact that the handsome man was only protecting her while she was here, but Sally probably had an idea, knowing the business he was in.

"That would be perfect. We always enjoy it when we can get Marcus to come to dinner, but it's not too often that we do."

Somehow that made Abigail feel better, and she wasn't sure why. She enjoyed the lunch with Sally, and they lingered over their dessert of coconut cake and coffee.

"I'd think it would be very lonely to travel alone," Sally said. "Don't you miss your friends?"

Truthfully, Abigail hadn't given her friends much thought. When she did, she could just imagine them discussing her broken engagement, and that wasn't something she wanted to think about.

"Actually, my life had become very busy, but I'm not sure any of it counted for much. I do miss my parents, though." More than she'd thought she would. Each day, she appreciated them a little more.

"I can imagine. I'm married, but I see my mother nearly every day. Are you planning on going home after you finish the business for your father?"

"No. I . . ." She liked Sally, and there was really no reason not to tell the truth. "I was planning on getting married. . .and it was called off. My fiancé is marrying someone else, and I just don't—"

"Oh, my dear. I am so sorry. I am just too nosy sometimes."

"You aren't nosy. It is all right. Actually, it feels good to tell someone about it. I just couldn't stay there."

"Well, I'm glad you are here. I would have wanted to do the very same thing," Sally said, endearing herself to Abigail.

Abigail found she could actually chuckle. "I just kept thinking that everyone in town would be talking about me behind my back, and I just couldn't face it. I don't think I'm a very brave person."

"I know I'm certainly not. Don't you worry. We'll find all kinds of things to keep you busy until you feel at home here. Why don't we go shopping soon? You can tell me how we compare to your hometown."

"Perhaps we can go on Monday?" Abigail had the rest of her week planned out, and she was sure Sally would want to spend Saturday with her husband; it would be nice to look forward to the next week, though.

"I'd like that. Just let me know what time is good for you."

"Let's plan on around ten, and then we can have lunch while we're out and keep shopping after or not."

"That sounds wonderful." Abigail was sure that since Marcus knew Sally, they'd be able to shop alone. . .well, except for whatever agent he'd have watching them from a distance.

❧

Marcus felt all right about leaving Abigail with Sally. He had his man in the hotel and knew they'd be watched well. But he found himself thinking about her all the way back to his office. He could get quite used to being with Abigail Connors on a regular basis. He had to keep reminding himself that the only reason he was seeing so much of her was because of her father. Otherwise, she would most likely rather be left to herself.

He was glad she wasn't planning on leaving once her work for her father was done. Jacob had told him that she was coming for an extended stay, and he hoped she didn't get homesick and decide to return anytime soon. Not because he'd been hired by her father. Marcus would be watching after Abigail Connors even if Jacob hadn't asked him to.

Arriving at his office, he called his mother to let her know that Abigail had accepted her invitation.

"Good. Did you tell her that it was a party in her honor?"

"Well, no. I didn't."

"Marcus!"

"Mother, it will be fine. She'll be pleased. She said she was looking forward to seeing you and Father."

"I think you'd better tell her when you pick her up, then."

"I will." Marcus could hear his mother's sigh on the other end of the line.

"You be sure to. We'll see you later, then."

He heard the click on the end and had a feeling she was a little put out with him. He probably should have told Abigail it was a party, but he'd not thought it was that important at the time. He turned his attention to the mail he'd picked up earlier. Shuffling through the letters, he pulled out the one that interested him the most. The agent he'd sent to Eureka Springs to look into Abigail's background, other than what Jacob had told him, had some information for him.

Marcus scanned the letter quickly, but there wasn't really anything there he didn't already know—except that the man Abigail had been engaged to was her widowed brother-in-law. From all accounts, she'd been in love with him for a very long time. And now he was set to marry someone else.

Leaning back in his chair, Marcus could see how that would be a devastating blow one would want to run from. He folded the letter up and slipped it into the envelope. He couldn't understand it. Abigail was lovely. She seemed a little brittle at times, but after all she'd been through, that seemed understandable.

There wasn't much he could do about the hurt she'd suffered except pray for her, and he bowed his head and did just that.

"Dear Father, I don't know the facts on Abigail's hurt, and perhaps I'm not meant to. But You know I'm a have-to-know kind of person, and I'll try to find out so that I can understand her better. In the meantime, I just pray that You help her through the pain she must be feeling. Please help her to get over her broken engagement and be able to have the kind of life You want for her. Please help us to make her feel welcome here, and while You are at it, Lord, I have a feeling I'm beginning to care a little too much for her. Please help me not to lose my heart to her. She's not likely to return any feelings I might have for her. Not right now, anyway. Please just help me to help her and keep her safe while she's here. In Jesus' name. Amen."

Abigail was surprised at how much she enjoyed the evening at the Wellingtons' on Saturday night, considering how nervous she'd been when she found out that it was a party in her honor. Mrs. Wellington was so gracious and kind to do something like this.

She'd been introduced to Dr. O'Malley and his wife and to one of the pharmacists in town, a Mr. Primm, and his wife. . .Donna, Abigail thought her name was. She knew she'd never remember them all, but by the end of the evening, she had a feeling she'd met most of the people she might need to know if she stayed for very long. She'd already met the minister on Sunday, but tonight, besides a doctor and a pharmacist, she'd met a lawyer and a banker and their wives. They were all very nice.

She had a feeling she'd be receiving invitations for other dinners and outings very soon. Once the last guest left, she turned to her hostess. "Mrs. Wellington, I can't thank you enough for having me tonight. My mother will probably cry when I write her about your kindness."

Mrs. Wellington patted her on the shoulder. "I just want you to feel at home in our town, dear. And I hope you will feel you can drop in on us anytime."

"But—"

"And don't you worry about formality. You are always welcome in our home. Always. If we are not here, you feel free to come in and stay as long as you'd like. In fact, I think you should just stay with us instead of at the Arlington, although it is a very nice hotel."

"How sweet of you. But I can't impose that way."

"Abigail Connors." Mrs. Wellington sounded so much like her mother that Abigail found herself fighting tears. "You are my dear friends' daughter. That means you are family. You would not be imposing in any way, but I will try to understand your need to be on your own. Or at least accept it."

She smiled, and Abigail couldn't help but chuckle.

"But," Mrs. Wellington continued, "I will be very hurt if you don't visit often and keep in touch."

"I can't think of anything I'd rather do," Abigail answered honestly.

"Good. Now, how would you like to come with me to a meeting at church next week? We are trying to find ways to help those who come here to make use of the springs but can't afford to stay in the hotels."

Marcus had told her about the free bathhouses, but Abigail hadn't really thought about those who might not be able to afford to stay indefinitely. And even if she had, at one time she would have put it to the back of her mind. She was a bit surprised to hear herself answer, "Yes, I'd be glad to go with you."

"Good. It is at eleven o'clock on Wednesday. After the meeting, we'll have a nice lunch."

Abigail had never been very demonstrative, but she found herself hugging the older woman. "Thank you. Being around you makes me feel as if I have family here."

Mrs. Wellington hugged her back. "That's exactly the way we want you to feel. I wish your parents could come for a visit."

Abigail grinned. "If I stay long enough, perhaps they will."

"Then we shall strive to keep you here," Mr. Wellington said.

Abigail looked over the older man's shoulder at Marcus, and something about the look in his eyes made her heart turn over. When he smiled at her and showed his dimple, that same heart seemed to do a sort of flip and dive that left her feeling more than a little breathless.

The feeling didn't leave her until long after she and Marcus had said good night from opposite sides of her door.

The next day at church, Abigail tried to ignore the way her pulse raced as she sat beside Marcus. She had to admit that she didn't mind having him escort her wherever they went. It was obvious that he was well-thought-of and respected by those people she'd met when with him. And if anyone had heard of her broken engagement, she certainly didn't think they'd bring it up, knowing she was a friend of the Wellington family. All in all, she was very pleased her father had hired Marcus, and knowing her father as she did, he probably took the family friendship into consideration when he did so. That way, people wouldn't just naturally assume he'd been hired to protect her.

She stood up when the rest of the family did to sing a hymn and chastised herself for thinking about Marcus when she should be paying attention to the church service. . .and for all the times she'd let her mind wander back home when she was in church. She'd been attending all her life and could remember when she'd been baptized. But it suddenly hit her that somewhere along the way, she'd only been putting lip service to her Christianity. It was time for that to change.

Chapter 7

Abigail's mother had written to let her know that Nate and Meagan had set their wedding date for the third of September, and while she'd shed tears over it, Abigail also felt relief that she hadn't destroyed their chance for happiness. Over the next few weeks, Abigail began to feel at home in Hot Springs. She'd been invited to several more dinners and had gone shopping a few times with Sally. But the time she'd enjoyed most was the hours she spent with Marcus and his family. She loved going to church with them and then spending the rest of the day at their home. Usually, others were invited for Sunday dinner, and she was beginning to feel comfortable around them as well. It was hard to believe she'd been in Hot Springs for more than a month and that it was now September.

The days were still warm, but the leaves were beginning to change on the hardwoods on the mountain across from her hotel. She still had no desire to return home, and she'd begun to think she might want to stay in Hot Springs permanently.

On the weekdays when Abigail went with Mrs. Wellington to her meeting at church, Mr. Wellington picked her up at the hotel, and then she somehow ended up going back to their home for the afternoon and evening. Marcus would join them for dinner and take her back to the hotel. It had become something she really looked forward to. . .more and more each week.

Over the last few weeks, she'd been studying her Bible in ways she couldn't remember doing back home, and this Sunday, she listened closely to the sermon John Martin preached. His subject was based on Philippians 3:13, on what Paul had said about *forgetting those things which are behind, and reaching forth unto those things which are before."*

"Brethren, we must not dwell on our past mistakes but on what we are doing now and in the future. We must forgive ourselves as we have asked God to do and as He has done. We are His children, and each day, we must give ourselves over to doing God's will and not our own."

As he finished his sermon and they stood to sing the invitational hymn, Abigail felt as if the minister had spoken just to her and decided she wanted to think about this sermon and read her Bible more.

The final prayer was said, and she followed Marcus out into the aisle.

"Wasn't that a wonderful lesson?" his mother asked from just behind Abigail. "I think one of the hardest things for us to do is to learn to forgive ourselves. John gave me much to think about."

Abigail couldn't imagine that Mrs. Wellington had that problem, for she couldn't envision that the woman had ever sinned. Yet she knew that as humans, everyone did. Still, compared to all she'd done. . .yet. . .

"You look very nice today," Marcus said, as he led her out to his buggy for the trip to his mother's.

"Thank you." Abigail could feel her cheeks heat up and wondered what it was about this man that could do that to her. She wasn't one to blush, but for some reason, she felt like a young schoolgirl when Marcus complimented her. She wanted to tell him how handsome he looked in his black suit, and she'd never found it hard to compliment a man until now. In fact, she'd found it quite easy. Had that been because she hadn't really meant it?

At the Wellington home, it felt quite natural to help Mrs. Wellington get Sunday dinner on the table. Like Abigail's mother, Mrs. Wellington tried to let her housekeeper take off on Sundays. Abigail was just now realizing that it was something she should have been doing with her own housekeeper all along.

She sighed. One more thing to feel guilty about. Then she remembered the sermon she'd just heard and had hope that she could put all of that behind her. For the first time, she truly believed that perhaps she could be forgiven her past mistakes—if she could become a different person than the one she'd been these last few years. It was something she needed to think more on—and she would as soon as she got back to the hotel.

❧

Marcus watched Abigail from across his parents' dining table. She was laughing at something his father had said, and she'd never looked prettier to him. He couldn't put his finger on when it began to happen, but each time he was with Abigail, she seemed to be changing in small ways that were hard to discern. She seemed. . .somewhat softer—less brittle? It was as if that hard edge she'd seemed to have the day he met her was fading away, and she didn't seem so much on guard. Much as he would like to think that it was because she felt safe and secure knowing he and his men were watching over her, he had a feeling there was much more to it than that. Besides, she still seemed a bit wary around him at times. And sometimes she still looked so vulnerable he wanted to take her in his arms and tell her that he'd never let anything happen to her.

As if I can control those kinds of things. All I can do is see that she is protected to the best of my ability, but if her heart is still broken, there is nothing

A LOVE ALL HER OWN

I can do about that.

The thought took him back a bit. Her broken engagement was none of his business; he knew that. Neither was her broken heart. Yet he wished he could do something—anything—to mend it so that she might look at him as someone besides the man her father had hired to watch over her.

"Marcus?" His mother broke into his thoughts, and he found that everyone was watching him. It appeared he'd missed some of the conversation while he was woolgathering.

"Yes, Mother?"

She paused with her fingers on her temple. "Well, I was going to ask you something, but as long as it took to get your attention, it appears I've forgotten what it was."

"I'm sorry, Mother." He couldn't help but chuckle along with her, though, when she laughed and shook her head.

"You looked as if you were miles away from here."

Marcus shook his head. "No. My thoughts were right here." On Abigail—where they seemed to stay these days.

Once Abigail was back in her room at the hotel, her thoughts on the minister's sermon fought to be heard. She barely tasted her tea for all the realizations that filled her mind. Before she could forgive herself for the past and go on, she had to make sure she'd asked God for His forgiveness.

And how far back did she need to go to know she had? The Lord knew she wasn't to blame for Rose's death. But she'd had that moment of hope that because of her sister's death, Nate might learn to love her. Abigail could no longer deny that she had coveted her sister's husband. A moan from deep inside escaped, and Abigail slid to her knees. "Oh, please, dear Lord, forgive me for wanting Nate for myself," she whispered. "And please forgive me for being so envious of Rose for all those years."

Abigail began to cry as she prayed. "Please. . .dear Lord. . .please forgive me. . .for drawing away from You." She wiped at the tears streaming down her face. "I didn't want to admit what You've known all along. I have been an awful person, Father. I tried to make Nate feel guilty so that he would marry me—and I almost succeeded. And now. . .I don't know if I ever really loved him or if I just wanted what was Rose's."

Tears flowed freely as she continued. "And if I hadn't been so hateful to Natalie that day, she wouldn't have fallen down the stairs. Thank You for letting her be all right now." Her sobs came from deep within her. "I'm so ashamed, Father. Please forgive me and help me to become the child You would have me be. I don't want to be the same Abigail who left Eureka Springs ever again.

171

I don't want to be that selfish or self-absorbed. Please help me. And please, please let Natalie and Nate and everyone I've hurt forgive me. All of this, I ask in Jesus' name. Amen."

Abigail stayed there, her head on the settee, until her tears were spent. She felt a peace settle inside her that she hadn't felt in years, and she knew the Lord had forgiven her.

∽

Marcus looked through his mail, and his attention fell immediately on the envelope from Eureka Springs. It was thick, telling him that his agent had found out more about Abigail. For a moment, he wondered if he should have gone this route. After all, just because he could find out almost anything about anyone didn't mean he always should, he supposed.

Abigail had become more than just the daughter of Jacob Connors to him. She was more than a family friend and certainly much more than his other clients. Marcus opened the envelope and pulled out the thick missive. He quickly scanned the pages and then read again, more slowly this time.

The Abigail Connors of Eureka Springs bore little semblance to the Abigail he'd come to know. He shook his head as he read. Apparently Abigail had, for the most part, lived a very selfish life in the last few years. She'd been mostly concerned with having a good time with her friends and convincing Nate Brooks to marry her. She'd nearly succeeded; but then her niece had an accident, and shortly afterward, her engagement was broken. Nate had recently wed another woman, a Meagan Snow. *Hmm, that still doesn't tell me who broke the engagement.*

Marcus got up from his desk and went to look out the window. From the sadness in Abigail's eyes when he first met her and the fact that her fiancé had married another woman, he had a feeling that Abigail hadn't wanted the engagement to end. But he had no real way of knowing. She'd changed some from when he first saw her, so it stood to reason that she wasn't the same person she'd been at one time. At least he hadn't seen any evidence of her being the kind of person this letter described her as being.

He picked it up and read it again. It seemed that before her sister died she hadn't been quite so concerned with her social life. It appeared there'd been a time when she hadn't been quite so self-absorbed. Perhaps the death of her sister. . .

He shook his head and dropped the letter on the desk. None of it really mattered. . .not now. The Abigail he'd come to care about didn't seem anything like the one his agent was describing now or in the last letter. And he had no way of knowing what was truth and what wasn't. All he could really go by was now. And be thankful that the Abigail he'd come to know was nothing like the old one. At least—he prayed not.

❧

Abigail felt like a new person. After confessing her sins to the Lord and asking for His forgiveness, she felt almost the same as she had the day she'd been baptized: brand-new and ready to begin a new life. She just had more of her own sins to try to forget and put into the past than she had back then. She knew the Lord had forgiven her. But she was finding it harder to forgive herself.

She'd written letters to both Nate and Meagan, asking for their forgiveness for trying to come between them when she knew they cared for each other. Abigail shivered just thinking back on all the ways she'd hurt them in her quest to get Nate to marry her. She couldn't blame them if they never forgave her. The letter she wrote to Natalie was even harder. She loved the child so much and had loved her since the day she was born.

> *Dear Sweet Natalie,*
>
> *How do I tell you how much I love you and how sorry I am that I caused your fall by raising my voice and hurting your feelings? I understand why you ran out of the room that day, and I will blame myself forever for your fall. I pray that you have healed completely by now.*
>
> *I do know that you think I caused your mama's fall that day of the fire, and I can see how you might. But nothing could be further from the truth. I can only tell you that my intention was only to get her to not go back upstairs when I grabbed her arm. I know it may be hard for you to believe that after the fall you had, but oh, my sweet, it is true. I only wanted her to come with us to safety. The Lord knows that is true.*
>
> *I love you and miss you with all my heart, dear Natalie. I pray that someday you will forgive me for causing your fall and love me once more. I will always love you.*
>
> *Love,*
> *Aunt Abby*

Abigail felt better once she'd handed the letters to the desk clerk the next morning, but she didn't hold out a lot of hope that she'd be forgiven. She'd been so awful to everyone. And she was having a hard enough time forgiving herself—how could they do it?

She read Philippians 3:13 repeatedly each night, and she was trying to put her past behind her—but Satan always reminded her of her sins in one way or another.

Still, she was faithful to take her worries to the Lord, and she was happier than she'd been in years. She wondered if it showed when Marcus arrived to take her to the Wednesday ladies' meeting at church. His father had a meeting, so Marcus picked her up and then they went to pick up his mother.

He kept glancing over at her until she finally asked, "What's wrong? Do I have a smudge on my face?"

His dimple flashed in a grin, and he shook his head. "No. You just look very pretty today. Not that you don't look nice all the time. You do. You just look . . .happy."

So, he did notice. And he thought she looked pretty. She could feel the color steal up her cheeks at his compliment. "I am happy. Papa is pleased with the reports that I've sent him on the bathhouses, and I feel I can relax and enjoy my stay now. I really like going to these meetings with your mother."

"She enjoys them, too. She says you are all making progress on finding ways to house those who need the help."

Abigail nodded. "Well, I'm not doing much, but these ladies are very determined to help those who've been sent here for treatment by their doctors but can't afford the bathhouses or the hotels. Several of the churches have members who have an extra room and have volunteered to take in boarders for free. Others are talking to the town leaders about what the town can do."

"There is a need. No doubt about that. Perhaps they should talk to the park superintendent."

Abigail nodded. "I think that would be a good idea, too. We can mention it to your mother."

His mother was waiting for them when they got to his parents' home, and once Marcus stopped the buggy, Abigail moved to get down so that Mrs. Wellington could sit on the front seat beside her son.

"Don't you move, Abigail," Mrs. Wellington said. "There's no need for all that getting down and getting back up into the back and getting settled. You stay right where you are."

"But I don't mind—"

"I know you don't, dear." She was at the buggy, and Marcus was helping her into the backseat. "But I do."

Marcus looked at Abigail and smiled. "Stay put. She can be real stubborn when she wants to be."

His mother chuckled. "Yes, I can be. I've found I've had to be a time or two in my life from living with you and your father."

Marcus took his seat beside Abigail and grinned. "Now she's saying that Papa and I are hard to live with."

"I did not say that, Marcus Wellington!"

They bickered back and forth all the way to church, but Abigail knew them well enough to know it was all done in fun and with love. She relaxed and let them entertain her all the way there.

❧

That evening, Abigail and Mrs. Wellington caught up Marcus and his father on the ideas the ladies were working on.

"We now have fifty families willing to house people who are in need," Mrs. Wellington said. "I've put our name on the list, too, Martin."

"I figured you would, dear," Mr. Wellington said.

"Well, since Marcus moved out and we can't convince Abigail to come stay with us, I wouldn't feel right if I hadn't."

Marcus laughed and turned to Abigail. "I knew she'd use us as an excuse. But don't you let it bother you any."

"No dear, don't. You both are saving me a ton of money this way," Mr. Wellington assured Abigail. "Lydia would be having me add a room to the house if she didn't have one or two free ones, wouldn't you, dear?"

Abigail had a feeling he was right, and she was even more assured when his wife agreed with him.

"Yes, I probably would have. Still, this won't be the answer forever. We have also decided to form a committee to go to the town leaders and also the reservation superintendent, as Abigail told me you suggested, Marcus. Surely, either the city or the United States government can help come up with a permanent solution."

"Yes, I agree they should. But these things take time, dear."

"I guess it's a good thing we are trying to begin the process, then," Mrs. Wellington said.

Mr. Wellington nodded in her direction. "It is, my dear. I am certain that you ladies will make these leaders sit up and take notice that something needs to be done."

❧

By the end of the evening, Marcus was convinced that the Abigail he'd come to care a great deal about was not the same Abigail whom his agent had reported on. Oh, she might be the same person physically, but otherwise, she was nothing like the woman described in the letters he'd received.

He'd just received a letter that day from her father, wondering if she seemed lonely and how she was doing and if she was adjusting to life in Hot Springs. Marcus felt he could honestly report that she seemed to be doing quite well. Over the last few weeks, he'd accompanied her to several dinners she'd been invited to, she'd insisted that she could go shopping with some of the lady friends she'd made, and he had let his agents make sure they were safe. He didn't want her to feel smothered. But as he came to care more for her, her safety was as important to him as it was to her father.

"Thank you for attending these meetings with Mother. It seems to mean a lot to her to have you with her."

"Oh, she'd do fine by herself. She feels quite strongly about doing something to help the sick who come here to get better. I'm sure my mother would do the same. Since I'm not a permanent resident, I don't feel I have much to say, but I'm glad to go and give your mother any support I can."

Her words had Marcus's heart beating hard against his chest. He didn't like the idea of her leaving. Was she planning on going back home soon? He couldn't bring himself to ask outright. "Have you given any thought to making Hot Springs your home?" Only as he waited for her answer did he realize how much it meant to him.

She leaned her head to one side and looked at him. "Not really. But I'm not in any hurry to leave." She shrugged. "I do like it here a lot. Maybe it is something I should give some thought to."

Marcus allowed himself to relax. She wasn't going anywhere for now. He had some time. . .to what? Convince himself that he didn't care about her—or convince her to stay?

Chapter 8

As Abigail got ready to meet Mrs. Wellington for lunch on Friday, she was looking forward to spending time with the woman she'd come to think of as family. While she did miss her parents and Natalie, she had no desire to go back to Eureka Springs. She'd started a new life here, and she was beginning to like herself again. She had a feeling that if she returned to Eureka Springs, she'd revert to the old Abigail: selfish and self-absorbed. She couldn't—wouldn't—let that happen.

She watched in the mirror as Bea put her hair up. "I still can't do that half as well as you do, Bea."

"It just takes practice is all. And it is easier to put up someone else's hair because you can see the back much better."

"Well, I might make myself look presentable, but I always feel I look much better when you do it." And she did. But somehow it didn't matter quite as much as it had at one time. In Eureka Springs, her appearance seemed to take up way too much of her time. Now she usually forgot what she looked like as soon as she was ready to leave the room.

Bea helped her on with her dress, a purple print with a sheer overskirt that draped to the back.

"You look lovely. Are you meeting someone special?" Bea asked.

"I'm meeting Mrs. Wellington for lunch here. She reminds me so much of my mother it's almost like having her here. I do miss my parents. I wish they would come for a visit." It suddenly came to Abigail that while she wanted them to visit here, she still had no desire to return to Eureka Springs.

"She seems a very nice lady," Bea said. She'd met her once when she'd accompanied Abigail to the drugstore. "I'm sure you'll have a wonderful lunch."

"I'm sure we will." Abigail picked up her reticule and an envelope and turned to Bea with a smile. She handed her the envelope. "This is your pay for last week. Thank you again for helping me, Bea. I really do appreciate it."

"You are welcome. I'm grateful that you hired me. I'll pick up your dresses from the hotel laundry and bring them up before I leave."

"I'll see you later, then." Abigail headed downstairs to meet Mrs. Wellington, who would be arriving at any moment.

She recognized all of the agents whom Marcus had assigned to her now. . .

at least she thought she did, but she'd been instructed not to speak to them unless she needed them. So she just glanced over and nodded an impersonal good day to the one currently on duty and then went to the front desk to check her mail. She had one letter from her mother, which she put in her bag to read later. She kept hoping she would hear from Nate and Meagan and Natalie, but she really didn't think she would. Before she could begin to dwell on the past again, she reminded herself that she'd asked for their forgiveness and that was what was important.

She turned to watch for Mrs. Wellington and found her entering on her son's arm. Abigail crossed the lobby and greeted her with a hug. "I am so glad you could make it today. I've been wanting to take you to lunch for weeks now."

"I've been looking forward to it, my dear."

"And I feel a bit left out," Marcus said. But Abigail could tell he was teasing from his tone.

"Oh dear. I'm sorry. You can join us if you'd like, Marcus," Abigail said with a smile.

He chuckled and shook his head. "No, thank you. I do have a meeting to go to. But thank you for the invitation. It makes me feel better. I'll be back to pick you up in a couple of hours, Mother."

"Your father said he can pick me up if you can't come back, dear. Just let him know."

"I'll be here, Mother," Marcus said, bending to kiss her on the cheek. "You and Abigail have a good lunch."

He waved good-bye to them, and Abigail led Mrs. Wellington to the hotel dining room where they were shown to a table looking out onto Central Avenue.

"Marcus has been telling me how good the food is here," Mrs. Wellington said as she looked over the menu.

"It's all excellent. I believe I'll have a salad and macaroni and cheese."

"That sounds quite good to me, too."

The waiter took their order, and the next hour and a half passed much too quickly as they enjoyed their lunch and conversation. Mrs. Wellington always entertained Abigail with stories of when she and Mr. Wellington and her parents were younger. It gave Abigail more insight into her family. By the time they finished their dessert of lemon pudding, Abigail felt she knew a side of her parents that she'd never been able to see.

When they left the dining room, they headed to the lobby to wait for Marcus to pick his mother up.

"Abigail! Abigail Connors!"

Abigail's heart sank when she recognized the voice calling out to her. She turned to find Jillian Burton, one of her best friends from Eureka Springs, standing at the hotel desk, evidently checking in.

"Jillian?"

"Why, it is you!" Rebecca Dobson said. Suddenly, Abigail found herself surrounded by half the group of people she'd spent most of her adult life with. There was Reginald Fitzgerald, Edward Mitchell, and Robert Ackerman. Abigail's heart seemed to stop beating, and for a moment, she thought she was trapped in her worst nightmare. But when Marcus came in to pick up his mother just then, she realized the nightmare was all too real.

❧

Marcus's heart stopped when he entered the hotel to find his mother and Abigail surrounded by people he'd never seen before. His agent was on his way to the group, but Marcus didn't wait for him as he strode into the middle and asked, "Abigail, do you know these people?"

The look in her eyes told him more than he was sure she wanted him to know. She knew them, but he wasn't sure she wanted to admit it.

"Of course she knows us!" a woman with curly red hair said rather indignantly. "We're her best friends!"

The color in Abigail's face seemed to drain, and for a moment, Marcus thought she was going to faint.

"It that right, Abigail?"

"I—yes, I know them." She turned in the circle and began to introduce them by name. Then she turned to Marcus and his mother. "Everyone, this is Mrs. Wellington and her son, Marcus. They are family friends."

All her friends from Eureka Springs smiled and were polite, but Marcus had a feeling they were sizing him up and wondering about the way he broke into their circle. Abigail hadn't introduced him as owning the Wellington Agency or explained that he was in charge of her safety, so he followed her lead and accepted that she considered him a family friend now.

"Please come sit with us while we wait for our rooms to be ready and our luggage to get here," Jillian said.

"I do need to get home, dear," Mrs. Wellington said. "You have a nice time visiting with your friends. Thank you so much for lunch."

"Oh, do you have to leave?" Abigail asked.

Marcus had a feeling that she didn't want to be left alone with these people, but his mother didn't seem to pick up on it. "I do. But I hope to get to know your friends while they are here."

Abigail turned to the group from home and smiled. "I'll be right back. I want to walk Mrs. Wellington out."

"Your friends seem quite nice, dear. Perhaps I can have them all to dinner one night?"

"That's sweet of you, but don't worry about it. I'm sure they have all kinds of plans," Abigail said as she walked with them to the door.

"I'll be back after I take Mother home, Abigail."

"You can stay here, dear. I can take a hack home."

"I'll get one for you, Mother." He turned back to Abigail. "I'll be right back."

Abigail nodded, but he couldn't tell if she wanted him to come back or stay away. It didn't much matter. He'd be back. He wasn't sure about those friends of hers. Not at all. It was a good thing Ross was on the job.

❧

Abigail pasted a smile on her face and went back to her friends. For some reason, it had never crossed her mind that they would show up in Hot Springs. They must have found out where she was and come to see how she was doing after her broken engagement. Now that she thought about it, it was a wonder they had taken until the middle of September to find her.

"It is so good to see you! You could have let us know where you were!" Jillian said when Abigail got back to the group.

"You didn't come just to see how I am?" Abigail knew these people. She'd never known them to take a trip to Hot Springs or anywhere else for that matter. Their lives were pretty wrapped up in the Eureka Springs social life, just as hers had been.

"Of course not. We didn't know you were here," Reginald said. "We've been hearing how much more advanced Hot Springs is and about the bathhouses here, the opera, the races."

"Eureka Springs has been pretty boring of late. . .especially with you gone," Robert said. He sounded just a little too smooth for Abigail.

"We wanted a change of scenery," Edward said.

"How are you doing, though?" Rebecca asked, letting Abigail know that she was most likely right about the reason for their visit.

"Very well." Abigail chose not to mention her broken engagement or Nate and Meagan's marriage. "Papa had some business he wanted me to attend to for him, and I've found that I like Hot Springs quite well."

"But you aren't going to stay here, are you?" Jillian asked. "You are coming home, aren't you?"

"I'm staying here awhile longer."

"Well, then. We must make it our goal to convince you to come back to Eureka Springs with us," Robert said. "But while we're here, I'm sure you can tell us the best places to go and all about the nightlife."

Nightlife and socializing. That was what they had on their minds. It was almost all she'd thought about at one time, too. But not now. Still, they were here, and they wouldn't leave her alone now that they knew where she was, too.

"There is a nice opera house here. I'm not sure what is playing now, but the desk clerk will know."

"Oh, I'll go check," Rebecca said.

"The hotel dining room is excellent, but there are other restaurants in town. Marcus will be able to tell you other places of interest when he returns."

"Marcus? The family friend?" Robert asked. He almost sounded jealous, but he certainly had no right to. Abigail had never given him any encouragement.

"Yes."

"My—he is quite handsome. Is he the reason you came here?" Jillian asked.

Abigail wanted to tell her it was none of her business, but instead she answered honestly, "No. But it is very nice to have family friends here."

Rebecca returned to tell them that there was a minstrel show playing at the opera house that evening, just as Marcus came striding through the hotel doors.

"You'll join us, won't you?" Jillian asked Abigail as Marcus walked up to the group.

"I don't know." Abigail hesitated. She didn't know whether to be relieved or worried at the realization that Marcus wasn't going to let her go anywhere, even with people she knew, without accompanying her. After all—he didn't know them.

"What don't you know?"

"Everyone wants to go to the minstrel show at the opera house this evening," Abigail explained to Marcus. Might as well invite him. Otherwise, everyone would wonder why he was with her. "Would you like to go with us?"

He looked into her eyes and said, "I can't think of anything I'd rather do."

Abigail's heart turned over, and for a moment, she forgot that he was just going along with her so that they didn't know he was really there just to protect her. *That* thought gave her heart a little twist in pain, and she was glad she didn't have to say anything as the group made plans to meet up in the lobby at seven.

❧

As Abigail waited for Marcus to pick her up, she couldn't remember when she'd been so nervous. On the one hand, she wanted him with her. If her friends thought she'd been moping around since her breakup with Nate, having Marcus as an escort should help put an end to that! On the other, she was afraid that her greatest fear would come true—that with her friends here, he would find out what kind of woman she used to be back home in Eureka Springs.

"Dear Lord, please don't let that happen. I don't want him to see me as I was but only as I am now." The knock at her door interrupted her whispered prayer, and she hurried to answer it.

Marcus stood looking quite handsome in his black suit and tucked white shirt with pearl studs and white cravat. She was glad she'd worn her favorite pink evening dress with white lace trim and a lace overskirt that draped to the side and cascaded midway down the skirt.

"You look very nice. Are you ready to meet your friends?"

"Thank you. I'm not sure about meeting my friends. I suppose I have no choice, though."

"You weren't expecting them, then?" Marcus crooked an arm for her to take, and they headed down the staircase.

"No! Of course not. I haven't corresponded with them since I left."

"Hmm."

"Yes. My thoughts exactly."

When Marcus chuckled, so did she, and by the time they reached the lobby, she was feeling a little better about the evening. Marcus wasn't the only one looking after her. The Lord had heard her prayer, and she would trust that things would go well.

They all had dinner in the hotel dining room together before going to the opera house, and her friends seemed to be on very good behavior. They had been known to get a little rowdy in the past, but perhaps the genteel atmosphere helped to subdue them. Abigail certainly hoped so.

Oddly enough, no one brought up Nate or his marriage to Meagan. Perhaps her friends cared more for her feelings than she'd given them credit for. More than likely, it was because they weren't sure they should in front of Marcus. Either way, Abigail still wasn't at all sure how she felt about them being in Hot Springs.

Marcus proved what a gracious person he was by talking to them all, asking about their trip, and generally showing an interest in them. No one suspected that he was a private investigator and was very good at putting people at ease. By the time they left for the opera house, Abigail could tell that they all liked him. Well, all except for Robert, who still seemed a bit jealous to Abigail.

The opera house was quite luxurious inside, and Abigail was a bit surprised that she hadn't been there before. But most of her evenings out had been in people's homes, and she'd come to enjoy that more than trying to find entertainment. Actually, she'd liked entertaining back at home, but most of her friends had preferred going out somewhere as opposed to hosting in their homes.

Several couples whom she'd met through Marcus and his parents were attending the event, and it was good to talk to them. Her friends seemed quite impressed that she knew so many people already.

"You seem to be fitting in here quite well," Robert said as they found their seats. "And most of who you know appears to be the town's elite."

Abigail felt her hackles rise as she took her seat between Robert and Marcus. "It wouldn't matter to me if they were or not. They are very nice people, and I like them a lot."

"My, you are touchy, Abigail. I didn't mean anything by my comment," Robert said.

But she knew Robert and what *was* important to him. Thankfully, the minstrel show started just then, and she didn't have to answer him.

The show was quite entertaining, and it felt good just to laugh after being so tensed up that afternoon. They were all still chuckling when they came out of the opera house.

"Well now, my good man," Reginald said. "Abigail has told us you would know the best places to go. Where do you suggest we go to get a cup of tea, coffee, or chocolate?"

"There aren't a lot of restaurants open this time of night. The Arlington serves until eleven, though. The Melrose Place is open, and there is a café around the corner that will be open for a while, yet."

"I think I'll just go back to the hotel tonight," Abigail said, knowing she'd have tea brought up soon.

"Me, too. All that traveling has made me very tired," Jillian said with a yawn.

"Well, if you are going back, so am I," Rebecca added.

"But the night is young," Robert said. "I'm not ready to retire."

"I'll see the ladies back to the hotel, if you gentlemen aren't ready to go yet," Marcus said.

"You're sure? Do you mind, Rebecca and Jillian?" Reginald asked. "I'm a bit too wound up to sleep just yet."

"It's all right—tonight. But don't make a habit of it," Jillian replied. "Go. I'm sure Mr. Wellington will see us safely back to the hotel."

That was all it took for the men to be on their way down the street, and Abigail wondered why she hadn't realized how...thoughtless they were before now. Had they always been that way? Abigail was certainly glad none of these men was her beau, as Reginald was Jillian's and Edward was Rebecca's. And although she'd let Robert escort her to a few functions in the past, she'd never considered him a beau. Even if she had, after this evening, he no longer would have been one.

Marcus procured a hack waiting outside the opera house and helped the ladies up, and then he took a seat beside Abigail. Jillian and Rebecca spent the ride wondering where the men might have gone and openly flirting with Marcus. Were their relationships that shallow?

By the time they got back to the hotel, Abigail was ready to go to her room, but Jillian and Rebecca had decided that they would like to go to the dining room.

"Won't you come, too, Abigail? We have so much to catch up on!"

Abigail shook her head. "Not tonight. I'm very tired."

"Well, you will spend some time with us tomorrow, won't you?"

"Yes, of course I will. I don't know how you two are still going after the train trip here. I was exhausted."

"Well, you were most likely depressed, too," Rebecca said. "After all—"

The none-too-subtle nudge from Jillian stopped Rebecca's next sentence, much to Abigail's relief. There was no telling what she was about to say. But the next words out of the woman's mouth were no help, either.

"I'm sorry. I—"

"Rebecca! Come on. I think that the dining room may be closing very soon." Jillian took her friend's arm and pulled her away, waving back at Abigail and Marcus. "We'll see you tomorrow, Abigail. It's been nice meeting you, Mr. Wellington."

Abigail's sigh of relief was audible. "I'd forgotten how. . ." *Irritating* was the word that came to mind, but Abigail didn't want to seem childish or mean-spirited. She shook her head and looked up at Marcus as he escorted her up the stairs. "Thank you for escorting me tonight. Their showing up here took me somewhat by surprise."

"They didn't know you were here?"

Abigail shook her head and shrugged. "No. I. . .just needed a change, and I. . .haven't felt the need to let them know where I am. I'm not sure what that says about our friendship."

Marcus didn't comment as they reached her room and he checked things out for her. She was relieved that he didn't ask any questions, although she wasn't sure what he was thinking about her. Although, that did bother Abigail, she'd been honest, and she was glad about that.

He handed the key to her and looked into her eyes. "I enjoyed being with you tonight. Your friends might take some getting used to, but I'll accompany you anywhere you want to go with them—and I would even if I weren't keeping you safe."

For some reason, his words made her feel like crying, and she wasn't sure why.

Chapter 9

Marcus wasn't impressed with Abigail's friends. Not at all. He especially didn't like the way Robert Ackerman watched her. The man had come looking for her; Marcus was sure of it. He'd been in this business too long not to put a few things together. Most likely, Ackerman had found out where she was and then convinced his friends to come with him so it wouldn't look as though he'd sought her out. The other option was that one of the other friends found out where she was and convinced everyone else to make the trip, and Ackerman invited himself along. Either way, the man was here to pursue Abigail. There was no doubt in Marcus's mind about that. The only thing he wasn't totally sure about was how Abigail felt about it. Oh, he had a feeling she hadn't been very happy to see them all today, but he wasn't sure how she would feel about it in the coming days.

On Saturday, she asked him to accompany her out to dinner with the group and give them a tour of the town so that they would know where they wanted to go. Marcus would have thought that the men had an idea from being out and about the night before, but he was more than glad to be with Abigail for any reason.

During dinner in the hotel, Marcus was less impressed than ever by the people Abigail called friends. The young woman called Rebecca seemed to want to rub salt into Abigail's wounds over her broken engagement—the one Abigail still hadn't told him about.

"Nate and Natalie look quite happy these days," Rebecca said over dinner. "Life with Meagan must agree with them."

Marcus heard Abigail's sharp intake of breath, and even Jillian recognized the insult. "Rebecca!"

Rebecca immediately put her hand over her mouth and said, "I'm so sorry, Abigail. I didn't mean to bring up a sore subject." But the look in her eyes said anything but that she was sorry.

"I'm glad to hear that they are all happy," Abigail said.

There was a sincerity in her voice that Marcus hadn't heard from Rebecca. Abigail may have been hurt by the other woman's words, but she seemed to truly be happy for her ex-fiancé.

"That is kind of you, Abigail, after all the hurt you've been through."

"I'm doing fine, Jillian. Thank you." Her smile was genuine, and her friend seemed quite surprised. Then their attention turned to Marcus, and he could tell they were wondering what kind of relationship he and Abigail had. Well, there was no way he was going to tell them her father had hired him to look after her. No way at all.

"I'm so glad to hear that you aren't pining after Nate," Robert said, leaning toward Abigail. "You deserve someone much better than Nate Brooks."

Marcus didn't like the gleam in the other man's eyes. He was more certain than ever that Robert would be pursuing Abigail in earnest. He hoped she could see through him, but he wasn't sure. He'd seen her when she first arrived, and whatever had happened back in Eureka Springs had saddened her deeply. He could only hope that she wasn't so vulnerable as to still be flattered by Robert's attentions.

Deep down, he knew that was as much for his sake as hers. The thought of her caring about another man wasn't one he wanted to dwell on. Not for even a minute.

$\backsim$

Abigail's heart had stopped when Rebecca brought up Nate and Meagan and her broken engagement. She'd quickly looked to see Marcus's reaction to the words, but his expression didn't tell her a thing. He was still unreadable as they returned after the ride around town. He excused himself to talk to Ross, who was on duty. "I'll be right back."

Abigail nodded and turned to the rest of the group. "Won't you all come to church with me in the morning?"

"What time is it?" Jillian asked.

"We'd need to leave here at nine."

"Nine! Oh my. I'm not sure I can make that, dear Abigail. That is a little early for me."

"For me, too," Rebecca said.

"Oh, don't count on us either." Edward took it on himself to answer for the three men.

"Well, should you change your mind, just meet me here in the lobby."

Jillian giggled and shook her head. "All right. But don't count on it."

Reginald and Edward escorted them up to their rooms, telling Robert that they would be back down shortly.

"Good night," Abigail called to them all before she went to the desk to check for mail, only to be a little disappointed that there was nothing from home.

"May I see you to your room, Abigail?" Robert sidled up to her and asked.

"No, thank you, Robert. You have a good evening." Abigail realized that at one time she might have been flattered by his attentions, but she didn't want Robert Ackerman to escort her anywhere now. She'd let him take her to the Crescent Grand Opening only because Nate had asked Meagan to go, but that had been out of sheer desperation. Now she felt bad that she'd used him that way, but there was just something about the man that she didn't trust. She was very relieved when Marcus came up to her and took hold of her elbow.

"I'll see Abigail to her room. Good night, Ackerman."

The other man didn't bother to answer—nodding, instead. But Abigail didn't like the look in his eyes. It gave her the shivers.

While she and Marcus climbed the stairs and he saw her to her room, she couldn't help but wonder what was going on in his mind. She wanted to address the fact that she'd been engaged, in case it was brought up again. Her friends might say they didn't know she was here, but she just couldn't believe them. And it was doubtful that Jillian or Rebecca would not bring up the subject of her broken engagement again.

But she didn't have to bring it up. Marcus did it for her. He handed her back her key after checking out everything in her room and looked down at her. "Your tea got here before you."

"Good. I can use a cup."

"I'm sorry your friends reminded you of a hurtful time."

"I assume you mean my broken engagement. . .as they were so eager to talk about."

"It can't be easy to have it brought up in the way they did. Are you sure they are your friends?"

Abigail couldn't help but chuckle. "I've been wondering the same thing. But it is all right. I am truly glad that Nate and Meagan are happy. They were meant for each other."

"Well, if you are all right with it. . .I just don't like to see others purposefully set out to hurt another."

Abigail caught her breath, for she couldn't deny that she'd done exactly that to Meagan on occasion. She sent up a silent *thank-You* that the Lord had forgiven her for it, and she still prayed that Meagan would. But how could she judge her friends for something she'd been all too guilty of in the not–so-distant past?

"I'm hoping it wasn't done purposefully."

"Well, they are your friends, and you know them better than I do," Marcus said. "I am glad for your sake that it didn't hurt as much as it seemed intended to do."

"Thank you, Marcus."

"Will you be attending church tomorrow?"

"Of course."

"Good. I'll pick you up at nine."

"See you then." Abigail backed into her room.

Before pulling the door shut, Marcus said, "Enjoy your tea. And lock the door."

She turned the key and heard him say, "Good night."

"Good night, Marcus." Abigail leaned against the door for a moment before crossing the room to pour her tea. Then she went to the window and pulled the drape slightly open, barely enough for her to see out. It had become a sort of game to watch for Marcus leaving the hotel at night. Tonight he was just coming out from under the portico—much sooner than usual. She supposed it was because he'd talked to his agent before seeing her to her room. She waited until he looked up toward her window and then turned to walk down the street.

She let the curtain down and took a sip of her tea. She'd come to depend on Marcus more with each passing day—and probably more than was good for her. But she was so glad that he was there with her the last few days, even knowing that he didn't approve of her old friends. She was finding that she didn't much approve of them either.

Her worry was that Marcus might judge her by the company she had once kept. And still was keeping by what he could see. Marcus was so unlike the men in her social circle, yet she wondered if she would have seen the difference a month or so ago. No. She wouldn't. And suddenly, she realized why. She was the one who'd changed. Not them. She wasn't the same Abigail she'd been when she left Eureka Springs. Part of her problem with her friends being there was that they reminded her of the woman she used to be, and that was not something she wanted to think about or go back to being. Never again.

She took another sip of tea and opened her Bible. It had become a nightly habit she didn't want to break. And tonight, she couldn't wait to get started. She'd just realized that the changes in her were because the Lord was working in her, and the joy she felt at that knowledge kept her reading late into the night.

❧

Marcus looked forward to driving Abigail to church. Other than when he saw her to her room the last two nights, there hadn't been a chance for any real conversation between just the two of them. And after the dinner with her friends the night before, his opinion of them hadn't changed from the first day. Well, perhaps it had gotten worse, but that was all. The two women could be very catty on occasion. Abigail might be trying to give them the benefit of the doubt, but on more than one occasion, he'd heard them tell Abigail how sorry they were about her broken engagement. But the look in their eyes told him they really weren't that sad, and they seemed a little disappointed that she seemed to be doing quite well. The men in the group seemed no different than a lot of the rich men who frequented Hot Springs, looking for a good time and a way to spend their money. It was all he could do to keep his mouth shut as he listened to some of the conversations going on around him.

Marcus always loved Sundays, but he was especially thankful for today, in that he would have Abigail to himself for the ride to church.

"Will your friends be coming to church later?" he asked as he helped Abigail into his buggy.

"No. They probably aren't even up yet. They never have attended church much."

"Oh, I see."

"I did ask them to come today, though."

She sounded a little defensive, and he quickly apologized. "I'm sorry, Abigail. I didn't mean to sound judgmental."

"It's all right. They were talking about going sightseeing last night. I let them know that I'd be having Sunday dinner with friends."

"I'm sure Mother would have been glad to have them over," Marcus said. And she would have; of that he was positive.

"Oh, I'm certain she would have invited them. But truthfully, I could use a break from their company for a little while."

It did his heart good to hear those words. "They do seem to be quite busy—"

"Searching." Abigail interrupted.

"What?"

"They are all searching."

"For what, do you think?"

"For ways to have a good time, for ways to entertain themselves, for happiness. All kinds of things. But they never seem satisfied."

Suddenly, he felt he had a little more understanding of why, in Eureka Springs, she might not have been the woman he'd come to know. If she was spending most of her time with friends like the ones he'd met, she wasn't keeping very good company as far as he was concerned. Not at all. It was a puzzle to him that she was even part of their social circle.

"How did you become friends with them?" As soon as the words left his mouth, Marcus wished he could take them back. The color seemed to drain from Abigail's face, and she sighed.

"Jillian and Rebecca are friends from my school days. I can't remember when we didn't do things together. Reginald and Edward became part of the group later, and Robert is fairly new to the group. I've only known him a few years."

"I'm sorry, Abigail. It really is none of my business. You are just so different from them. I just wondered."

"It's all right."

But it wasn't. She still looked agitated when they arrived at church. Marcus thought Abigail looked about ready to bolt out of the buggy without his help. By the time they reached the inside, though, she seemed calmer. He'd try to think before he asked another question about her friends. It was obvious to him that she wasn't really comfortable with them being here in Hot Springs—but his questioning had made her even more uncomfortable, and his personal curiosity was no excuse. None at all.

❧

Abigail felt herself relax as she listened to the lesson and spent the afternoon with the Wellingtons. It was good to be with people who felt like family and who she knew really cared about her.

"How is your visit with your friends going, Abigail?" Mrs. Wellington asked over Sunday dinner.

"Fine. They are on the go a lot, though."

"I suppose they want to see what our town offers compared to what they are used to at home," Mr. Wellington suggested.

"Possibly," Abigail said, but she really thought they just came to find out how she was dealing with the heartache of knowing Nate had married Meagan. Thankfully, she was much better than they expected. For that matter, she was much better than even she thought she'd be by now.

"Abigail asked them to come to church, but they had some sightseeing they wanted to do," Marcus said.

"I'm sorry they didn't join you. I would have been glad for them to join us for Sunday dinner," Mrs. Wellington said.

Mrs. Wellington was one of the most gracious women Abigail had ever known, but she was more than a little relieved that her friends weren't with her. She wasn't sure what the Wellingtons would have thought of them. She didn't think they'd be any more impressed with them than Marcus was, and she didn't want them wondering about how they could be her friends as Marcus obviously had.

"There is a lot to see around here. Did they say where they wanted to go?" Mr. Wellington asked.

"They'd asked me about some places, and I suggested the Thousand Dripping Springs, Chalybeate Springs, and Mountain Valley Springs," Marcus said. "But the men seemed most interested in the McComb Racetrack."

Abigail was sure they were. And she wasn't going to let herself feel bad that she hadn't gone with them. Just because the old group from home was here didn't mean she had to entertain them or miss church and being with her new friends for them. After all, she hadn't asked them to come to Hot Springs. She would be nice to them, and she would spend some time with them. But she didn't have to revert back to the Abigail she'd once been. And with the Lord's help, she wouldn't.

By the time Marcus took her home, she was feeling more like the Abigail she wanted to be. She hoped that her friends were still out or that they'd retired to their rooms. It had been a good day, and she didn't want to run into them that evening. She was relieved that they weren't in the hotel lobby, and even though she would have liked to have spent more time with Marcus, Abigail didn't tarry downstairs for fear of running into them.

"I'm glad you were able to spend the day with us," Marcus said after he'd checked out her room. "My parents look forward to your company."

"It's become one of the highlights of my week," Abigail said. But she couldn't bring herself to tell him that seeing *him* was the highlight of each day for her.

"Mine, too." The look in Marcus's eyes had her heart skipping a beat. . .or two. He pushed away from the door frame. "Benson will be on duty tomorrow, but if you need me, have the desk clerk telephone me. They have the number. Otherwise, I'll be here around noon."

"Thank you, Marcus."

He grinned and grazed her cheek lightly with his knuckle. "You're welcome, Abigail. Good night."

"Good night," she whispered back.

She hurried to the window and watched until she saw him reach the street. But this time when he looked up, it was as if he knew she was watching. . .and he gave a little wave. *That man. His smile. . .his touch.* Abigail drew a sharp intake of breath. Why, she was. . . She turned quickly, stopping the thought she knew was there when a knock sounded on her door. She assumed it was her tea being delivered, but she was mistaken. She swallowed the moan that begged to escape at the sight of Jillian and Rebecca.

"My, you've been gone a long time," Jillian said, sweeping into the room.

"I spent the day with the Wellingtons."

"Oh? With Marcus or his parents?" Rebecca asked, taking a seat on the settee.

"With all of them."

"Then he really is a family friend?"

"Yes, he really is." She knew he was her father's friend, and she felt he was hers as well.

"Hmm. How close a family friend?"

"I don't see how that is any of your business, Jillian," Abigail said.

"Well, Robert has been wondering and wanted us to ask."

"It certainly isn't any of Robert's business."

"Abby, what is wrong with you?" Rebecca asked. "You've changed."

"And why would that be something wrong with me? Perhaps it's a change for the better." She couldn't help but smile at their expressions. It seemed she'd just given them a concept they couldn't understand.

"You really aren't that upset about Nate, are you?"

"I told you I was happy for him and Meagan."

"But. . .but. . .you never talked to us about it. You just up and left town."

"I am sorry I didn't see you before I left. And I was upset at first. But I've come to see that Nate and I were not meant for each other."

"But, Abigail, you loved him for so long." Rebecca looked at her in surprise. "How can you be over it so quickly?"

That gave Abigail pause for thought; she suddenly knew the answer, but she wasn't about to talk about it now. She just shook her head. "I really don't want to discuss it."

Abigail could tell Rebecca was frustrated that she wasn't getting an answer. Her huge sigh told it all. "I suppose we might as well go." Rebecca looked at Jillian. "You know how stubborn Abigail can be."

Oddly enough, her words didn't upset Abigail. Instead, she chuckled, garnering puzzled expressions from both women.

"You *have* changed," Jillian said. She leaned her head to the side and looked at Abigail. "And perhaps it is for the better after all." They exchanged a smile before Jillian motioned to Rebecca. "Come on. We aren't getting any more information out of Abigail tonight. We can talk tomorrow."

Abigail walked them to the door. "What did you all do today?"

"Just a lot of boring sightseeing," Rebecca said. "We did take a picnic from the hotel dining room, and that was nice. Other than that, it is about as boring here as it is at home on a Sunday."

"Maybe you should have come to church with me—that would have started your day off right."

Jillian looked at her closely. "Perhaps we should have. See you tomorrow. You'll meet us for lunch in the hotel?"

"All right. See you then." Her tea arrived just after they left, and Abigail was more than ready for a cup. It had been hard to avoid answering their questions when all she wanted was to be left alone with her thoughts. She hurried to get ready for bed, and then in her comfortable wrapper, she curled up on the settee with her tea and thought back over the evening and the answer to why she had gotten over Nate so quickly. There was only one answer: She had been more in love with the idea of loving Nate than she had been in love with him. She wasn't sure that what she'd felt for him was even love . . .not when Marcus Wellington could make her feel the way he did with just a smile, a look. . .or a touch.

Chapter 10

Robert Ackerman was waiting for Abigail when she came down to join the group for lunch the next day. "Everyone has already gone in and acquired us a table. I told them I'd wait for you."

He crooked his arm, and etiquette insisted that Abigail slip her hand to his forearm. But when he pulled her hand farther and put his other over it, she felt a chill pass down her spine. What was it about Robert that bothered her so? She glanced around quickly and found Ross watching from across the room. He nodded, letting her know he'd be there, and she relaxed somewhat. Marcus or one of his agents was never far away, and just knowing that gave her a feeling of security she'd never fully realized until now.

She and Robert were shown to the table where the others were waiting for them, and Abigail was relieved that the only two chairs saved were not next to each other. The girls had saved her a seat at one end of the table so they could talk to her, and the men had left Robert one at the other end. Breathing a sigh of relief, she greeted everyone warmly. "Good morning. . .or afternoon. Did you all have a good day yesterday?"

"We missed you," Robert said plaintively from the other end of the table. "I felt like a fifth wheel along with these four."

Abigail wanted to say he was the one who'd chosen to travel with the four-some. It wasn't her responsibility to keep him company. And then it dawned on her that it sounded as though he'd thought that once they got to Hot Springs, he wouldn't be the odd number in the group—and that must mean that he'd known she was there. She chose not to comment on that revelation, however. "It's a beautiful day today. What do you all have planned?"

"I wanted to do some shopping," Jillian said.

"We thought maybe we could do that and the men could. . .find something else to do," Rebecca said.

"Well now, that's not fair," Reginald said.

"Why not?" Rebecca asked. "We did what you all wanted yesterday. And we don't expect you to go shopping with us. Surely you can find something to do on your own."

Abigail couldn't help but giggle at all the sputtering from the men. She wondered if the long courtship Rebecca and Jillian each had with their beaus wasn't getting a bit old. After all, they'd been courting for more than a year now—in Rebecca's case, nearly two—and still no wedding dates had been set.

There was a bit of tension at the table as they ordered their lunch, and Abigail was more than ever convinced she didn't want to go back to Eureka Springs and run around with this crowd. Oh, she cared about them and would pray for them, but she no longer was interested in spending her days in boredom, waiting for the next exciting event to come along or someone to come up with a way to take one's mind off the fact that all they were really doing was searching.

"I wish you all had come to church with me yesterday."

Total silence fell for a few moments, and then Jillian spoke up, "I kind of wish we had, too."

The waiter brought their meals just then, and the subject was changed. Abigail wished she had the courage to ask one of the men to say a prayer, but from the way all except Jillian had looked at her when she'd mentioned church, she didn't think it would be well received. So, as she silently prayed for their meal, she asked the Lord to work in their hearts the way He'd worked in hers to show her that all that searching she'd been doing had really been for Him.

The conversation got back to the afternoon's activities, and the men decided to go visit one of the bathhouses. "You might want the desk clerk to see if you can get into a bathhouse. They stay pretty busy," Abigail said.

"What are you ladies going to do?" Reginald asked.

"We're going shopping," Jillian said.

"But you will join us at the opera house, won't you?" Robert asked.

"Oh yes, I forgot to tell you," Rebecca said, turning to Abigail. "The night clerk told us that Bailey's big production of *Uncle Tom's Cabin* is here this week until Saturday when Lillian Russell will be here starring in the title role of the comic opera *Patience*."

"I'll think about it. Perhaps I'll go."

Robert looked a bit perturbed that Abigail hadn't said for sure, but she wanted to talk to Marcus to make sure he could accompany her before she committed herself to going with them. She certainly didn't want Robert thinking he'd be escorting her.

She was very relieved when Marcus showed up just as they finished and entered the lobby. Abigail turned to Jillian and Rebecca. "I need to talk to Marcus a moment before we go shopping, all right?"

"Certainly. Why don't you see if he'd like to come with us tonight?" Jillian suggested. "The show starts at eight, and we'll meet for dinner here at six."

Abigail could have hugged the woman for suggesting that she do exactly what she intended to. But this way, she wouldn't have to answer questions about how she felt about him. At least she hoped not. Those were questions she wasn't quite sure she wanted to answer yet. "I might just do that."

"Jillian! Why did you do that?"

Abigail heard Robert's aggravated-sounding whisper to her friend, but she ignored it as she met up with Marcus, who'd been talking to Ross.

"Good afternoon," he said. "Did you have a good lunch?"

Abigail smiled but admitted truthfully, "I've had better. I'm going shopping with Jillian and Rebecca this afternoon, but they all want to go to the opera house tonight. Would you be available to escort me?"

"Of course I will. Ross will be watching out for you this afternoon, all right?"

"That will be fine."

He nodded and smiled. "Good. Have a good afternoon, and I'll see you this evening at. . .what time?"

"It starts at eight. But we're having dinner here at six. Can you join us then?"

"I'll be here."

Abigail's heart gave a little jump when he smiled and showed his dimple, and she found herself looking forward to the evening very much. "Good. I'll see you then."

❧

Marcus watched as Abigail went back to her friends. He gave them all a wave and turned to Ross. "She's going shopping with the ladies. Just keep an eye out, okay?"

"Sure. Long as I don't have to carry their bags, I'm happy." Ross laughed. "I'll let them get out the door and then stay out of sight."

"Abigail knows you'll be there, but it's better to try not to be seen in case her friends get curious. I'm going to do a little checking on a few things, and I'll talk to you later."

Ross nodded and went back to his paper reading. Marcus figured his men were more aware of what was going on in the town and country than most of the people who visited Hot Springs, with all the newspaper reading they did.

Marcus headed back to his office with the express intent of looking into Robert Ackerman's past. Something about that man set him on edge, aside from the way he looked at Abigail. Perhaps it was just his personality, but if there was something there—if Abigail was somehow in danger—he needed to find out.

Her other friends had all checked out. They were just part of the rich and, to his mind, idle: always in search of something more, something better. Abigail had been right. They were searching for all the wrong things. He was so thankful that she realized that now, because he didn't think she had in Eureka Springs.

Marcus looked over the scheduling of his agents. He'd insisted that they all get telephones put in their homes in case he needed to get in touch with them in a hurry. It had helped immensely when he needed to change schedules. He looked over the agents he had hired. He picked up the receiver and turned the crank to get the operator.

"Miss Opal? Could you get me through to the Morrison house?"

"Certainly, Marcus. Hold on."

Marcus waited to be connected to Ben Morrison, one of his best agents, who'd just returned from an assignment in Little Rock.

"Ben," Marcus said when he answered. "I need you to go to Eureka Springs. I need you to check out someone for me."

"Marcus, I can't do it. Doc says the baby can come any minute. I can't leave Melanie right now. I hope you understand."

"Of course I do. Don't worry about it. I hope everything goes well. Let me know when she has the baby."

"I will. Thanks, Marcus. I appreciate it."

"No problem. I'll get someone else." Although he didn't have a clue who—all his other full-time agents were on assignments. Luke came in just then from checking the mail and the telegraph office. Maybe it was time to give the young man another assignment. He'd been hinting that he thought he was ready to do some real investigating. Marcus couldn't really argue with that. He'd taught him about all he needed to know, and experience was the only thing he was lacking. Luke had been eager to learn all Marcus had taught him, and he was chomping at the bit to get away from his desk and into the field. It was time he put what he'd learned into practice.

"Luke, want to go back to Eureka Springs on assignment?"

His huge grin told Marcus all he needed to know. "Are you serious? Of course! What do you need me to do?"

"A little investigating."

If anything, the younger man's grin grew bigger as he nodded.

Marcus gave him what information he had on Robert Ackerman. "He may be clean. But I have a feeling there's more to him than he wants anyone to know about, so dig as deep as you can. If you have to go somewhere else to get more information, let me know."

"Yes, sir. I'll get on it. When do you want me to leave?"

"As soon as you can get packed and get on a train." Marcus opened the safe he kept in the office, pulled out some cash, and handed it to Luke. "This should see you until you get back, but if you do get low, telegraph me and I'll get some money to you."

"All right." Luke pulled out a pocket watch and looked at it. "There's a train leaving this afternoon. I'll go pack and catch it."

"Good. Let me know when you get there and keep me updated. If you find out anything I need to know quickly, telegraph me. Otherwise, I'll be looking for your report by mail."

"Yes, sir. You'll be hearing from me as soon as I get there."

Marcus watched Luke walk out of his office and knew he'd put the right man in charge. . .even if he was the only one he had available.

❧

For the most part, Abigail did have a good time shopping with Jillian and Rebecca. Still, she was finding that they just weren't quite as humorous or fun as they'd once been, and she had a feeling they'd certainly say the same about her. She took them to the shops she'd enjoyed going to with Sally, but they weren't very impressed.

"Don't you have a dress shop like Meagan's here?" Rebecca asked.

Jillian nudged her, but it didn't seem to faze her. "She's making quite a name for herself in Eureka Springs. I've ordered several things for this fall, but she can't get to them yet because she's so busy."

"Rebecca! I'm sure that Abigail doesn't want to hear about how successful the woman who stole Nate from her is!"

Only then did Rebecca act as if she didn't know her words could hurt. "I'm sorry, Abigail. But you did say you are happy for them."

Abigail took a sip of her tea and wondered if Rebecca was testing her. She was glad she could answer honestly, "I am happy for them now. But at first, I wasn't. I was devastated when I left Eureka Springs. But I've come to realize that a lot of the hurt I've gone through in my life has been caused by my own actions and choices."

"What do you mean?" Jillian asked.

Abigail shrugged. She wasn't sure she could trust her deepest feelings with these two women she'd once confided in. "Let me just say that the Lord has shown me a few truths about myself in the last few months."

"What kind of truths?"

"I've been able to see how self-absorbed I have been. To see that I was just putting lip service to my Christianity, that I was always thinking about myself and what I was going to do next that would be entertaining." Although her words didn't paint a pretty picture, Abigail wanted them to know that she wasn't the same person who left their hometown.

"All I was concerned with was what I wanted." *And how I could make Nate fall in love with me when I wasn't really in love with him. I only thought I was.*

That thought gave Abigail pause. That was exactly what she'd been doing. And how unhappy she would have been had all that happened? Two people who didn't really love each other married because of what she only thought she wanted! *Thank You, Lord, for making sure that didn't happen!*

"But Abigail, we've all done that. Just because you want to have a good time doesn't mean you are a bad person," Rebecca said.

"Of course not. But it is when it is all one is concerned with. When it takes away from enjoying doing for others, spending time in God's Word, and trying to live the life He wants me to live—"

"What has happened to you?" Rebecca said, looking at her as if she'd never seen her before. "You aren't the Abigail we knew."

"I'd say I'm sorry, Rebecca," Abigail said. "But that wouldn't be true. I like the person I'm becoming here in Hot Springs, and I don't want to go back to being the old Abigail."

"And who is the cause of all this change? Is it Marcus Wellington? I'll admit he's a very handsome man and would be a nice catch for any woman."

Rebecca just didn't understand, and Abigail doubted that she could make her. Although she agreed with everything Rebecca said about Marcus, her change wasn't because of him. She gave all credit to the Lord. "No. Marcus doesn't have anything to do with what's happening with me—except perhaps that I'm glad he didn't know me back in Eureka Springs. The Lord is the One who is changing me, and I'm ever so happy that He is."

Both ladies seemed at a loss for words, and Abigail had a feeling that she'd given them something to think about or that they didn't want to hear any more when Jillian said, "I guess we'd better get back to the hotel so that we can get ready for tonight."

"Yes, let's," Rebecca readily agreed.

Abigail was glad to go back, too. She almost dreaded the evening ahead and would have tried to bow out had it not been for the fact that Marcus would be with her. She'd told the truth that he wasn't the one who had anything to do with the change in her. . .but there was no denying that he had a lot to do with the fact that she was enjoying her stay in Hot Springs and had no desire to go home.

⋍

Abigail looked lovely when Marcus came to pick her up. She was dressed in a bluish green dress that brought out the color of her eyes and made her skin look like velvet, and he was more than proud to escort her back downstairs to meet her friends. "You look quite beautiful this evening."

"Why, thank you, Marcus. You look very nice this evening, too."

"Thank you." He pulled her hand through his arm and looked into her eyes.

He loved seeing the color creep up her neck onto her cheeks when he complimented her. It made her look even prettier.

Ackerman, Mitchell, and Fitzgerald were in the lobby when they got there, but it was Ackerman who hurried over and reached for Abigail's hand. He brought it to his lips, and Marcus's fingers itched with the urge to grab her hand out of his.

"You look lovely as always, dear Abigail," Ackerman said, looking deep into her eyes.

The man was a creep, and Marcus was relieved to see Abigail pull her hand away and put it behind her back.

"Thank you, Robert." She looked around the lobby. "Have Rebecca and Jillian come down yet?"

"Not yet, but they'd better hurry, or we are going to be late."

"We're coming," Jillian called from the staircase as she and Rebecca hurried down.

After a somewhat hurried dinner, they all went out to the tallyho the men had rented to take them to the opera. There was some juggling for position, with Ackerman obviously trying to sit by Abigail. The man succeeded, but as Marcus was on the other side of her, he didn't worry about it overly much. He had a feeling that Abigail didn't like the close proximity of the other man any better than he did. At least he certainly hoped not. As far as he was concerned, her friends couldn't leave Hot Springs soon enough. Especially Ackerman.

Chapter 11

By the time Marcus took Abigail back to her room that night, she was very relieved to get away from the people she'd once considered her best friends.

"Are you all right?" Marcus asked. "You were awfully quiet tonight."

She shook her head. "Sometimes I don't feel I know my friends anymore. I mean. . ."

"You aren't anything like them, Abigail."

Oh but she had been, and one of her biggest fears was that Marcus would find out just how much like them she had been. "We just don't seem to have as much in common as we once did," she answered honestly. "And Robert—"

"Is he bothering you when I'm not around?"

"He just. . ." She shivered. "I don't like it when he is close to me."

"Don't worry about it. I will take care of him."

Abigail's heart flip-flopped against her chest at the look in his eyes. "I—thank you. I don't know how much longer they will be here, and I just don't want to have to keep warding off his advances."

"You won't have to. The next time I see him, I will make it perfectly clear he is to leave you alone." Marcus pushed a loose curl from her cheek, and his touch sent her pulse to racing. "Don't lose any sleep worrying about Robert."

"I won't." Abigail sounded a bit breathless to her own ears.

"Sleep well." He handed her the key, and a current of electricity shot up her arm. "Lock the door."

She could only nod and do as she was told.

"Good night," Marcus said from the other side of the door.

"Good night."

Her tea arrived only minutes after she'd watched Marcus leave the hotel. She couldn't help but smile when she wondered what he'd do if she actually threw back the drapes and waved when he looked up. He'd probably grin that smile that made her heart beat double time and wave back.

She quickly got ready for bed and then poured herself a cup of tea. She sat down and took a sip and sighed. She wasn't sure how much longer she could spend time with the people she'd once considered her best friends without letting them know they no longer were. She had nothing in common with them now. Their constant pursuit of fun seemed childish, their constant gossiping about people they knew was irritating, yet. . .it hadn't been that long ago that she'd been just like them.

Had she really been as boring and self-absorbed as they were? Abigail's heart twisted in her chest at the truth that was there. Yes. She'd been all those things, too, and she certainly had no right to judge her old friends. Instead, she should be trying to help them, but how? Jillian was the only one who had seemed interested in the changes in her. Rebecca seemed disturbed by them. And Abigail wasn't even sure that the men had noticed, not that it mattered. The only man whose opinion mattered to her right now was Marcus Wellington.

Abigail sighed and took a sip of tea. The better she got to know him, the more certain she was that she was falling in love with him. But could he ever feel the same about her? Probably not if he ever found out what an awful person she'd been. Abigail slid to her knees and prayed, "Dear Lord, please don't let him find out. With Your help, I am no longer that woman, and I never want Marcus to know how selfish and horrid I was. In Jesus' name, I pray. Amen."

❧

Keeping in mind that she wanted to help her old friends see there was more to life than the search for excitement, over breakfast the next morning, Abigail asked Jillian and Rebecca to accompany her and Mrs. Wellington to the Wednesday meeting at church. Rebecca immediately turned down the offer, but Jillian took her up on it.

"I'd like to meet some of the people you think so highly of, and I noticed the free baths when we've been out and about. I think it's wonderful that some women are trying to help those who are coming for health reasons but can't afford to stay in the hotels."

"I'm not doing that much. But I love being around Mrs. Wellington and the other ladies who try to help others. You know, our mothers do the same thing in Eureka Springs. Wonder why we never got involved?"

"That is a good question, Abigail," Jillian said.

"Well, they are involved. They don't need us," Rebecca stated. Then she waved a hand as if that should be the end of the subject.

"There will always be a need to help others. Our parents won't always be here, Rebecca," Abigail said.

"Humph! What's wrong with you two? I wanted to go on a picnic today. The men have gone to look at some horses for sale, and I won't have anything to do."

"Come with us then."

But Rebecca dug in her heels. "No. I'll just visit one of the bathhouses and get a massage and then take a nap. See you both later."

"Don't mind her," Jillian said as they watched Rebecca flounce off. "I really want to come with you. I want to meet these people who've become your friends here. I miss you, Abigail, but you seem so happy here that I think maybe you should stay."

"I've been thinking of looking for a house. I do love it here."

"You aren't looking to become Mrs. Marcus Wellington?"

Abigail was suddenly at a loss for words. How could she answer that? It seemed Jillian had looked inside her heart and found her deepest wish. . .one she hadn't really let herself think about. "I—"

Mr. and Mrs. Wellington arrived just then to take them to church, and Abigail was saved from answering. *Thank You, Lord. I know the answer, but I don't want to put it into words right now.*

As always, Mrs. Wellington was gracious and very happy that Jillian was joining them. Jillian seemed to really like meeting everyone, and instead of going back to the Wellingtons for the rest of the day as Abigail usually did, the three women had lunch at a small café near Marcus's office.

"It is so nice to meet a friend of Abigail's," Mrs. Wellington said to Jillian. "We love having her here. You aren't going to try to talk her into going back to Eureka Springs, are you?"

"No, ma'am. I can't speak for the others, but I'm not. Abigail seems happier than I've ever seen her, and I think she should stay right here. Besides, if she's here, I'll be able to come and visit her when I need to get away."

Abigail had been holding her breath as Jillian spoke, hoping she wouldn't go into detail about how she'd changed. Now she realized that Jillian truly did care about her and what was best for her. She patted her friend's hand. "You'll be welcome anytime." It was nice to know that she meant it.

❧

Marcus was glad to know that Abigail didn't like Robert Ackerman's advances any more than he did. It would be his pleasure to put a stop to them. All he'd needed was to know that Abigail wanted them stopped as much as he did.

During the next week, he made sure that he interrupted each and every conversation Abigail and Robert had. It didn't matter if it was in the lobby of the Arlington or in the hotel dining room; Marcus was by her side at any sign of irritation on her part. Before long, he could tell from just a certain look or smile that she needed him. But the man was persistent; Marcus had to give him that. If Ackerman wasn't trying to get Abigail to sit by him, he was trying to get her to go for a walk to see the town at night. And no matter how many times Marcus heard Abigail tell him no, the man refused to be fazed.

Did these people have no life to go to back in Eureka Springs? They'd been in Hot Springs for nearly three weeks now. That they were wealthy was obvious from the way they spent money, but surely the men had businesses to return to. Marcus couldn't wait until the day he would hear them say goodbye. Why Abigail agreed to so many outings with them was beyond him, but at least she saved her Sundays for him and his family.

"I almost talked Jillian into coming today," Abigail said on their way to church that Sunday.

"Really?" Jillian bothered Marcus the least of any of Abigail's friends. She had manners and truly seemed to like being around Abigail.

"Yes. But she didn't make it down in time. I suppose she slept in again. Or Rebecca teased her so much that she decided not to come."

They'd arrived at church, and Marcus was helping her down from the buggy. "I know it would have been good for you to have her with you, but I have to admit I look forward to Sundays even more than usual."

"Why is that?"

He looked into her eyes and told her the truth. "Because it is the only day of the week I get to see you without them."

"Oh."

He wasn't sure if she was pleased at his answer or not, but he loved watching a warm flush of color deepen in her cheeks. As the day passed, he didn't think she was upset with his words, for she seemed to relax and enjoy herself as always with his family and the other church members his mother had invited for Sunday dinner.

The afternoon passed pleasantly as they played croquet and checkers and enjoyed lemonade and cookies. He hated to see it come to an end and hoped that he and Abigail wouldn't run into any of her friends when he took her back to the Arlington. At first, he thought he was going to get his wish, but before they were ten feet into the lobby, he heard Ackerman's voice as he came from across the room.

"Abigail! We've been waiting for you to get back. Come sit with us."

Marcus heard Abigail's soft moan as she turned to greet Ackerman. "You knew this is Sunday and I'd be gone all day."

Ackerman didn't even rise as Marcus and Abigail walked over to the group. "That doesn't mean we have to like it, my dear. After all, we did come all this way to see you."

"Oh? I thought you didn't know I was here."

"Yes, well, you are here, and so are we, and we missed you today."

"You all could have come with me." Abigail spread her hands to include the whole group.

Marcus couldn't remember when he'd heard so much twittering as they made excuses.

"I overslept," Jillian said. "I meant to come."

"Well, we were out late, and I hadn't even cracked an eye open by ten o'clock this morning," Edward said.

Marcus was certainly glad they hadn't come along, but he knew he shouldn't feel that way. It was Sunday, after all, and it was hard to come away from one of the minister's sermons and not have much to think about. It always did him some good, so he couldn't see how it would do Abigail's friends any harm.

"You know I don't attend church often, Abigail." Robert's smile turned Marcus's stomach. He didn't know how much more of this man he could take.

"Now how would I know that, Robert?"

When Abigail's eyebrow went up, challenging the man to answer her, Marcus bit his lip to keep from laughing.

"We've known each other for a while now, Abigail," Robert said, sounding condescending to Marcus.

"We don't know each other that well. Anyway, it was a good lesson today."

"Yes, well, perhaps next Sunday, we'll go with you." That same tone. Marcus had to clench his fist to keep from using it on the man. *Lord, help me here. Please.*

"Yes, we should do that," Jillian added. "If we aren't gone by then."

"Are you talking about leaving?" Abigail asked.

"Well, we've been thinking it is time to get back home," Rebecca said.

"Yes, there are several events we don't want to miss," Reginald said. "You should come back with us."

"Oh yes, Abigail. Please, won't you do that?" Rebecca asked.

"No." Abigail smiled and shook her head. "I'm not ready to go back yet. I like it here."

Marcus breathed in a silent sigh of relief. Deep down, he'd been worried that Abigail might decide to go back with them.

"But your home is there, your family is there, and *we* are there," Robert said. "Surely you miss all of that."

"I do miss my family. But I've just been able to see you all. I don't want to go back right now."

Robert folded both arms together and sat back in his seat. Marcus had never seen a grown man pout before, but there was no other way to describe the look on Ackerman's face.

"Well, I will be glad if you decide to come back, but you seem very happy here, and I'm glad for you," Jillian said.

"I don't understand you at all," Rebecca said. "It's a nice town and all, but it's not home!"

Abigail chuckled. "I believe you are all getting homesick."

"Not quite yet," Reginald said. "But we must return at some point soon."

"Yes, soon," Rebecca said. "I don't have that many cool weather clothes with me, and the nights are getting chilly."

"You could always buy a new jacket," Jillian said.

"I could, but I don't want to. I'm having Meagan Brooks make one for me."

"Oh."

Silence descended on the group at the mention of the Brooks name, and Marcus found himself holding his breath, waiting to see what Abigail would say.

"I don't blame you. She's quite talented."

He could have laughed out loud at the look on Abigail's friends' faces at her compliment for the woman who'd married her ex-fiancé. They just couldn't seem to believe she was being so gracious.

No one seemed to know what to say, and Abigail turned to him. "I think I'm ready to go up now. I'll see you all tomorrow."

Robert was immediately on his feet. "I can see Abigail to her room, Wellington. I'm on the floor above her, and I'm not going back out tonight. No need for you to bother yourself."

"Thank you but no, Ackerman. I will see Abigail to her room, and it is certainly not a bother. Good night, everyone." Marcus clasped Abigail's elbow and steered her toward the staircase.

"Thank you," Abigail whispered as he led her away from the group.

But they weren't left alone. Ackerman hurried up behind them and grabbed Abigail's free arm.

"Look, Wellington. Abigail and I have been friends a long time. I'd like to see her up."

Marcus threw his hand off Abigail's arm, gently pulled her hand through his arm, and looked Robert in the eye. His voice was soft but firm. "I will see that the lady gets to her room safely, Ackerman. I always do."

"Oh?"

"Yes."

"Should I take that to mean you are courting our Abigail?"

Marcus had about had it with Robert Ackerman, and it was time to set some limits. "I don't think that is any of your business, Ackerman, but you can take it to mean anything you want. Just be clear on this. Your advances to Abigail are unwelcome, and I will be the one you answer to should you make any more."

Robert backed off, his hands raised. "I understand. Completely."

"I'm not sure you do, but as long as you keep your hands to yourself and quit bothering Abigail, everything will be just fine."

Marcus hoped Abigail wasn't upset with his implication that they were courting. But if it kept Robert away from her, that was what mattered. He wasn't sure how she felt about it, as she was silent as they ascended the stairs and walked down the hall to her room.

❧

Abigail's heart was pounding so loud she was afraid Marcus might hear it. For a moment, she'd thought he and Robert might come to blows. But it looked as if she wouldn't have to worry about Robert bothering her anymore.

Marcus checked her room out as usual. When he came back to the hall and handed the key back to her, he surprised her by asking, "Are you upset with me?"

"Not at all. Why would I be upset with you? I think Robert finally got the message not to bother me anymore, and I can't thank you enough, Marcus. It was getting to the point that I dreaded seeing him at all. Truthfully, something about him frightens me a little. I don't know what it is, but—"

"Don't worry about him. I won't let him get near you again."

"Thank you," she whispered, and her pulse began to race at the look in his eyes as he bent his head.

"You are welcome." His head dipped toward her, and he lifted her chin to look into her eyes. Her eyes closed the moment his lips touched hers, and Abigail realized her heart had wanted him to do just that for weeks. She couldn't keep from responding, and he pulled her into his arms and deepened the kiss. She wasn't sure who ended it, but she had a feeling it would be a long time before she quit feeling the sweet touch of his lips on hers.

"I. . ." For the first time since she'd known him, Marcus seemed to be at a loss for words. He took a step back and then reached out and gently touched her lips. "I. . .I'd better go. Sleep well, and lock your door."

Abigail backed into the room, her eyes never leaving his. He pulled the door shut, and she inserted the key and turned it with trembling fingers.

"Good night, Abigail." His voice was deep and husky from the other side of the door. "Sleep well."

"Good night, Marcus." She didn't know how she was going to sleep at all after that kiss. Abigail sighed and leaned against the door, her hand over her heart. She was in love with Marcus Wellington. And whatever she felt for Nate Brooks was nothing compared to what she felt for the man who'd just claimed her heart with one kiss.

Chapter 12

Marcus came back downstairs, hoping not to run into Abigail's friends again. But there they were, still chatting and laughing. He had to wonder if they were waiting until he came back down. Now that he thought of it, many times the men were just leaving the hotel when he came back from seeing Abigail to her room.

The idea that they were waiting to make sure that he did come back down quickly didn't sit well with him. How dare they think that he and Abigail—*I have no proof that is what they've been wondering. None at all.* Still, he had a feeling that was exactly what they'd been doing.

He took a moment to say good night to them and went to talk to Ross, who was on duty. He didn't even bother to keep his voice down, as the only people in the lobby were he, Ross, and Abigail's friends.

"Keep an eye out," he said to Ross. "If anyone bothers her, you know what to do."

Evidently, Ross had enjoyed witnessing the earlier exchange between Marcus and Robert. He grinned up at Marcus. "I certainly do."

"I'll be looking for your report tomorrow."

"You'll get it," Ross said.

When Marcus turned to leave, he nodded once more to Abigail's friends, and he couldn't miss the look of dislike on Robert's face. Well, too bad. Marcus didn't trust the man one bit, and he hoped Robert realized that he was having someone watch after Abigail.

The men might not be going out tonight—after all, it was Sunday—but he had tailed them one night after the ladies retired for the evening, just long enough to know that they spent most of their nights gambling at one of several clubs in town. That was one of the downsides of a growing resort town in which rich people thought they needed the same kind of entertainment they had back home. Some of those amusements would be better left back there, as far as Marcus was concerned.

He walked out of the hotel and looked up at Abigail's window. The light was still shining, and he wondered if she was having her tea and if she was thinking of the kiss they'd just shared. He knew he wasn't going to forget it anytime soon. He shouldn't have kissed her. . .because now that he knew how sweet her lips tasted, he'd be wanting to kiss her again. And again. Of that he had no doubt.

⚓

"So, Marcus is afraid I'll make myself a pest, is he?" Robert asked Abigail first thing the next day as soon as she came downstairs.

Reginald and Edward began a conversation with each other, but Abigail had a feeling they were listening to every word as she asked, "What do you mean?"

"It appears he's hired someone to make sure I don't bother you." Robert nodded in the direction of Nelson, who'd come on duty that morning. "I'm sure he's been watching me. There was another here last night."

"There are men sitting in this lobby all the time, Robert. I believe your imagination has gotten away from you."

Jillian and Rebecca came down just then, and they all headed toward the dining room, with Robert taking the lead, obviously out of sorts.

"What is he upset about now?" Rebecca asked.

"He thinks Marcus is having him watched."

"Well, it wouldn't surprise me any if he is, after last night when Marcus told him he'd be seeing you to your room," Jillian whispered to her as they were being shown to their table. "Marcus doesn't want him around you."

Abigail's heart did a little flip. After that kiss she and Marcus had shared, she hoped Jillian was right.

"Then again, maybe he's going to watch Robert on his own." Jillian nodded in the direction of the hotel lobby.

"What?" Abigail turned to see Marcus enter the dining room with a smile. Her stomach felt like a hundred butterflies took flight as he crossed the room to their table. He wasn't looking at anyone but her.

"May I join you?"

"Of course."

He pulled up a chair beside Abigail, and Robert had no choice but to move his chair down. "Since your friends think they might be leaving soon, I decided to take off work the next few days so I can accompany you wherever you want to go with them."

"Why how nice of you, Wellington," Robert said with a sarcastic tone.

"It is very nice of you, Marcus. We'll enjoy your company," Jillian said.

"Thank you, Jillian."

The others in the party added their welcome to Marcus, but it was obvious that Robert especially wasn't pleased as he kept silent and gave his attention to the menu.

"Well, what shall we do?" Rebecca asked in a voice that sounded slightly whiny.

"What haven't you seen yet?"

"There can't be much more," Edward said. "I think we've been to every bathhouse in town, and we've been to the races—if you can call it that. We got to see some trial runs, but the season actually ended at the McComb Racetrack before we got here. We've been to the opera several times."

"We're going again on Friday evening," Reginald said.

"Well, what can we do today?" Rebecca asked. "I'm always up for shopping, but I think I've been to every shop in town."

"How about a picnic tomorrow?" Marcus suggested. "The weather is very pleasant in late September, and I know several places that you might not have been to yet."

"I like picnics," Abigail said. "We can have the hotel pack us one."

"Yes, we did that the first Sunday we were here," Jillian said. "It was very good."

"Let's do that, then," Rebecca said.

The waiter came to take their orders, and once he left the table, the subject changed back to what to do that day.

"Why don't we just take a ride around the countryside?" Abigail asked. "I haven't seen it all. The National Reservation is large; perhaps we can take a ride up Hot Springs Mountain and see the view of Hot Springs from there."

Several other ideas were thrown out, but Abigail found she didn't really care what they decided to do. Marcus would be with them all day, and that alone made anywhere they might go more special.

❧

On Friday afternoon, Marcus sat at his desk and rubbed the bridge of his nose as he pored over the detailed reports Luke Monroe had brought to him. He'd received a telegram from Luke on Wednesday evening, letting him know that his suspicions were on target: Robert Ackerman had a past, and it wasn't pretty. Luke had left Eureka Springs that same evening and was sitting across from him now.

"Good work, Luke."

The younger man beamed at the compliment. "Thank you, sir. I'm glad I could get some usable information for you."

Marcus looked at the paper in front of him and nodded. "I'd call this usable. First thing we have to do is talk to the chief of police. I put in a telephone call earlier." He glanced at the clock on the wall. "He's supposed to be here anytime. I didn't want to go there. I don't want Ackerman or any of his friends to see me go into the police station. We can't let Ackerman know that we're on to him."

"No, sir, that wouldn't be a good thing. I was afraid to put all the details in a telegram, but I worried all the way back that maybe I should have."

"I needed the proof you've brought me before I could do anything. I did ask the chief to see if he had anything on Ackerman, but nothing turned up."

"And of course that's because he's going by a different name now."

Marcus nodded. "You know, Luke, you did as good a job as any of my seasoned agents would have. Not everyone would have dug as deep as you did to come up with Ackerman's true identity. You've learned well."

"Does that mean you'll be using me in the field a little more often?"

"It definitely does." Marcus was proud of the young man. He had the makings of a great agent and had already proved himself.

"I'll be ready."

A knock on the door signaled the police chief's arrival, and Marcus welcomed him into his office.

"Wellington, you don't ask for a meeting unless it's something worth my while. What have you got?"

"Have a seat, Chief." Marcus motioned to the chair beside Luke in front of his desk. "This young man has just come back from Eureka Springs after investigating a man who's here in Hot Springs. A Robert Ackerman, formerly known as John Baxter. Ever heard of him?"

"Actually, that name is familiar, but I don't know from where. Who is he?"

"A dangerous man." Marcus slid Luke's report and a WANTED poster over to the chief. "And someone you might be interested in putting behind bars. I certainly am."

Marcus had put an extra man to watching Abigail ever since he'd had the run-in with Ackerman on Sunday evening. Now he was more than glad he had, but he wouldn't rest until the police had him in custody. The chief scanned Luke's report. "I see he's been living off the wealth of others for quite a while. He's apparently married several rich young women and inherited their wealth after they all died of mysterious causes." He looked up from the paper. "All except for the last one. She was shot, and he's wanted for her murder. He's been wanted for murder for over two years?"

"Yes, sir," Luke answered.

"And this man is the Robert Ackerman you asked me to check out." The chief looked at Marcus. "The one who is staying at the Arlington?"

"He's one and the same."

"Is he there now?"

"Last I heard from my agent, he and several of his friends had gone out of the hotel." Thankfully, Abigail wasn't with them. His mother had invited Abigail and her lady friends over for tea, so at least he didn't have to worry about her being anywhere near Robert. "I do know where he will be this evening though."

"Well, let's come up with a plan. This man needs to be put behind bars, and the sooner the better. I don't want a murderer running around my town for one more day."

Marcus was pretty sure he wanted it even less than the chief did. "I've been thinking about that. . . ."

Abigail opened the door to Jillian and Rebecca, who had come to Abigail's room to have Bea help them with their hair before going to the opera that evening. The young maid had been able to make a little extra money while they'd been there. While Abigail had wanted to learn to do some things on her own and had actually needed Bea less as time went on, Jillian and Rebecca had used her services in helping them get ready quite often since they'd arrived. Bea was happy to make the extra money, and they were happy they had someone to take care of them.

"I do hate to leave tomorrow," Jillian said as she waited for Bea to finish with Rebecca's hair. "Do you think you'll be home for Christmas? Surely you'll be home for that!"

"I don't know," Abigail said. She did miss her parents; she also wanted to see Natalie so badly, but there still had been no response from the child she loved as her own. Still, she didn't want to go back to Eureka Springs. She especially didn't want to go back if Natalie didn't want to see her. "Maybe my parents will come here. The Wellingtons would love to have them come for a visit, and that way I could stay here."

"But don't you ever want to come back?" Rebecca asked.

"I don't know. I do like it here very much."

"You like Marcus Wellington," Rebecca stated.

Abigail looked in the mirror and pinched her cheeks, trying to give an excuse for the color that rushed up her face. "Marcus is a family friend. I've told you that."

"Yes, you did say that. And I believe he is," Rebecca said. "But I think there is more to it. Robert does, too."

"Oh, Robert! He's just upset that I don't want to have anything to do with him."

"Mmm. But—"

"Rebecca, leave Abigail alone about all that. I wouldn't want Robert's attentions, either. And how she feels about Marcus is none of our business."

Dear Jillian. If there was one person she was going to miss, it would be she. She'd proven to truly be a friend. Abigail smiled at her now as Bea began to work on her hair. Perhaps it was time to change the subject. "Did you enjoy tea at Mrs. Wellington's?"

"I did," Jillian said. "Very much."

"So did I," Rebecca said. "She is a nice lady, and so were the others she'd invited to meet us. Too bad she didn't do that when we first got here. Most likely, we'd have been invited to their homes, too."

Have I always found something to complain about? Abigail wondered. It seemed Rebecca couldn't say anything nice about anyone without adding something negative. Surely she wasn't always that way. Abigail was more than relieved when the two women went back to their room to finish getting ready, and she sent Bea with them, happily. At least she'd finally learned how to dress herself!

❧

Marcus ran a finger along the starched collar of his shirt. He hadn't paid a bit of attention to the musical. All he'd been thinking about was keeping Abigail safe when the plan he and the chief had come up with went into action. When the curtain came down on the final act and the gaslights were turned up, he was relieved to see the agents he'd assigned to the opera house in position. They were there in case Ackerman became suspicious before they got outside. Marcus knew police officers were stationed just outside the door, waiting for him to give the signal.

He and Abigail were behind Ackerman, who was behind the others in the group. Marcus noticed Ackerman looking around as if he suspected something was up and held his breath as they went through the doors to the outside. Once they'd cleared the doorway, he stepped in front of Abigail to shield her in case there was trouble and called out, "Ackerman!"

When the man turned, four policemen immediately surrounded him and had him in cuffs. "What is this? What's going on! Wellington, you have something to do with this?"

The chief came up to him. "John Baxter, you are under arrest for the murder of Marie Baxter."

"What! My good man, I am Robert Ackerman. Just ask my friends here. They'll tell you!"

"His name is—," Reginald began.

"John Baxter," the chief interrupted. "He's only been going by Robert Ackerman for about two and a half years. How long have you known him?"

"About two years," Edward replied.

"And do you know where he came from?"

"Well. . .I . . ."

"He came from Kansas, where he shot and killed his last wife." The chief turned back to Robert. "Take him away, boys. Let's put him where he belongs."

"You had something to do with this, didn't you, Wellington?" Robert yelled as they took him off.

Marcus didn't bother to answer. He breathed a sigh of relief that no one, especially Abigail, had been hurt. He turned to look at her. She and her friends couldn't seem to take it all in.

"I. . .can't believe it!" Rebecca shook her head. "I just can't."

"He murdered someone? How can that be?" Jillian asked.

"I—" Abigail shook her head. "I don't know what to say. He—I—"

"Let's all go to that little café around the corner and talk about it," Edward said. "I can't believe he's been part of our crowd and we never suspected that he could be a criminal."

"Could they have the wrong man?"

"I don't think so," Marcus said. "There is a lot of evidence against him."

"Is Robert right?" Reginald asked. "Did you have something to do with his arrest?"

"I told the chief I knew where he'd be tonight."

"Then you helped, didn't you?" Edward stated.

"And if you knew a murderer was right under your nose, you wouldn't have?"

"Why—I suppose I would."

"Let's get off the street and go talk," Rebecca said.

"I don't want to go anywhere but back to the hotel," Abigail said. She looked up at Marcus and asked, "Will you see me back to the hotel, please?"

"Of course."

"I'm much too wound up to sleep," Jillian said. "I—we need to decide if we are leaving tomorrow or if we should stay. . . ."

"I'll see Abigail back to the Arlington," Marcus said.

"Are you sure you won't come with us, Abigail?" Jillian asked. "We're just getting some coffee and dessert."

"No, thank you. I'm not up to it tonight," Abigail said. "Knock on my door and let me know what you decide, or if it's too late, I'll see you tomorrow."

As the others headed in one direction, Marcus and Abigail headed toward the hotel. But when he pulled her hand through his arm, she looked up at him and said, "I want to know it all, Marcus. Now."

Chapter 13

Marcus chuckled. He'd had a feeling Abigail would have some questions. He just prayed she wouldn't connect it all back to the fact that he'd been investigating her along with her friends. "What do you want to know?"

She shook her head and shrugged. "I'm not sure. I knew that I didn't like being around Robert. . .but that he was a murderer? I went to a ball with him in Eureka Springs once! It's just so hard to believe."

She shivered, and Marcus pulled her a little nearer. "Are you cold?"

"No. I'm just so appalled that he could do something like that. I had no idea. None of us did."

Marcus didn't doubt that for a moment. That she was truly stunned to find out about Robert was obvious, and he had to admit that he was relieved she had no prior knowledge of the man. But she was paler than he ever remembered seeing her. "Look, why don't we go into the dining room and have some tea to settle your nerves?"

She hesitated only a moment before she nodded. "Yes, that will be fine. A cup of tea sounds good. I just didn't want to discuss it all with the others."

Nor did he. Marcus asked for an alcove table so that they wouldn't be disturbed, and once the waiter had taken their order, he turned to Abigail. "I did have a hand in getting him arrested. I admit that I haven't liked him from the first. Just something about him put me on edge."

"I can understand that. But how did the police know about him?"

"I told them."

"How did you know about him?"

"I had him investigated. I sent an agent to find out what he could about him."

"Oh. . ."

"Abigail, when you've been in this business as long as I have, sometimes you just get a feeling about people."

"I suppose that makes sense."

The waiter returned with their tea, and Marcus waited until he'd poured them both a cup and left before continuing the conversation. "I'm sorry if my having him checked out bothers you. I just became worried about your safety when he was around, and I—"

"Oh, I'm not upset with you, Marcus. I. . .it's just hard to believe that someone I saw often socially is a murderer." She shivered again. "How—what exactly did he do?"

"He's made a career out of marrying rich young women. Three, to be exact. But they died from mysterious causes, and we think he poisoned them. All except for the last one. He shot her and ran."

"Oh. . ." Abigail put a hand to her chest. "He just shot her?"

"Yes. After making sure he cleaned out all of her accounts."

"I. . .I'm at a loss for words."

"I know. That kind of temper. I knew he'd been pursuing you, and I wasn't sure what he was capable of. From the first, something about him just. . . didn't set well with me." He didn't tell her that a lot of his dislike for the man was personal. He had never liked the way Robert looked at Abigail. . . not from that first day. He'd come to Hot Springs to find her. Marcus had no doubt of that now.

"Go on," Abigail prompted.

"Once my agent got back into town with the information, I contacted the police chief, and we came up with the plan for tonight. I didn't want one more day to pass with him in this hotel with you."

"Well, now that we know what kind of man he is, I certainly wouldn't want to have him here either." Abigail shivered. She sipped her tea and was silent for several minutes before continuing. "Thank you for. . .watching over me, Marcus. I know Papa asked you to, but I don't think I've ever told you I appreciate that instead of leaving it all to your agents, as you could have, you've done a major part of looking after me when I'm sure you had other things that needed your attention. Not only that, but you've put up with my friends when I know you haven't really wanted to. I. . .thank you."

Marcus reached across the table and took her free hand in his. "Abigail, you don't need to thank me. You are a fam—"

"Family friend. I know you say that. But when I got here, only my parents were the family friends. And I was a very spoiled, bitter woman. I'm sure that you wondered just what you'd gotten yourself into by telling my father you'd keep me safe."

"I think you were going through a rough time." Marcus hesitated and then admitted, "Your father told me you'd just gone through a broken engagement."

"Oh? What else did he tell you?"

He hurried to assure her that her father hadn't given him her life history. "That you needed to get away and that you'd be checking into some business for him."

He could see her relax and felt like a heel. What would she do if she knew he'd had her and the rest of her friends investigated? That he knew she wasn't the woman she'd been when she arrived in Hot Springs? How would she feel knowing that he knew a lot about her, but it didn't come from her father? Should he tell her now?

No. She'd been through enough just finding out a friend of hers was a criminal. He didn't need to stress her more right now. But he had to tell her before she began to put it all together. And he had to pray that she would forgive him when he did.

❧

As Marcus saw her to her room, Abigail felt totally safe and cared for. Something about being with this man made her feel special. That he'd had Robert investigated because he was concerned about her safety gave her hope that he might care about her as more than just an. . .assignment.

She'd canceled her nightly tea order on the way out of the dining room. She'd enjoyed sharing her tea with Marcus, although he only drank one cup to her two. It was a nice way to end the evening, and she hoped that once her friends went back to Eureka Springs, they might be able to end an evening like this more often. Of course it could be that once her friends left town, she'd see less of Marcus, too. That thought didn't set very well with her. Not at all.

Marcus took her room key and checked everything out for her as usual, and Abigail realized how much safer she felt knowing he always made sure her room was safe.

"Here you are." Marcus handed the key to her. "I hope you sleep well after all the commotion this evening."

"I think I will. Thank you for seeing me back safely."

"You're welcome." He leaned against the door frame. "Are you sure you are all right? You still look a little pale."

"I'm fine. It is just a shock to know that we've had a criminal in our midst . . .and that we befriended him."

"I'm sure it is."

"What will happen to him now?"

"I imagine he'll be taken back to Kansas to stand trial."

"Which is what he deserves."

"Yes, it is. Are you going to be all right?" Marcus tipped her chin to look into her eyes, and her heart remembered the last time he'd done that. It had ended with him kissing her. . .his head dipped toward her now, and her heart began to pump at double time. Surely he could hear it. She closed her eyes—

"Abigail! You *are* still up!" Jillian and Rebecca came rushing down the hall toward her room. "We were hoping you would be. You should have come with us!"

Marcus moaned and stood straight. "Your friends have the worst timing. . . ."

Her heart did a flip-flop at his words. She didn't like the interruption any better than he did.

"I felt a little better by the time we got back, and we had tea here," she said, explaining why she and Marcus were just now getting to her room.

"Maybe we should have come with you," Jillian said with a sly grin.

"You could have." Abigail raised an eyebrow at her friend. "I believe you were the ones who wanted to go elsewhere."

"You're right," Jillian conceded with a giggle.

"I'll let you ladies talk over the events of the evening and check in to see how you are in the morning."

"Good," Jillian said. "We can tell you good-bye then, Marcus."

"We've decided to leave on the afternoon train," Rebecca explained.

"Oh?" Abigail tried not to sound too happy, but she truly wouldn't be sorry to see them go.

"Yes. Reginald and Edward are ready to get back. Besides, it would just seem. . .strange to stay now, with Robert in jail," Rebecca said.

"And they can't wait to get home and tell everyone about what happened," Jillian added.

"Oh, Jillian, you act like we are a bunch of gossips. You can stay here if you want." Rebecca flounced into Abigail's room.

Marcus backed away and gave them all a salute. "I'm sure you all have much to talk about. I believe I'll leave you to it. Good night." He smiled at Abigail. "I'll see you tomorrow."

"Good night." Abigail couldn't blame him for making a quick exit. She didn't want to be in the middle of this conversation. Jillian followed Rebecca into Abigail's room, and she had no choice but to join them.

"I just can't believe that Robert is a criminal!" Rebecca said, dropping down on the settee and throwing an arm over her forehead. "Surely they have the wrong man."

Have I always been that dramatic? Abigail wondered. "I don't think they do, Rebecca."

"How could we not have known he was that kind of man?" Jillian asked.

"Because, *that* kind of man goes to all kinds of lengths to make sure no one does know."

"I suppose so. But it's just so. . .disturbing."

"What all did Marcus know? Was he in on the arrest?"

"I believe the police chief wanted his assistance."

"And he put us all in danger to capture him? Surely they could have found a way to do it when Robert was alone."

"And when would that have been, Rebecca?" Abigail asked. She didn't like the implication that Marcus didn't care about their safety when she knew he did. "The police had people all over the place. Not to mention that Marcus was right with us. I'm sure we were in no danger—no more than we've been in all this time we've accepted him into our homes, anyway."

"Abigail is right," Jillian said.

"I suppose," Rebecca grudgingly admitted.

An hour later, Jillian and Rebecca finally went to their room. They'd discussed Robert's arrest from beginning to end at least three times and why none of them had seen what kind of man he really was. Abigail was weary from hearing it, but it was hard to turn her mind off as she got ready for bed. She was very relieved that Robert was no longer there to frighten her. The events of the evening left Abigail with mixed feelings. On one hand, she was appalled to find out about Robert. And she was disgusted that she'd had anything at all to do with him. Yet she was thankful that she wouldn't have to put up with any more of his advances. No wonder she'd been frightened of him. Maybe it was because her relationship with the Lord had strengthened and she was finally listening to the instincts He gave her. At least she hoped they were right because she was beginning to think that Marcus might actually care about her, too.

She knelt beside her bed and prayed, "Dear Lord, thank You for this day. Thank You for letting Papa ask Marcus to protect me. I know I fought it at first, but I was wrong. He has done a wonderful job of keeping me safe. Thank You for letting him find out about Robert and for helping to capture him before he hurt anyone else. Please watch over Jillian, Rebecca, Reginald, and Edward on their way home. I pray that they let You work in their lives as You have in mine, Father. I believe Jillian wants You, too, and I pray that the others will, as well. Please watch over Marcus and his family, and thank You for bringing them into my life. If it be Your will, please let Marcus care about me the way I care about him. I love him so. In Jesus' name, I pray. Amen."

Chapter 14

When they all gathered in the Arlington dining room for lunch the next day before her friends left on the afternoon train, Abigail was more than a little pleased that Marcus joined them. Of course, the talk was still all about Robert.

"Edward and I went to see him this morning, and they've already taken him off to Kansas!" Reginald said.

"Why would you do that?" Abigail asked.

"You went to see him?" Rebecca asked. "Why? He's a—"

"I don't know." Edward sighed and shook his head. "We just felt we had to find out more, I suppose. To be truthful, I'm glad that we didn't see him. I have no idea what I would have said. I feel he played us all for fools."

"We were taken in, to be sure," Reginald said. "But I was surprised that he was gone already."

"I imagine the chief didn't want to chance his escape. No one likes the idea of a murderer on the loose," Marcus said.

"True, true," Reginald agreed. "How did you become involved, Wellington?"

Marcus shrugged. "I had a feeling about him from the first, and I sent an agent to find out what he could."

"It was that easy? Why hadn't he been found out before now?"

"I'd assume it was because no one else became suspicious enough to check into his background."

The waiter brought out their food just then, and the conversation stopped until he'd left.

"You sent an agent? What kind of agent? What exactly is it you do, Wellington?" Edward asked.

Suddenly, Abigail realized how truly self-centered her friends were. None of them had ever inquired about what Marcus did for a living. Not one. They must have thought he was one of the wealthy with time on his hands just like they were.

"I own Wellington Agency."

"And. . .it is what kind of agency?" Reginald asked.

"It is a detective/protective agency."

Reginald sat back, seemingly stunned. It was all Abigail could do not to laugh. How shallow they were. Had they but asked...

"You investigate people for a living?"

"Yes, if there is a need. My agency also protects clients. I assumed you knew, but that was probably egotistical on my part. Although my firm is getting more well-known all the time, it will never be the size of the Pinkerton Agency."

"I assumed you all knew, too. I'm sorry." Abigail looked at Marcus. "I should have told them."

"No need, really."

"Well, not unless we're the ones being investigated." Reginald laughed. "Of course, we aren't wanted for anything other than having a good time. It's good to know who to call on should we ever be in need of your services."

"Do you only have the one office here?" Rebecca asked.

"At present. But I'm getting ready to open one in Little Rock, and I'm thinking about opening up one in Eureka Springs, too."

"My, what interesting stories we have to tell back home," Edward said. "I'm assuming you've been protecting our Abigail while she's here, but why? She never needed protection at home."

"Yes, my firm is making sure Abigail stays safe while here. At home in Eureka Springs, she had her father and friends"—Marcus looked Edward in the eye—"and she knew almost everyone in town, but she'd never been to Hot Springs, and it was new to her. And, last but certainly not least, she is a family friend, after all. That is all the reason I'd need to watch over her."

"Yes, well, that's been quite obvious during our visit. Not something more the two of you want to tell us, is there?"

Abigail's heart stopped when her gaze met Marcus's. The look in his eyes was for her alone. She felt it deep inside.

"If there's anything we feel you need to know, Edward, we'll telegraph you," she said.

Rebecca laughed. "I think you've been properly put in your place, Edward! Let's change the subject. Talking about Robert gives me the shivers. When do you think you'll be coming home, Abigail? Surely you'll be there for the holiday season. I'm sure your parents are expecting you for Thanksgiving, and that's less than two months away."

"I'm not sure. I'll let you know when I do, though."

"Yes, we must keep in better contact now that we know where you are," Jillian said. "I will miss you so!"

The talk turned to their plans for the holidays and how many events were planned, but Abigail didn't feel left out. She had no desire to attend most of the events they talked about. For the present, she only wanted to be here...

where the man she'd come to love sat next to her. He bent toward her now and whispered, "I know you are going to be lonesome without your friends for a while, at least. Would you have dinner with me tonight?"

"That would be very nice, Marcus. I'd love to." There was nothing she'd rather do.

❧

No one was happier to see Abigail's friends off at the train station that afternoon than Marcus. And he was more than a little thankful that Abigail was standing beside him and not on that train, waving back at him with them. He couldn't bear the thought of her going back to Eureka Springs, and it was time to tell her how he felt. But when he did, he had to tell her that he'd investigated her. That he knew all about her life before she came to Hot Springs. . .and he just wasn't sure how she was going to take it all. *Dear Lord, please let me know when and how to tell her.*

"Thank you for seeing them off with me, Marcus," Abigail said as he saw her back to the hotel.

"You are welcome."

Abigail checked with the desk clerk and was pleased to be handed a packet of letters from home.

Marcus walked her to her room and, after checking everything out, he asked, "Will you be all right until I pick you up for dinner? Would you like to go see my mother?"

"I always love seeing your mother, but Jillian and Rebecca kept me up late last night. I think I'll just rest for a while and read my mail. I may need to answer some letters."

"All right. I didn't want you feeling too lonesome with everyone gone."

"I'm sure I'll feel a bit at loose ends for a few days. . .although to be truthful, I was ready for them to go. All except for Jillian—I do hate to see her leave. I found out that she is a true friend."

"I'm glad. But I know Mother and Father will be glad to see more of you, too."

"Spending Sundays at church and with your family have been the highlight of my week. I do wish my friends had come to hear some of John Martin's sermons while they were here. I think if Jillian had stayed a little longer, she would have. . .but the others. . ." She shook her head. "But it's not them who have changed. It's me."

Marcus knew she was right, but now wasn't the time to tell her. He could only pray that the Lord would show him when that was. "I'll be back to take you to dinner at seven, then."

"I'm looking forward to it."

Marcus's heart swelled at her words, and he knew he'd be counting the hours before he saw her again.

❦

Abigail undid the packet of letters and shuffled through them. There was one from her parents and. . .her heart turned over when she saw the name of the sender of the next letter. Nate had answered her letter! Had he forgiven her? She was afraid to open it for fear that he had not, but she had to know. Her fingers shook as she slit it open with her letter opener. She sat down at the writing desk and pulled out the letter:

> *Dear Abigail,*
> *I thank you so much for your letter. Of course I forgive you—I know that you never meant me harm. My question is, will you forgive me? I should never have asked you to marry me knowing that I loved Meagan. It was wrong of me, and I am so very sorry for the pain I caused you. I know that you have always had Natalie's best interests at heart, and I know how much she means to you. Please know that Meagan and I have been explaining much to her. . .and I know that she loves you.*
> *From your letter, I know that you will be glad to know that Meagan and I are very happy, and we wish that for you as well. We pray that you will find someone who loves you in the way you deserve—for you have much love to give. You will always be welcome in our home, and we hope that you will return soon. Your mother and father miss you a great deal.*
> *Thank you again for your letter.*
> *Sincerely,*
> *Nate*

Abigail noticed a page behind the first. It was a letter from Meagan. If anything, Abigail's fingers shook even more as she began to read:

> *Dear Abigail,*
> *Thank you for your letters to us all. Please rest assured that you have been forgiven. As I've come to hear more about you and your help with Natalie through the years, I understand even more how much she means to you. Please know that you are always welcome in our home, as Nate said in his letter. You always will be. As Natalie's aunt, you are family. She loves you and misses you a great deal. May God bless you and*

keep you. We do pray that He will bring someone in your life to make you as happy as we are.

Sincerely,
Meg

Abigail found that she couldn't stem the tears of happiness that flowed. It was several minutes before she could see well enough to open the next letter. It had no name as the sender on it, but it was postmarked Eureka Springs; she prayed that it was the one she needed most of all. She opened it, and her heart leaped at the realization that this one was indeed the letter she'd truly been waiting for. She had to keep wiping at her eyes as she read the childish handwriting:

Dear Aunt Abby,
   I do forgive you. Please forgive me. I know it wasn't your fault that Mommy fell down the stairs. You were trying to save her, too. Like you saved me. I know that you love me, and you didn't cause me to fall down the stairs. I ran too fast and tripped. Please don't blame yourself. I love you, too. Please come home soon.

Love always,
Natalie

Finally, Abigail knew she'd been forgiven. Her Natalie still loved her. Abigail gave in to the tears and let herself cry long healing sobs. *Thank You, Lord.*

⁓

When Marcus arrived to take Abigail to dinner, she opened the door to him with the most beautiful smile he'd ever seen. She'd never looked lovelier. The dress she wore was different shades of purple, although he was sure it had some fancier name. Whatever it was called looked beautiful on her. Her skin glowed, and her eyes were shining in a way he'd never seen before. Maybe her friends should have left a week or so ago, if their going had this kind of effect on Abigail.

"You look beautiful tonight," he said.

"Thank you." She gathered her bag, and after making sure the door was locked, they headed downstairs. Marcus had made reservations for them and asked for an out-of-the-way table that overlooked the street. Abigail liked looking out at the streetlights, and he wanted somewhere fairly quiet. Last night had been the only evening in weeks that he'd had her to himself for any length of time, and they'd spent that talking about Robert Ackerman. Marcus wasn't going to miss her friends at all.

They were shown to a corner table that had a view of the street yet was more private than some of the others. He held Abigail's chair for her and then sat down across from her. The waiter placed menus in front of them and then left them alone.

"Were you able to rest this afternoon?" She looked. . .more refreshed and alive than he could ever remember.

"I didn't take a nap, but I can't remember when I've had a better afternoon. The letters I received gave me joy."

Marcus wanted to ask about them but didn't feel he had the right to yet. And once he told Abigail about looking into her past, as he knew he must, he might never have that right.

✎

Abigail had never experienced a more perfect night. She didn't know if it was because of the forgiveness she'd received from her letters or from Marcus sitting across from her. She had a feeling it was a combination of both. From the time Marcus had picked her up, she'd felt more special than she ever had in her life. The look in his eyes told her that he found her attractive, that he was happy being with her, too. She was beginning to believe that she could put her past behind her and look to a future.

She'd let him order for her, and they had the same meal they'd enjoyed on the first night they'd eaten together. Only this time, it felt special—as if it were their meal, their evening.

"I have to tell you that I wasn't real sorry to see your friends take off." His dimple flashed as he grinned at her.

She couldn't help but laugh. "They can be quite—"

"Irritating to be around—I'm sorry, Abigail. I shouldn't have said that. I'm sure they aren't irritating to you, but it got a little tiring not being able to. . ." Marcus stopped and shook his head. "Never mind. I guess I just resented the fact that I rarely saw you without them."

At his admission, Abigail's heart turned to mush. He'd missed being with her. . .just as she'd missed him. Hope soared inside that what she was feeling—what she hoped *he* was feeling—was real and not just a dream.

Chapter 15

Marcus sat beside Abigail in church the next day, disgusted with himself. He hadn't been able to bring himself to tell Abigail about looking into her past the night before. It had been such a perfect evening—one he'd remember forever. He'd told himself that he'd waited this long; surely he could wait a little longer.

The sermon was one he needed to convince him he had to tell Abigail everything. Minister Martin preached on secrets and truth. The verse that seemed to speak to Marcus's heart was Luke 8:17. *"For nothing is secret, that shall not be made manifest; neither any thing hid, that shall not be known and come abroad."* He could not put off letting Abigail know he'd had her life looked into any longer. She would eventually find out. He knew that. But even more, he didn't want to keep a secret from Abigail ever again, and he wanted her to know she could tell him anything.

He would tell her tonight when he took her back to the hotel. It was time. But in the meantime, he was going to enjoy the afternoon with her at his parents' home. He loved Sundays. It was the only day of the week that he was able to spend the whole day with Abigail.

Now he watched her from across the table and knew without a doubt that this was the woman he wanted to marry. And he had a feeling his parents wanted the same thing for him.

"Are you going to miss your friends, dear?" his mother asked Abigail.

"Not terribly. I will miss Jillian the most. But the rest of them are easier to take in small doses, I've found. I'm sure they feel the same about me after this visit."

"I don't know how anyone could tire of being in your company, Abigail," Marcus's father said. "We enjoy you immensely."

"Well, I think I've changed from the friend they counted on me to be. I. . . have changed in the last few months, and although I like the changes, I'm not certain that they all do."

"We all grow at different paces. . .in all kinds of ways."

"It was time I did some changing," Abigail said. "And I believe I had to leave home to do it. I'm not sure that I ever would have if I'd stayed in Eureka Springs."

"Well, I know you will want to go back to see your parents, but we'd love to see you make your home here."

"All of us would like that," Marcus said, his gaze catching Abigail's and holding it. He watched the delicate color flush her cheeks and hoped that what he thought she might feel toward him was right.

The afternoon went by much too fast, as the days were getting shorter, and after sharing a light supper with his parents, they decided it was time to head back to the hotel. It had turned cooler out, and his mother insisted that Abigail wear one of her light jackets on the way back.

"Are you warm enough?" Marcus asked as they headed back to the hotel.

"Yes, thank you. It's a lovely evening, isn't it? I love this time of year." The streetlights were being lit as he drove down Central Avenue, and lights were being lit in houses up the hillside.

"Would you like to take a drive, or are you too tired?"

"I'd love to take a ride."

Marcus steered the buggy past the Arlington, taking it to the right at the Central Avenue and Fountain Street split, then following Park Avenue past the Waverly Hotel and the Hays House, which was undergoing renovations. He turned and made the circle back.

"Oh, it's lovely at night from up here!"

"Yes, it is." *But nowhere as beautiful as you are.* Her eyes were sparkling as bright as the stars she was looking at. Marcus wanted to tell her his thoughts, but he had to be truthful with her. The longer he put it off, the more he feared she'd never forgive him. When they arrived back at the Arlington, he wanted to delay the moment of truth as long as he could and thought about asking if she wanted to go to the dining room for a cup of tea. Instead, he walked her to her room as always, checking it out and then coming to stand in the hall beside her. "If you aren't too tired, I'd like to talk to you about something."

"No. I'm not tired. What do you want to talk about?" Abigail asked.

Upholstered benches had been placed here and there in the wide hallway, and he motioned her to one. "Would you like to sit?"

"Do I need to?"

"I'm not sure how you are going to take what I'm about to say."

"Let's sit, then."

Marcus led her to the bench and sat down beside her. "Abigail, there is something I should have already told you."

"What? What is wrong? Is there more about Robert?"

"No. No, this has nothing to do with him. It has to do with you."

"With me?" She looked at him with a question in her expression. "What is it?"

Marcus found he couldn't sit still. He got up and paced in front of the bench. "I'm afraid I'm not very proud of myself."

"What have you done?"

"I'm not sure it's what I have done as much as what I have not done."

"Marcus! What are you talking about? Tell me."

He dropped down on the bench beside her and took one of her hands in his. "Robert isn't the only one I had checked out."

"The rest of my friends—you investigated them, too?"

"I did. And not only them—"

Abigail jumped to her feet, pulling her hand from his. "You checked into my background, too?"

He hesitated. Oh, how he wanted to deny it. But he couldn't. He looked her in the eye. "I did. I wanted to know more about you so that—"

"No! I don't want to hear any more. You know all about me. You know how—"

"Abigail, there was no—"

"No. I can't believe you didn't tell me—"Abigail rushed into her room and slammed the door.

"Abigail. Please, listen to what I have to say."

"Go away, Marcus. Just go away."

He thought he heard her begin to cry, but he couldn't stand outside her room and pound on the door until she opened it. He couldn't compromise her reputation that way. "I'm sorry, Abigail."

Silence answered him from the other side of the door.

⌒

Abigail let the tears flow. All her hopes of a future with Marcus were gone. Had never really been—not after he found out what kind of woman she'd been back home. She readied herself for bed without even realizing she did, her thoughts on all that Marcus must have learned about her.

The maid arrived with her nightly pot of tea, and Abigail motioned for her to set it on the table.

"Are you all right, Miss Connors? Can I get you anything?"

"No. Please. Just. . .thank you. . .but just go. I'm all right."

"Yes, ma'am."

Abigail poured a cup of tea but found she couldn't drink it. She sat but found she couldn't sit still. She paced her room. Back and forth in front of the fireplace. What was she to do now? Her heart twisted so tightly she thought it would surely break. She'd known Marcus was protecting her because her father asked him to. . .but she'd begun to feel that he had come to care for her just as she did him. It no longer mattered that he'd started out looking after her because of her father.

But now. . .to find that he'd had her investigated, asked questions about her, found out what a horrid, selfish person she was. She shuddered. All her dreaming about a future with him had been just that. A dream. There was no way a man like him would fall in love with a woman like she'd been. How could he see her as the woman she'd become now after all he'd found out? And how could she stay in Hot Springs knowing all that he knew?

After a sleepless night, Abigail got out of bed as soon as it was light outside. At some time in the middle of the long night, she'd come to the conclusion that it might be time to go back home. She'd only thought it would be hard to stay in Eureka Springs and watch Nate and Meagan start a new life. To stay here and see the disappointment Marcus must feel after just learning about how selfish, conniving, and hateful she'd been. . .

No. She couldn't do it. She had to leave. Much as she loved Hot Springs, she couldn't stay under those circumstances. Couldn't watch what might have been caring for her turn to disgust. She hurriedly dressed and then pulled the cord to alert the desk that she wanted service. Then she began packing. She knew there was a midmorning train to Eureka Springs because her friends had debated taking it or the later one. She wanted to be on the earliest one she could get.

When the maid came up, she was pleased to see it was Bea, but she was sad, too. She'd come to like the young woman. She had written a letter of recommendation to the hotel manager, suggesting that he put Bea on full-time when an opening came up. And she'd left a note with a large tip for her. That was the least she could do.

"What is it, Miss Connors? You are up awfully early!"

"Yes, I've decided to go home. I need to have the clerk procure me a ticket on the morning train to Eureka Springs. Would you let him know? And then can you come back and help me pack?"

"Of course. But oh, I do hate to see you go! I thought that maybe you'd be marrying and staying in Hot Springs."

Abigail turned quickly to keep Bea from seeing her tears. That was exactly what she'd been hoping for, too. "I guess that isn't to be."

❧

Marcus hadn't slept at all. He'd tossed and turned until he finally flung the covers off and got up to pace his room. But that did no good, either. Finally, just before dawn, he'd gotten dressed and gone for a walk, praying for an answer to his distress. Surely Abigail would hear him out today. Last night, she'd never let him tell her how he felt about her, never let him explain that none of her past mattered. Of course, he really couldn't blame her. For the first time, he realized how invasive his profession could be and how he wouldn't like it if someone had been poking into his past for no reason other than that they just wanted to know.

It gave him pause. He knew he provided a needed service. Had he not had Ackerman investigated, the man could still be free to hurt someone else. And what he had found out about Abigail's other friends was only because of wanting to know more about her. But he shouldn't have looked into her past. Her father had given him all the information he needed. Yes, he wanted to know why she was so sad, and though he'd wanted to help her, he should have asked her. . .not gone about it the way he had.

Before he got to the Arlington, he knew something was wrong. Nelson was pacing back and forth outside the hotel.

"I had the desk clerk ring through to the office for me and had Luke see if you were in your apartment. Ross followed Miss Connors to the train station. She left a half hour ago. She had the clerk reserve a ticket to Eureka Springs for her. I have a hack hired. Let's go!"

Both men hurried to the hack, and Marcus didn't even ask Nelson why he thought he should be going, too. At the moment, all he could think of was stopping Abigail from taking that train. "To the train station as fast as you can get there!" he told the driver.

Both passengers were flung to the back of their seats as the driver proceeded to do just as Marcus had asked. When the driver reined the horse in at the station, Marcus left payment to Nelson. He'd settle up with him later. He ran into the building and scanned the crowd of people either just coming in or getting ready to leave. Finally, he saw Ross motioning to him several yards ahead.

"Where is she?"

"Over there." Ross nodded across the room where Abigail was sitting, her head bowed and her eyes closed. "Her train isn't due in for about twenty minutes."

Marcus sighed in relief. She was still here. "Thank you, Ross."

He prayed with each step he took. *Dear Lord, please let her hear me out. Please let her forgive me. I ask Your forgiveness, too. And I ask that if it be Your will, I can convince her to share her life with me.*

He took the seat beside her, and she didn't even look up. He braced himself for the possibility that she might run from him, and then he took a deep breath. "Excuse me, miss. I'd like to ask your forgiveness if you can find a way to give it to me."

Abigail opened her eyes and started to rise. Marcus put a hand to her shoulder. "Please hear me out, Abigail. Please. I love you so."

She did stand then, shaking her head. "No. How could you? You've just found out all the bad there is to know about me."

Marcus jumped to his feet, his hands on her arms, looking deep into her eyes. "None of that—"

"You know how selfish and manipulative I've been in the past," she continued. "You know how I tried to get my sister's husband to marry—"

"No, Abigail. Don't—"

"—me when he loved someone else," she continued as if she didn't hear him. "You found out how I was just like the rest of my friends, only wanting to have—"

Marcus couldn't stand hearing her talk about herself that way. He stopped her the only way he knew how. He pulled her into his arms and pressed his lips against hers, stopping her words and trying to show her that none of what he knew mattered. Finally, she responded, and he deepened the kiss. It was several moments before he raised his lips from hers, and then he looked into her eyes. "I love you, Abigail. With all my heart. *None* of what I found out matters. You aren't that woman, and you haven't been for months."

"But—"

His fingers stilled her lips. "No buts. I love the woman you are. I shouldn't have looked into your past. But when you got here, you were so sad. . . . My only excuse is that I wanted, needed to know why. But I had no right. I should have asked you, not taken it on myself to find out. I knew as soon as I got the report that you weren't the same woman you'd been when you left Eureka Springs. That was made even clearer when your old crowd came into town."

"You didn't just find all this out when you looked into Robert's past?"

Marcus steeled himself for her wrath. "No. I knew before they ever got here. And I watched as you changed, a little each day, into the woman I've fallen in love with. Please, Abigail. Don't go. Please forgive me and give me a chance to win your love."

❧

Abigail felt her heart would explode with joy. Marcus loved her. And he'd fallen in love with her, knowing about her past. She shook her head. It was too good to believe.

"Oh, please don't say no, Abigail," Marcus said. "Just think about it—"

Her hand came up to cup his jaw. "I don't need to think, Marcus. I love you, too. I thought that you couldn't love me because—"

Marcus claimed her lips once more, cutting off her words and convincing her of his love. When he raised his head, he looked into her eyes and said, "No more talk about your past. From now on, there is only the future. Please, Abigail, will you do me the honor of becoming my wife?"

"Oh, Marcus, yes. Oh yes, I will." She stood on tiptoe and sealed her promise with a kiss meant to leave him with no doubt that she meant every word.

Epilogue

October 16, 1886

Abigail had no desire to go back to Eureka Springs for the wedding. As soon as possible, she wanted to be married in Hot Springs, in the church where she'd begun to change and where she'd fallen in love with Marcus. She'd waited much too long for Nate to fall in love with her. She didn't want to wait one moment longer than she had to before becoming Mrs. Marcus Wellington.

She wrote home and asked her mother and father to come and bring the dress Meagan had made for her. She didn't want to wait to have another made, and neither did Marcus. They just wanted to get married as soon as possible. She'd hired Bea to come work for her and Marcus as housekeeper in the home they were having built. It would be ready to move into when they returned from their wedding trip to Europe.

They were married on a crisp fall day, and Abigail was overjoyed to have her family there to share the day with her. Marcus's parents were trying to talk hers into coming back for Thanksgiving, and Abigail hoped they'd stay through Christmas, too.

But what made her heart sing and made the day even more perfect as she walked down the aisle toward her groom was that Natalie went before her, sprinkling flower petals along the way, while Nate and Meagan sat beside her parents.

To be given so much—forgiveness from those she'd hurt so badly and the love of a man who loved her as she was. Her heart overflowed with happiness as she and Marcus said their vows, and her hand trembled as he slid an emerald ring that had belonged to his grandmother on her finger. All her dreams were coming true.

As soon as the minister declared them husband and wife, Marcus claimed her lips in a kiss that sealed their promises to each other. Her heart felt as if it might burst with happiness as they turned and walked back down the aisle. When they arrived in the church foyer, her new husband pulled her into his arms and whispered, "I love you, Abigail Wellington," just before his lips claimed hers once more.

Abigail kissed her new husband back and thanked the Lord above for the blessings He'd rained down on her—especially for forgiving her, for changing her, and for giving her a love all her own.

A LOVE TO CHERISH

Dedication

To my Lord and Savior for showing me the way,
To my family for encouraging me along the way,
I love you all.

Chapter 1

Eureka Springs, mid–January 1902

Becca Snow entered the home she'd lived in for most of her life, wondering if she'd live there for the rest of it. She took off her winter coat and hung it on the coatrack, hoping to slip upstairs without being seen.

But the pocket doors separating her sister's dress shop from the rest of the house were open, and her mother had the best hearing in town. "Becca, dear. Come have some tea with us, and tell us about your day," she called.

Becca sighed and forced a smile to her lips as she entered the room and took the cup of tea her mother had already poured for her. Afternoon tea had been a family tradition ever since she could remember. "Good afternoon, Mama, Meagan, and Sarah. My day was fine." It was just a day as all of them had become for her. No problems, but no excitement or joy of doing her job anymore. It seemed she just went from one day to another. "How was your day?"

"Busy but good," her sister Meagan said.

Becca took a tea cake to go along with her tea and sat down in one of the chairs flanking the settee where many of the shop's customers sat and went over her sister's designs or the latest fashion magazines before placing an order.

Meagan had started her dressmaking business sixteen years earlier to help out her family after their father died. She continued with the business even after she married banker Nate Brooks, and she'd made a name for herself in Eureka Springs. The dress shop had thrived, with their mother and sister Sarah coming into the business as well. Becca had helped out in the shop after school and on Saturdays until she went to college, but she'd never wanted to be a seamstress or designer like her sisters. Now, with Meagan's daughters, fourteen-year-old Lydia and twelve-year-old Eleanor, becoming involved in the sewing, Becca was glad she hadn't wanted to go into the business. Not to mention that Sarah, who'd been married to Mitch Overton for two years, had found out she was expecting a few months ago. If the baby was a girl, then she might well want to be part of the business, too.

The shop had made a very good living for them all and provided travel abroad to visit the fashion houses in Paris and even for Becca's education so that she could become what she'd always dreamed of—a teacher. And she would always be thankful. She did love teaching, but it was harder to go about her normal routine now that her dreams had died along with her fiancé.

Becca sipped her tea in silence as conversation flowed around her. She couldn't think of anything to add to it and was hoping that she could escape before her mother or siblings commented on her quietness. No wonder her life was boring—she'd become boring, too.

"Becca? Dear, are you all right? You haven't heard a word we've been saying."

She looked up to see her mother looking at her with concern in her eyes. Her sisters were watching her closely, too. "I'm sorry. I must have been wool-gathering." Becca stood and put her cup back on the tray. "I'll take these to the kitchen for you."

"Not now, dear." Her mother took the tray from her. "Please sit back down. We need to talk to you."

"You all look so serious. What did I do?"

"You haven't done anything, Becca. We just worry about you," Sarah said.

That brought tears to Becca's eyes. "I'm sorry."

"Oh, Becca. We're sorry that you've had to go through so much sorrow. We just want to help," Meagan said. "Mama told me that you feel you might do better if you could get away from Eureka Springs."

"I've wished that I could. At least for a while," Becca admitted. "It's not that I want to be away from you all. I would miss you. But. . .it's just so difficult to . . ." She swallowed hard and looked at her sister. "And I don't know—will I ever feel happy again—anywhere?"

Her family quickly gathered around her in a group hug, and that was more than she could take. Becca gave in to the tears she thought she'd used up months ago. Several minutes passed before she had them under control, and once she was down to a sniff or two, her mother poured another cup of tea— her answer for any stressful situation—and brought it to her.

"We have an idea that might help you, dear. We were talking about it earlier today."

"What is it?"

Meagan pulled out a newspaper. "Natalie's aunt Abigail knows you've been struggling and sent this to us. There is an opening for a high school teacher in Hot Springs. Or at least there was a week or so ago."

Becca took the newspaper and scanned the help-wanted ad in the *Sentinel Record*. She tried to tamp down the hope that sprang in her heart. "Do you think the position is still available?"

"I don't know, but I can have Nate find out if you want me to."

Becca looked at her mother and sisters. "I think I need to get away for a while. It's not you all. It's this town and the. . ." She couldn't keep her voice from wobbling, and she hated that she wasn't stronger. She took a deep breath and finished. "The memories."

Her mother hugged her once more. "I will miss you terribly, Becca. But I want you to be happy, to get your joy of life back. If moving to Hot Springs will help, then I want you to go. It's not all that far by train. My goodness—we've been to Europe and back."

"Thank you, Mama," she whispered. "But what about you? I don't want you to live here all alone."

"That's something we were going to tell you at dinner," Sarah said. "With the baby coming, Mitch and I have been talking about buying a home. The small apartment we are in now won't be large enough for long. Mama said we could move in here until we could save enough money to buy something. So we would be here with Mama, and you wouldn't have to worry about her—not that you should anyway. Meagan and I would make sure Mama is all right."

"I know. But still—"

"Girls, I am perfectly able to take care of myself. But Becca dear, Sarah is right. There is no need for you to worry about me. She and Mitch will be here with me."

Becca could hardly believe that she might really get her wish. She looked at her older sister. "Will you have Nate see what he can find out?"

"I'll get him on it right now." Meagan hurried to the telephone and rang through to the operator. After getting the bank's switchboard, she was connected with her husband. Several minutes of conversation followed before she hung the receiver back on its hook and turned to her family.

"Nate is going to send Marcus Wellington a telegram. He'll get back to us quickly about it."

Becca was almost afraid to hope, but if the position was still open, it seemed this might well be the answer to her prayers. Her stepniece, Natalie, Nate's daughter, came into the shop just then, bringing a couple of beautiful hats she'd designed. Unlike Becca, she'd wanted to go into the fashion business along with the rest of the Snow family, but her true love and talent lay in making lovely hats to go with her stepmother's creations.

Once she found out that Becca was thinking about applying for a teaching position in Hot Springs, she became very enthusiastic. "Oh, Becca! That would be wonderful. I love going to Hot Springs. It's about time I visited my aunt and uncle. If you are there, I'd have even more reason to pay them a visit."

Becca could feel a bud of excitement beginning to open but was afraid to give in to it. What if the position was already taken or she didn't get it? Instead she busied herself with taking the tea tray to the kitchen, setting the table while her sisters helped their mother with dinner, and waiting for Nate to pick up Meagan.

By the time he got there, however, the possibility that she could start a new life away from the memories of Richard and what could have been had her praying that it would be so.

When Nate arrived, Meagan brought him back to the kitchen, and Becca turned from taking the biscuits her mother had made out of the oven.

"I telegraphed Marcus, and he's already gotten back to me. The teaching position is still open, and they haven't had many applications at all. With this being the middle of the school year, there aren't that many people looking for a job. But they need someone soon. One of the married teachers had to resign because she is. . .with child. The principal has been teaching the class, and he's desperate to hire a good teacher."

"You mean there is a possibility that I might get the position?"

"Becca, if you want it, I'm almost certain you will get it," Nate said. "Marcus was going to talk to the principal tonight and said he'd get back to us first thing tomorrow. He and Abigail will give you a high recommendation, I know."

For the first time since Richard had died, Becca felt a flicker of joy. *Dear Lord, please, if it be Your will, let me get this teaching position.*

～

When Becca got home from work the next day, she learned that Nate had word from Marcus. He'd talked to the principal himself and also to the school superintendent. Going on the Wellingtons' recommendation and desperate to have a teacher, they were quite willing to hire Becca—provided she could be there in two weeks' time.

"I'm not sure I can do that," Becca said. "I can't leave my school in a bind."

"I saw Molly Bryant at the soda shop just the other day. She is back home and hoping to find a teaching position next year," Sarah said.

"Really?"

"Ring her home and see. If she hasn't found anything yet. . ."

Becca hurried over to the telephone and asked the operator to connect her to the Bryant home. In moments she heard Molly's voice on the other end of the line.

After welcoming her sister's friend home, Becca got right to the point. "Sarah says you want a teaching position next year."

"Yes, I'm hoping to find one," Molly said.

"Would you be willing to start earlier, if possible?"

"I'd love to. But I talked to Superintendent Mallard just the other day, and he said there wasn't anything now."

"Well, there will be once I give them my notice. I'm taking a position in Hot

Springs, if the school can find someone to take my place."

"Really?"

Becca smiled at Molly's squeal of excitement and held the receiver away from her ear for a moment. "Really. But I haven't given notice yet. I'll do that first thing tomorrow. May I give your name as a possible replacement?"

"Oh, Becca, yes, please do."

"I will be glad to." Thrilled was more like it. If they allowed Molly to take her place, she could be beginning a new chapter in her life very soon.

"And please thank Sarah for mentioning me."

"I will. Hopefully by this time tomorrow, we'll both have what we want." Becca ended the conversation and turned back to her family with a grin. "I think it's all going to work out."

She prayed that it would. By the time she went to bed that evening, her hopes were high that she could get away from the daily routine that brought back so many painful memories. Each time she passed the police station or the bank or saw Richard's parents at church or in town, memories of him came flooding back. The past year had been so very hard.

She'd made it through one holiday after another—but just barely. She'd managed to get through Thanksgiving by being thankful for the family who had gotten her through the worst of her sorrow. But Christmas had been hard, and now the New Year was here...but it loomed long and empty for her without Richard. She didn't know if moving away would help, but she desperately wanted—needed—to find out.

❧

The next afternoon Becca raised her hand to knock on the principal's door and paused to whisper a prayer. "Dear Lord, please let Mr. Johnson see how much I need a change and be open to letting Molly take my place. You know how badly I need to get away."

Her light knock was answered with a "Come in."

She smoothed her skirts and took a deep breath before entering. The secretary was at her desk right outside the principal's inner office.

"Becca, what brings you here this afternoon?" Caroline Green asked.

"I need to speak with Mr. Johnson, if he's not too busy, please."

"I'm sure he'll see you. Wait here, and I'll see." Caroline knocked on the door separating the two offices, and stuck her head in. "Mr. Johnson, Becca Snow would like to speak to you, if you have the time."

"Why of course I do, Miss Green. Send her right in."

Caroline motioned for Becca, who quickly crossed the room and entered the office. "Good afternoon, Mr. Johnson. Thank you for seeing me."

She was aware that Caroline went back to her desk but left the door open, as was the custom when one of the female teachers met with the principal.

"Good afternoon, Miss Snow." He motioned for her to take the chair across from his desk. "What can I do for you?"

Becca sat down and folded her hands in her lap. "Mr. Johnson, I would like to take a teaching position in Hot Springs, and I—"

"Oh no, Miss Snow. We don't want to lose you."

"I'm sorry, sir. It isn't that I don't want to be here. It's just—I feel I must get away from. . ." Becca sighed. "The memories are—"

"It's all right, Miss Snow. I do understand." Mr. Johnson leaned back in his chair. "In fact, I expected something like this after you lost your fiancé. But I was beginning to think that maybe you were through the worst of it all."

"I'm sorry."

"My dear Miss Snow, there is no need to apologize. You've been through a great deal in the last year. You will be able to finish the term, won't you?"

"They would like me to start as soon as possible." She bit her bottom lip, waiting for his reply.

"That does present a problem, doesn't it?"

"Not necessarily. Miss Molly Bryant is back home and looking for a teaching position. She asked Superintendent Mallard about next year a few weeks back, but of course there were no openings at that time."

"Molly Bryant. Yes, I remember her. This means a lot to you, doesn't it, Miss Snow?"

"Yes, sir, it does."

He nodded. "Ask Miss Bryant to come in to see me tomorrow. In the meantime I'm having a meeting this afternoon with Superintendent Mallard and will talk to him about the situation."

Becca jumped up from her chair and would have hugged the man if propriety allowed for it. Instead she simply smiled and said, "Oh thank you, Mr. Johnson. I will speak to Molly as soon as I get home. I'm sure she will come in tomorrow."

"I'll see you tomorrow also. Perhaps we can have this settled by the end of the day. Good day, Miss Snow."

❧

Luke Monroe looked up as his employer entered the office of the building Luke managed when he wasn't off on assignment. Through the years they had become good friends and didn't stand on ceremony. "Marcus! You must have a good assignment lined up for me to show up this early in the day."

Marcus Wellington owned Wellington Agency, the private investigative/protective agency Luke worked for. Marcus spent most of his time in the new office he'd had built farther down on Central Avenue. The office Luke was using had been the first office of the Wellington Agency. Now offices were spread across the state, and Marcus was debating whether or not to expand.

The older man took a seat across from Luke. "It's not exactly an assignment for you. More like a favor to ask."

"You have it. You know that." Marcus couldn't ask anything of him that Luke wouldn't try his best to do. He owed the man his very freedom. After being falsely accused of a crime when he was much younger, Luke had been proven innocent only through Marcus's investigation of the events. Not only had Marcus gotten him out of prison, but he had also taught Luke all he knew about being a private investigator and put him in charge of the building where his office and apartment were located, giving Luke a place to call home. All Luke wanted was to make as much of a difference in someone's life as Marcus had made in his.

"I was wondering if you have a vacant apartment in the building?"

"I do. The Wilsons just moved out. I haven't had time to call anyone on the list, though."

Marcus nodded. "Good. Abigail's niece has an aunt by marriage who has taken a teaching position at Central High School, and while Abby and I are going to invite her to stay with us, I've a feeling she's going to want a place of her own."

"I'll make sure to have it aired out and cleaned, then."

"I'd also just ask you to keep an eye on her. She's never lived totally on her own for any length of time, and she's recently suffered some heartache."

"I understand. I'll be sure to watch out for her. When will she be arriving?"

"I believe Rebecca and our niece Natalie will be here in a week or two. Abby is so excited about it. She can't wait to see Natalie and is hoping to convince her to open a hat shop in town. She'll most likely be spending a lot of time with Rebecca while she's here, and that's another reason I'll feel better about Rebecca living here if she doesn't choose to stay with us. I know you'll watch out for them. They won't have to be watched around the clock, but this is a new town to them and—"

"I understand."

"I knew you would." Marcus stood to leave. "You are a good man, Luke. I always feel better when I put you in charge of something."

Luke was glad he did. But he wasn't so sure he felt the same way this time. It was one thing to investigate people or protect people who came to Hot Springs. But to have the responsibility of keeping someone connected to Marcus's family safe. . .well, that was a big one. He'd do his best though. It was the least he could do after all Marcus had done for him.

Chapter 2

Almost two weeks later, on the twenty-ninth of January, Becca was on her way to Hot Springs along with her stepniece, Natalie Brooks. She wasn't sure who was more excited—herself because she was moving to a new place and getting away from painful memories, or Natalie because she was getting to show her stepaunt a town she loved.

The trip hadn't been bad at all with Natalie to keep her company. They'd left Eureka Springs the evening before, and Natalie's father had paid extra to get them a private sleeping booth. They'd talked long into the night, like two schoolgirls on their first outing alone. Finally the rocking motion of the train had lulled them both to sleep, and it was only the porter's knock on the door the next morning announcing that breakfast would be served in the dining car in half an hour that stirred them.

They hurriedly helped each other become presentable before joining the other travelers heading to the dining car. Becca knew they both looked nice in the traveling dresses her sister had made them. Meagan had insisted on furnishing her with several new outfits, and the brown and cream dress she had on was one of her favorites.

Becca's appetite had been almost nil since Richard's death, but as the waiter set their breakfasts in front of them, she found that she was suddenly very hungry. It was a welcome change, and after a silent prayer, she took a piping hot biscuit and buttered it.

"Mmm. This is very good."

"Yes, it is," Natalie said. "Traveling always makes me hungrier than usual."

Becca took a sip of steaming coffee and looked out the window. The scenery was a little different from home, but not so much that she felt she was in a strange land, and with Natalie along, she hadn't had a chance to miss her family yet.

The morning sped by as they took their time with breakfast and visiting with other travelers. By the time lunch came around, Becca was filled with anticipation of arriving in Hot Springs. She could barely contain her excitement through the next few hours and was glad she had Natalie with her for company.

They freshened up as best they could and took their seats for the last half hour before their arrival. "I'm so glad you came with me, Natalie."

"I'm just happy you are moving here. I'll miss you so much, but I understand your need to get away. I can at least see you when I come to visit Aunt Abby and Uncle Marcus."

Becca's memories of Natalie's aunt weren't all that good—she'd been awful to Becca's sister Meagan back before Meagan had married Nate. Then Abigail had moved to Hot Springs and married Marcus Wellington. Meagan said that Abigail had changed for the better, but still, Becca was a little nervous that she'd be staying with the couple until she could find an apartment or boarding-house to live in. At the same time, she was thankful to have a place to stay.

"It's kind of them to invite me to stay with them. I'll begin looking for a place as soon as I can, though."

"There isn't any hurry, Becca. I'm sure you'll be welcome there as long as you want to stay."

"I won't want to wear out my welcome."

Natalie shook her head and laughed. "You won't. Just wait and see."

Becca could only hope her stepniece was right. The enormity of what she'd done by leaving her teaching position for one in a town she'd never visited and where she really knew no one was beginning to sink in. And yet, so was the relief she felt that she didn't have to pass by daily memories of broken dreams. She'd been praying for guidance and hoped she was doing the Lord's will by moving. And she reminded herself that she wasn't alone. She had Him with her no matter where she went.

As they neared the town that would be her new home, Becca prayed, *Dear Lord, please forgive me for not always remembering that You are always there for me. I know You have been—I couldn't have made it this last year without You. I admit to being nervous about this move. Please give me peace in knowing that You will always be there to guide me, and please help me to do Your will in all that I do. In Jesus' name, I pray. Amen.*

"Look, Becca." Natalie pointed out the window. "Hot Springs is just around the bend up ahead."

Becca held her breath, waiting for a glimpse of the town she'd be claiming as hers soon. The winter scene allowed for seeing the city long before the other seasons would have. Becca's heart began to pound as she saw the first rooftops in the distance. She could make out light spirals of smoke coming from their chimneys, and as the train rounded the bend, the downtown area came into view. She took in everything she could as the train slowed and entered the town set inside Hot Springs National Park.

The valley between two mountains seemed to narrow as the train made its way to the depot. Before the train came to a stop, Becca and Natalie stood and brushed their skirts and pinned on the hats Natalie had made to match their traveling outfits.

As they made their way down the aisle and stepped off the train, Becca felt the peace she'd prayed for and smiled. She might not know anyone here, she might not know her way around, but she would never be alone.

❧

Abigail Wellington stood beside her husband and waited for her niece to alight from the afternoon train. She couldn't wait to see her. She'd loved Natalie as if she were her own since the day she was born, and she didn't see her near often enough, to her way of thinking. Perhaps with her stepaunt, Becca Snow, who was only four years older than Natalie, moving here to take a teaching position, Natalie would come to Hot Springs more often. Abigail hoped so.

In the meantime she hoped she could befriend Becca Snow, the sister of the woman who had married the man she once thought she loved. Abigail felt it was the least she could do to make up for the pain she'd once caused Meagan and Nate. She knew she'd been forgiven years ago, and not a day went by that she didn't count her blessings because of it. But if she could do something to help Meagan's sister feel more comfortable in Hot Springs and help her feel at home, then she wanted to do it.

As if he knew how she felt, Marcus squeezed her hand. "It will all be fine, my love. We'll do all we can to help Becca adjust to being away from her family. And Natalie will be here to help her settle in. By the time Natalie goes back to Eureka Springs, Becca will feel she's part of our family, too."

"Oh, I hope you are right, Marcus. The poor girl has suffered so much heartache in losing her fiancé. I just can't imagine. . . ." She shook her head. "I hope the move here will help her get over her loss and enable her to look to the future with joy."

"Look, I think I see Natalie—isn't that her just about to step down?"

"It is." Abigail hurried forward. "Natalie! Natalie, dear, over here!"

Her niece spotted her, and Abigail was rewarded with a huge smile. "Aunt Abby!"

Natalie hurried down the steps and ran toward her. Abigail greeted her with a hug and looked over her niece's shoulder to see Becca Snow standing quietly behind her. "Becca?"

At the younger woman's nod, Abigail smiled and gave her a hug also. "Welcome to Hot Springs. We hope you'll love our city as much as we do, don't we, Marcus, dear?"

"We certainly do. Welcome to our town, Miss Snow," Marcus said.

"Oh, please call me Becca, Mr. Wellington. I am looking forward to starting my new position and getting settled in. Thank you both for letting me stay with you until I can find a place of my own. I really appreciate it."

"We're very glad to have you," Abigail tried to assure her. "We can talk more about that at dinner. I'm sure you are both tired. Marcus will take care of getting your things delivered to the house, and we'll get you home so that you can both freshen up before dinner."

Soon they were all in the surrey and on their way back to the house. "You both look lovely," Abigail said. "Natalie, are those hats some of your own creations?"

"They are," Natalie said, nodding. "I made mine and Becca's to match our traveling suits."

"They are beautiful. You are very gifted, Natalie. I'd like you to make one or two hats for me while you're here, if you have time."

"I'd love to do that, Aunt Abby. If you aren't in any hurry, I'm sure I'll have time once Becca begins her teaching position."

Abigail laughed. "No, I'm not in any hurry at all. I want to keep you here as long as possible. You take all the time you need." She glanced over at Becca. "I am very thankful that you are moving here, Becca. I am hoping that Natalie will be visiting more often now that you'll be here."

"Oh, you don't need me to get her here. She was very excited about coming to see you, Mrs. Wellington."

"Please, you must call me Abigail—or Abby, as Natalie does. We want you to feel comfortable around us and know that you can turn to us for any kind of help at any time, Becca."

"Thank you, Mrs.—Abigail. It will be good to know there are people I can turn to if needed."

❧

After a light tea so as not to spoil their dinner later, Becca was shown to a beautiful room across the hall from Natalie's. It was done in blue and white and was quite inviting. It even had a private bath. Her luggage was waiting for her, and Becca was glad for the chance to freshen up and change into a modest dinner dress.

Abigail and her husband were very gracious, and Becca had no doubt they were trying to make her feel comfortable. Her sister Meagan had assured her that they would be, and it appeared she was right. In the meantime Becca was very thankful that she had a place to stay and that Natalie was with her. Desperate to have her, the school had given her a little more time than they'd originally wanted to. She was to start teaching in less than two weeks, on Monday, the tenth of February, and that didn't give her long to find a place of her own and get moved in. She hoped the Wellingtons would have some recommendations for a nice boardinghouse or apartment building she would feel safe in.

Natalie swept into her room. "Are you ready to go down for dinner? It smells wonderful. I think Aunt Abby had her cook make all of my favorites."

"I'm sure she did. It's obvious that she is thrilled to have you here." Becca pinched her cheeks and checked her hair in the mirror. "I'm ready. I don't want to be late to dinner my first night here."

Natalie led the way downstairs, and Becca was introduced to Marcus's parents, who'd been invited, too. They seemed very nice, and as they went into the dining room, Becca began to relax and think she'd made the right decision to move.

Natalie was right. Her aunt had made sure all of her favorites were served, and the resulting feast reminded Becca of Thanksgiving at home. Everyone seemed quite interested in Becca's new teaching position.

"You are teaching at the high school? How do you like teaching young people, Miss Snow?" the older Mrs. Wellington asked.

"I love teaching, Mrs. Wellington. I've found teaching upperclassmen quite enjoyable."

"The principal, Edward Fuller, is a good friend of ours, and I can tell you that he is more than a little relieved to be able to get back to his work and let you do the teaching." Mr. Wellington chuckled.

"I am just so thankful that you let us know there was a position open. I really needed a change." Becca didn't want to go on about the past. She was sure everyone here knew about Richard's death and—

"We're glad you came here, dear." Mrs. Wellington reached over and patted her shoulder. "I'm certain your students are going to love you—especially after dealing with Edward. He's a wonderful person and a great principal. He's a very good teacher, too, but he readily admits that he is finding it hard to do both jobs."

"I'm sure it is."

"Oh, I think it is probably good for him. Reminds him of what it's like for the teachers," Mr. Wellington said.

Becca smiled and broached the subject uppermost in her mind. "I was wondering if any of you could recommend a nice boardinghouse or apartment building for me to check into."

"My dear, there is no need to hurry. You are welcome here as long as you would like to stay," Abigail said.

"Yes, you are, Becca," Marcus added. "You are more than welcome to stay here. There is no need to worry about finding a place right now."

Becca sensed they were sincere, but she felt it was time she was on her own. She couldn't take advantage of their kindness. "I thank you so much. You are very kind and gracious. But as I plan on making Hot Springs my home, I really believe I need to find a place of my own."

"You young women are getting to be so independent these days. I don't know whether to be excited or afraid for you," the older Mrs. Wellington commented.

"It's exciting, isn't it?" Natalie said.

"I'm not sure it would be for me, were I your age, dear," Mrs. Wellington stated. "I was taught that a young lady married and took care of the household. But I can see where it would be very exciting for those of you who've had training to do something else—at least for a while. I still hope that you will get married one day."

Not knowing what to say, Becca took a bite of her food, barely tasting it. She knew the older woman didn't mean to bring up hurtful memories, but she suddenly lost her appetite. She'd wanted to be married much more than she wanted to be a teacher, but that wasn't to be after Richard's death.

She hadn't realized that quiet descended after Mrs. Wellington's remark until the woman gasped and said, "Oh my. Becca, I am so sorry, my dear. I didn't mean—"

"It's all right, Mrs. Wellington. I know you didn't. Please don't worry about it."

"I can't believe I was so—"

"Mother Wellington, you are one of the kindest women I've ever known. We all know you meant no harm. But we do want you to know how sorry we are at your loss, Becca," Abigail said. "And while we truly would love for you to stay with us indefinitely, if you feel you would be more comfortable on your own, then we will do our best to help you find a safe place to stay."

"Thank you, Abigail. I do believe that will be for the best. I appreciate your hospitality more than I can say, but I don't want to disrupt your daily lives forever."

"Well, since it is your wish to be on your own, I may have the answer," Marcus offered.

"Marcus, what do you have in mind?" Abigail asked.

"There is a vacancy in my building downtown. I checked with Luke, and he agreed to hold it just in case Becca chose to be on her own. I haven't mentioned it because I didn't want her to think that we didn't want her here."

"Oh, I love that building," Natalie said. "I used to enjoy going there with you and Uncle Marcus, Aunt Abby. I always thought it would be wonderful to live in one of the apartments there."

"Oh, Marcus, that is a wonderful idea. With Luke right there on the premises, that may be the answer," Abigail said.

"You have an apartment building?" Becca asked.

"Yes. It's right downtown and not that far from the school," Marcus explained. "You can walk or use the trolley to get there. It is where my first office was, and I lived in an apartment there before Abigail and I were married. Luke Monroe manages the building for me now, and I know we'd all feel better knowing you were in that building. I could recommend some boardinghouses, too, but you'd only have a room there, where the apartment would provide you with a home, small though it might be, and I get the feeling that is what you would like."

"That sounds wonderful." Becca really didn't like the idea of living in a boardinghouse—except for having meals provided. She wasn't a very good cook. But she didn't like the idea of being confined to a room all of the time. She could learn to cook. And as large as Hot Springs was, there was sure to be restaurants when she got tired of her own cooking. "Do you think I might be able to see it tomorrow?"

"Of course. I'll telephone Luke after dinner and let him know we'll be coming over after breakfast."

"Thank you all so much. It is wonderful to have you all to turn to." Becca found her appetite had returned. She was starting on a new adventure, and she had to put the past to the back of her mind.

⌒

The next morning Luke was on the lookout for the Wellingtons and their houseguest. He'd made sure the apartment was cleaned and aired out just as he'd promised Marcus he would. He'd always liked that each apartment in the building had nice windows and lots of light. This one had the added advantage of looking out onto Central Avenue, just as his did.

Consisting of a nice-sized parlor, a dining room, a small kitchen with its own window, a large bedroom, and a private bath, he thought it would appeal to just about anyone who didn't have children. Some of the apartments in the three-story building had two bedrooms, and a couple of families with one or two children lived in them. Mostly though, single working people who wanted to live close to their work rented the apartments. Only one other lady lived there alone. A widow who worked at the bookstore, she kept pretty much to herself. Maybe if Miss Snow took the apartment, Mrs. Gentry would feel more comfortable.

He wondered what Miss Snow was like. He didn't know many women who were dependent on themselves for their livelihood. Marcus had told him that she'd suffered a heartache of some kind, but Luke didn't feel he should ask for details. He didn't even know how old she was, but if she was Natalie's aunt, she could be Abigail's age. It really didn't matter. He'd promised Marcus he would keep an eye on her, and even if she decided not to take the apartment, he would find a way to watch out for her.

He heard Marcus's voice in the foyer and knew he'd find out soon. He opened the door to welcome them into his office. "Good morning, everyone. It's a beautiful day out, isn't it?"

"Good morning, Luke. It's good to see you," Abigail said. "You remember Natalie, don't you?"

"Of course I do. How are you, Natalie?"

"I'm fine, thank you for asking. I'd like you to meet my aunt. She's my step-mother's sister and my best friend, Becca Snow. Becca, this is Luke Monroe."

Luke had been trying not to stare at the young woman ever since she walked inside his office. She couldn't be more than a few years older than Natalie, and she was quite pretty, with large green eyes and reddish hair. He had a feeling it wasn't going to be a hardship to watch over her.

She smiled at him, showing twin dimples. "Pleased to meet you, Mr. Monroe."

No, watching over Miss Snow wasn't going to be hard at all.

Chapter 3

How do you do, Miss Snow? Marcus tells me that you've come to Hot Springs to teach."

"Yes, I have. I'm looking forward to teaching high school very much."

Luke Monroe's smile reached his eyes, and Becca's pulse quickened as he took her hand. "I hope you'll like it here in our fair city."

"I like what I've seen so far," Becca said. Mr. Monroe seemed to be a very nice man, and though his smile warmed her heart, Becca didn't welcome the feeling and hoped the small talk was about to end as she slipped her hand out of his. She really wanted to see her possible new home. Evidently it showed, because Luke went to his desk and retrieved a key.

"I'm sure you are anxious to see the apartment we have available."

"Yes, I am."

Luke motioned to them all to follow him into the elevator that stood ready to take them up. "Marcus just had the elevator put in a couple of years ago, and all of our tenants love it. But there are stairs, too, in case it breaks down or one doesn't want to wait for it."

Becca stepped into the wire cage and enjoyed the ride up to the third floor. She quite liked elevators. Most of the ones in use in Eureka Springs were in hotels and banks, and she didn't have much opportunity to use them. But if she took the apartment, she'd be able to ride it each day.

The elevator stopped long before she was ready for the ride to end, but she was anxious to see the apartment. She hurried off and waited for the Wellingtons, Natalie, and Mr. Monroe to join her in the hall.

As they made their way down the hall, Becca fought the memory of the plans she and Richard had made to build a home. The life she would be living here would be so very different from what she'd hoped for just over a year ago, and she wondered if she'd made a mistake in leaving her family and everything familiar to her, just to get away from the memories. Could she ever really get away from them?

Luke stopped at an apartment that faced the street and turned to her. "I'll unlock the door and show the apartment to you. After that, I'll let you look around all you want."

"Thank you." Becca held her breath while he turned the key. What if she didn't like it? She didn't want to upset the Wellingtons or Natalie.

Luke opened the door, and from the moment she walked inside the small foyer, Becca loved the apartment. The parlor was large and airy with sunlight streaming in from the large bay window. Her spirits lifted immediately. The room was furnished with a nice divan and comfortable chairs. And the bay window was huge. A nice-sized round table and two chairs looked right at home in it. Becca knew she would eat most of her meals right there. She could also see herself sitting there, grading papers and looking out onto the street below, and when it got colder, she'd move to sit near the fireplace to read or work. The room had a cozy feel, and she knew she could think of this place as home, especially after she added the personal touches she'd brought from Eureka Springs—with more to be sent once she had a place of her own.

"It's very nice." She crossed the room to look out of the window. "I like how it looks out over Central Avenue."

Natalie joined her. "Oh look, you can see Bathhouse Row from here. I love the magnolia trees. In the summer they smell so sweet and their blooms are very big."

Becca turned back to Luke. "I'm sorry; let's see the rest of it."

"There is a good-sized dining room to your right—"

"Oh look, Natalie, there are big windows on two sides. I love the light in here." Becca followed Luke into the room, while Natalie, Marcus, and Abigail came in behind her.

A buffet sat along one wall next to a dining table that could easily seat eight. It would be nice to have Natalie and the Wellingtons over for dinner—if she learned to cook well enough. "It's beautiful—it really is."

"Let me show you the kitchen," Luke said. Back in the parlor, he turned to the room next to the dining room. "It's quite functional, I think. The one in my apartment is just like it, and I've found it to be easy to cook in."

The kitchen had a small range, a sink, and a small icebox on one side and a long row of cupboards with a soapstone countertop along the other side. There was even a small window at the end.

"This is the service door," Luke said as he opened another door to the hall. "Coal for the range will always be here, you can put your trash in the receptacle for the janitor to collect, and your grocery deliveries should be left here for easy access."

"I think it will be quite workable. I like it." Becca smiled.

"Now to the bedroom and bath. They are across the way." Luke motioned to the doorway on the other side of the parlor. "I'll let you take a look and leave you to discuss things in private. I'll be in my office when you are through."

"Thank you," Becca said. "I don't think we'll be too long."

"Take all the time you need," Luke offered. He gave a little salute and turned to leave.

"I think I'll come back down with you, Luke. We'll leave the ladies to it," Marcus quickly added.

Abigail smiled at her husband. "That's a good idea, dear. I'm sure you and Luke have business to discuss, and that way Becca won't feel rushed."

"That's what I was thinking," Marcus said. He chuckled as he and Luke left the apartment.

Abigail's laughter was light and full of joy. "He is such a wonderful man. And he can almost read my mind. I was hoping they would leave us to look over the apartment at our leisure."

She led the way into the bedroom, Becca right behind her. "Oh, how nice and big it is. And another window—I do love lots of light."

The furniture was a matching set of bird's-eye maple, and a comfortable reading chair and table sat in a corner by the window. There was even a closet to put her clothes in.

Becca passed through the door next to it and found a bathroom that would be her very own. She whirled around and smiled at Natalie and Abigail. "It's just wonderful. The furnishings are all so beautiful. I never expected anything so nice."

"You're right. I think it is perfect for you, Becca," Natalie enthused. They slowly made their way back into the parlor, and Natalie turned to her aunt. "I just don't remember these apartments being quite so nice, Aunt Abby. And I didn't realize they were furnished."

"They are very nice, aren't they? Marcus did just have the bathrooms installed earlier this year, and that has made them the nicest apartments in town. Not all of them have furniture, and I confess I had a hand in furnishing this one. The last renter had no furniture, and there were so many things in our attic. I had Luke come and get enough to make it livable."

"Oh, I love it all. You have impeccable taste, Mrs.—ah. . .Abigail."

"Thank you, Becca. I'm glad you like it. But we have more things in the attic—a lot of furniture and decor items that you might be able to use. We'll go up and let you choose what you might like. I just didn't want you to walk into a completely empty apartment."

"I can't imagine changing anything you've picked out." Becca looked around. "Thank you so much." That the apartment was furnished was a blessing. She certainly didn't have the funds to furnish a place this size—and certainly not with the quality of furnishings Abigail had brought to it.

"Are you going to take it, Becca?" Natalie asked.

"I'd be crazy not to, don't you think?"

"Well yes, I do. But the decision isn't mine."

Becca grinned and shook her head. Natalie never had been one to hide her thoughts. From the time they first met when Becca was ten and Natalie was six, they'd been good friends. When Natalie's father married Becca's sister, they'd been thrilled to be family. "Let me take one more look around, and then we can go talk to Mr. Monroe."

The apartment felt like home. Becca couldn't imagine finding any place that would feel more comfortable. Besides, there weren't that many apartments available. There were some boardinghouses, but at twenty-six, Becca felt she wanted somewhere to call her own. And this just seemed right to her. As she moved through each room once more, she said a silent prayer that she was right and that, if she was wrong, the Lord would let her know—quickly.

❧

Luke wasn't at all surprised when Marcus told him what to tell Becca the rent was. He was giving her a substantial discount. But as he'd done much the same for Luke—even charging him nothing at first, but telling him it was part of his pay—he wasn't going to question him about it.

"Yes, sir."

"We all know that teachers don't make that much money, but she is almost family, and Abigail wants her to stay here. She's hoping that we'll get to see more of Natalie with Becca here."

Luke nodded. "That's a possibility. They seem quite close."

"Becca is four years older, but she's always been there for Natalie, and for that reason alone, Abigail would want to do all she could to help her settle in here. Besides, the town needs good teachers, and I've heard she's a very good one."

Luke wondered at why the knowledge that Becca Snow was four years older than Natalie caught his attention, but it did. That put him at ten years older than her instead of the fourteen that he'd assumed on first meeting her, given that she and Natalie seemed so close. Ten years didn't seem quite so bad—

"Luke. Luke, the ladies are here," Marcus said.

Luke jumped to his feet. "Ladies, please come in. What did you think, Miss Snow? Will the apartment suit you?"

A smile lit her face just before she said, "Oh yes, it does. I just hope I can afford it."

When Luke named the figure, she seemed speechless. Then she repeated the figure, and he nodded. "Yes, that's right."

Becca looked as if she might cry as she turned to Marcus and Abigail. "I can't let you do that for me. I know how much apartments go for in Eureka

Springs, and—"

"Becca, please," Abigail said, "we can well afford to do this, and it is something we very much want to do. You are part of Natalie's family and, as such, part of ours. We'd like to give it to you rent free, but I know you wouldn't allow us to do that."

"But I—"

"Oh, Becca," Natalie interrupted. "Take it. It's perfect. Don't let a little thing like too low a price keep you from living here." Everyone laughed.

"Well, put that way, how can I possibly refuse?" Becca turned to the Wellingtons and spread out her hands. "Thank you. You won't be sorry. I will take very good care of it, as if it were mine, and—"

"It *is* yours, Miss Snow." Luke handed her the key. "Rent is due on the first of each month."

Becca stood, clasping the key close to her chest while Natalie squealed and hugged her. "Let's go take another look and see what else we need from Aunt Abby's attic."

"Natalie! At the price they are charging me, I don't think I need to take anything else from your aunt and uncle."

"Don't be silly. Aunt Abby will come with us."

"Go on," Marcus said to his wife. "You three have a good day. I need to get to my office, and I know Luke has things to do. How about we meet you all back at the house for dinner?"

"That will be wonderful," Abby said. "May I use your phone to call Bea and let her know you'll be joining us, Luke?"

"Certainly. Thank you for the invitation." He certainly wasn't going to turn down a dinner invitation to the Wellingtons any more than Becca Snow was going to turn down the apartment they were offering her. He was beginning to think that looking after Miss Snow might be the most entertaining assignment he'd ever been given. Becca Snow had already brought a feel of springtime to the Wellington Building. She was young and fresh and beautiful.

❧

The rest of the day seemed to fly by after Becca, Natalie, and Abigail left the apartment building. They went to lunch at a new tearoom in town, and the discussion was all about how to make the apartment even more comfortable than it already felt.

While they waited for their lunch orders, Abigail and Natalie helped Becca start a list of what she might need apart from what was already there.

"You'll need curtains at the windows so no one can see in at night," Natalie said.

"And you need bed linens and a few table lamps and tableware," Abigail stated. "I'm sure we can find anything you need in our attic. We'll take a quick look when we get home."

"Mama will be sending some of my personal things from home, and I have a trunk full of things for when Richard and I got married. I'll arrange to have it sent soon."

"Well, I have plenty you can use until your things arrive. I'm so sorry about your loss, dear," Abigail said once more.

"Thank you. It's been hard. But I think moving here will help a lot. I hope so anyway."

"It will help once you start teaching and meet others. You'll meet quite a few people at church on Sunday, and Marcus and I want to give a dinner party to introduce you to some of the people you'll be working with, too."

"Oh, Abigail, you've done so much already. There is no need to do that. But thank you."

"I love giving dinner parties, Becca. Hosting one to make you feel more at home here will be a joy."

Their lunch came just then, a steaming pot of tea and egg salad sandwiches. Abigail poured the tea and changed the subject back to the apartment and the basics of what Becca might need.

"Your utilities are included in the apartment, but you might want to have a telephone installed. There is one down in the lobby, but there isn't much privacy there."

"I'll contact the telephone company this afternoon then."

"Remember that Luke can let them in if you aren't available. In fact, I can have him take care of it for you, if you'd like."

Becca shook her head. "I'm sure there will be a deposit of some kind. I'll go by when we leave here."

By the time they'd finished eating, Becca had a list of all the things she'd need for the apartment, another list of things to do, and Abigail's recommendations on where to get what. There was a grocer not far from the Wellington Building, as well as a pharmacy. Plenty of other shops were within walking distance, too.

Abigail hired a hack to take her home while Becca and Natalie set out on foot to go to the telephone company and see how far it was to the high school from the apartment. Becca could take advantage of trolleys to get her to work if the walk was too far or the weather was bad.

It didn't take long to arrange for the phone company to install a phone the next week, and after finding the high school, Becca thought she'd enjoy the walk on a good day. She and Natalie took a trolley back to Abigail's home, and Becca found she liked this town more each day. She couldn't wait to get all moved in and begin teaching again.

By the time they arrived back home, they only had time for a quick look at what was in Abigail's attic before it would be time to dress for dinner—but it was enough to know that there was plenty up there to furnish several apartments.

"I almost wish I was moving here, too, Becca," Natalie said as she moved around the furniture, lamps, boxes of whatnots, and any number of other things from her aunt's former homes.

"You could, you know." Becca picked up a lamp she thought would look wonderful in her new bedroom for a closer look. "Wouldn't it be fun to have apartments in the same building? You could open a hat shop here. I'm sure it would do very well."

"It's a thought. Maybe I'll talk to Aunt Abby and Uncle Marcus about the possibilities and where the best location might be. And maybe I'll get up enough nerve to ask Papa what he thinks." Natalie sighed and shook her head. "Somehow, I don't believe he'll be as excited about the prospect of my moving away as I am."

"Probably not. But it would be so nice to have you here." Becca set the beautiful lamp back down carefully.

"I know. I'm going to miss you when I go back home. But I think you made the right decision for you. I think getting out of Eureka Springs will be good for you and—"

"Natalie, dear, are you up here?"

"Yes, Aunt Abby. Is it time to get ready for dinner?"

"It is." Abigail stepped inside the huge attic. "As you've seen, I have more than enough for you to choose from, Becca. We'll come up in the morning when there is better light. But dinner will be ready in less than an hour, and Marcus and Luke should be here anytime now."

As they headed down to the second floor, Becca realized she was looking forward to many things for the first time in a very long time.

She and Natalie hurried to change into something more fitting than their day dresses for dinner. She was sure that she wouldn't dress for dinner in her own place. She would eat a simple supper and most likely wear what she'd worn to work that day. But she was at the Wellingtons, and they dressed for dinner each night. Becca knew that was what wealthy people did. They changed clothes for almost any activity during the day. She did when really necessary, but she didn't see the need in having a new outfit on every time she left the house.

Only because her sister was such an excellent seamstress, Becca had a wardrobe befitting of someone much wealthier than she was, and never had she appreciated it so much as now. Tonight she chose a dinner gown of green silk.

It was one of her best colors, and she'd been told it made her eyes darker and brought out the red in her hair.

Natalie knocked on the door just as Becca was finishing her toilette, and they went down the stairs together. It appeared that Marcus and Luke were waiting for them when they entered the parlor, for Abigail whisked them all into the dining room.

It wasn't until Becca was seated next to Luke Monroe that she realized how much she'd been looking forward to seeing him again.

Chapter 4

By Wednesday of the next week Becca still couldn't believe the apartment was hers. The weekend had passed quickly: She and Natalie and Abigail had rummaged in the attic on Saturday afternoon, and on Sunday she'd gone to church with them all and been welcomed by so many people she couldn't begin to remember all of their names. But Abigail had invited several people back for Sunday dinner, and Becca had met the principal she'd be working for. Mr. Fuller and his wife were so nice she found she was quite excited about starting to work and anxious to get settled in her apartment.

Despite her objections, the Wellingtons were charging her only half a month's rent for February, saying they wanted her to have plenty of time to move and get settled in comfortably. They insisted that she stay with them until the telephone was installed and she had moved all she might need over to the apartment. She'd begun to move in on the first, the day after she rented it, bringing in a few things from the Wellingtons' attic each day after. She was expecting a crate to arrive anytime with the things her mother was sending. She'd see what she needed after that. Abigail had told her that she was welcome to take anything else she needed, but they'd done so much for her already that she didn't want to take more.

The apartment had begun to feel like home. They'd found curtains to hang at the windows and lamps for the parlor and bedroom. Abigail had several sets of tableware in the attic, too, and had told Becca to choose a set she liked. But Abigail's china—even that in the attic—was very expensive, and Becca didn't feel right asking for it. Finally Abigail insisted she take a set of genuine Haviland china that had been made in Limoges, France. It was beautiful, heavily embossed and traced with gold, its design one of sprays of pink roses.

Becca had tried to refuse, but even Natalie had insisted she take the set, and now her stepniece was busy unpacking the delicate pieces and handing them to Becca to put in the sideboard in the dining room.

"I can't wait to come to dinner here, Becca. What fun it will be to see your table all set with china and—"

"I've got to learn to cook first, Natalie," Becca replied.

"You can cook. I've seen you in your mother's kitchen."

"You've seen me helping Mama. She did show me how to make some things when Richard and I became engaged." Becca swallowed hard and blinked at the sudden tears that formed.

"I'm sorry, Becca. I didn't mean to bring up hurtful memories." Natalie patted her on the shoulder.

Becca sighed. "It's all right. I was just going to say that I hadn't kept up the lessons afterward. I'm just hoping I can remember what she did manage to teach me."

A knock on the door was a welcome interruption for Becca, and she hurried to the foyer. Thinking it was probably Abigail, she was surprised to see Luke Monroe standing there, a large box propped up on his shoulder. The beat of her heart sped up as it usually did when he smiled at her.

"Good morning, Miss Snow. You've had a trunk and several boxes delivered just now. I wanted to make sure you were here before I brought them up."

Becca backed up and made room for him to come in. "Please just put it down anywhere, Mr. Monroe. I should have let you know to expect them. I'll come help you bring them up."

"No. They are too heavy for you. I'll get them. Just tell me where you want the trunk, and I'll bring it up next." He smiled once more, but Becca could tell from the tone in his voice that he meant what he said.

"If you could put it in the bedroom, at the end of my bed, that would be nice."

"Certainly. And the other boxes?"

"Just put them here in the foyer. And thank you, Mr. Monroe."

"You are quite welcome. It is no problem whatsoever."

"Luke! How are you today?" Natalie came out of the kitchen. "What do you think of the apartment? It is looking quite homey, don't you think?"

For a moment Becca felt a twinge of jealousy that the younger woman knew Luke well enough to call him by his first name, and then she became unsettled that it mattered to her. After all, he was the manager of her apartment building—not a lifelong friend. No. Friends didn't make one feel quite the way Luke Monroe's smile made her feel—all fluttery and nervous.

Luke looked around the room and nodded. "It does look quite comfortable. Makes me feel mine could use a little sprucing up."

Natalie laughed. "Yours probably just needs a woman's touch. When are you ever going to get married, Luke?"

"Natalie!"

"It's all right, Becca. I've been after Luke to find a wife for several years. He's quite used to my impertinence. But I'm afraid he's never going to take my advice."

Luke laughed and shook his head. "I'll bring the trunk up shortly."

"Thank you. I'll leave the door unlocked."

When he left, Becca turned to Natalie. "I can't believe you talked to him that way, Natalie. Why, it was quite—"

"Honest. He does need to get married. He would make someone a wonderful husband."

"Have you set your sights on him, Natalie?"

Natalie's giggle quickly turned to full-blown laughter. "No. Luke is like an uncle to me. I've known him since I was six or seven, Becca. I could never think of him that way. But I do care about him and would like to see him happily married one day. Besides, he's fourteen years older than I am."

"Lots of women are married to men older than them."

"Yes, well, fourteen years seems a bit much to me. Ten wouldn't be so bad, though." She grinned. "No, ten wouldn't be bad at all. In fact, I think that would be just about right."

Becca realized where her friend was going with her thoughts. "Don't even think about it. Not for one moment, Natalie. I'm not looking for romance. I just want to get over heartache."

The younger woman patted her on the shoulder. "Oh I know. And that takes time. But it doesn't appear that Luke is looking, either. And who knows what could happen?"

Becca was long used to her stepniece's romantic notions, and she knew the best way to handle them was to pretend she didn't understand what Natalie was hinting at. So she just sighed and went back to the kitchen—and tried not to think of what could happen. . . .

～

Later that day Becca went to the grocer down the street to stock her kitchen. Abigail had told her that Morton's Grocery Store carried a fine variety of goods.

She chose things she knew she could cook fairly easily. Bacon and eggs along with a loaf of bread would work for several meals. She bought staples like flour, sugar, coffee, and tea. She picked up some canned vegetables and some potatoes, thinking she'd like some fried with onions as she'd seen her mother do. It sounded good for supper. By the time she'd selected other items, Becca felt she could survive several days on her own cooking. She'd spotted several nearby cafés where she could go if she got tired of the few things she knew how to cook.

After arranging for her groceries to be delivered, Becca stepped out of the grocer's, her mind on getting back to the apartment before the delivery boy got there. She turned to the left and collided with a man on his way in. He brushed her to the side and attempted to move.

"Oh, I am so sorry," she said a bit breathlessly as she steadied herself. "I wasn't watching what I was doing."

"Should watch more closely," the man muttered, his eyes boring into hers for one brief moment before he tipped his hat down over his eyes and entered the store without acknowledging her apology. Well, she tried. Something about the man looked familiar to her, but she was sure she'd never met him before. Maybe he had relatives in Eureka Springs.

She shrugged and hurried on her way, excited to be spending her very first night in her apartment. With her things from home unpacked and put up, it really felt like home. It would be the first time she'd ever stayed by herself—Natalie had offered to stay with her, but she'd turned her down. She needed to get used to being alone, and she was actually looking forward to it.

She took the elevator up with Mrs. Gentry, whom she'd just met that morning.

"Good afternoon, dear. Did you get everything unpacked?"

"I did. I've just ordered groceries to be delivered, and I'm staying in the apartment tonight."

"Well, I hope you like it here. It's a very safe building—Luke sees to that—and you'll feel quite safe here after a while."

"Oh, I already do." And she did. She'd met several more of her neighbors besides Mrs. Gentry, and Luke Monroe was just down the hall. She had nothing to fear in this new home—nothing at all.

❧

Harland Burrows looked back to see what direction the young woman who slammed into him went. He'd seen that young woman before—he was sure of it—but he couldn't remember just where. He'd lived in Hot Springs for several years now, and it was possible he'd run into her. Still, she was very attractive, and he was sure he would have remembered meeting her. But from the way the hair had stood up on the back of his neck when her eyes met his, he didn't think it had been a good meeting.

"Harland, good day to you. That caviar you ordered came in just this morning," Ned Morton, the grocer, said.

"Hello, Ned. It is a fine day out. I need to add a few more things to the order." He handed the man his list. "It's not a lot, so I can take it with me."

Ned looked over the list and handed it to one of his clerks to fill. "This won't take long."

"Say, that young woman who just left here—I'm sure I know her, but I've forgotten her name. Can you tell me what it is?"

"The pretty one who just left?"

Harland nodded. "Yes, that's the one. I just can't place her."

"First time she's been in here." Ned pulled out a sheet of paper. "She paid cash, so I don't have a name. Just that she lives in apartment 312 in the Wellington Building."

"Well, perhaps it will come to me. If she's new in town, maybe she just looks like someone I know. I'll think on it." He waited for Ned to fill his order, but he couldn't get the woman out of his mind. He'd seen her somewhere before. In his line of business, he depended on remembering the people he'd run into. He had to.

❧

Luke Monroe made it his business to know as much as he could about the people who lived in his building, and as much as possible, he kept up with what was happening in their lives and how they were doing. Most of them had come to feel like family to him.

But there was something different about Becca Snow—a feeling he had each time he saw her that had nothing to do with how he felt about the other renters in the building. And it had nothing to do with the fact that Marcus had asked him to watch over her. It was all about the way his chest tightened when he was around her and how his heart beat faster when she smiled at him. He looked forward to seeing her each day.

When he'd taken her trunk and several boxes up earlier, he was impressed by the warmth and coziness of the apartment. She was making it hers in a way that told him she was someone to whom home and family meant a great deal. What he assumed were family pictures were set here and there, with several hung on the wall. The place had an inviting feeling that made him want to linger. But Miss Snow and Natalie were still busy unpacking and he had work to do, so he'd gone back to his office, only to find himself thinking of how pretty she'd looked as she thanked him for his help and saw him out the door.

There was no way around the fact that she was on his mind quite often. Having her, Natalie, and Abigail in and out of the building while she was moving in had him listening for the lilt of Becca's voice or the sound of her laughter. Still, he told himself that he didn't need to get too interested in the young woman—Marcus knew about his background, and while he trusted Luke to watch out for her, Luke wasn't sure he'd ever approve of him courting Becca. And even if the Wellingtons had no objections, that didn't mean Becca's family wouldn't. In fact, Luke was sure that they would, and he needed to remember it. It was the main reason he'd been able to keep from giving his heart to anyone. There weren't many people who would want a man who'd spent time in prison for a son-in-law—even if he had been cleared of all charges.

But as he watched Becca enter the lobby and head to the elevator, he knew it wasn't going to be easy to stop thinking about her. When she saw him and smiled, he thought it was going to be near impossible.

Chapter 5

It was getting dark by the time Becca put away all her groceries and thought about what she wanted for her supper. She still had boxes to unpack—books from home and some personal items—so she decided to scramble some eggs and make toast.

Becca loved her kitchen, and she liked that there was a window at the end of it. She opened it just a bit for fresh air, and she could see out to where streetlights were coming on down below. Seeing several lights at windows across the way made her feel safe and not so alone.

Deciding to fry some bacon so she would have grease to cook her eggs in, Becca slipped several pieces in the skillet and set it over the burner. She'd always been a little afraid of stoking the fire in a stove and had depended on her mother to do it. But she managed, and minutes later she was proud that she had cooked the bacon without burning it too badly. It was just nice and crispy. Then Becca put slices of bread into the oven and began scrambling her eggs. The eggs were just the way she liked them when she slid them onto a plate alongside her bacon.

But when she turned to retrieve her toast, black smoke was seeping out of the oven. She quickly grabbed a mitt and pulled the pan out, but the toast was black and the pan was hot. She dropped it alongside the skillet, and the mitt caught on fire. "Oh no!"

Becca hurried to the window and raised it higher, but before she could throw the mitt out the window, the curtain caught on fire. Suddenly Luke burst into the kitchen, and she could only watch as he grabbed the curtains and the mitt, dumped them into the sink, and pumped water on them. The grease in the skillet suddenly flamed up, and Becca felt frozen to the spot as she watched Luke grab the lid and slam it on top of the skillet, quickly smothering the flame.

Only then did she let go of the breath she'd been holding. She began to tremble as she looked at Luke. "Thank you. I—I'm sorry. . .I'm so sorry. I could have burned down the whole building."

"But you didn't. It's all right."

Becca shook her head. She was shaking all over. "No. It's not. I—" She began to sniff.

Luke quickly gathered her in his arms. "Oh, don't cry. It *is* all right. Nothing burned down. The only loss is the curtains and mitt, and I'm sure you can replace them without any problem."

His kindness only made her want to cry more, and as much as she enjoyed the comfort of his arms, his nearness was doing nothing to end her trembling. She blinked back the tears and stepped back. He immediately dropped his arms to his sides.

"I don't know why I thought I could do this. I should have paid more attention to Mama's teaching. I don't know how to cook."

"No? Those eggs look just fine, but they are probably a little cold by now. And the bacon is crisp, just the way I like it." He lifted a piece and took a bite. "Just right. But it's kind of smoky in here. Let's raise some windows, and I'll take you out to eat. I was coming to see if you might like to celebrate moving in, anyway."

"Your timing couldn't have been better. I don't know what I would have done if you hadn't shown up. Now the Wellingtons are going to ask me to move, and I can't blame them. I—"

"Miss Snow, I'm glad I showed up, too. But there's no need to worry about the Wellingtons. I'll not be running to them with any tales. All is well. Let's go eat, and by the time we get back, hopefully there'll not even be a smoky smell. Gather your jacket, and I'll raise the windows."

Becca was so grateful that he wouldn't be telling Marcus and Abigail that she'd nearly burned the place down that she didn't even argue with him. She headed for her room to freshen up and grab her reticule.

"You might want to raise the windows in there, too," Luke called from the dining room. "It might be chilly when we get back, but I'll show you how to turn up the radiator when we return."

Becca did as he suggested, and in a matter of minutes they were seated at a restaurant just around the corner from the building. She had to admit that sharing a meal with Luke Monroe held a lot more appeal than eating cold bacon and eggs.

∾

More than once on the way to the restaurant, Luke told himself he shouldn't have invited Becca Snow to dinner, and now that he was sitting across from her, he knew he was right. Still, he was glad that he had. They'd been shown to a table for two in an alcove that looked out onto the street.

It was nice to have company for the meal. Had he planned to cook for himself tonight, most likely he would have chosen the same menu she had, only he liked making an omelet and fried potatoes to go along with it. But more often than not, he chose to eat out as opposed to eating at home alone. Somehow, seeing other people doing the same thing made him feel less lonely.

"What do you recommend?" Becca asked.

"Everything on the menu is good, but I like the roast beef special."

"I'll have that then."

The waiter came to take their order, and Luke requested the special for both himself and Becca. When the man left, Luke turned to Becca and found her gaze on him.

"Thank you again, Mr. Monroe. I really didn't know what to do when the curtains caught on fire. How did you get there so fast? And what alerted you to the fire?"

"Actually I'd come to see if you needed anything. I wanted to show you how to work the heat, and I did want to invite you to dinner, too. I smelled something on fire, and. . .I just happened to time it right."

"You certainly did. I can't bear to think of what might have happened had you not shown up when you did."

Neither could he. To think that she might have been badly burned. . .or worse. No. He wouldn't let himself think about it. "I'm thankful that I was there. Let's not think about what might have happened and be thankful that it didn't. Will you pray with me?"

"Yes, please pray," Becca said and bowed her head.

Luke looked at her bowed head for a moment before bowing his own head. "Dear Lord, we thank You that Miss Snow was not hurt earlier tonight. We thank You that nothing was burned that cannot be replaced. Please be with Miss Snow as she starts her new teaching position and help her to settle into her apartment and feel at home here in Hot Springs. Thank You for bringing her here. We thank You for the food we are about to eat. Most of all, we thank You for Your plan for our salvation. In Jesus' name. Amen."

"Amen," he heard Becca whisper from across the table.

"Are you excited about starting work next week?"

"I am. Thank you for praying about it. I can barely wait to meet my students and get to know them. I've met Mr. Fuller, and I'm anxious to meet the other teachers, also."

Their meals arrived just then, and conversation stopped until the waiter left the table. Then Luke waited to see if Becca liked her meal.

"You were right. This is very good."

"I'm glad you like it. Back to our conversation. . .I'm sure everything will go quite well at your new school. I'm sure everyone is anxious to meet you, too. What made you want to be a teacher?"

"I loved playing school with Natalie. I was always the teacher, and she was the student. But I didn't plan to be a real teacher—I thought I would become a seamstress like my sisters and mother."

"Why didn't you?"

Becca chuckled and shook her head. "I found I hated sewing. It was much too solitary for me. And I had the hardest time threading the needle. Besides, there was really no need for another seamstress in the family. The business didn't need that many of us. But I will always be thankful to my sister's business, for it provided me the education to become a teacher."

"Then this isn't the first time you've lived away from home, is it?"

"Oh no. It's the first time I've been on my own or lived by myself. I went to the Industrial Institute and College in Mississippi along with one of my friends who had family there, but of course I lived in a dormitory with other students, so I was never alone."

"Are you nervous about spending your first night alone?"

"No." She shook her head, and Luke decided he liked the way the light caught the reddish highlights in her hair.

"Good."

"I might be nervous if I weren't in an apartment building. But there are others all around, and everyone seems very nice."

"They are. You'll find that the tenants watch out for each other, and I make sure the building is safe. We have a guard day and night, and they make certain it is safe as well."

"That is good to know. I should have asked more questions before I moved in, I suppose, but the apartment felt so homey to me that I felt safe from the moment I walked in. As it turned out today, the building was safer before I moved in. It wouldn't surprise me if the other tenants don't ask me to leave."

Luke had to laugh with her. It was refreshing to find a woman who could laugh at herself. "The tenants aren't going to know you caught anything on fire. And it's not the first time an apartment has had smoke billowing from under the door. Mrs. Gentry burned some cookies a few weeks back. It happens."

"Well, I'm afraid it might happen more if I don't learn to cook soon."

"You really don't know how?"

"Well, I can cook a few things. But. . ." She shook her head. "Not many. Mama did try to teach me, but I'd like to learn more. I guess it just comes with doing it. She suggested that I find a copy of Fannie Farmer's *Boston Cooking-School Cook Book* and told me that it would teach me all I need to know. I hope she's right."

Luke was tempted to tell her he could teach her, but he stopped himself from doing so. That would mean spending more time with her, and he had a feeling that was something he should try not to do. She was much too captivating for his own good.

When they arrived back at the apartment, Becca was relieved that it no longer smelled like smoke. Luke helped her close the windows and showed her how to manage the heat and light the fireplace. "It should be toasty in here before long."

Becca followed him to the door. "Thank you for putting out the fire, for the meal, and for everything."

"You are quite welcome. Thank you for joining me for dinner. I don't much like eating alone."

"It was nice to have company."

"Good night. Lock up good."

"I will. Good night."

Becca saw him out and made sure to lock up behind him. It had been a very pleasant evening. She had almost forgotten how nice it was to go to dinner with a gentleman. And Luke was certainly that—and a handsome one, too. Surprised at that thought, Becca hurried into the kitchen to clean up the mess she'd left behind.

She hadn't thought of a man that way since Richard, and she wasn't comfortable thinking that way about another man now. Still, she had to fight to keep thoughts of Luke at bay, and she was glad when her telephone rang. It was Natalie, wondering how everything was going.

"Everything is fine. I'm cleaning up the kitchen now, and I'm going to take a nice bath after that."

"It sounds as if you've settled in quite well," Natalie said. "I am almost envious of you. Especially since I've decided to go home."

"You are going back so soon?"

"Well, I have an ulterior motive. I'm going to try to talk Papa and Mama into letting me open a hat shop here. I think it's time I was on my own, too. And I'm going to miss you so, Becca."

"What do you think your parents will say?"

She could hear Natalie's deep sigh over the telephone wire. "I don't know. But I want to try."

"You know you can move in with me, if you need to."

"Of course I know you would welcome me in. But I want to be on my own, just like you are. I think it is time. After all, this is the twentieth century. And I have no suitor in sight. It's time I take on the responsibility of making my own living."

"Oh, Natalie, I'm not sure your papa will agree with you. Remember, my papa died when I was young. Our situations are different."

"Don't you want me to move here?"

"Of course I do. I just don't want you to be disappointed if—"

"I know. And I'll try not to be. But say a prayer that Papa will listen to me at least."

"I will. When are you leaving?"

"Tomorrow afternoon. Aunt Abby wanted me to ask you to lunch."

"Of course I'll come to lunch. Tell her thank you. Your aunt and uncle have been wonderful to me, Natalie. I will be forever grateful to them."

"Come about noon. I'd better go pack. I want to get home and get back here as soon as possible. Seeing you start all over here makes me want to do something new. I feel I'm going to become a spinster if I stay in Eureka Springs."

Becca had to keep herself from saying that she would most likely be the spinster of the two of them—not Natalie. After all, she was four years older, and her plans for marriage had died with Richard. But somehow she didn't think those were the words Natalie wanted to hear. Instead she said, "I'll be praying they agree to let you come here, Natalie. For your sake and mine, I'd love to have you nearby."

"That's what I wanted to hear. See you tomorrow."

"See you then." Becca replaced the receiver and went back to the kitchen. It would be nice to have Natalie in the same town. She was going to like it here. She was sure she was going to like her new school, and she loved her apartment. And it didn't hurt at all that Luke Monroe managed the building.

Her thoughts turned to the man who'd saved her from catching the apartment—not to mention herself—on fire. Her heart thudded at the memory of how afraid she had been when the curtains caught on fire. When Luke had suddenly showed up and saved her and the building, she'd felt as if the Lord had surely brought him at just that time and for that reason.

Standing there in the kitchen with her memories, Becca couldn't help but think of how it felt when Luke had held her for that brief moment or two when she'd nearly given in to tears. She'd felt safe and comforted, and it hadn't been easy to step out of the circle of his arms. It hadn't been easy at all. But at the same time, she felt guilty that she'd enjoyed being held by Luke when, just over a year ago, she'd been engaged to marry Richard.

But Richard was gone, and nothing was going to bring him back. Was she to live the rest of her life alone and lonely? That was something she didn't want to think about. Not now, at any rate. Right now she wanted to go take a bath in her very own tub and go to sleep in the first place she could call her own.

Becca gathered her robe and nightgown and went into the bathroom. She almost pinched herself to make sure she wasn't dreaming. Marcus and Abigail had spared no expense when they'd remodeled and had the bathrooms put in. She'd only hoped for an indoor toilet and a basin, expecting to have a communal tub down the hall somewhere, but to have her own tub, well, she felt as if she were living in pure luxury.

She turned on the water and added some bath salts to it. She wasn't going to think about the past tonight. And she wasn't going to worry about the future. She was going to soak in her very own tub and thank the Lord above for her blessings.

*

Luke had a hard time going to sleep. All he could think about was Becca Snow. She was so pretty and so very real. She didn't put on airs and gush like a lot of the women he knew. She seemed to be comfortable with who she was, and it was refreshing to be around her.

When he'd come down the hall to see if she needed anything, he'd noticed the smell of smoke right away. But it wasn't until he got close to her door that it seemed the smell and smoky air was coming from her apartment. When he'd heard her yell, "Oh no!" he hadn't waited to knock. He'd grabbed his master key and let himself in.

When he'd run into the kitchen to see flames grab the curtains and Becca standing so close to them, his heart had stopped. He could remember asking the Lord for help, and then he went into action. There was not one doubt in his mind that his prayer had been answered. He'd been able to put the curtains out before they caught anything else on fire and put out the skillet fire before it had a chance to do damage. But it'd been such a close brush with disaster; he knew it would be a long time before he forgot it.

That Becca had held herself together when he was pretty sure all she wanted to do was dissolve into tears said a lot about her character. He'd followed his first instinct when he'd seen the sheen of tears in her eyes and tried to comfort her. That had been his first mistake. When she'd moved away, his arms had felt empty, and he knew he'd remember the moment for a very long time. The second mistake had been in asking her to dinner, but he knew he'd do it again in a minute. He couldn't remember enjoying an evening more.

Still, he reminded himself that he had to quit thinking of her—at least in the way that he was. This was not a woman he could ever hope to court and not one he could ever hope to marry. But somehow none of that mattered when it came to thinking about Becca Snow. He simply couldn't seem to put her out of his mind.

Chapter 6

O n Sunday morning as Becca got dressed for church, she felt totally at home in the apartment and was excited about beginning her new position the next day. The last few days had been busy. She'd had lunch with Natalie and Abigail, and she'd gone to the depot with the Wellingtons to see Natalie off on Thursday. As they'd waved good-bye until the train rounded a bend and couldn't be seen any longer, Becca didn't know who had hated to see Natalie leave worse, her or Abigail.

The older woman had linked her arm with Becca's and said, "I'm going to miss Natalie so, and I know you are, too. You know Marcus and I were never able to have children, and I've always thought of Natalie as more than a niece."

"I know. Hopefully she'll get to come back soon."

"That is what I'm praying for. But I don't want you to become a stranger. Please. Marcus and I enjoy having you around, and we'd love to have you think of our home as yours on Sundays. We have several people over after church for Sunday dinner each week. His parents used to do it, but we've sort of taken that over from them in the last few years. It was becoming too hard for Mother Wellington."

"Thank you, Abigail. I would love to join you for Sunday dinner. Thank you for the invitation."

Becca had kept busy on Friday and Saturday, getting more settled in and buying new curtains for the kitchen. When she'd asked Luke for a ladder so that she could put them up, he'd put them up himself.

He'd asked about her plans for the weekend, and she'd told him that she was going to the Wellingtons for dinner after church. He'd immediately asked if he could escort her since he was always invited for Sunday dinner, too. "It's the one day of the week I never have to decide whether to cook for myself or go out somewhere. I love it. Since we're both going to the same place, we might as well go together."

Although Becca wasn't sure why her heartbeat sped up at his suggestion, it made perfect sense to her, and she saw no reason not to agree. "I suppose we might as well. I can meet you in the lobby—what time do we need to leave?"

"We'll catch the trolley and need to leave about nine."

"I'll be on time."

Now as she dressed in a blue and cream Sunday dress, one of the many new ones Meagan had insisted she needed, Becca was grateful for many reasons. She was grateful for the invitations from both Abigail and Luke, and she was grateful to her sister for providing her with a fashionable wardrobe. It occurred to her that she'd never had to worry about whether she had the latest styles or not. She'd always had them because her sister and mother had a knack for knowing what they would be even before they made it to Eureka Springs.

She left her apartment for the elevator to take her down to the lobby, and a few moments later as she stepped out of the elevator and looked at the clock in the lobby, Becca was relieved to see that she was a few minutes early. She hated to be late when someone was expecting her.

Luke was waiting for her, and he smiled as she approached him. "Good morning, Miss Snow."

"Good morning. I hope I haven't kept you waiting."

"No, not at all. But I will say I'm surprised at your promptness."

"Oh? Why is that?"

He smiled down at her. "Most women I know think it's fashionable to keep a gentleman waiting."

"Oh. Well, I suppose I could learn to do that, but I was taught to be on time if at all possible."

"Then you were taught well, and I appreciate it. We'll have no problem at all catching the trolley. Thinking you would be a little late, I gave you an earlier time than needed. In fact, we'll have to wait a few minutes for it to get here. I apologize. Next week you can wait until a quarter after nine, if you'd like."

Luke truly looked apologetic, and Becca found herself wanting to make him feel better. "No need to apologize. It's all right. But I'll take the extra minutes next Sunday."

Realizing that he was planning on accompanying her to church again next week gave Becca a good feeling deep inside. And after his coming to her aid the night of the fire and promising not to tell anyone how close she'd come to burning the building down, putting curtains up for her, and offering to accompany her to church, she had no doubt that she had made a new friend. One she could count on.

⤴

There was no way Luke couldn't enjoy the interested looks he and Becca got as he led her to the pew he normally sat in. It was right behind Marcus and Abigail, and he'd been sitting there for the last ten years. But he'd never sat there with a woman he'd brought to church. He motioned for Becca to enter first and then took a seat beside her. He could hear the twitter of whispers behind them.

Becca had sat with Natalie and the Wellingtons the Sunday before, and he was sure she'd been noticed. He certainly hadn't been able to concentrate on the sermon that day. But today she was sitting beside him, and he was enjoying knowing that many of his church family were more than a little curious about how that came to be. When he'd first begun going to church there, several of the older women had tried their hand at matchmaking, but nothing had developed. He was pretty sure that they'd given up on him long ago.

And truly, Becca sitting beside him changed none of that, but he wasn't going to deny that he very much liked the fact that she was sharing a hymnal with him—even though all they ever would or could be was friends. It seemed he had to keep reminding himself of that fact.

He forced himself to listen to the sermon, and as usual, it was very good. The minister, John Martin, spoke about Ecclesiastes 3:4 and about there being "a time to weep, and a time to laugh; a time to mourn, and a time to dance." He couldn't help but notice that Becca was listening intently.

Marcus had told him that Becca had suffered a heartache but not exactly what. Luke hoped that what she was hearing would help her through whatever had caused her grief, and he prayed her heart would heal.

By the time he and Becca left the Wellingtons' that evening to go back to the apartment building, he couldn't remember spending a more enjoyable Sunday. The meal had been wonderful, as always. They'd played parlor games afterward and had a light supper before he and Becca left. The day in itself wasn't that much different from many he'd spent at the Wellingtons'. What had made it so memorable and enjoyable was Becca's company. She truly was delightful to be around.

"I had such a good time," Becca commented as they walked to the trolley stop near the Wellingtons'. "Thank you for escorting me home, Mr. Monroe."

"You are welcome. But since we see so much of each other, do you think you might just call me Luke? Calling me Mr. Monroe makes me feel old."

"Old? Why, you aren't old. But if calling you by your last name makes you feel that way, of course I can call you Luke. Only if you call me Becca, though."

"I can do that." He'd been thinking of her as Becca for days now. "Becca it is, then."

The trolley stopped, and he held Becca's arm to steady her as she ascended the steps. He followed her to an empty seat and sat down beside her. He was quite a bit older than Becca—ten years by his best estimation. Just one more reason to keep his distance from her, but he wasn't doing a very good job of that. Still, he couldn't avoid her—even if he wanted to. She lived in his building, and he'd been asked to watch over her. Surely no harm could come in being friendly. He'd just have to make sure he didn't let what he felt for her go beyond that. But as Becca smiled up at him, he knew that was not going to be an easy feat. Not easy at all.

"Thank you for helping me the other night and for not letting everyone know how I almost caught the apartment on fire. I've had nightmares about setting the whole building on fire."

Luke shook his head. "I've had nightmares about *you* catching on fire."

"Oh dear, I am sorry. Only your quick thinking and actions prevented that."

"Well, let's put it out of our minds. Are you nervous about tomorrow?"

"I am, a little. But I'm excited, too. And I'm ready to go to work. I'm not used to. . .having all this time to myself."

"Are you homesick?" He certainly hoped not. He'd not like to see her go back to Eureka Springs.

"No. I miss my family, but I love the apartment. And I like Hot Springs better each day, although I haven't seen a lot of it yet. I probably used the wrong words. I should have said *leisure time*. I like being busy, and I love teaching."

"That's a very good thing for your students." The trolley stopped a block from the apartment building, and they got off and walked briskly down the street, as the night air had begun to cool quickly.

The night watchman greeted them as they entered the building. "Evening, Mr. Monroe, Miss Snow."

"I'll see Miss Snow to her apartment and be back down shortly, George." The watchman had noticed someone lurking around the other side of the street for several nights in a row and had told Luke that it seemed the man was watching their building. Luke wanted to know if he'd been back tonight, but he didn't want to mention it in front of Becca.

"You don't have to see me to my door," she said. "I'll be fine, and I'm sure you have things you need to do."

"Nothing that can't wait until I see you safely inside."

He walked her to the door and waited until she unlocked it and stepped inside. "I hope you have a very good day tomorrow. I look forward to hearing all about it."

"Thank you. I'm hoping it goes well, too. I'll let you know. Thank you for taking me to church and seeing me home."

"You're welcome. I can't see any reason for us to go separately when we're both going to the same place, can you?"

Becca shook her head. "It wouldn't make much sense, would it? But thank you anyway."

"You're welcome. I'll be waiting to hear how your first day goes. I'll wait for you to lock up. Good night."

"Good night," Becca said, shutting the door.

He heard the key turn in the lock before he headed back downstairs to talk to George. He prided himself that he kept this building safe, and he didn't like the idea that some stranger was watching the comings and goings of the tenants. The Wellington Building was known as one of the safest apartment buildings in the state, and he wanted to make sure it stayed that way.

Abigail sat at her dressing table, brushing her hair while Marcus sat in front of the fire, reading. "Marcus, dear, did you notice the way Luke tried to keep from looking at Becca today?"

He chuckled. "No. I noticed how often he did look at her."

"You did notice, then. I think he's interested in her."

"It's about time he found someone. But I'm not sure Becca is ready. After losing her fiancé. . .you never know how long that might take."

Abigail sighed. "You are right. I wouldn't know what to do if something happened to you. Of course we are married, and Becca lost Richard before they married, but I don't know how much difference that would make."

Marcus shook his head. "No, neither do I. But in my mind, there is no doubt that Luke is interested in her. I think he's trying not to be, but as you and I both know, trying *not* to care for someone doesn't always work."

Abigail met her husband's eyes in the mirror and smiled.

"That is very true. I would hate for Luke to get hurt. I so want to see him happy. I think he longs for a family, for someone to love." She put her brush down, got up, and sat down beside her husband. He pulled her into his arms and kissed the top of her head.

"I'd like to see the same thing. And Becca is just the kind of woman he needs."

"Let's pray that her heart heals and that she is open to falling in love again—with Luke, of course."

"We can do that. You've turned into quite a romantic, my love."

"*You've* turned me into a romantic. And I just want to see Luke and Becca as happy as we are."

"That would be nice." Marcus tipped her head up and lowered his lips to hers.

"Mmm, yes, it would. . . ," Abigail said, just before his lips touched hers.

Becca woke early the next day. She was both excited and apprehensive about her first day at Central High. She hoped her students liked her and that the other teachers were easy to get along with. She dressed with care in a brown and cream dress that made her feel businesslike. She pulled her hair up in a french twist, thinking it made her look older. Although she wanted to establish who was in charge from the very first, she preferred to do it by the way she handled herself, and she hoped by the end of the day her students would realize she was firm but fair.

Although she'd gone in and met Mr. Fuller, been shown her room, and been given the curriculum the week before, he had asked her to come a little early today so that he could show her around more fully and introduce her to the other teachers. By the time she entered the school and made her way to the principal's office, she was pretty certain that she was much more nervous about meeting her students than they were about meeting her.

The secretary seemed pleased to see her again.

"Oh, I am so glad you are here, Miss Snow. It will be so nice to have Mr. Fuller in his office full-time so that I don't have to run down the hall every time I need to ask him about something or someone telephones him. I know he has been looking forward to this day, too."

She showed Becca into the principal's office right away, and Mr. Fuller stood as soon as she entered his office. It was obvious he was happy to be able to turn his class over to her, and he quickly put her at ease. "Miss Snow, I can't tell you how glad I am that you've decided to join our faculty. So are our teachers. They are eager to meet you. Come with me. They are waiting in the teachers' lounge."

He led her to a room just across from his office and introduced her. "This is Miss Becca Snow, who has come to relieve me in teaching the literature classes. Please make her feel welcome so that she will stay with us."

Everyone chuckled at his words, but she felt genuinely welcomed as he introduced her to each one. Becca knew she'd never remember all their names, but she tried to connect faces to names as she shook each hand.

The nice lady with hair that was graying was Mrs. Ella Richards, and she taught geography. The short blond who looked about the same age as Becca was named Lila Baxter, and she was the domestic science teacher. The redhead was Jennifer Collins, who taught Latin. Then there was Gene Landry, who taught algebra, and Harold Green, who taught geometry.

By the time she'd met the rest of the teachers, she was getting confused about who taught what but was assured she'd know them all better by the end of the week.

"Or next, anyway," Miss Collins said. "It took me two full weeks to get it all straight."

"And we'll help you remember. Don't worry at all if you call us by the wrong name," Miss Baxter added.

Everyone was so kind, offering to help in any way they could, that by the time Mr. Fuller took her to meet her students, Becca was sure she'd fit right in.

"I think you'll find the students are very easy to get along with and eager to learn," Mr. Fuller said as they walked up the stairs to the second floor. They passed several clusters of students, and Becca was pretty sure they knew she was the new teacher. Although they didn't speak, most of them smiled at her.

"I've enjoyed teaching them. It's just that I don't feel I'm doing justice to either them or my duties as principal. I think you'll enjoy the class, but if you have any concerns or questions, please don't hesitate to ask."

He stopped at a room at the end of the hall, and Becca was happy that there were so many windows and lots of light in the room. "I've left lesson plans for you for the next few weeks so that you didn't have to do all of that right away and you can see where we are."

"Oh thank you. That will help immensely."

"You're welcome. I know how hard it can be to step in midyear. I really didn't think we'd find anyone this late in the year. I do hope you like it here, Miss Snow. I think you'll find the students are well behaved." He chuckled. "Most of them, anyway. I made up seating charts for each of your classes and will stay with you today to make sure no one tries to confuse you. Some of the boys certainly aren't above pulling a few pranks. I also made up a list of those I think might see how far they can push you in the first few weeks, and if one even tries, send them straight to me."

"Yes, sir. Don't worry. I will."

The bell rang, and true to his word, Mr. Fuller stayed with her, making sure everyone took the right seat. Then he introduced her.

"Class, this is your new teacher, Miss Snow. She's come all the way from Eureka Springs and is an excellent teacher. I'm sure you are going to find her much more pleasant to look at than me. Please make sure she doesn't regret her decision to move here."

Becca noticed that he smiled to take the sting out of his words before he cleared his throat and said, "I have enjoyed teaching each one of you this year. I believe you will all go far in life, and remember; I'll be watching to make sure you do. And just as it was here, my office door is always open to you."

It was obvious why he had such a good reputation as a principal. He deeply cared about each one of these young people. It appeared she had a lot to live up to in this class.

The morning passed quickly, and Becca enjoyed having lunch with the other teachers. If anything, the afternoon went by even faster, and by the time she caught a trolley back to the apartment, Becca was sure she was going to like teaching at Central High. For the most part, she didn't think she'd have any problems with her students. The girls all seemed very sweet and nice. The boys. . .were boys. Overall, they seemed well behaved, too, with the exception of two or three, and she thought they were just a little mischievous. Time would tell.

⤳

Burrows had been watching the Wellington Building for days and only this morning had seen the woman come out and take the trolley. He stepped on the trolley at the back, took a seat, and unfolded the newspaper he'd brought with him. He pretended to read while he waited to find out what stop she would get off at. It was near the end of the line when she stepped off and headed toward the high school.

Hmm. Apparently she was a teacher. He couldn't remember any teachers he'd met recently. He had to find out where he'd run into her. For some reason, he hadn't been able to get the young woman out of his mind. But perhaps it wasn't here. He was out of town a lot in his line of business. Maybe she'd just moved here. But how was he to find out? Maybe he could pretend to be interested in renting an apartment in the building. That was it. He'd walk right in and talk to the manager. He had business to attend to, but he'd go there this afternoon. Perhaps he'd see the young woman again and remember where it was he'd seen her before. It was imperative that he find out.

At two thirty Burrows rode the trolley back to the Wellington Building and walked right in as if he had every right to be there. The day watchman looked up from his desk. "May I help you, sir?"

"Yes. My name is Harland Burrows, and I'd like to talk to the manager about renting an apartment. I've heard good things about this building."

"I don't believe we have any openings right now, but you can talk to Mr. Monroe. He might put you on a waiting list. I can see if he has time to see you now, if you'd like."

"Yes, I would. Thank you." This might be easier than he had thought.

The guard picked up the telephone, and in minutes Burrows was shown to the manager's office.

"Mr. Monroe, this is Mr. Burrows. I told him I didn't think we had any openings, but he'd like to talk to you about putting his name on the waiting list."

"Come in, Mr. Burrows," the building manager said. "Derrick is right. We have no openings at present, but you can put your name on a list. That won't guarantee that you will get an apartment or when one might become available. What it will guarantee is that we will get in touch with you if your name is next on the list when we have a vacancy. Would you like to do that?"

"Yes, I believe I would."

"I'd need you to fill out an application." Mr. Monroe handed him a form to fill out.

Harland looked it over and began to fill it out.

"Would it be possible for me to see an apartment or floor plan?"

"I have a floor plan I could show you. Would you be needing a one- or two-bedroom apartment?"

"Perhaps a two-bedroom. I'm out of town often on business. The wife likes to have her family come to visit occasionally, especially when I am gone."

Mr. Monroe slid a floor plan of the building over to him. Harland couldn't ask for anything more. It gave the room numbers of each apartment and the layout. The building manager pointed to an apartment in the middle of the building. "This would be a two-bedroom floor plan. They are all alike but could be reversed, depending on which one became vacant."

Harland looked it over. Obviously they were very nice apartments—much nicer than what he was renting now. But what he really paid attention to were the room numbers. Apartment 312 was a corner apartment looking out over Central Avenue. That was what he'd wanted to know. "These are very nice."

"Yes, they are the nicest apartments in town. We don't have an empty one for long."

Harland stood up, hoping to take the floor plan with him, but Mr. Monroe held out his hand. "I'm afraid I need that back. It's the master copy, and it stays here."

"Yes, of course." He didn't really need it. He'd seen enough. "Thank you. I look forward to getting that call one of these days."

"Good day, Mr. Burrows."

Harland left the office and turned just in time to see the young woman come through the door. When she looked at him and he met her gaze, he was even more positive that he had seen her before. But where? He pulled his hat down low and hurried out the door. He had better find out, and the sooner the better.

Chapter 7

By the time Becca stepped off the trolley and entered the apartment building, she realized just how very tired she was. She didn't know if she had the energy to make even a light supper.

A man came out of Luke's office just then, and Becca thought he looked familiar. When he pulled his hat down over his eyes, she remembered where she'd seen him. It was at the grocer's the day she'd moved in. But she'd thought he looked familiar then, too. She sighed. Well, he would this time. After all, she'd run into him twice already.

Luke came out of his office just as she reached the elevator.

"Who is that man?"

"He's Harland Burrows. He came to inquire about an apartment. Why?"

"Oh, I've just run into him before, and he looks very familiar to me. But I don't recognize the name." She smiled and shrugged. "He probably just looks like someone I've met before."

Luke nodded. "That happens to me, too. How did your first day go, Becca?"

"It went very well, thank you. But I'm quite tired. I must have become lazy during the last few weeks. I'd forgotten how much energy it takes keeping up with high school students. They are very bright, and they ask a lot of questions."

"Why don't you let me treat you to dinner then? Don't you think you should celebrate your first day teaching here?"

"Oh, I can't let you do that."

"Why not?"

"You just took me out to dinner the night of the fire."

"I'm not talking about taking you to dinner. I'm talking about making you dinner. I'll bring it to you."

"You will make me dinner?" His thoughtfulness touched her heart, and she could hear her voice soften. "That would be nice. But only if you let me return the favor soon."

He smiled. "I rarely turn down a dinner invitation, Becca. Of course I'll let you return the favor. I'm roasting a chicken. I'll bring it over about six. Just set a table for us."

"All right. Thank you. I wasn't looking forward to frying eggs again." Suddenly Becca wasn't quite so tired. She found herself looking forward to dinner with Luke and to having someone to talk with about her day.

～

Becca set the round table in front of the bay window with the china and crystal she'd brought over from the Wellingtons' and the silverware her mother had sent. She'd been filling a hope chest for years, but after setting up housekeeping here, she'd realized that she hadn't accumulated anywhere near as much as she thought she had for her marriage to Richard. Of course there would have been wedding gifts, and they would have bought things to fill out what they didn't have, but Becca realized that it was over years that people accumulated all they needed to live in the lifestyle she now enjoyed due primarily to her family and the Wellingtons.

While she waited for Luke, she made iced tea and straightened the already-neat parlor before going to the bathroom to freshen up. She still found it hard to believe that she was living in such a nice place. She dampened her comb and ran it over her hair, straightening the wayward curls that liked to spring up around her face.

Each time she came into this room, she almost felt guilty. Until a year or so before, she and her mother had been using an outdoor privy. Meagan and Nate had practically begged her mother to let them put a real bathroom in, such as they had in their new home. Finally, with a little help from the urging of Becca and Sarah, Mama had given in.

Becca decided to count herself blessed that she was able to live in such a fine fashion, but at the same time, she felt quite spoiled. She prayed she'd never take all this for granted.

A knock on the door had her hurrying through the apartment to answer it. Luke was standing there with a grin on his face and a huge picnic basket on his arm. "At your service, miss. May I ask where you would like me to set up our meal?"

He grinned and raised an eyebrow, and Becca couldn't help but laugh. She motioned to the table. "Right over there. I thought it would be nicer than the dining room. It's a little formal, and this is more—"

"This is just right. I don't have a table like this, but I have a chair in my bay window, and it's where I usually eat, too. Dining rooms are nice if you are having more than two people to dine, but with two people, one at each end of a long table, it seems. . ."

Too far away was Becca's first thought, but instead she said, "A long way to pass the potatoes. I'm not sure either of us has arms long enough for that."

Luke threw back his head and laughed. "You are absolutely right. But how did you know I brought creamed potatoes?"

"I didn't, but those are my favorite kind. Let me help you get this on the table. My mouth is watering at the aroma." She helped him set out the roast chicken, potatoes, and peas. He filled their plates while she poured iced tea into the goblets. Then she took her seat, and Luke said a blessing before they began to eat.

Becca took her first bite and closed her eyes. "This is delicious. I can't believe you cooked all of this. But oh, thank you. I am getting so tired of the few things I know how to cook."

"You really don't know how to cook? Or are you just frightened after the grease fire?"

"A little of both, I suppose, but mostly the latter." Feeling the need to explain about her lack of cooking skills, she added, "My older sisters helped Mama in the kitchen the most. I set the table and did the dishes a lot, but I seemed to have missed out on learning all Mama could have taught me."

"I'll show you how to safely light the burners and the oven. And I'll be glad to teach you what I know about cooking."

Becca nodded. "I'll take you up on the offer. I'm going to pick up a copy of Fannie Farmer's book, too, this weekend. I meant to do that on the way home today, but I was so tired that I forgot."

Luke nodded. "It would be good to have. But there is no need to hurry. I can help you this week. It would probably be better to work in your kitchen so that you know where everything is and how your range works. After we eat, I can see what you have on hand, and we'll make up a menu for the next few days. Then I'll come over and help. Don't worry about what you don't have. If we're going to eat our cooking together, I can buy what we need."

Becca thought her mother would disapprove of her having Luke over so often. It might not have been approved behavior when Mama was young, but it was 1902, after all.

She took another bite of chicken. If she could learn to cook even half as well as this, she would be quite comfortable asking people over for dinner. And she was bound to want to, once she got to know more people from her new church family and the high school faculty—not to mention the Wellingtons and Luke.

Besides, Luke had never treated her in any inappropriate way. He'd been helpful and friendly, but she would expect nothing less from the manager of the building and the employee of the Wellingtons. In fact, several times she'd wondered if he was only nice to her for those reasons. She'd hoped that he liked her for herself, and she had begun to think of him as a friend she could talk to, someone she could count on.

She wasn't totally comfortable with the way her heart jumped when he smiled at her. Or the way she looked forward to seeing him each day. But Luke didn't know how he made her feel, and at any rate, he seemed to be only acting out of kindness and friendship. At the moment, that was exactly what she needed.

"Thank you, Luke. If I ever get to the point that I can make chicken taste this good by myself, I'll cook the whole dinner for you."

"I'll certainly agree to that, Becca. What time would you like me to come over tomorrow?"

"Whenever you need to. You know how long it takes to prepare a meal. I still don't know how you time it all to be ready at the same time."

"You will. I'll be here around five thirty."

They finished the meal, talking about what Becca had on hand and what they could make, then Luke helped her clear the table, gathering his dishes to take home. But Becca wasn't about to let him take home dirty dishes. The least she could do was wash them for him. She did that while he took stock of her pantry.

They worked in silence, her washing and drying dishes and repacking his basket and him making a list of menus for the week. It was a comfortable feeling. . .not awkward at all. *Yes,* she thought, *right now Luke is just the person I need to be around—a friend who expects only friendship in return.* She found herself looking forward to the next day—not just because of her new job but because she would be able to spend the evening with Luke.

❧

Becca's day went very well on Tuesday. She began to think she might be able to put names to faces fairly soon, thanks to Mr. Fuller's seating chart. His lesson plans would prove to be invaluable to her also. These first few weeks would be much easier if she didn't have to create her own plans. It would give her time to assess where her class as a whole was and how fast she could expect them to move through the material she had left to teach for the year.

She was finding that being in a new school in a new town, meeting new people, and learning the rules and regulations she was expected to observe at school, while exciting, was a bit more tiring than she'd thought it would be. Actually she hadn't thought about the adjustments she'd be making when she decided to move. All she'd wanted to do was get away from painful memories.

She hadn't been able to escape them altogether, but she'd had so many new experiences that thoughts of what could have been didn't come quite so often, and when they did, she got busy with something that took her mind off it all. And yet, she felt guilty that she wasn't thinking of Richard quite as much these days. She knew she'd loved him, and the heartache she'd suffered had been deep and lasting—so much so that she didn't know if she would ever be able to fall in love again. Certainly she didn't want to give her heart to anyone who had a dangerous position: not another policeman, not a fireman, not anyone who put his life on the line by choice.

But the memory of what Richard looked like had begun to fade, and she had to pull out a photo of him to remember. Yet what good did that do? It only served to make her sad. He wasn't here, and the life they'd planned could never be. In the last few months Becca had come to accept that fact. Now she found she was longing to look forward to the future once more.

And today she was anticipating her first cooking lesson from Luke. She could just imagine what her mother would have to say about it. As she stepped off the trolley and walked the short way to the Wellington Building, she chuckled. She wasn't sure that was something she wanted to share with her mother. . .not just yet anyway.

She hurried up to her apartment and unlocked the door. As she walked in, she found a note had been slipped under her door. She picked it up and read the masculine handwriting. "I'll be a little late. I'm picking up a few things at the grocer's. You can peel a couple of potatoes, cut them into cubes, and put them in a pan of water, if you'd like."

"I should be able to do that," Becca said out loud. She changed into a dress more appropriate for cooking and put on one of the aprons her mother had sent from home. By the time Luke knocked on the door, she was feeling quite domestic.

She opened the door to him and found that he had his arms full. "Oh, Luke, what have you got there?"

"You were a little short on a few things, and if we're going to be cooking, I wanted to make sure you had everything we might need."

"I bought the staples Mama always said to have on hand: flour, sugar, salt, and pepper."

"Your mother was right. But you also need baking powder and soda and some spices for flavoring."

Becca led him to the kitchen and helped him unload his bags. As she pulled out nutmeg, cinnamon, ginger, and cloves, she could remember her mother using them back home. She just wasn't sure in what dishes the different spices were used. How could she have lived in that home for all those years and not learned to cook more than she did? Well, she was going to learn now. That was all there was to it.

She turned to Luke. "What do you need me to do?"

ᔥ

Becca looked adorable in her ruffled apron. She could just stand there looking pretty and talk to Luke while he cooked for her if she wanted to. But she really did seem to want to learn to cook. From her talk of her mother cooking and her sister helping with her education, he didn't think that she'd been raised in the same kind of luxury Abigail had been. He was certain that she came from an upstanding family, but he vaguely remembered that they had fallen on hard times at some point and that was why her sister had gone into the dressmaking business.

Perhaps the fact that she came from that upbringing was why he related to her so well. . .but none of that changed the fact that he had no business dreaming of her at night or thinking of her first thing in the morning. He shouldn't have offered to help her learn to cook, but he wasn't going to back out now, not when she was looking at him so expectantly.

"You have the potatoes ready to boil. We'll drain most of the water and add butter and parsley to them once they are done." He put the pot on the range and showed her how to operate the damper to control the amount of heat. "I'm sure you know how to do this—"

"No, that's not the way I was doing it. This range is a little different from the one at home." She watched him closely. "I'll try to remember how you did it."

"I can show you again anytime." He turned toward her. "Once the potatoes come to a boil, we'll move them to a cooler spot and let them simmer. Then I'll let you be in charge of them."

"I think I can manage. What are we having with them? I have some bacon—"

"We'll save that for another night. I bought a couple of pork chops. We're starting fairly easy and are just going to fry them."

"Mmm, I do like pork chops," Becca said as she watched him unwrap the white butcher paper to reveal two thick chops.

"But first we're going to mix up some biscuits."

"Oh my. Biscuits—I'm not sure that's starting out easy."

"They aren't hard. You'll see." He pulled a piece of paper out of his pocket. "Here is an easy biscuit recipe. We'll need a bowl and two cups of flour measured into it."

Becca pulled out a bowl and her measuring cups. She carefully measured the flour into the bowl.

"Now we need four teaspoons of baking powder and a half teaspoon of salt. I'll make sure the oven is hot enough while you are doing that."

"And now what?"

"Now you cut up two tablespoons butter into the flour mixture."

"Oh, I remember Mama doing that. She used two forks." Becca pulled two out of a drawer, and after putting two cubes of butter in the bowl with the flour mixture, she began pulling the forks in opposite directions across the butter.

"That's how I do it."

"Milk next?" Becca smiled up at him.

"You do remember. Yes, a cup. We're going to make it easy and just drop them onto a buttered pan. Next time we'll roll them out. Don't add the milk just yet, though. I need to get the chops started. Where is a skillet?"

Becca pulled one out of the cupboard and handed it to him. Luke took the skillet and put it on a burner, then he carefully slid the chops into the skillet and seasoned them with salt and pepper. "We'll have to watch them closely so they don't burn. Once they are browned, we'll let them cook slowly. The potatoes are boiling, so you can move the pot over to the side of the burner so they can simmer."

Becca did as he suggested, and the rolling boil quickly settled down to a gentle simmer. "Do I add the butter now?"

She really was eager to learn, and it made him more determined to teach her. "Not yet. We'll do that a little later. Part of putting a meal on the table and having everything ready at one time depends on learning how long each thing takes to cook. Mostly it just takes practice."

"How do you know when to turn the pork chops over?"

"You can lift a corner and see how it is doing. Or you can nudge it like this." Luke pushed at one of the chops with his fork, and it didn't want to move. "It needs a little more time."

"What about those biscuits? Should I add the milk and drop them on the pan?"

"Yes, please. I'll watch the chops." But he also watched Becca. She was concentrating so hard on mixing the dough that she seemed unaware of his presence. Then she turned around and found him looking at her.

"Ah, is the dough ready to drop?" she asked, delicate color flooding her cheeks.

"Yes, I think so. You can put them on the pan." He turned back and checked the chops. This time the chop slid easily, so he turned it over and did the same with the second one. He was thankful that he hadn't let them burn while he was watching Becca.

"I think this is the way my mother did it when she was in a hurry," Becca said, taking a spoonful and dropping it onto the pan by pushing it off the spoon with her finger.

"I'd say she probably did. You are doing fine." He checked the chops and moved them to a slower-cooking burner. "Now we'll let the chops cook slowly while the biscuits bake."

Becca nodded as she dropped the last biscuit onto the pan. "I think they are ready."

Luke opened the oven door so she could slip the pan in. "Now we can butter the potatoes. I brought a can of peas we can heat up, too."

Becca brought out another pan, and Luke opened the peas and dumped them into it. "We can heat these up and add a little butter to them. Mama didn't add much else, if I remember right."

"You can be in charge of them while I show you how to butter the potatoes," Luke said. He drained most of the water off them, salted and peppered them, and then added some butter before putting them back over a low fire. He chopped some parsley and added that to the pan. "The water and butter will cook down and make a good sauce while the parsley will give a little more flavor and add some color."

"Everything smells wonderful. I'll fill our glasses and take them to the table, along with the butter. Would you like some honey to go with the biscuits?"

"Yes, please. The chops are almost done, and I think the biscuits are, too." When Becca came back from setting things on the table, he asked, "What do you want me to put them in?" Had he been by himself, he would have just slapped it all on a plate and been done with it, but he didn't suggest that approach.

"Well, I know it's not the way we'd be doing it at the Wellingtons'—or even at home, for that matter—but why don't we just fill our plates and take them to the table? I have a basket we can use for the biscuits."

She was a woman after his own heart. "That's how I'd do it if I were at home."

"Well, I probably should have it set up all proper and everything, but right now just getting it on the table seems a great accomplishment."

"That's how I feel after working all day." Luke pulled out the biscuits that had baked to a golden brown, and then he dished up the chops while Becca added potatoes and peas to each plate. "And you've done great tonight. The biscuits smell wonderful. Next time I'll let you fry the chops."

"Oh, you will?" Becca smiled at him from over her shoulder as she headed for the parlor with her plate and the basket of biscuits.

If he didn't know better, he'd think she was being flirtatious. But she'd given him no indication that she thought of him in that way. None at all. Luke sighed and followed her out of the kitchen.

❧

Becca bowed her head while Luke said a prayer over their meal. She tried to concentrate on what he was saying instead of thinking how handsome he'd looked in her kitchen. She hadn't been prepared for the way she felt just having him in the small area, as they'd moved around each other while they worked together. It was quite enjoyable, and she was very proud of the meal she and Luke had prepared. He had done most of the work, but he'd let her do enough that she felt as if she truly had cooked. . .and cooked well. The biscuits were light and fluffy and tasted as good as any she'd eaten. She was looking forward to rolling them out next time so that they looked as good, too.

"Mmm, the pork chops are just how I like them."

"They are good, aren't they?" Luke agreed with a smile. "But not as good as your biscuits. How do you like the potatoes?"

"Thank you. About the biscuits, I mean. I like the potatoes, and I think I could make them on my own."

"You can do this whole meal on your own. I'll leave the biscuit recipe with you, just so you have it to go by."

"I think that is part of the problem. I didn't write things down while my mother was trying to teach me. But the real issue is that I mostly watched and didn't do."

"Well, you are going to do fine, because I'm going to let you do most of it."

Becca took another bite of pork chop. It was very good: crisp on the outside, moist on the inside, and seasoned just right. "I hope you don't expect anything this good—at least not just yet."

She looked out the window and thought she saw someone under the light across the street looking up, but when she stared more carefully, the person had moved on. She didn't know if she'd imagined it or not, but for several evenings she'd thought the same thing. She shook her head and sighed.

"What is it?"

"Nothing really. I just thought I saw someone outside looking up this way. It's probably just my imagination."

Luke looked out the window. "Was it a man or woman?"

"A man. The last few evenings I've thought someone was watching from across the street, but when I looked again, he was always on his way up the street. Besides, it's no crime to look up at a building. I do it, too. I'm sure it was just my imagination." She felt a little silly even bringing it up.

"Well, it might be, but it never hurts to be sure. Don't hesitate to let me know if you think someone is watching your windows again. The Wellington is a safe place to live, and I want to keep it that way. But we need to know if that reputation is threatened in any way. Don't ever feel anything that bothers you is too small to tell me."

Luke made her feel much better, but still she wanted to change the subject.

She didn't like the idea that someone might be out there watching her windows. "I'm sorry I don't have anything for dessert."

"With biscuits as light as these and butter and honey, who needs a fancy dessert?" Luke said, making her feel as if he couldn't want for more. By the time she saw him to the door after he insisted on helping to clean up the kitchen, Becca was beginning to think this man was too good to be real.

Chapter 8

By that Thursday Becca had learned how to roll and cut out biscuits and make mayonnaise and chicken salad—on Wednesday they'd used the leftover chicken from Monday night—and tonight she'd learned to make an omelet and fry bacon without burning it. All in all, she thought she was off to a good start. Well, she had burned the first few pieces of bacon, but Luke had showed her how to regulate the heat again, and the next batch was cooked just right.

When he'd left that night, he'd said, "Tomorrow is Friday, and...I...ah... I know that we aren't sweethearts, but it is Valentine's Day, and well, you are new in town, and I think we should celebrate a week of you learning how to cook. Will you let me take you to dinner?"

She'd been trying hard not to think about the next day being Valentine's Day. But she hadn't been able to banish it from her thoughts entirely, and she'd dreaded spending the evening alone, thinking about Richard and what could have been had he lived. Luke's invitation would enable her to spend the evening in the company of someone besides herself, and she was thankful for it.

Becca's heart seemed to do a little dive into her stomach as she watched the color rise on Luke's cheeks while he waited for her answer. Why, he was unsure of what she would say. While they weren't sweethearts, they'd become friends, and it would be a whole lot less lonesome if they spent the evening together. "That would be very nice, Luke. Thank you."

Over the last few evenings she'd found that she liked the man very much ...and could be in danger of losing her heart to him if she wasn't very careful. Now as she dressed for her dinner with Luke, she took care with her hair and wore a dinner dress that she'd worn only once before, but she loved it. It was a Worth-inspired gown of red silk with black trim. Her sister was such a wonderful seamstress that Becca was sure many would think it was an original Worth gown. She was just glad that she didn't have to pay the Worth price.

She felt wonderful, and when she opened the door to Luke a few minutes later, his expression told her what he thought before he spoke. "What a beautiful gown," Luke said. "You look lovely tonight, Becca."

"Thank you, Luke. You look very nice, too." He had on a black overcoat with a black fur collar over a black suit, a wing-collared shirt, and a black silk tie. He didn't just look nice; he looked quite handsome.

He helped her on with her black cloak trimmed in fur and then pulled something red out of his pocket. "This is just because I wanted to give you something to celebrate your first week of teaching and how well you are doing with your cooking. You can open it later if you want." He handed the prettily wrapped package to her.

She took it and turned it over in her hand. "Oh, Luke, you shouldn't have. But since you did, may I open it now?"

"Of course you may."

Becca tore open the wrapping to find not candy as she'd expected but a leather copy of Fannie Farmer's cookbook. "Oh, Luke, thank you. I was going to pick up a copy tomorrow."

"I know. But I wanted to get it for you. It seemed fitting since I'm helping you learn to cook. Besides, I figured I could learn a few things, too."

"I know I can learn a lot from it. We'll go over it later." Becca laid it on the table in the bay window. "Thank you so much. I can't wait to use it."

She knew they weren't sweethearts, but when Luke locked the door for her and cupped her elbow with his hand as they walked to the elevator, she felt more special than she had in a very long time. He'd hired a hack to take them to the restaurant instead of taking the trolley, and that only added to the special feel of the evening.

He'd made reservations at the Park Hotel. Its dining room was quite beautiful, with windows on three sides. It was said to be one of the nicest in the city. They were shown to a table for two, and on this night in particular, Becca was glad to have Luke as an escort. The room was full of couples, the ladies dressed in their finest and the men dressed much like Luke.

They were handed menus, and Becca looked over the choices. They seemed very expensive, and she wasn't sure what Luke could afford. "Would you order for me? I don't know what is best."

"I'd be glad to. Their fillet of beef is excellent. It's served with potato croquettes and peas, but the meal starts off with mock turtle soup and ends with ice cream and nut cake."

"It all sounds wonderful."

Luke nodded, and the waiter seemed to appear out of nowhere. Luke gave him the order, and he left as quietly as he'd come.

"How did your day go?" Luke asked.

Becca knew he would raise this question, for he'd asked her each day this week when he'd come for a cooking lesson. "It was very nice. The school held a secret Valentine exchange. During lunchtime the students could go into each room and put a card on the other desks, just one or all of them. But they had to take turns. I ate my lunch at my desk and made sure that only one student at a time came in. Then right before the last class was dismissed, they could open their cards. Some had more than others, but everyone got several, and they all seemed quite happy."

"Good. I would hope no one was left out," Luke said. "So overall do you think you are going to like teaching there?"

Becca nodded. "I already do. I'm glad I made the move. I needed—"

The waiter chose that moment to bring their soup, and Becca was glad of the interruption. It had been a lovely evening, and there was no need to put a damper on it by bringing up Richard's death.

As soon as the waiter left the table, Luke said, "Please pray with me." He bowed his head and prayed. "Dear Lord, we thank You for this day and that it was a good one for Becca. Thank You for the beautiful day You've blessed us with, and help us to live each day to Your glory. We thank You for the food we are about to eat. Most of all, we thank You for our salvation through Your Son and our Savior. It is in His name we pray. Amen."

They began eating their soup, and talk turned to cooking. "Thank you again for the cookbook. I'd like to have the Wellingtons over for dinner once I learn to cook a little better."

"That won't be long. You are a fast learner. I looked through Mrs. Farmer's book, and the instructions seem very clear and easy to follow."

Becca chuckled. "That's what I need. How did *you* learn to cook so well? Did your mother teach you?"

"I learned some from her, but she died when I was young. Actually, I learned most of what I know from the Wellingtons' cook. When I liked something, I asked how to make it, and she was always willing to tell me. I have a box full of recipes. Sometimes I'd go into the kitchen while she was making a meal and she would show me what to do."

He told her of several disasters in his kitchen. "I might not have caught my kitchen on fire, but I've burned several things to a crisp. The first chicken I tried to roast shriveled on its bones, and I caught a steak just before it burst into flames."

By the time they'd finished their meal, Becca's sides were sore from laughing. It had been a very long time since she'd enjoyed an evening as much as this one. When Luke smiled at her from across the table, her pulse began to race, and she wondered if perhaps her heart was on the mend after all.

Suddenly she wanted to know all about Luke: where he was born, how he came to work for Marcus, why he hadn't married and had a family yet. But it wasn't until they were on their way back to the apartments that she got up enough nerve to ask about him.

"I'm sorry about your mother, Luke. Is your father alive? Do you have any siblings?"

"No, I have no brothers or sisters, and my father died several years ago."

"Are you from Hot Springs?"

"No. I was born in Fort Smith. But once I went to work for Marcus, I moved here. I consider Hot Springs my home now."

"It does seem to be a nice place to live. I think I'll be considering it home before long, too. How did you come to work for Marcus?"

"Oh, I met him not long after I left home, years ago. He took pity on the young man I was and offered me a job working for him. I owe Marcus a great deal. I've never doubted that I made the right decision—not once in all these years."

She didn't have enough nerve to ask why he'd never married. Instead she decided she was just glad he hadn't.

As they finished their ride home in the quiet of the hack, Becca thanked the Lord above that she'd found a real friend in Hot Springs. Luke had helped her feel at home here, keeping her from being terribly homesick. This might not have been the kind of Valentine's Day most women dreamed about, but she would always remember it as one of the most special she would ever have.

❧

Luke thought back over the evening and realized that he could tell himself that he and Becca Snow were just friends all he wanted; he'd be lying to himself, as it was all he could do to keep from pulling her into his arms when he said good night.

Yet after the questions she'd asked, he was more convinced than ever that he had to stop the growing feelings he had for her. He hadn't been able to tell her that he'd gotten in with the wrong crowd and ended up in jail for a crime he hadn't committed. He hadn't been able to bring himself to tell her that he met Marcus when the man had gotten him out of jail all those years ago. He hadn't been able to tell her that he owed Marcus Wellington his very life.

He'd been afraid she'd look at him with disdain in her eyes, and he didn't think he could bear that. And even if she didn't reject him, she was a lovely, wonderful woman who came from a very good family. Once they found out, he was sure they would discourage her from having anything to do with him. Then there was the age difference. While he had no doubt that she thought of him as a friend, he was sure she wouldn't be thinking of him as a suitor—and deep down, that was really what he wanted to be.

He shouldn't be spending as much time with her as he was. Instead he should be distancing himself from her. But that was the last thing he wanted to do.

Yet he should tell her about his past—he knew he should tell her. And he would. . .soon.

❧

Over the next month Becca and Luke got to know each other even better. When they were spending two or three evenings a week together with her cooking lessons, it seemed the most natural thing to accompany each other to church and then to the Wellingtons' on Sundays.

Luke never failed to ask how her day went at school, and Becca had come to look forward to talking over the day with him and asking about his. From what he told her, he stayed busy running the building and helping Marcus with various projects from time to time. With Luke's help and her new cookbook, Becca was beginning to feel she could ask the Wellingtons over soon. Maybe she would start with some of the teachers at school.

Tonight she and Luke were making Maryland Chicken using a recipe from the cookbook he'd bought her. It was fairly easy, and while it cooked, Luke made a salad and Becca made biscuits. She was quite proud that she could roll them out now and that they were as light as a feather.

She'd put green beans on earlier, seasoning them with bacon grease, onion, and garlic like her mother's recipe called for—one from a batch of recipes in the last letter her mother had sent. Becca found she liked cooking very much, and she pored over her new cookbook, looking for things to try.

"Now that spring is almost here, how are your students doing?" Luke asked. "Have they been up to any antics?"

"No. None that I know of, anyway." Becca liked teaching at Central High more each week. Her students were getting used to the way she did things, and they all seemed to like her.

He chuckled. "Well, be on the watch. If my memory serves me, spring is when young men seem to want to pull a few pranks."

Luke took the chicken out of the oven, and Becca slid her biscuits in the oven beside the potatoes so they'd be ready at the same time. "I'll be on guard. Oh! Have you heard about an alligator farm that is being made? That's been all the talk at school. The teachers have been talking about taking an outing with the students once it's up and running."

"I have heard about that. It's going to be out on Whittington Avenue. I've driven by there a few times. The city council decided to let it come in to give tourists who come to Bathhouse Row something else to do for entertainment."

"Hmm. I'm not sure watching alligators is what I would choose to do, but my students are all excited about it. I don't know exactly where it is. I know my way around this area, and I know how to get to church, school, and the Wellingtons', but there is a lot I still haven't seen of Hot Springs."

"The weather is getting better each day. Perhaps we can go for a drive on Sunday afternoon. I'll take you around and show you where the alligator farm will be and all the other places you haven't seen yet."

"That would be quite nice. I'd like that, thank you."

By now, she and Luke had a routine of setting the table together and going back to the kitchen to fill up their plates. When the biscuits were done, Luke dished up the chicken while Becca added the green beans and croquettes to the plates. Then he took the plates to the table by the bay window, and she brought in the biscuits.

He pulled out Becca's chair and seated her before taking the one across from her. He said a blessing before the meal, and Becca realized that it was the evenings they cooked together and shared a meal that she enjoyed the very best.

Besides Sunday dinner at the Wellingtons', she and Abigail had lunch together most Saturdays, and occasionally she'd been invited to a dinner party at their home. But it was these weeknights she shared with Luke that she looked forward to the most, and she knew that her life would be very lonely without his company. But she was afraid she'd become too dependent on him.

She looked over to find his gaze on her. "What is it?"

"I don't think you are going to need many more lessons. You are becoming quite a good cook, Becca."

She could feel the color flood her cheeks at his compliment. "Thank you. But I still have a lot to learn. Besides, how will I know how I'm doing if I don't have someone to try out my cooking?"

Luke grinned and shook his head. "Oh, I didn't say I wouldn't be here. . .just that I think you've learned about all I can teach you. I think I'll be learning from you from now on."

"I think we'll both be learning from Fannie Farmer."

"I do believe you are ready to have the Wellingtons or anyone else you'd like to have over whenever you wish." He took a bite of chicken.

"I've been thinking about that. I thought I might have some of the female teachers over one night before I ask the Wellingtons."

"I think that's a very good idea."

"Maybe I'll ask them for Saturday evening. But what will you do?"

"The same thing I did before you came into my life. I'll have dinner out."

"That sounds lonesome." She hated to think of him being alone. Of course they didn't eat every meal together, but they did it often enough so that she felt bad for having a dinner party without him.

"Sometimes it was. But you need to be doing things with people your age. I shouldn't be monopolizing all your time."

"My age! Age doesn't matter, and I haven't noticed a difference. Luke, I wouldn't even be thinking about having anyone over if it weren't for you. You've given me the confidence to do it."

Luke didn't quite seem himself tonight. Over the last day or two he'd seemed a little different, and Becca couldn't quite put her finger on what it was. Perhaps he was tired of spending so much time with her. Maybe he thought she was too immature for him. Those thoughts had her heart twisting in her chest, and Becca suddenly realized that she was very close to falling in love with Luke. But he hadn't given her any indication that he might care for her in that way, and from his conversation tonight, he seemed to want to distance himself from her.

"Luke, have I done something to upset you?"

"Of course not. Why would you ask?"

She shrugged. "It just seems as though you. . .maybe I've been monopolizing *your* time. I suppose I have. You had a life before I moved here, but I haven't let you live it. I'm sorry, Luke."

"Becca, you are talking nonsense. I didn't have much of a life before you moved here. But I'm ten years older than you are, and my life is what it is. You've begun a new life here and are just getting to know other people. I don't want you worrying about me just because you want to have your friends over for dinner or you want to go out with them. But you haven't done anything to upset me."

Becca knew Luke was trying to reassure her, but instead she felt more unsettled than before. There was something in the tone of his voice that didn't match the words he was saying, and she had to force herself to finish her meal. Something was wrong. She just didn't know what it was.

Chapter 9

Luke woke in the middle of the night. Or rather he gave up trying to sleep. All he'd been doing was tossing and turning. The evening had started out wonderful, and the meal had turned out delicious. But something had gone wrong somewhere during his and Becca's conversation, and he wasn't sure what it was or exactly when it had happened.

He couldn't figure out why Becca thought she might have upset him in some way, and when she'd asked about it, it was all Luke had been able to do to keep from pulling her in his arms to assure her that she hadn't. But he didn't have that right, and he was afraid that such a gesture might end their friendship forever. While he could never hope to win Becca's love, he wanted her friendship. She'd livened up his life more than she would ever know, and the thought of not having her in it was something he just didn't want to think about.

Still, he didn't think his words had convinced her that she hadn't done anything to upset him, and he wasn't sure he hadn't made things worse. She'd seemed quieter for the rest of the evening. While they had talked about this and that, it wasn't the easy conversation they'd had earlier, and he'd taken his leave a little earlier than usual.

He was upset with himself—for letting himself fall in love with her, for letting himself look forward to any time at all in her company, and for beginning to dream that she might someday return his feelings.

He knew better—especially if she ever learned of his past. He needed to distance himself from her, now more than ever. But he didn't want to. . .didn't think it was possible that he even could.

❧

By Sunday things seemed back to normal with Luke, and Becca was relieved. True to his word, he'd telephoned her after her dinner guests had left on Saturday night to find out how it went.

Her heart had skipped a beat when she heard his voice, and it did the same now when she met him in the lobby to go to church. His smile seemed genuine, and she wanted nothing more than to believe that everything was all right as they headed outside to catch the trolley.

She'd dressed with care in her favorite green silk Sunday dress. It had pleats down each side of the flat front and the back, which had a small train. She brought her parasol along and a matching reticule.

"It's going to be a beautiful day. Are you ready for a little sightseeing after lunch?"

For the first time that morning Becca breathed easy. He hadn't mentioned the planned outing last night, and she'd thought he might have forgotten or decided that it wasn't a good idea. "I am looking forward to it very much. Do you think Abigail and Marcus might join us?"

"I don't know. We'll have to see if they have others over." He put his hand on her elbow to assist her in stepping up into the trolley and followed her down the aisle.

Becca sat next to the window and thought she saw the man who seemed so familiar to her across the street. "Isn't that the man who wants to rent an apartment in the building?"

Luke leaned in front of her to look out, but by then the man had pulled his hat down over his eyes and was walking down the street. "It might be. I'm not sure." He settled back down in his seat, and Becca released the breath she'd been holding. His nearness had her heart beating so fast she could barely breathe.

Seemingly unaware of the effect he had on her, Luke kept talking. "We aren't going to have any openings for a while. Well, there is one that might come open in a few months, but Marcus asked me to hold it in case Natalie moves here. And even if she doesn't, Mr. Burrows's name isn't that high up on the list. We have quite a long one."

"How did I get in so easily?"

"Marcus asked me to hold it for you."

"How nice the Wellingtons are." She owed them for more than their hospitality. She owed them for making it possible to get to know this wonderful man.

"Yes, they are. They've helped more people in this town than anyone knows. I've learned much from them. They don't just talk about their faith. They live it."

Becca thought about his words and agreed with him. Whatever kind of woman Abigail had been at one time, she'd grown into a wonderful, giving, caring Christian woman. Meagan had been right, and Becca was glad. She'd come to think of Abigail as a good friend.

The Wellingtons greeted them warmly when Becca and Luke slipped into the pew beside them.

"Good morning," Abigail whispered. "Isn't it a gorgeous day out? Spring will be here before we know it."

"Next week," Becca whispered back. "I love this time of year."

"So do I, and I've noticed some of our trees are already blooming. Others are just about to. You moved here in the dead of winter, but you'll soon see how lovely Hot Springs really is," Abigail said quietly.

The service started just then, and Becca pulled her attention to it. She already felt at home here. The members had all been so welcoming, and she thoroughly enjoyed listening to Pastor Martin speak. His lessons never failed to touch her heart and make her contemplate how she could be a better Christian. Today was no different. The pastor's sermon was about how studying the Word was the only way to stay true to it. By the time the service was over, Becca was determined to read her Bible daily. She'd gotten out of the habit since her move, and it was time to get back into God's Word.

Sunday dinner at the Wellingtons' was most enjoyable as always, but Becca was looking forward to the drive Luke had promised her. It had been quite cold when she arrived in January, and most of February was, too. But March was giving way to warmer days, and Becca was anxious to see what the landscape looked like all in bloom.

The Wellingtons had asked several other people over for dinner, so of course they couldn't go with Becca and Luke. However, Abigail had some suggestions on what Luke should show her.

"I'll never forget the drive when Marcus took me through town, past Bathhouse Row, up Central Avenue to Ramble and back down Park. The view was stunning. I'm sure it will be the same now. And of course the national park is always a wonderful place to spend an afternoon. It's really a great place to picnic. We'll have to do that soon."

"Actually, what I need to do is invite you and Marcus over for dinner. Please let me know when you have some free time on your calendar."

"Oh, Becca, we'd love to have dinner with you. I'll look over our schedule, but I think we are free this Friday, unless that is too soon for you."

"No. That would work beautifully."

"I'll telephone and let you know for sure later this evening."

"Wonderful!"

It was only when she and Luke were in the hack he'd borrowed from Marcus that Becca became nervous about the invitation. "What was I thinking, Luke? I mean, Abigail and Marcus have a cook who can make anything and could work anywhere. I can never hope to make anything as good as she does."

"Yes, you can. You make several things just as well now. Your roast chicken is as good as any I've tasted. You could serve scalloped potatoes and green beans or corn. Your biscuits are great. Sometimes a simple meal is much more satisfying than one of many courses."

"You'll be there, won't you?"

"Of course, if you want me. And I'll help in any way you need."

"Thank you, Luke."

The rest of the afternoon was very pleasant. Becca loved riding past Bathhouse Row, with all its magnolia trees lined up outside the buildings.

"You'll love the huge blossoms in the summer. They smell wonderful in the heat of the day. Or will you be going home for the break?"

"I might go visit, but I don't want to lose the apartment, and if this is to be my home now, I think I'll spend most of the break right here. I'm hoping my mother might pay me a visit."

From there, Luke turned onto Fountain Street and up to the park. "This is North Mountain. Although the park is under the jurisdiction of a superintendent, elected officials govern the town."

"I knew Hot Springs was part of the park, but I didn't know how it was governed." It was lovely. Luke pointed out the different drives and walks with seats at different intervals. Horse trails had also been developed for those wishing to ride through the park. Becca spotted violets and purple spiderwort peeking out from under the trees, the hickory and oak just beginning to leaf out, the green of the pines among them standing out against the clear blue sky. Sprays of pink phlox added to the color, making Becca anxious to see the park again in a few weeks and discover what else had bloomed.

The chatter of squirrels mixed with the calls of cardinals and blue jays and the sweet song of a mockingbird. It was wonderful to be outdoors.

"Oh, it's so peaceful and beautiful up here. What a wonderful place."

"It is very nice. I don't take the time to come up here as often as I should. I suppose I take some of what Hot Springs has to offer for granted."

They took several different roads winding up and around, and at the last turnaround, Luke headed the buggy back down the mountain. By the time they came out of the park, the sun was beginning to lower over West Mountain.

"Why don't we stop at the Arlington Hotel for a light supper? Then I can take you up Central on the ride Abigail liked so much."

Becca didn't want the afternoon to end. "That would be very nice. Thank you."

The Arlington Hotel was right at the edge of the park on the corner of Fountain Street and Central Avenue. She'd never been to the hotel before but had heard it was very luxurious and that the dining room was excellent.

On entering, Luke led her through the rotunda, and she couldn't help but be impressed. Its walls were finished with oak, and the chandeliers were beautiful. Easy chairs and sofas were positioned near the fireplace. They practically begged for one to sit and talk.

"The height of the resort season for Hot Springs is from January to June, and some of the hotels will close during the slower season. But the Arlington has always stayed open all year around. This is where Abigail stayed when she first came here. She and Marcus come here on special occasions."

"Really?"

He nodded. "Her father had hired Marcus to watch over her when she came here. Things have changed a lot in the last decade. It wasn't common for a young woman to travel alone then, and he wanted to make sure she was safe." He chuckled. "I'm not sure he meant for them to fall in love."

"But it is a wonderful match."

"Yes, it is. And I think Mr. Connors was very happy with the outcome."

They reached the dining room and were shown to a table in an alcove that looked out onto the avenue. Streetlights were coming on, and it felt cozy and private. The waiter must have assumed they were a couple instead of just very good friends. Becca surprised herself by thinking that she wished he were right.

They looked over the menu, and then Luke suggested the chicken with rice. It would be served with soup, macaroni with tomato sauce, and lemon pie for dessert.

"That sounds good. Although I'm not sure it would qualify as light," Becca said.

"Perhaps not. But it is very good."

And it was. The meal, enhanced by the atmosphere, was one of the most enjoyable she'd ever had. Still, she wouldn't trade evenings out at an elegant hotel with the ones she and Luke spent cooking together, discussing their day. No. She wouldn't trade them at all.

After dinner, they came out of the hotel to find that the night was cooling down. But Luke pulled out a lap robe to place over her for the ride up Central over to Ramble and then back down Park Avenue to Central again. Luke stopped at the top of the hill, and just as Abigail had said, the view was spectacular. Night had fallen, and the lights from downtown twinkled from below while the stars in the sky shone brightly in the evening sky. The moon was big and bright and beautiful.

"It is lovely, isn't it?" she breathed.

"It is. I'm glad Abigail suggested that we take this drive."

"I'll have to thank her."

"So will I."

Luke drove the horse and buggy back to the Wellingtons', and after visiting for a few moments, Marcus drove them back to the apartment building.

Luke escorted Becca back to her rooms and unlocked the door before handing the key back to her.

"I want to thank you for a really wonderful day," Becca said.

He shook his head. "It's I who should be thanking you. It has been a very special day for me—one I'll remember always."

He couldn't have said anything that would have touched her more. She looked up at him. "So will I."

"Becca—" Luke bent his head and tipped her chin up. His lips softly grazed hers, but before Becca could respond, the sound of the elevator being summoned from another floor startled them both. Luke quickly straightened up and cleared his throat. "I suppose I should let you go in. You have to be alert to keep up with those young people you teach."

"They do keep me on my toes." But a few more minutes wouldn't have made much difference.

"Good night, Becca. I'll see you tomorrow. Thank you again."

"Good night, Luke." She went inside, shut the door, and locked it, her pulse racing. She leaned against the door and touched lips that still tingled from his kiss. Luke had kissed her. He really had.

The week sped by, and after a hectic day on Friday, Becca found herself hurrying home to put away the chicken she'd just bought. Something had happened that morning that had her a little flustered, and she tried to tell herself it was nothing and put it to the back of her mind when Luke showed up to see if she needed help with anything. She'd asked him to make a mayonnaise to dress the salad she was preparing, and while he was stirring it up, he asked how her day went.

"You seem a little. . .flustered. You aren't nervous about the dinner with the Wellingtons tonight, are you?"

"No. At least I don't think so. I—something happened on my way to school today that bothered me a little."

Luke stopped stirring and gave her his full attention. "What happened?"

"That man that I can't place. . .the one who looks so familiar to me and wants to rent an apartment here. . ."

"What about him? Has he approached you?"

She shook her head. "No. But he was on the trolley this morning. He was standing at the back when I got on and I—" She shook her head. "It's probably all my imagination, but I felt like he was watching me. I can't explain it. I got the shivers, but the trolley stopped, and when I looked back, he'd gotten off. I'm sure it's nothing, and I don't know why running into him bothers me, but it does."

"If you see him again, you let me know right away."

"I'm sure it's nothing, Luke."

"If it makes you feel uncomfortable, it's something I want to know about."

"Hopefully I won't run into him again. Unless he eventually lives in the building."

"That isn't going to happen, Becca. Not now. Not ever."

A knock sounded on the door, and Becca went to answer it. She sighed. So much for putting it all to the back of her mind. But somehow in telling Luke all about it, her spirits had lightened and she was able to greet the Wellingtons with a smile.

Chapter 10

Becca entered the small café and waved to Abigail from across the room. She still wasn't sure why her friend had telephoned and invited her to lunch when they'd just had dinner together the night before. But it really didn't matter; she always enjoyed lunching with Abigail. They hadn't gotten to the point of exchanging confidences yet, but she felt they might one day. Maybe Abigail had heard something from Natalie. They hadn't been able to talk much about her last evening.

"I'm so glad you could join me at the last moment," Abigail said when Becca took the seat across from her. "Marcus had a meeting, and well, I just thought it would be nice to get together with you and thank you again for that delicious meal last night."

"You are very welcome. Thank you for coming. I'd been wanting to have you and Marcus over. I know there is no way I'll ever be able to repay you for all you've done for me—"

"Oh, Becca, we don't want repayment. If anything we—I—am so thankful that you've become my friend after all the pain I caused your sister before I left Eureka Springs."

It was the first time there'd been any mention of the heartache Abigail had caused Meagan, but Becca knew about it. Abigail had wanted her brother-in-law, Nate Brooks, for herself after her sister died, and she'd been manipulative and quite horrid to Meagan in trying to keep Nate from falling in love with her. But he had fallen for Meagan, and—the details always became a bit blurry to Becca because she'd only been ten at the time—it all ended with Abigail leaving town and Meagan and Nate getting married.

Abigail had asked for Meagan and Nate's forgiveness long ago, and they'd given it to her. Meagan had told Becca that Abigail had changed over the years, and that was obvious from the kindness she'd shown Becca. But evidently Abigail still felt bad about the events of the past, and she trusted Becca enough to confide in her now.

"Abigail, all that happened long ago. Meagan and Nate speak quite highly of you. You've been so very good to me, and I consider you a wonderful friend. Please put all of that in the past where it belongs. You know that the Lord wants you to accept that you've been forgiven by Him and by Meagan and Nate?"

"I try to forget it, and of course I know I've been forgiven. For that I am truly blessed. But one thing I've learned is that our actions always have consequences. One of them is that we have to live with the wrong we do. I am thankful that Meagan and Nate have had a happy life and am so blessed that Marcus and I do, too. But I did cause a lot of pain for so many back then, and it is something I can never go back and undo. That's the consequence I must live with."

"I understand." Things in Becca's life that she regretted doing popped up in her memory from time to time. "I think we all must deal with that. But we must remember to do as Paul says—forgetting those things that are behind us and going forward toward the goal. That's not it exactly, but you know what I'm saying."

"I do. Becca, I can't tell you how much it means to have you here. I can see why Natalie loves you so much. And speaking of her, I just received a letter from her this morning. While Nate hasn't come around to her moving here, he has said she can visit whenever she wants, and she's hoping to come for Easter. If not then, she says she's coming for sure in May."

"But that is wonderful. It will be so good to see her again. I do miss my family. But with friends like you, Marcus, and Luke, and our church family, I feel more at home here each day."

"It was very good of you to invite Luke for dinner last night."

"Oh, Luke and I have dinner together often."

"You do?"

Becca decided it was time she did some confiding of her own. "Yes. He's been teaching me to cook."

"Luke?"

Becca chuckled at the expression of surprise on Abigail's face. "Yes. He took pity on me my first day of teaching at Central and made dinner for me. It was then that he found out I didn't know much about cooking, and he offered to teach me. He's been collecting recipes from your cook through the years."

Abigail laughed and shook her head. "Well, of all things! Who would have thought that Luke would be a good cook? I just assumed that he ate out a lot, and I wished he'd come eat with us more often. I'll have to tell Cook that he put all her recipes to good use."

"He certainly has. With his help I began to remember some of what Mama had tried to teach me, and with the help of Fannie Farmer's excellent cookbook, we're both learning even more."

Abigail clapped her hands together and smiled. "I'm glad that you and Luke have become such good friends. Marcus and I think of him as family, and I've often thought he seemed lonely. But now that I think about it, he's been much. . .happier in the last few weeks. I think that it might have started when you came into town."

"Oh, I'm sure that's not the reason." Becca only wished it might be.

"Well, I think it is. And there is not a doubt in my mind that it has been good for him to have you around."

For a moment, Becca wanted to tell Abigail of her growing feelings for Luke, but then she decided against it. If Luke didn't feel the same way, it might put Abigail in an awkward position, and Becca liked the way their friendship was growing. She'd keep her thoughts on Luke to herself for now.

The next week found trees and flowers blooming all over the place. Spring was in evidence everywhere, and Becca felt the change deep inside. Each day had become a new adventure that she looked forward to. The Saturday before Easter, she and Luke went on a picnic and took another drive, this time over to Whittington Avenue to see what progress was being made on the alligator farm and to see the Whittington Amusement Park at the head of the avenue.

The alligator farm looked almost ready from what they could tell. They couldn't see any alligators, but the farm was set to open soon. Plans were underway at the high school for an outing later in the spring.

They walked around the outside of the amusement park, which hadn't opened for the season yet, and as Luke talked about all the amusements it offered, Becca found herself looking forward to its opening.

"The park has a summer theater and a music stand, along with a bicycle track, a baseball park, and even a new electric merry-go-round," Luke explained. "In the summer this is a very busy place. They also have concerts twice a week. We'll come over and see a play or listen to the band when it opens for the season, if you'd like."

Luke's smile had her stomach feeling as if a hundred butterflies had just been released inside, and Becca couldn't think of anything she'd rather do than spend a day here with him. "That would be very nice."

Becca's heart felt lighter than it had in a long time, and she was looking forward to the next day. She and Luke were going to the Wellingtons' for a potluck Easter dinner, and she was taking a coconut cake she'd finally perfected. Luke had declared it better than Abigail's cook's. Becca had tasted that cake, and he was giving her high praise indeed.

Becca's sister had sent her a new dress for Easter. It had arrived just the day before, but Becca hadn't opened the package until she had returned home from picnicking and sightseeing with Luke. When she'd unwrapped it,

Becca thought it was the most beautiful dress she'd ever seen. It was pink linen trimmed in white, and Natalie had sent a hat to match. Now as she turned this way and that in front of the mirror, Becca was sure it was the prettiest dress she'd ever had.

Instead of Luke meeting Becca in the lobby, he came to get her so that he could carry the basket she'd placed the cake in. As they walked out of the building to the buggy he'd rented from the livery down the street, Becca was in high spirits. Although it was still cool this time of day, the sky was cloudless and the sun shone bright, promising a warm and beautiful day.

Luke put the cake under the seat, securing it so that it wouldn't get jostled on the way to church. She much preferred riding in the buggy on Sundays. He'd been renting one ever since their first ride to the national park, and she and Luke had begun taking an afternoon drive each Sunday after they left the Wellingtons'. She especially enjoyed having a light supper with him at one of the hotels before going home.

Becca knew she'd come to count on Luke more than she should. . .come to care for him too much. But now she couldn't imagine going a whole day without seeing him.

They got to church just as the Wellingtons drove up, and after Luke helped her down, she turned to find Marcus helping someone besides Abigail down from his buggy. She began to smile as she hurried over. Natalie had come for Easter.

The two friends hugged, and Natalie exclaimed, "Oh, Becca! It is so good to see you."

"I was hoping you were coming. Over lunch the other day, Abigail and I were talking about when you might visit." Becca patted the lovely hat Natalie had made her. "Thank you for this beautiful creation. When did you get in town?"

"You're welcome. I arrived early yesterday," Natalie said. "I didn't call because I wanted to surprise you. So Aunt Abigail had the package delivered to you. Becca, Eureka Springs is just not the same place without you, and I've missed you so."

"I've missed you, too."

Natalie looked behind them at Luke, who was talking with Abigail and Marcus. "Not too much, I'm sure. I hear you and Luke have been keeping company."

For a moment Becca was taken aback that Abigail had told her, but when she looked back and saw the older woman shrug and mouth *I'm sorry*, she couldn't be angry. She knew how persistent Natalie could be when she wanted to know something. She smiled at Abigail to show her there were no hard feelings and linked her arm with Natalie's as they headed inside the church. It was wonderful to have her here, and she couldn't wait to hear news from home.

The church service was one she'd remember for a very long time. Pastor Martin made Jesus' death, burial, and resurrection come alive for Becca, and from the sniffling around her, she knew she wasn't the only one who needed the reminder of all that had been sacrificed for her salvation. She prayed that she would keep the memory close to her and not have to be reminded. . .but that she would think upon it each and every day.

The potluck dinner at the Wellingtons' was held outside, where tables had been set up in the backyard, under the oak trees that had leafed out over the past few days. The temperature was just right, not too cool nor too hot, and Becca enjoyed compliments on her cake from all of those around her.

It wasn't until after the surplus of food had been put away that Becca and Natalie got to talk about home.

"How are Mama, Meagan, Sarah, and all my family doing?"

"They are fine. Sarah just glows. She's very happy. But they miss you terribly—almost as much as I do. Well, maybe the same. They are hoping you'll come home for a few weeks this summer. Or perhaps they'll try to come here." Natalie leaned close and whispered, "If I can convince Papa to let me make the move, I'm sure they'll come often."

"Are you making any progress on that front?"

"Maybe a little. I was hoping you might write Mama and see if you could have her talk to Papa. I mean, she is your sister, after all, and you could assure her that you would watch out for me, couldn't you?"

"I suppose I could try."

"Oh, thank you, Becca."

"I can't promise the outcome, though."

"I know. Just try, please."

"All right, I will." It would be good to have Natalie living in the same town.

❧

Luke and Marcus concluded their meeting at the Wellington Agency, and Luke headed back toward the Wellington Building. The assignment he was going on was one he knew he could carry out. He was being sent to Little Rock to track down a suspect in the robbery of one of the Wellington Agency's best clients. Neither Marcus nor the client wanted the police called in unless—or until—their suspicions proved true.

While Marcus had filled Luke in on what he wanted him to do, all Luke could think about was that he didn't want to go, and he'd never felt that way about an assignment before. But he owed Marcus so much; there was no way he was going to try to get out of it. He just wished he didn't have to leave right now.

As he neared the building, he recognized Becca coming from the other direction, and he suddenly knew why he didn't want to go. He didn't want to leave her.

"Good afternoon, Becca. Where have you been?"

"Oh, I had a wonderful lunch with Abigail and Natalie, and then I went to the grocer's to pick up a few things. I thought I might make a beef stew tonight. Want to join me?"

"Becca, I won't be here this evening. I'm sorry."

"Oh, why, that's all right. I shouldn't have assumed—"

He liked that she had and hurried to reassure her. "No, I'm glad you did. It's just that I'm leaving on the evening train for Little Rock."

"Little Rock? But why?"

"Marcus is sending me on an assignment."

She shook her head. "Assignment?"

"Look, let me help you with your bags, and I'll explain when we get upstairs."

Becca released her grip on one of the bags and kept the lightest one as they went into the building. Mrs. Gentry was just getting on the elevator, and she greeted them cordially.

She smiled at Becca. "Isn't Mr. Monroe a good landlord? He's always willing to help carry up packages or deliver messages. I have a friend in another building, and she says their apartment manager barely speaks to them."

"Oh, that's a shame," Becca replied.

"It is indeed."

"Well, I must tell you that I'll be out of town for a while. But Mr. Easton will be filling in for me."

"Mr. Easton?" Becca asked.

"Yes, he's Marcus's assistant, and he fills in for me when I have to be out of town. We've found it works better than having a full-time assistant manager here."

"He's a very nice man, too," Mrs. Gentry said. "But we will miss you, Mr. Monroe."

It wasn't until they entered Becca's kitchen and put the bags down that she turned to Luke and asked, "Are you going out of town on business for the apartments?"

"No, of course not. I'm on assignment for the Wellington Agency."

"You—you're an agent? An investigator?"

"Why yes. I thought you knew that."

"How would I have known? Oh, I knew you worked for Marcus—I mean, you manage the building for him. But I didn't know that you were an investigator. You never talked about it—never once mentioned it." Becca's voice was low and measured.

She was upset; there was no question about it. But Luke didn't understand why she would be so distressed that he worked for the Wellington Agency. She knew what Marcus did for a living. He shrugged and shook his head. "I thought you knew by now that I was one of the Wellington agents, Becca. I wasn't trying to keep that from you. It just isn't something I normally talk about. But why does it bother you so?"

"It's a dangerous job."

"It can be. But I've been doing it for a long time, and I stand here before you—"

"I lost my fiancé just over a year ago," she said, as if she hadn't heard what he'd said. "He was killed in a bank robbery."

The pain in her eyes was real, and his heart went out to her. "I am truly sorry about your loss, Becca. I wish I'd known. I knew you'd gone through some kind of heartbreak, but I didn't know how to ask you about it. We don't have to talk about it now if you don't want to."

"No. It's all right. In a way, it's good to be able to talk about it. At home my family treats me with kid gloves, as if they are afraid to mention Richard's name to me. I'm not sure that helped me. That is why I moved here—I had to get away from the memories." She took a deep breath before continuing. "Richard was a policeman in Eureka Springs. I'd gone to the bank with a deposit for my sister. I was unaware that it was being robbed until I saw the man turn away from the teller window, a gun in one hand and a bag of money in the other. Before he got to the door, it opened, and Richard burst in. But the robber shot him before he had a chance to. . ." Her voice dwindled off.

Luke waited.

Becca sighed and shook her head. "Richard died in my arms."

Luke released a large breath. "Becca, I am so sorry. That had to be devastating."

Becca began to cry, and he pulled her into his arms. He had to try to comfort her. Someway, somehow. He rocked her back and forth. But he could tell she was still crying. He leaned back and tipped her face up. Her tear-filled eyes broke his heart, and he couldn't keep himself from leaning nearer and capturing her lips with his. When she responded, he deepened the kiss and began to hope that she might return his growing feelings for her.

But then she pushed him way. "No! I never wanted to fall in love with anyone who would willingly put his life on the line in his profession. Not a policeman, not a fireman, not a soldier—no one who puts himself in danger. I promised myself I wouldn't. I don't think I could take the fear of going through that kind of loss ever again, Luke."

Her eyes were swimming in tears, and Luke didn't know what to say next. He certainly couldn't blame Becca for feeling the way she did. Most likely he'd feel the same way had someone he loved died in his arms. No, he couldn't blame her. But he wished she didn't feel that way. With all his heart he wished it.

"I'm so sorry, Becca. I wish I'd mentioned earlier that I also worked as an investigator for the Wellington Agency, but with your connections to the Wellington family, I truly thought you knew. It wasn't something I tried to hide." But he was aware that most people in town thought that he just managed the Wellington Building for Marcus. And that was the way Marcus wanted it. Now that he thought about it, it was probably the reason Becca didn't know.

"Once I proved myself to Marcus, I was promoted to handle some of the harder cases that usually take me out of town. I'm not sent on a regular basis, but when Marcus asks me to take an assignment, I know he wants someone he can depend on to get the job done." Luke made himself stop talking. By the closed look on her face, he figured he was making things worse.

From the way she'd responded to his kiss, he felt she cared about him. But he also knew that being an agent for the Wellington Agency fell into the category of all the things Becca had just said she wanted nothing to do with. All he could do was pray that the Lord would help her change her mind.

There seemed to be nothing left to do but take his leave and say, "I'm sorry. I'll. . .ah. . .I'll see you when I return."

When he got to the door, he turned back to see her wiping her eyes. "I will be back, Becca. That you can count on."

Chapter 11

Luke threw his things in a valise, his desire to leave town totally gone. All he wanted to do was go back to Becca and make sure she was all right. But he couldn't let Marcus down—he owed the man his life. He'd never felt so torn in his life.

He took his case down to the office and waited until Easton showed up. Most likely the watchmen could handle anything that came up, but he felt better knowing someone else was on the premises or nearby. Easton lived down the block and could get there in a matter of minutes if anything happened in the middle of the night.

Luke had never worried overly much when he left, but that was before he'd been asked to watch over Becca Snow and before he'd fallen in love with her. He just wanted her to be safe. He suddenly remembered Becca telling him about seeing Burrows again, and he wondered if he could be the man George had seen several times. He didn't want to leave town without alerting Easton and Marcus to the situation. After putting through a telephone call to Marcus and being assured that a man would be stationed across the street around the clock, he felt better about leaving. But only marginally.

Once he was on the train to Little Rock, Luke tried to think positively. Maybe this was a good thing: to put some space between them. As upset as she was at him and given her reasoning, he hoped that what he felt for her was simply because they'd been spending so much time together. Maybe being away would show him that he didn't care as much as he thought he did. Yeah. And maybe he'd wake up in a different city and forget the kiss they'd just shared. She might say she didn't want to fall in love with—no. She had used the word *wanted*. She said, "I never *wanted*." Not *I didn't want*, or *I don't want*. Not *I never want*, but "I never *wanted* to fall in love." Those were the words she used. Could she possibly have meant that she had already fallen in love? Or was he just grasping at thin air?

∽

The first day Luke was gone, Becca tried to tell herself that she was angry with Luke for not telling her that he was a Wellington agent. The next day she was mad at herself for not realizing what should have been obvious. The day after that she just wanted Luke to come back. She missed him more than she wanted to admit, and she worried about him even more. She prayed night and day for him to come home safely.

She'd never felt so torn in her life. She did not want to care that much about the man, but she couldn't get him or his kiss out of her mind. And it didn't help that everywhere she looked she could see him—in the kitchen, where they'd prepared so many dishes, and at the table by the bay window, where they'd eaten those meals. In the elevator, in the lobby, on her way out of the building each morning, and on her way in each afternoon—everywhere she went—she found herself looking for him and then getting angry with herself for caring.

She asked Natalie over for dinner because she just couldn't sit at the same table by the bay window without missing Luke even more.

"This is delicious, Becca. You did learn to cook."

"Yes, finally. I'm glad you like it." Then, because she felt she should be honest, she added, "Luke taught me a lot."

"Luke did?"

"Yes. Seems he'd been gathering recipes from your aunt's cook for a long time. He really is very good at it."

"Mmm. And so the two of you have been cooking together a lot?"

"Often, yes."

"Isn't he out of town on an assignment for Marcus?"

"Yes." Becca got up to clear the table and bring in dessert.

"May I help?"

"No. I'll be right back." She didn't want Natalie to see the tears that had sprung to her eyes. She cut the chocolate cake she'd made the day before and put the thick slices on dessert plates.

She'd no more than set them down when she sighed. "Oh, I forgot the coffee. I'll be—"

"I'll get the coffee, Becca. You sit down. I didn't come over tonight to have you wait on me. You worked all day."

Becca didn't argue—there would have been no point. Natalie was already in the kitchen. Instead, she dropped down into her chair and looked out on the street. Even with Natalie's company, which she always enjoyed, she was lonesome.

Natalie brought the coffee to the table and poured them both a cup before taking her own seat—or rather, Luke's seat. "Becca, you seem a little on edge tonight. Is something wrong?"

"No, not really. I'm sorry. I just. . .I didn't realize that Luke worked for the Wellington Agency. I thought he just managed this building for Marcus."

"Oh. I can see how that would. . .unsettle you, especially if you didn't know."

"It shouldn't. What he does for a living is really none of my business."

"But of course you care; you've become good friends, Becca. I guess we've all known about Luke's job for so long it never occurred to us to explain."

"There was no reason you should have. Not really. It just surprised me."

"It's more than that. It is really upsetting you."

Memories flashed before Becca, swift and clear, of the night he'd put out the fire, of him bringing supper to her, teaching her how to cook, taking her sightseeing, and. . .the kiss that she couldn't seem to get out of her mind.

"Becca? Have you fallen in love with Luke?"

She looked at her stepniece and best friend. "Oh, I hope not."

"He's a good man, Becca. He would make a wonderful husband."

Becca found herself shaking her head. "I know he's a wonderful person, Natalie. But what he does can be dangerous, and I. . ." Becca sighed and shook her head. "I can't let myself fall in love with him, Natalie. I just can't."

But deep down she was afraid she was very close to doing just that. She had to get over it. Time apart would be good for her. She had to find a way to distance herself from him. What he did was, or could be, as dangerous as Richard's profession. She didn't even know what kind of assignment he'd gone on. . .because she'd gotten too angry to ask. Still, she found herself sending up a silent prayer. *Dear Lord, please keep him safe, whatever he's doing and wherever he is. Please watch over him and bring him back soon. In Jesus' name, I pray. Amen.*

⌒

After Becca's dinner with Natalie, the Wellingtons took pity on her and had her over for dinner for the next two evenings. She wondered when Luke would be coming home, but it wasn't something she felt comfortable asking Marcus, so she just waited and worried in quiet.

But she could have hugged Abigail when she asked, "Marcus, have you heard from Luke lately?"

"I had a telegram from him today. Just that he was near to completing his assignment and expected to be back next week."

Since this was Friday, Becca's spirits lifted with the news that he could be home as soon as Sunday. She might want to distance herself from him, but that was emotionally. She wanted to see him back home and know that he was all right. . .and the sooner the better.

Becca was thankful that when she returned from the Wellingtons', she had her work and that it was midterm and she had tests to grade that week. At least that kept her busy for the evening after she got home.

On Saturday she went to lunch with Abigail and Natalie, and they arranged to pick her up for church the next morning. She was grateful for the ride, but coming down to the lobby with no Luke there to greet her left Becca feeling more lonesome than ever.

She did manage to enjoy the afternoon at the Wellingtons' even though it had begun to rain while they were in church. She and Natalie spent the afternoon sipping tea and talking. Becca listened as Natalie told her about her dreams to open a hat shop in Hot Springs—and that she thought she was close to talking her papa into agreeing to let her try it.

"With Aunt Abby here and now you, too, he's finding it harder to find reasons why I shouldn't move. And he knows I'm not happy in Eureka Springs. Many of my friends have married and moved away. I just don't feel I belong there anymore. I want a change."

"What is it you two are talking about?" Abigail asked as she swept into the room.

"My moving here."

"Oh, I like that subject, don't you, Becca?"

"I do."

"You seem a little down today, dear; is anything wrong?"

For a moment Becca thought Abigail was talking to Natalie until the younger woman said, "She's missing Luke, Aunt Abby."

"Natalie!"

"Well, you've been moping around for days now. I think you—"

"Natalie, dear, if Becca doesn't want to talk about it, then we shouldn't bring it up."

"It's all right, Abigail. It's just that I. . .well. . .I. . ." She didn't know what to say next. She did miss Luke. Much as she tried not to, she did. More with each passing day.

"If you want to talk about it, we are here for you. Anytime. I just don't want you to feel you have to. And as for missing Luke, I miss him, too. It's about time he got back."

"She doesn't want to miss him, Aunt Abby. That's part of the problem."

"Oh?"

"Natalie, you've said quite enough now. I'll tell Abigail the rest."

"Yes, ma'am," Natalie said. But Becca saw the smug smile she tried to hide and realized that Natalie had just accomplished precisely what she had set out to do.

"I think I may have come to care for Luke more than I should. . .and I didn't realize he was also an investigating agent for the Wellington Agency until the day he left. I suppose I should have, but I didn't."

"Oh, my dear. No, there is no reason why you should have. And I am so sorry we didn't make it known to you. But Becca, why would Luke working as an agent distress you so?"

"When I lost Richard, I promised myself that I would never fall in love with anyone who put himself in danger willingly. But I—I just don't know what to do. I want Luke to come home safe, but I feel I must distance myself from him. I just don't think I can take the worry and the fear of going through all that heartache all over again."

Abigail sank down on the couch beside her and hugged her. "Oh, Becca, I do understand. It would be devastating to lose someone else you love. I believe that is a normal reaction to what you've been through. But I also know that no matter how much we might deny our true feelings, the heart doesn't lie. I know you haven't asked, but the best advice I can give you is to take it to the Lord and ask Him to help you to know what to do. And be assured that He does have a plan for you."

❧

Luke had never struggled with an assignment the way he had with this one. Thoughts of Becca were never far away. He tried hard to keep them at bay while he was working. But the desire to get back home spurred him into concentrating on the job at hand. From the leads Marcus had given him and the contacts he'd made from those, Luke found out that the man, whose real name was Charles Williford, lived a double life. Here in Little Rock, he was married with a wife and two children, and from all accounts he was an upstanding citizen and good neighbor.

He worked as a newspaper reporter for the *Arkansas Democrat-Gazette*, where he covered the social life of the Little Rock wealthy. It was also how he found out where and when the rich of that city would be going to Hot Springs or other resorts in the state. But he also pretended to be a businessman from up North, who came to Hot Springs for an occasional weekend for the health benefits of the baths.

Williford would find out which of Little Rock's wealthy families were staying in Hot Springs over a weekend or two, and he would make a trip there himself. But he was careful to come back so that he would be at work when, the next Monday, reports came in from Hot Springs that one of Little Rock's elite had been robbed while on vacation.

Luke had wired Marcus and gotten the orders to tell the police in Little Rock what he'd found out. After a meeting with the chief of police, Luke had agreed to help capture the man.

Now, as he walked into the newsroom and asked a lady he thought might be the receptionist where to find Mr. Williford, policemen stood at every entrance and exit of the building.

The young woman pointed to a row of desks. "His desk is about midway down the aisle. You can go on back."

"Thank you," Luke said. As he walked through the room, he checked to see where the closest exit was. It was near the back and had a frosted-glass window in the door. He was pretty sure the shadow he saw was of uniformed police—at least he hoped so, because experience told him that Mr. Williford would take off as soon as he realized what Luke was questioning him about.

The man's head was bent over his Underwood typewriter, and his fingers were tapping away. He was larger than Luke had expected. Luke cleared his throat, trying to get the man's attention, but he kept right on typing. "Mr. Williford, may I have a word with you?"

"Be with you in a minute," he said without looking up. "Take a seat."

Luke did just that. He sat looking at the burly man and wondering why he would have turned to a life of crime when he had a good job and—

"What can I do for you? Got a social event you want to put in the paper?"

"No. I just came to ask you a question or two. I've been told you might know someone I'm looking for."

"Oh? Who is that? And who are you?"

"My name is Luke Monroe. The man I'm looking for goes by the name of Gibson. Dub Gibson." Luke watched the color drain from the man's face, telling him what he needed to know.

But old Charley kept his composure; Luke would give him that. The man shook his head. "Nope. Never heard of him."

"Are you sure? The desk clerk at the Hale House in Hot Springs says he was given your name as a contact in case he ever had any juicy stories about the hotel's clientele. Gibson told him you'd pay well for a good story."

"Well, maybe I did business with someone he knew, but like I said, I don't know anyone by the name of Gibson."

"Oh, I think you do. In fact—"

"Mr. Monroe, I've told you I don't know him. I've got work to do. Now kindly leave before I call the security guard."

Luke stood. "Why don't you call him on over? I'm sure he'll be interested to know what the Wellington Agency has to say about Mr. Gibson and you."

The man pushed back his chair and stood. He was big, just as Luke had thought. And tall. He had at least four inches on Luke, who was close to six feet, and probably weighed fifty pounds more. "I just want to talk to you, Gibson."

"Well, I don't want to talk to you."

Luke let the man's words sink in. It sounded like Williford had just admitted he was Gibson. "Got something to hide?"

"Why, you little pip-squeak. . ."

Williford came toward Luke like an enraged mama bear. Luke stood his ground. "You aren't going to get away with it, you know."

"Elliot," Williford bellowed. "Get this man out of here, or I will."

Evidently Elliot was a guard, and he was standing up by the door Luke had come in through. He headed their way but not before he knocked on the door.

"What is it, Mr. Williford?" The front door opened, and two policemen burst into the room.

"Why, you little traitor!" Williford yelled at the guard. He grabbed Luke's shoulder.

Before Luke could throw a punch, Williford threw a blow at him that had him seeing stars, then he knocked Luke out of the way, sending him flying across one desk and plowing into the corner of the next one. Luke's head felt as if a starburst had gone off inside, but he didn't have time to think about it as he pulled himself up and got his bearings. He felt a little light-headed, but he had to see this through. Williford was headed for the back exit closest to his desk. Luke followed.

"Stop, or we'll shoot," one of the cops behind him yelled before he passed Luke. Luke came up in the rear as they moved closer to Williford. The man was almost at the door. He yanked it open and ran right into the two policemen waiting for him. He was handcuffed in a matter of seconds and taken into custody.

His hate-filled eyes met Luke's gaze. If looks could kill, Luke knew he'd be dead.

"Mr. Monroe, sir," one of the policemen said.

"Yes?" Luke was feeling a bit nauseated.

"I think we better get you to a doctor."

"Why?"

"Sir, your head is bleeding."

Luke reached up and felt the wetness. He brought his hand down and saw that, indeed, his head was bleeding. But that wasn't the only place that was hurting. He'd hit his right shoulder on the corner of the desk, and he had no doubt that it would be giving him trouble for some time to come. "I think you are right."

"I'll take you. Then we'll go back to the police station. I think you can add some charges of your own to the long list Williford already has."

Luke nodded and found it hurt to do even that. He felt a little sick as he looked at his arm. His arm would heal, and he'd be all right. The job he'd been sent to do was almost done. But most important was that he'd get to go home very soon. "I think I can add some charges. Let's go."

Chapter 12

Burrows followed the woman to the post office. It had become imperative that he find out if she remembered him. His future here could be at stake. This was his home, and he'd felt safe here for the past two years. He'd never liked robbing banks in the places he lived. He liked living here. His wife was happy, and it made a good base from where to work. He didn't want to have to move away. He thought he knew who this woman was. He'd done some digging in his files after he saw her when he was leaving the Wellington Building that day.

The newspaper photograph was grainy, but he was almost positive that it was her. The picture had been taken right after the robbery at a bank in Eureka Springs more than a year ago. In her arms she was holding the policeman he'd killed. The caption said her name was Rebecca Snow and she was a teacher. It all made sense; he'd followed her to the high school, so this woman must also be a teacher. But still, the young woman here could just look like the one in the paper. The hairstyles were different, and in the picture he couldn't see her eyes because she was looking at the man in her arms.

Yet he couldn't be totally sure. Just because he thought she was the same woman didn't mean that she was. He watched her go inside the post office. Now was the time to find out. He stepped into the building. She'd approached the postmaster and waited for him to get her mail, then she handed him several letters and turned to leave. Their eyes met before he could turn away.

She got to him and stopped. His heart dropped. Did she know?

"Excuse me, sir. You seem very familiar to me, but I can't place you. I—"

"Sorry, miss. I've never met you before." He tried to stay calm and moved past her to buy some stamps. He could only hope that she left. His heart thudded as he turned to leave. She was gone. He breathed a sigh of relief before he rushed out of the post office. He could see her a block away, and he turned in the opposite direction. If she was the same woman—and he was almost certain she was—it would only be a matter of time before she remembered just where she had seen him. It was time to make a trip to Eureka Springs and see if Miss Rebecca Snow still lived there. His steps quickened as he headed to the train depot. He'd take the next train out.

A LOVE TO CHERISH

All the way down to the Arlington Hotel, where she was meeting Natalie and Abigail for lunch, Becca tried to place where she'd seen the man she seemed to run into on a fairly regular basis. She pretty much went to the same places—the grocer, the post office, the bookstore, school, church, and of course, the Wellingtons'. Probably she'd passed him on the street going to one or the other of those places, and that was why he'd looked so familiar to her when she'd bumped into him at the grocer's that day.

But while that reasoning made sense to her, she could not get rid of the feeling that she'd seen him before she arrived in Hot Springs. Something about the man just sent shivers down her spine, and she didn't know why when she didn't even know who he was. Becca sighed and shook her head. What did it all matter anyway—other than to keep her mind off Luke?

Becca knew what she was doing. She was trying to occupy her thoughts with anything or anyone besides Luke. She missed him more with each passing day, and it was nearly impossible to keep from thinking about him.

She reached the Arlington and was glad to find that Natalie and Abigail were there ahead of her. With Luke gone, she didn't look forward to much except being at school and spending time with her two best friends.

"We were getting worried about you," Abigail said when Becca was seated across from her.

"What took you so long?" Natalie asked.

"I had to run to the post office to mail some letters home."

Her nights were the loneliest without Luke around. She'd reverted to having a very light supper, after which she pored over her cookbook or caught up on her letter writing to her mother and sisters. She'd just received one from her mother the day before. "Remember you asked me to write Meagan? And Mama is talking about coming for a visit—I'm trying to convince her to do that. I wish she would. I do miss her."

"What is the news from home? Anything exciting? I haven't heard from Mama and Papa since last week."

Becca tore into her letter and skimmed it for news she could report. "Everyone is doing fine, according to Mama. She says Sarah is growing larger each day, and they've wondered if she might have twins. They run in Mitch's family, you know."

"Oh, that would be something, wouldn't it?" Natalie asked.

"Mama says there is a new minister in town, Natalie. Why didn't you tell us about him?"

The younger woman shrugged. "I didn't know you'd be interested. He's young."

"Mmm. Mama says he is very nice looking, too. And that he seemed quite interested in you." Becca was sure Natalie blushed at her words. "She thinks he may be the reason you came back to Hot Springs."

"Why, I came back to see you and Aunt Abigail. I. . .he. . ." Natalie stopped and shrugged again. "He would like to court me. I'm just not sure how I feel about that. I mean, I don't think I am meant to be a minister's wife, but he . . .well, he is a very good man and. . ." She sighed. "I'm hoping the Lord will help me decide what to do."

"That is the best thing you can do, dear," Abigail said, looking from Natalie to Becca. "The Lord has someone in mind for each of you. I know from experience it is much better to let Him bring two people together than to try to make something happen. Much better." She took a sip of tea and smiled before adding, "I think you'd make a very good minister's wife, Natalie dear."

Becca felt that Abigail had been talking about herself and Marcus and also about Meagan and Nate. And while her friend's advice was good, Becca knew firsthand how hard it was not to want to control one's heart. She didn't want to care so much about Luke, but she was getting nowhere telling herself not to care. She could fight her feelings all she wanted, but that didn't stop her from thinking about him. And it didn't keep memories of his kiss at bay.

Were these thoughts and feelings God's will for her and Luke? She didn't know. And if he didn't come home soon, how was she ever going to find out?

"Becca?" Natalie brought her out of her thoughts. "Did you hear what Aunt Abby said?"

"I'm sorry. I must have been woolgathering. What did you say, Abigail?"

"I was saying that I believe Luke will be home soon. Marcus had a telegram from him, and he was quite pleased with Luke's work."

Becca's heart did a little somersault before righting itself in her chest. Luke was coming home. "Did he say when he'd be coming back?"

"No. And the telephone rang just then, and I forgot to ask. I'm sorry."

"Oh no. There is nothing to be sorry about." Luke would be home soon, and that was what mattered. Had she not come to lunch today, she might not have known. Just the knowledge that she would see him before long and that he was all right made the day brighter and her mood much lighter.

❧

After lunch Becca, Natalie, and Abigail did some shopping, and by the time they parted company, Becca was in much better spirits. Perhaps Luke would be home tomorrow or at the very least by Monday. She didn't know how she would react when he saw him. She only knew that she wanted him back here at the Wellington Building, helping her to cook, being in her life. . .as the person who'd become her very best friend.

That she felt more for him than that, she tried not to think about. And she tried not to dwell on what his kiss meant about the way he felt. All she really knew was that she missed him and couldn't wait to see him again.

"Good afternoon, Miss Snow," George said as she entered the building.

"Good afternoon. It's a beautiful day out," Becca said. She wanted to ask if Luke was back, but one look at his office showed that he wasn't. As she headed toward the elevator and glanced into the office, it was Mr. Easton she saw. She gave him a wave and stepped onto the elevator.

There was no way to know what train Luke took out of Little Rock, and he might not be on one yet. There was nothing to do but wait. . .and pray that they were still friends when he got back.

She met up with Mrs. Gentry in the hall. "Good day, Mrs. Gentry. How are you doing?"

"I'm fine, dear. I'd be better if Mr. Monroe would get back in town."

"Oh, do you need something? Can I help? Or I'm sure Mr. Easton would."

"I don't need anything. I just miss seeing Mr. Monroe. He's always so kind, and he checks on me. I haven't seen Mr. Easton checking on anyone since Luke went away. I don't like it when Luke goes out of town. It's just lonely without him around."

Becca felt exactly the same way. "It will be good to have him back."

"Yes, it will. I'm on my way down to the Townsends'. I told them I would watch their children tonight. It's their anniversary, and they are going to dinner at the Arlington."

"That's very nice of you."

"It's nice of *them*. It gives me something to do besides crochet. These hands get a little stiff if I keep at it too long." The older woman waved and went on her way, leaving Becca to think how selfish she'd been. Instead of feeling sorry for herself because she didn't have Luke to share a meal with, she could have invited Mrs. Gentry over, and they'd both have been a bit less lonely. She might be new in town, but Mrs. Gentry was a widow without any family around from what Becca could tell. She was ashamed that she hadn't made more of an effort to get to know her neighbors and promised herself that she would do better from now on. She'd spent too much time moping around her apartment with Luke gone and more than enough time thinking about a man she only wanted as a friend.

Disgusted with herself, Becca put up her purchases and went to fix a light supper. But frying bacon and eggs only served to bring Luke to mind once again. She couldn't help but remember the night she'd nearly set the kitchen on fire and Luke had come to her rescue.

He hadn't ever told a soul about her mishap. Nor had he teased her about it. No. Instead he'd offered to teach her to cook. Becca's heart filled with. . .love? No. She didn't want to love Luke—didn't want to love anyone who put his life in danger as Richard had. She didn't want to live with that fear. . .never again.

She took her supper to the table where she and Luke had shared their meals and looked out onto the street below as she had so many times. But the spot felt even lonelier tonight, so she picked up her plate and headed toward the dining room. But that table was so big, she didn't even sit down. Finally, she made her way back to the small table at the end of the kitchen and sat down to eat. But the eggs were cold, and she'd lost her appetite, so she scraped her plate and washed dishes.

Streetlights were coming on when she went back to the living room. She picked up a book she'd purchased that afternoon, *Kim* by Rudyard Kipling. She'd heard it was an excellent book and had been looking forward to reading it. But hard as she tried to get interested in it, she just could not concentrate. She found herself listening to the normal sounds of the building. She heard the elevator stop on her floor and held her breath, hoping to hear footsteps come her way, signaling that Luke was back, but the footsteps seemed to go in the other direction.

Becca sighed and set the book down. She'd been so confused since Luke left. She truly didn't want to fall in love with him, but she was afraid she was more than halfway there. If it wasn't meant to be, she needed to stop thinking about him. "Dear Father, please help me. I don't know what to do. I know I care too much for Luke, unless it is in Your will that I do. I don't want to. You know why. I'm not sure I can give my heart to someone who chooses to put his life in danger again. I. . .I don't want to lose anyone else I love. Please help me to put Luke out of my mind or show me that it is in Your will for me to care about him. Please let me know what to do. And please let Luke get home safely. In Jesus' name, I pray. Amen."

A knock sounded on the door, and her heart jumped. Could it be Luke? She hurried to answer the door, and what she saw when she opened it made her gasp.

❦

Luke knew he looked bad, but if he'd known Becca would be so shocked, he'd have waited to come see her. Her eyes were huge and sorrowful as they took in his black eye and the bandage on his forehead.

Her hands were over her mouth, but she moved them long enough to say, "What happened to you?"

"It isn't as bad as it looks," Luke said. "I promise."

She didn't seem convinced. "Who did that to you? What happened, Luke?"

"May I come in?"

"Of course." Becca stepped back, but her eyes never left his face. Good thing she couldn't see his shoulder and upper chest where he'd hit the desk.

She motioned for him to take a seat in the chair by the fireplace, and she took a seat on the footstool in front of him. "Did you have to have stitches?"

"A few. I'm fine, Becca, really. If it makes you feel any better, the bad guy is in jail."

"I would hope so. Are you going to tell me what happened?"

There didn't seem to be any way around it, so Luke launched into a detailed account of his assignment. Becca listened intently, but when he got to the part where Williford knocked him across the room, she jumped up and put her hand to her throat, her eyes filling with tears.

"Becca." His voice had her turning away. Luke stood and turned her toward him. Two teardrops slid down her cheeks as she looked into his eyes. "Becca, I am all right. I'm right here with you. I came back, just as I said I would."

She began to sob, and Luke pulled her into his arms. He tipped her face up and bent his own until their lips met. The taste of salty tears was on her lips as she kissed him back before quickly pulling away and brushing at her tears. But she'd responded just enough so that finally, in his heart, Luke knew that Becca cared for him, too.

That knowledge brought its own set of problems. She knew he was an agent for Marcus, and she didn't like it one bit. Yet she didn't know about his past, and he couldn't bring himself to tell her now. For once he did, he feared the two of them would have no future.

Chapter 13

Burrows had been in Eureka Springs for just over a week before he had his answers. He'd watched the Snow home every day, but he'd never seen anyone come out who looked like the woman in the picture.

Finally, he'd gone to the high school and pretended to be a parent who was checking out the education system in Eureka Springs before making a move to the city. The principal, Mr. Johnson, had been very nice and had taken him around the school, introducing him to many teachers, but there hadn't been one named Snow, nor was there anyone who looked like her teaching there.

As he got ready to leave, he finally learned all he needed to know.

"I thank you, sir, for showing me around."

"You are welcome, Mr. Burrows. I can assure you that we have an excellent staff and student body here. Your child—did you say it was your daughter or son who'd be attending?"

"Ah. . .I have both," Burrows lied. "A boy and a girl."

"Well, I assure you they will be happy here. I look forward to welcoming them personally. Where is it you said you'd be moving from?"

"Hot Springs, sir. A city not totally unlike your own."

"Ahh. We lost one of our best teachers to your town. A Miss Snow transferred there in the middle of the year. It was certainly our loss and Hot Springs's gain. Perhaps one of your children has her for a teacher."

"Hmm, I don't believe so, but I will ask. I'd best be on my way. Thank you again, Mr. Johnson. You've given me all the information I need."

The two men shook hands, and Burrows walked outside. He felt almost giddy, realizing that he'd found out all he needed to know. How easy this had been. He should have come here right from the first. Now all he had to do was go back home and wait for the opportune moment to take care of Miss Snow.

❧

Over the next few weeks, Becca and Luke slipped back into their routine of cooking and eating together most evenings. Her world finally felt back to normal. . .although it really wasn't. And while there wasn't another kiss, there was no way to deny that their relationship had undergone a subtle change.

She had no doubt that Luke cared about her, but since the night he'd come home, he seemed a little distant at times. And she went from being elated that

Luke was home and seemed to have missed her as much as she missed him, to feeling panic that his profession was one that would take him away fairly often and that he would be no safer than the fiancé she'd lost in the line of duty.

Still, she couldn't stop her heart from turning to mush each time she saw the fading bruise around his eye and on his forehead. He could have been killed in that brawl. Oh why did life have to be so complicated? Why did her feelings for Luke seem to grow with each passing day. . .no matter how hard she tried to keep them at the friendship level?

Every day she prayed for the Lord to show her what to do, to let her know if she and Luke were meant to be together or not. If not, most likely she needed to find another place to live. She wasn't sure she could stay in the same building, seeing him every day and wanting to be with him more all the time.

Thoughts of Luke were never far away, and this warm first day of May, as she and other teachers took their classes to the newly opened alligator farm as one of their May Day events, was no exception.

The reptiles weren't very appealing to Becca, but her students thought they were quite entertaining. The boys did anyway. The girls still kept their distance as the owner, Mr. Campbell, showed them around. He pointed to a male and female sunning themselves onshore.

"Just don't get too close," he admonished.

Becca knew the girls would heed his advice; it was the boys she worried about as they lagged behind and pushed each other a little closer to the gators.

"It looks like they have armor on," Milly Roberts said. She'd become one of Becca's favorite students and was quick to learn.

"And they are really ugly," Elizabeth Miller added.

Becca chuckled. "I agree completely, girls."

But when Mr. Campbell brought out a hatchling that was only about eight inches long, they all gathered around the man.

"Oh how cute. Perhaps they just get uglier with age," Milly said.

"They do seem to, don't they?" Mr. Campbell agreed. "Perhaps it's because they aren't so dangerous at this age."

"How fast can they move?" Elizabeth asked.

"Across land about eight miles an hour for short distances, but not as fast if it's more than a few yards, and in water they can go about ten miles an hour."

Suddenly a commotion from the shoreline of the pond caught their attention. As they hurried in that direction, it seemed that one of the boys had climbed over the fenced-in area and had fallen in, and one of the alligators was headed down the embankment to join him. Another boy had found a huge limb somewhere, and several of the boys took hold of one end while holding it out over the boy so they could drag him back up the embankment. Mr. Campbell and one of his assistants ran to help.

Once the boy was onshore, his teacher took control of the situation and headed the group back to the school. Becca breathed a sigh of relief that none of her students had been in danger; it put a damper on the afternoon though, and everyone seemed in one accord to end the excursion.

Becca gathered the students she was in charge of and they started back to school. When they came out of the gate, her heart did a little flip to see Luke standing there. When she'd mentioned the field trip to him the night before, he'd said he might join them, but she figured he was busy.

"Looks like I missed all the excitement." He grinned at Becca. "What happened?"

Luke seemed impervious to the curious glances he was getting from her students, but Becca wasn't. She was sure she'd be asked all kinds of questions about him, so it would be best just to introduce him. "Everyone, this is Mr. Monroe. He is a friend of mine."

She quickly introduced the students around them by first names, and after a chorus of "Pleased to meet you" from everyone, she went on to explain about the boy falling in the pond.

"Wish I'd seen that." Luke chuckled along with the other males in the group.

"It was quite frightening for a few minutes when the big old alligator headed toward him," Jennifer said. "But thankfully, some of the other boys pulled him to safety."

"Yes, well, I guess that would be frightening," Luke agreed. He bent low and whispered to Becca, "I still wish I'd been here to see it."

She smiled and shook her head.

"Well, I guess I'll go back to work. I'll see you later?" he asked, looking into her eyes.

For a moment Becca forgot young people surrounded them as she smiled up at him. "Of course."

Luke tipped his hat and went on his way as Becca and her students made their way back to school.

"He's very handsome, Miss Snow. Is he your beau?" Milly asked.

Was he? Becca didn't know how to answer other than to say, "We're just good friends. I don't have a beau."

"Oh, that's too bad," Elizabeth said. "You look very good together. He seems quite smitten with you."

Becca only knew that she was quite smitten with him.

Luke left Becca and her students, fully aware that they could see he was quite infatuated with their teacher. He couldn't hide how he felt. He was in love with Becca Snow. No doubt about it. She was on his mind every waking moment, and most of his dreams centered on her, too. And from the way she'd responded to his kiss the night he came home and the way she'd looked at him just now, color stealing up her neck and onto her cheeks, he was pretty certain she felt the same way.

But she seemed to be trying hard not to. He was also sure of that. Luke didn't think she could control her heart any more than he could. At least for now. But once she found out about his past, that could be a whole different story, and he knew he had to tell her. He might lose her, but he couldn't live with himself if he didn't tell her the truth.

He got back to the building just as Marcus was walking out.

"Did we have a meeting today? I'm sorry—"

"No. We didn't. I just thought I'd stop by and visit awhile. Why don't we go have coffee at the corner café that just opened down the street? I hear they have really good pie."

"Sounds fine to me." Luke hoped he wasn't about to get another assignment, at least not yet. He couldn't remember ever wishing that until just now, and he knew it had to do with Becca. He didn't want to leave her again, at least not until he knew how she felt about him.

They reached the café and gave their orders for coffee and cherry pie before Luke asked, "How are Abigail and Natalie? Has she decided to open a shop here?"

"She's looked at a few places, but Natalie doesn't really seem to be decided on moving just yet. And she's wondering if Becca might decide to go back to Eureka Springs now that the school year is almost finished."

Luke's heart seemed to stop. *Dear Lord, please don't let that happen.* "Has Becca said anything about it to her?"

Marcus shook his head. "Not that I know of. And from what I can tell, Becca loves teaching here. She mentioned that she hopes some of her family will come for a visit this summer. I'm not sure what Natalie is basing her thinking on. Abigail mentioned that there was a possibility of a romance for her back home."

"Becca?" Luke held his breath, waiting for Marcus's answer.

"No. Natalie."

"Oh." Luke breathed a huge sigh of relief. "Well, I certainly hope she is wrong about Becca moving back home."

"Ahh. It's that way, is it?" Marcus grinned at him.

Luke sighed. He'd spoken without thinking but decided it was time he talked to someone about it; he couldn't think of another person he trusted as much as he did Marcus. He didn't beat around the bush. "I've fallen in love with her."

"I thought that might be the case. She's a wonderful woman, Luke. You couldn't choose anyone whom Abigail and I would be happier for you to fall in love with."

"Now the trick is to find out if she could ever feel the same way."

"You don't know?"

Their pie and coffee arrived just then, and Luke waited until the waitress left the table to answer. "I believe she does. But she doesn't want to."

"Why not?"

"She thinks my work with the agency is as dangerous as her fiancé's was. You knew he'd been shot in a bank robbery, didn't you?"

"I didn't know all the details, but I knew he was a policeman who'd been shot."

Luke nodded and took a sip of coffee. "I suppose it's natural for her not to want to care for someone who could be in danger. But what I do is nothing like being a policeman, fireman, or soldier."

Marcus looked over the coffee cup he'd just brought to his mouth. "I don't suppose those bruises that have just faded gave her much confidence," he said before taking a sip from the cup.

"No. Good thing she never saw the rest of them." Luke forked a piece of pie into his mouth and chewed.

"She hasn't sent you on your way, telling you to leave her alone, has she?"

"Not yet."

"Then all is not lost. Have you told her how you feel?"

"That I love her and want her to be my wife? No."

"Why not?"

"Because when I do—or before I do—I have to tell her about my past."

"Your past? Luke, you were cleared of any wrongdoing."

"I know. But still, I was in prison, and she's such a genteel woman. . . ." He shook his head. "Even if she didn't have a problem with it, her family might."

"Well, I agree she should know. But I don't think it is going to be the problem you perceive it to be."

"Then there is the difference in our ages—"

"I've seen the way she looks at you, Luke. I'm pretty certain your age is not a problem at all. And just so you know, Abigail thinks Becca is in love with you."

Luke's heart swelled with hope, and he silently prayed that Marcus was right on all counts. Then another thought came to him. "What if Natalie is right, and Becca moves back home this summer?"

"I don't think that is going to happen. But if she does, then you'll know she's not ready to risk her heart again. You need to tell her about your past and how you feel about her. Only then will you know how she feels. It is something better found out now rather than later."

"I know. I'll talk to her soon."

"I think you should."

"I'll do it tonight." Luke dreaded it with every fiber of his being, but Marcus was right. He could no longer put it off.

Chapter 14

By the time Becca got home that afternoon, she was certain that all of her students and most of the teachers thought Luke was courting her—no matter how hard she tried to convince them otherwise.

She thought her students had lots of questions until she went to the teachers' lounge after school.

"Was that your beau, Becca?" Jennifer Collins asked.

"No. He's a good friend though. I'd mentioned that we were going on a field trip today, and he came by."

"You didn't see any young man coming to the alligator farm just because I was there." Lila Baxter gave an exaggerated sigh. "I could only wish to have someone that nice looking spending time with me."

"He is very handsome," Mrs. Richards said. "And I've been around a long time. I know that lovelorn look when I see it."

Becca laughed, but she could feel the color steal up her face as she shook her head and said, "Really, he's just a very good friend."

"Then you need glasses, Becca. The man doesn't want to just be a friend to you. And from what I saw, you care more than that, too," Jennifer said.

Becca couldn't very well deny the truth, so she said nothing. She just gathered her things and shook her head as she left the room.

She'd been praying very hard to know what to do. She could no longer deny that she cared deeply about Luke. She did. But she was so afraid of losing someone else she loved that she felt paralyzed about what to do.

Still, it didn't keep her pulse from racing when she saw Luke that evening. She told herself it was all the talk about him being her beau and courting her that had her reacting the way she was. She didn't go around thinking in those terms, but now that they'd been brought up, she couldn't seem to get them out of her mind.

Thankfully, he didn't seem to notice how flustered she was as they worked together in her kitchen to prepare supper. They'd made a soup from leftovers from the night before, and he'd brought crusty bread to go along with it.

They talked about the outing and what she thought of the alligator farm.

"If it hadn't ended so abruptly, perhaps I would have enjoyed it, but trying to keep up with students made it a little hard."

"I can see how it would. It's springtime, and young men get a little silly."

"Oh?" Becca looked up to see his gaze on her. A small smile played around his lips.

"Yes."

Something in his expression had her asking, "Why is that?"

"Because their thoughts turn to love."

"Really?" Becca caught her breath at the look in his eyes.

"Really. It happens with grown men, too. Becca, I must tell you something."

Her heart felt as if it had stopped. "All right. Go ahead."

"There are some things you don't know about me. Things I must tell you before. . ."

She nodded and waited.

Luke released a big sigh and stood up. He put his hands in his pockets and looked down at the floor for a moment before sitting back down across from her. "When I was about sixteen, my mother passed away. My papa seemed to lose interest in everything after she died. . .including me."

"I'm so sorry, Luke." Becca's heart went out to the lonely boy he must have been. She reached out and touched his hand.

He put his larger one on top of hers and grasped her fingers. He shrugged and continued. "I was on my own most of the time, and I. . .well. . .I hung around some older boys sometimes. They liked to pull pranks, and when I was with them, I went along. Until the night they wanted to rob a store."

Becca gasped, and Luke got up from the table again. It was obvious that this wasn't getting any easier for him to tell. "I didn't go with them. I told them no and went to my aunt Carrie's, my mother's younger sister. She'd been trying to talk to me, tell me I was in with the wrong crowd. I finally knew she'd been right. Anyway, going to her house turned out to be the best thing I could have done. I knew my papa wouldn't know if I was at home or not. He'd taken to drinking by that time, and well, anyway, I stayed the night with Aunt Carrie and Uncle Jerome and went home the next morning."

Becca breathed a sigh of relief that he'd known where to go. "I didn't know you had an aunt. Does she live here?"

"No. She lives up in Fort Smith. That's where I'm from."

"Oh, I remember you telling me that. What happened then?"

"Nothing for several days. Then the cops showed up and arrested me for the robbery."

"But you weren't even there."

"No. I wasn't. But my so-called friends said I was and that I was the one who did it. Once Aunt Carrie knew what happened, she contacted the police and told them I was at her home that night, but they said it didn't matter; I could have robbed the store before I went to her house. She saw an advertisement in the newspaper about the Wellington Agency when it was just starting out, and she wrote to Marcus and asked him to investigate. She didn't think he'd answer, but he came all the way up there to talk to her. She didn't have much money but gave him what she could and said we'd pay him back as soon as we could."

"Of course Marcus took the case."

"Yes. And to make a very long story short, he found witnesses who saw four boys on the corner that night but saw that one had left earlier—before the store was robbed. That was me. But they beat up the shopkeeper so badly he nearly died. His memory was fuzzy, and he couldn't be certain who attacked him, at first. Thankfully, he finally remembered before it was all over with.

"It took several weeks, but Marcus cleared my name. That alone would have indebted me to him, but then he offered me a job to learn from him and a place to stay—to get away from Fort Smith and start life over here in Hot Springs. But most important of all, he led me to the Lord. I don't think I can ever repay him for all he's done for me."

Becca could certainly see how and why he would feel so beholden to Marcus. "Oh, Luke. I'm so sorry you had to endure all of that and that you had to spend time in prison for something you didn't do."

"But what would your family think?"

"My family?" Becca wasn't sure what he was getting at. He'd told her so much, and she understood him much better now but. . .

"Would they ever allow me to court you?"

Becca's heart filled with love for this man. She cared so very much for him . . .but. . .

"Becca? You do believe me, don't you?"

"Yes, Luke, of course I believe you. And my family would approve of you; I am sure of that. But I. . .I. . ."

Luke stood. "I think I understand. You don't care about me in that way—" He turned to look out the window.

Becca jumped up and went over to him. She reached out and touched his shoulder. "Luke, that is not what I am saying at all. It's just that in the last few weeks, you've revealed things about yourself to me that, well, they are very important, and I can't help but wonder what else you haven't told me about yourself. What else is there about you that I should know?"

❧

Luke looked down into the eyes of the woman he wanted but was afraid he'd never have. "The only thing left that I haven't told you. . .the only thing that you need to know. . .is that I love you. With all my heart."

"Luke, I—"

"It's all right, Becca. I know now that there is no chance for us. I think I've known it all along, but I wanted so badly to be wrong. Now that I've told you about my past, I realize that you deserve someone who can offer you so much more than I can. You don't need someone in your life whose past could come back to haunt your future. Even though I was cleared, some people would wonder about it all if they found out I was once in prison. I can't ask you to take that on."

"I'm sorry. I just wanted to know what else—"

"There is no need to be sorry. And there is nothing else to tell. You've endured so much with the death of your fiancé, and I can understand how you would have reservations about my career. But I can't think of another career I would want, and I do feel loyal to Marcus. He taught me all I know, and he counts on me. I wish things were different." He saw the sheen of tears in Becca's eyes, but she didn't say anything. He didn't want her pity. He only wanted her love. It seemed that wasn't to be.

"I will always love you, Becca. But I know I am not right for you. I can only now wish you the very best life has to offer and let you find what that is." With that, Luke walked out of her apartment and down the hall.

Everything in him cried for her to open that door and call him back—for her to tell him she loved him, too. He felt she did. But evidently she still didn't want to, and there was nothing else he could say to change that fact.

He unlocked his door and waited a second. He heard no sound of a door opening, no call to bring him back. He walked in and sat down in his favorite chair. His heart felt as if it were being squeezed and wrung out, and he wasn't sure what to do other than pray. "Dear Lord, please help this pain go away. I knew that my chance to win Becca's heart was not good, and I didn't want to fall in love with her. But I do love her, Lord. Please help me to give up gracefully and be happy for her no matter who she chooses to spend her life with. You've blessed me with more than I ever dared dream, and I thank You for all that You've given me. I just ask that You continue to watch over her as I feel I must try to pull back from spending so much time with her. I value her friendship and would pray that we can still be friends, but please help me to get over the hurt of knowing that's all she feels for me. In Jesus' name, I pray. Amen."

Luke felt only marginally better after praying, but he trusted that the Lord would answer.

He felt bad that he hadn't stayed to help Becca clear the table and clean up the kitchen as he usually did, but he just couldn't stay. Now all he wanted to do was go back. Should he go apologize and help her wash dishes? He stood up and started toward the door. Then he stopped. What was he doing?

His telephone rang just then, and his heart jumped. He strode over and picked up the earpiece from its hook. Maybe it was Becca. Maybe—he spoke into the mouthpiece. "Hello?"

"Luke?"

His heart fell at the sound on the other end of the receiver. "Good evening, Marcus. What can I do for you?"

"We need to talk. I've just had a report from Nelson, and it also concerns Becca. It may be time for you to go on another assignment. Can you come over now?"

Maybe it was just what he needed, to get out of town and away from the heartache he was experiencing. "I'll be right there."

❧

Becca stood frozen to the spot as Luke walked out of her apartment. Her heart seemed to shatter into a million pieces as she watched him leave. She wanted nothing more than to run after him and tell him she loved him, too. Yet she was afraid of the depth of love she felt for him and petrified that something would happen to him, just as it had to Richard. What was she to do?

She made herself clear the table and put on an apron to wash dishes and clean up her kitchen, wishing with all her heart that she could get past the fear of loving again and embrace the life Luke offered her. He'd looked so. . .hurt and alone when he left. Now all she could think was that she didn't want him to think she didn't care.

Becca dried her hands and took off her apron. She had to tell him. But it was getting late, and it wouldn't look right to be knocking on his door at this hour. Instead, she placed a call through the operator, but he didn't answer. At first Becca thought it was because he thought it was her. But then she reminded herself that Luke ran this building and worked for Marcus. He would answer his telephone.

She hung up her earpiece and sighed. Perhaps he'd gone for a walk. Men could do that this time of night. There was nothing to do but wait until tomorrow. She could only pray that it wouldn't be too late and that he would still care.

Chapter 15

The next few days were some of the longest Becca had ever spent. She'd awoken the day after Luke told her he loved her only to find a note slipped under her door telling her that he had been called off on an assignment for Marcus and that he wanted to talk to her when he got back.

She had problems concentrating at school all that day, and her students asked her if she was all right. The weekend was no better. Saturday loomed long and lonely, and not even her lunch with Natalie and Abigail helped. Natalie had decided to go back to Eureka Springs to decide if she really wanted to move or stay there and see what happened with her and the new minister.

"I'm just having a hard time knowing what to do." She chuckled and shook her head. "I know I am very spoiled. I always have been." She looked at her aunt. "And you've done your share."

Abigail smiled and nodded. "I have."

"I know that it's time I grow up and make a decision about what I want to do with my life," Natalie said with a sigh. "But then I think that there might be a chance for true love for me back home, and I feel I must see what transpires, if it is possible that I could be a good minister's wife."

"Well, you know I am going to miss you greatly," Abigail said. "But it is your life, and I just want you to be happy no matter where you are. Come back and visit as often as you can."

"I will certainly do that. But I have to admit that I do miss Papa and Mama and Lydia and Eleanor. And I am hoping that Becca will come home for a month or two this summer."

Becca had thought she might go home to visit for a week or two, but now that things were so unsettled between Luke and her, staying here for most of the summer might not be an option. But she'd be back. She'd come to love Hot Springs and her students. She might have to find another place to live if things got too uncomfortable. She hoped that didn't happen, but there was no way of knowing until Luke returned. Still, she wasn't going to commit to any certain length of time with her family right now.

"I wasn't thinking of that long a visit right now," Becca said. "But school isn't out yet, so you never know."

"Well, since I'm leaving next week, why don't we spend the rest of the day together? We could go to that new moving picture show that is in town."

"That sounds good. Then you could come back and have dinner with me after the movie. You could stay over, and we could go to church together tomorrow."

"I'd like to stay over," Natalie said. "But don't think for a minute that I'm going to let up on getting you to come back home for longer than a couple of weeks."

Abigail and Becca looked at each other and laughed. Abigail shook her head. They both knew just how persistent Natalie could be.

Abigail decided against going to the movie, but she offered for her and Marcus to pick Becca and Natalie up the next morning for church.

"That would be nice, thank you," Becca said.

"It seems the least we can do since Marcus sent your escort out of town," Abigail said.

Becca didn't quite know what to say. It was possible that Luke wouldn't want to escort her anymore—not after last night. She was thankful that Natalie filled the silence.

"We'll be over to collect my overnight bag when we get out of the movies, Aunt Abby," Natalie said as they got ready to go their separate ways on the boardwalk outside.

"Why don't you both have dinner with us? That way you won't have to prepare anything when you get home. In fact, why don't you collect Becca's things and stay overnight with us? That would be so nice."

Becca had a feeling Abby was more upset than she let on about Natalie's going back home. She probably wanted to spend as much time with Natalie as she could before her niece left. As for herself, it would be a wonderful distraction that would keep her from listening for every footstep down the hall and wondering if Luke might be home. She smiled at Abigail. "That would be very nice. Thank you. We'll pick up my things and come over after the movie, then."

Abigail hugged them both before she left, and she whispered to Becca, "Thank you, sweet friend. I know you understand. Just don't you decide to leave, too."

She waved to them both and went in one direction while they took off in the other.

❧

By Monday, Becca was even more thankful than usual that she had Natalie and the Wellingtons in her life. Staying with them through the weekend helped keep her busy, but it couldn't keep thoughts of Luke out of her mind. He was always there, waiting to fill any moment of silence.

Tonight, as she made her supper, her thoughts flitted from the first time they met to every moment they'd spent together since. Cooking together, going to church, and spending Sunday afternoons at the Wellingtons' and going for rides. Having supper at one of the hotels. His kisses. She remembered everything up to and including the night before he left and his declaration of love quickly followed by his insistence that he wasn't right for her. She didn't think she'd ever forget the expression on his face when he left that night. Now she just wanted him home so that she could tell him she loved him, too—enough so that she would accept that he felt he must continue to work as a Wellington agent and would leave his safety in the Lord's hands.

She had to tell him how she felt. He was a wonderful man who loved the Lord and tried to live his life in a way that gave glory to God. He was kind to everyone. She couldn't remember him being rude to anyone at any time. And he loved her.

Her heart swelled just thinking about the honor of having him love her. Yes, it was natural that she might fear for his life after what happened to Richard, but she'd come to the conclusion that she'd have to deal with it. And with the Lord's help, she would. Luke was her very best friend, and he was the man she wanted to spend the rest of her life with. She just wanted him home so she could tell him so.

Perhaps he'd be back tomorrow. She straightened up her parlor and emptied her trash into the receptacle outside the kitchen. She moved through the doorway then turned to lock the door, when the man she kept running into suddenly appeared and grabbed the side of the door.

"Good evening, Miss Snow," he said.

Sudden fear gripped her. Becca tried to push the door, but the man was too strong and pushed back. He burst into the kitchen brandishing a gun, and Becca finally knew where she'd seen him. She turned to run, pushing anything in front of her away, trying to trip the man up.

"Stop or I'll shoot!" the man said, dodging a lamp she threw.

"No!" Becca screamed.

❧

Luke's nerves were strung taunt. He'd been waiting for days to get this thug, and he prayed tonight was the night. Things had been put on hold over the weekend when Becca had stayed with the Wellingtons. Marcus hadn't planned on that, and while they were both glad she was safe, it wasn't going to help them get the man when he made his move.

But he was ready, too, of that they were certain. Nelson had followed the man to Eureka Springs and found that he was watching the Snow family home and the school Becca had taught at. When Burrows caught a train back to Hot Springs after his visit to the school, they figured he was ready to make a move. The only thing they didn't know was why he was watching Becca so closely.

Now as Luke stood inside his darkened office and looked outside, waiting for Nelson's signal that Burrows was about to make a move, he prayed silently. *Dear Lord, please keep Becca safe. I know we have men stationed everywhere, but anything can happen. We don't know what this man wants or how dangerous he is, but You do. Please watch over her and let us get to him before he gets to her. I pray this in Jesus' name. Amen.*

He saw the flicker of a match being lit from across the street and knew that Burrows was making his way toward the building. Luke signaled to George to move up the back way while Luke hurried up the main staircase to stand in a darkened alcove where he could see the front door to Becca's apartment. He waited for Burrows to come up the stairs and approach it. And he waited.

But Burrows wasn't coming. What if. . .

Luke remembered that he'd shown the man a floor plan of the building when he'd inquired about an apartment. What if he came up the back way and went to—

"No!"

Luke took off in a run at the sound of Becca's voice. *Dear Lord, please let me be in time.* He kicked the front door and burst in.

❧

The front door flew open, and Luke ran in, pushing Becca into the hall before he tackled the man who'd shot Richard and left him to die in her arms. Men seemed to come from nowhere—two coming in from the kitchen door and two more behind Luke.

Becca prayed with everything she could as she watched Luke wrestle the gun away and hold it on the man while two of the men helped subdue the man who was still trying to fight. One of the other men called the police, and another stood guarding her. Becca assumed they were all agents of the Wellington Agency.

Her heart felt as if it were going to burst right out of her chest as Luke led her back into the apartment and set her down on the couch. "We've had a man tailing him for several weeks, and we finally put it all together," he said. "That's the man, right? The man who robbed the bank and shot your fiancé?"

Becca could only nod and whisper, "Yes. But I didn't remember him until tonight when he burst in the service door with his gun. It all came back to me then." Becca shuddered and began to tremble at the memory. She was still breathing hard when the police showed up. Two of them handcuffed the man and took him out while one stayed behind.

"Miss Snow? I need to ask a few questions, if you are up to it."

"She's pretty shaken, officer. I could bring her down to the station tomorrow if—"

"No, Luke. It's all right. I can talk now," Becca said.

There was a knock on the open front door, and they looked up to see Mrs. Gentry. "Are you all right, dear?"

"I'm fine now, thank you. I just need to answer a few questions."

Mrs. Gentry came inside. "Well, I'll go make you a cup of tea and straighten up a bit while you talk, if that's all right."

"That would be wonderful. Thank you." Becca felt like crying, but she didn't know if it was because of the woman's sweetness, because she'd been so frightened, or because Luke was home and sitting beside her, holding her hand. There wasn't time to think about it as the officer began asking questions. She tried to compose herself.

"Miss Snow, do you know this man we know as Burrows?"

"I don't know his name, but I've run into him several times since I moved here."

"Did you know who he was?"

"No. Not until tonight. He always looked familiar to me, but I couldn't place him until tonight when he burst into the apartment."

The policeman was writing everything she said down on a tablet, and he paused to finish his notes before asking another question. "Who is it you believe him to be?"

"I believe he is the man who robbed a bank in Eureka Springs around a year and a half ago. He also killed my fiancé, who was a policeman and tried to stop the robbery. Richard died in my arms."

The officer looked at her. "Richard Melton?"

"Yes."

"I remember that well. Richard was my wife's cousin. I'm sorry. I'm sure this is very hard on you."

"Thank you. I'm all right now. Do you have any more questions?"

"I think that does it for now. Obviously he must have been after you because he was afraid you would remember him. He has several other aliases, and I'm sure we'll link him to other robberies before we're through. But he did himself in this time. He'll get what's coming to him—I can assure you of that. We'll need to talk to you later and most likely will need you to be a witness, but I think that's all for now."

"Thank you," Becca said. She was beginning to shake harder, and she knew it was just a delayed reaction to all that had happened that night.

Luke saw the policemen and the other agents out while Mrs. Gentry brought a pot of tea to Becca and poured her a cup. "I'm so glad you are all right. I've noticed that man from across the street several times. If I'd known he was after you, I'd have called the police, my dear."

Becca patted her hand. "There was no way to know. Please don't feel bad. Thank you so much for the tea. It is just what I need." She barely managed to lift the cup and saucer without sloshing tea over the side. After a few sips, she began to feel better.

"I'll be going now, dear. But if you need anything, don't hesitate to let me know."

"Thank you, Mrs. Gentry."

Luke came back just as Mrs. Gentry left, and he stood looking at her for a moment before taking the cup and saucer and putting them on a side table. Then he took her hands in his and pulled her up into his arms. "I was so afraid I wouldn't get here in time. Oh, Becca, I don't know what I would have done had anything happened to you."

"You saved my life, Luke. I don't know what would have happened had you not been here. Most probably I wouldn't be here. I believe he would have killed me if you hadn't come just then."

"I think that was his intention. And while I want to say that you were never in any danger, you were. Part of that was my fault. I forgot I'd shown Burrows a floor plan and didn't realize he might use the service stairs. I should have. I am so sorry he got as close as he did. The plan was to stop him before he could get to you."

"It wasn't your fault. And I'm safe now." Becca had never felt so protected and secure as she did standing in the circle of Luke's arms. "I—Luke, I missed you so. I've found there is no guarantee for anyone to be safe. I can't live my life in fear of what might happen any longer. I love you, too, and I am so sorry that I didn't tell you the night you told me how you felt—I—please forgive me—"

Luke pulled back and looked into her eyes. "Did you say you love me?"

Becca nodded. "I hope you haven't changed your—" She couldn't say any more because Luke cut her off with a kiss that answered her question quite satisfactorily. He still loved her. *Thank You, Lord*.

When she broke off the kiss and looked into his eyes, she could see how much he cared.

"Becca Snow, I love you more now than ever, and I expect to love you more each day. I will resign from the agency, if you will marry me."

Becca's eyes filled with tears of love and gratitude. Not only had he saved her life and captured that man who took Richard's life, but he was also a very forgiving man. He still loved her, and he wanted to spend the rest of his life with her. He was even willing to change his profession for her. But she couldn't let him do that. "Luke Monroe, I love you with all my heart, and there is no need to resign from the Wellington Agency. I found out all too well tonight that it comes in very handy to have a Wellington agent watching over me. I can't ask you to give it up. And yes, I will marry you and love you for the rest of my life, and I'll trust the Lord to keep you safe."

As Luke's lips claimed hers once more, Becca thanked the Lord above for giving her a love to cherish.

A Letter to Our Readers

Dear Readers:

In order that we might better contribute to your reading enjoyment, we would appreciate you taking a few minutes to respond to the following questions. When completed, please return to the following: Fiction Editor, Barbour Publishing, Inc., P.O. Box 719, Uhrichsville, OH 44683.

1. Did you enjoy reading *Brides of Arkansas* by Janet Lee Barton?
   ❑ Very much. I would like to see more books like this.
   ❑ Moderately—I would have enjoyed it more if _____
   _____
   _____

2. What influenced your decision to purchase this book?
   (Check those that apply.)
   ❑ Cover   ❑ Back cover copy   ❑ Title   ❑ Price
   ❑ Friends   ❑ Publicity   ❑ Other

3. Which story was your favorite?
   ❑ *A Love for Keeps*   ❑ *A Love to Cherish*
   ❑ *A Love All Her Own*

4. Please check your age range:
   ❑ Under 18   ❑ 18–24   ❑ 25–34
   ❑ 35–45   ❑ 46–55   ❑ Over 55

5. How many hours per week do you read? _____

Name _____

Occupation _____

Address _____

City _____ State _____ Zip _____

E-mail _____

HAWAIIAN DREAMS

Surf's up in Hawaii, where romance is running rampant. Will three unattached women say aloha to love for keeps?

Contemporary, paperback, 352 pages, 5⁵⁄₁₆" x 8"
ISBN 978-1-60260-331-8

—————————————————————

SIERRA WEDDINGS

Challenges abound for a female cop, an accident victim, and a model as they seek men with whom they can build a future free of the haunting past.

Contemporary, paperback, 352 pages, 5⅜" x 8"
ISBN 978-1-60260-637-1

Please send me _____ copies of *Sierra Weddings* I am enclosing $7.99 for each.
(Please add $4.00 to cover postage and handling per order. OH add 7% tax.
If outside the U.S. please call 740-922-7280 for shipping charges.)

Name _____

Address _____

City, State, Zip_____

To place a credit card order, call 1-740-922-7280.
Send to: Heartsong Presents Readers' Service, PO Box 721, Uhrichsville, OH 44683

SEASIDE ROMANCE

Finding their true loves requires daring leaps of faith for each of three women from Rhode Island's seaside communities of old.

Historical, paperback, 352 pages, 5⅜" x 8"
ISBN 978-1-60260-636-4

_____